ONCE A
MONSTER

ONCE A MONSTER

ROBERT DINSDALE

MACMILLAN

First published 2023 by Macmillan
an imprint of Pan Macmillan
The Smithson, 6 Briset Street, London EC1M 5NR
EU representative: Macmillan Publishers Ireland Ltd, 1st Floor,
The Liffey Trust Centre, 117–126 Sheriff Street Upper,
Dublin 1, D01 YC43
Associated companies throughout the world
www.panmacmillan.com

ISBN 978-1-5290-9737-5 HB
ISBN 978-1-5290-9738-2 TPB

1 3 5 7 9 8 6 4 2

A CIP catalogue record for this book is available from the British Library.

Typeset by Palimpsest Book Production Ltd, Falkirk, Stirlingshire
Printed and bound by CPI Group (UK) Ltd, Croydon, CR0 4YY

Visit www.panmacmillan.com to read more about all our books
and to buy them. You will also find features, author interviews and
news of any author events, and you can sign up for e-newsletters
so that you're always first to hear about our new releases.

For Mum, and for Dad

It's one of those nights when rain lacerates the city and every familiar sight is obscured. You've been out in thunderstorms before, but not like this. Tonight, the old rivers beneath London rage and rise up. Gas lamps flicker and die. Caught out on a night like this, a faithless man might find God (if only for the sanctuary of one of his churches); a thief might find honour (if only for the shelter of a Newgate cell). But you don't have to worry about that, because you're one of the lucky ones, watching from the window, the heat of a hearth-fire prickling at your back. Tonight, you get to curl up with a book and read this story. There are people out there who have to live it.

Minos is one of them. Spare a thought for him as he shambles through the storm – for he'll be left for dead by chapter's end, and after that, who knows what will become of him?

The giant has known he is being followed since he took shelter in the alley behind St Anne's. There among the cowering street dogs, he sensed a presence: four cowled men, watching from alley's end. Fellow vagabonds, you might think, caught out in the storm – but Minos has been hunted before, and he knows them instinctively for what they are. There are different kinds of street dog in the world, so he bows back into the storm.

The North Marsh Low Lodgings are not so very far away, but the city is different on a night like this. Watch how the wind turns the trees at St Anne's to a frenzy of motion. Narrow your eyes, like Minos does, against the sleet driving into you at every conflux of roads. London is a deceitful city; what is navigable by day proves more devious by night – and, on a night like this, more devious yet. Without gas lamps or stars, there is little way of knowing north from south, or east from west; the city is hidden behind a constantly shifting cascade, so you must trust instead to the sensation of cobbles beneath your feet, the soles of your work-boots threadbare and thin.

Onward he goes. Left he turns; then right. Forward he ploughs; then back. It is strange how the whole of London devolves down to the few inches in front of your face, the ability to put one foot in front of another. Indeed, it is only by the strobing lightning that he realizes his hunters still shadow him at all. If only that lightning might illuminate the palaces at Westminster, perhaps he could find his way home. Instead, it reveals four cutpurses fanning out around him, a fifth somewhere ahead.

Instincts take over. *Animal instincts.* Yes, he has enough of those. He takes flight into tighter alleys – there are enough places to lose yourself in a tangle of London backstreets – but a man like Minos will always stand out.

Somehow, he reaches the river.

On its banks, the storm lifts squalls from the water and casts them around in wild, disordered furies. Minos tries to get his bearings – but being lost is a state of mind as well as body, and it takes too long to pick out the silhouette of the abbey. By then, the men are already around him.

'He's a big one,' says the first.

'But there's five of us,' says another.

Minos sees the cudgels in their hands. Leather straps. A length of lead pipe. Then: the flashing of knives. Something in his body remembers the touch of steel, and he rubs at a furrow of scar tissue by the nape of his neck.

'Is he going to say anything?'

'He's one of those oafs. He's got the body, but he doesn't got the brain.'

'Is he even going to fight back?'

They have their eyes on the satchel over his shoulder. Just as the cutpurses constrict around him, Minos tosses it into the water at their feet.

Inside it, they find the four shillings and sixpence he got paid at the end of shift – but men like this are never satisfied without a fight; men like this always believe there's more.

So they set about him.

How many times has this happened? He rolls with each blow, recoils at the knives plunged into his side, cradles himself as they set about him with steel-capped boots.

The only moment he tries to resist is when, satisfied with their work, they drag his brutalized body to the water's edge. The river is high tonight. He can hear it surge and roil. He opens his lips to plead with them, but discovers, somehow, that he knows no language. Everything has been taken from him. Again.

Seconds later, he is submerged, and all the world is a

kaleidoscope of grey, feathered only by red where his life's blood leaks out.

The water pummels and turns him around. He does not know, any longer, which way is up or down. But that doesn't matter, because he is already falling. Falling into dreams older than time. Falling into history and myth. Falling into memories that, if he lets them, will trap him like a maze.

Listen carefully, because that is where this story begins.

Volume I

Enter the Labyrinth

1

Water's Edge

Nell wasn't ordinarily the first to awake in the cramped, frigid attic above the Water's Edge. At ten years old, and four years since she slept in a bed made up by a mother's kindness, she had got used to the shifting of bodies around her, the sulphurous stenches that too often populated the night. But last night had been different. The rain sluicing through the roof slates and collecting in the tin pails, the wind roaring along the backstreets of Ratcliffe – all of that meant she hadn't slept at all. Instead, she'd reached into the straw mattress, pulled out the two satin slippers she kept hidden there and stroked them, imagining the possibilities of the world that used to be.

Then, before another soul awoke, she pushed the slippers back into the mattress and waited for dawn. No sleep tonight – not for Nella Hart.

That was why she was the first to the river that morning.

That was why it was Nell who found the body, washed up on the shore.

She was poking it with a stick when the rest started arriving, pouring out of the lodging house attic with their bellies full of bread and beer. Storms worked strange magics on the river. The waters danced wild, and things were dredged up from below – not just the coal and iron ingots that were their usual trade, but treasures which had sunk to the bottom and lain undisturbed with the years. Plenty of treasure in that river, said old Murdstone. Find me a treasure and it will transform your life.

'What you got there, Nell?' asked one of the older boys. His name was Noah. He said his father had danced the turncoat's waltz at Newgate, but the others said he'd too often been seen selling himself at the Executioner's Dock for that to be true.

Nell shrugged. They'd all seen dead bodies before. You didn't spend your life picking through the tidal mud of the River Thames and not, occasionally, see the half-face of some unfortunate staring back at you. She poked it with a stick again. It was bigger than most. From a distance, she'd thought it the hull of some sunken river barge; it was only when she got close that she understood it was a man. Most of his flesh was covered in silt, but there was no doubting the enormity of the creature. Twice as tall as old Murdstone, and three times as broad. He could have closed one of those enormous hands around Nell's neck and touched fingertips on the other side.

'Well, go on then,' said Noah, 'into his pockets, Nell.'

Nell looked back. Most of Murdstone's crew were here now, but not yet a sign of the old man himself. A collection of eleven ragged faces looked curiously upon her; eleven pairs of eyes egging her on.

Murdstone said there was no such thing as ghosts. You couldn't desecrate the dead because the dead had done their own desecrating, by leaving their mortal bodies behind. 'So

8

get digging,' Murdstone used to say. 'Pockets and linings. Belt buckles and bootstraps. Take the coat off his back, if it's worth a thing.'

Nell got down on her knees, then lifted the man's enormous arm so that she might reach the pockets of his overcoat. Most of these were filled with river mud as well.

'You'll have to do better than that,' Noah scoffed. 'He's got a belt, ain't he? Check his teeth. Might be a false set in there. Murdstone'll buy you a fish supper, for a set of false teeth.'

Nell recoiled at the idea of reaching into the man's jaws, but the thought of a fish supper was, at least, a restorative. Noah seemed sweet on the idea himself; he was ready to reach for the cadaver when one of the other boys shouldered him out of the way, grunted, 'It's Nell what found it,' and goaded Nell on with his eyes.

Nell crawled to the head of the corpse, whispered a plea for forgiveness, and took hold of the man's lower jaw.

Almost immediately Nell knew something wasn't right. She'd never felt a man's face like this before. His jaw seemed more prominent than it ought, his brow ridged and starkly defined. She supposed the river could do terrible things to a body. Or perhaps he'd been brutalized before being tossed in. She screwed her eyes against the slimy horror of it, pushed her fingers between his lips – and then felt the whisper of something on her fingertips, the whisper of something that was surely not the wind.

'Go on, Nell!' Noah crowed. 'Get your hand in there, or by God, I'll—'

'Stop!' Nell cried. She was suddenly aware that, of all the faces gathered on the shore, she was the youngest – and, by rights, had no cause to be shouting at anyone at all. But she knew what river wind felt like: cold and sharp, coarse with the touch of sand. This thing she felt on her fingertips was warm and dewy. It came from within.

'He's alive,' she said, and dropped her head to his breast to hear the distant tolling of a heart. 'I don't know how it happened, but he's still alive!'

Benjamin Murdstone – former rag-gatherer, former inmate, former gentleman, and current master of mudlarks from Woolwich to the Wapping dock – would have been at the river already, if only Tetterby the nightman hadn't been waiting. Directly outside the Lowood coach house where Murdstone spent his nights, Tetterby stepped into the road, thrusting a young woman in front of him. By the porcine look they both shared, Murdstone took her immediately as his daughter. 'You've got to take her,' Tetterby began. 'You swore you'd help an old friend.'

Friends, thought Murdstone. At the estimable (and esti-mated – for how can a foundling ever tell?) age of seventy-three, he'd made a lot of friends. Lost a lot too. He'd had friends in the street dens, friends in the palaces of Mayfair, friends in the rankest cells of the Marshalsea – and the one thing he'd learned was that friendship was just another kind of trade. 'What's wrong with adopting her father's profession?'

'It isn't work for a girl.'

Murdstone said, 'You've let ideas get in your head. Never a more dangerous pastime than that. Who's to say it's no trade for a girl? I know a dozen pure-finders on these streets, and all of them women. If there's a healthy living in what foul dogs leave behind, there's a healthy living in night-soil as well. I don't see how it makes a difference what hand scoops it up.'

Tetterby shuffled closer. 'She's a hard worker.'

'She'd get her hands dirty with me as well. You can't keep 'em clean for ever. You're forgetting, Tetterby – there's as much slurry in what she'd do for me as what she'd do for you. The river flows with it.'

Murdstone would have marched away, if only his body had let him. He limped, instead, along the Lowood road, leaning heavily into his driftwood cane. Tetterby, leaving his doleful daughter behind, had little difficulty catching up.

'You think you're better than me, Murdstone. Better than my family.'

This barely needed stating. Life, Murdstone had often observed, was made out of choices. A man ought not to be judged on the misfortunes that bedevil him, but on the choices he has made. And there stood Tetterby the nightman, a man who had spent twenty years chained to his barrow – choosing, every day, to go begging door to door for shit. There was no shame in sewage; Murdstone himself had waded through enough. The difference was: Murdstone and his mudlarks sifted in the filth of the river for the treasures that might transform their lives; to Tetterby and his ilk, filth was the treasure itself.

Murdstone looked again at Tetterby's daughter. He supposed he could always use more hands on the river – but more hands meant more mouths, and more mouths were always a problem. Some trades were worth it; some trades were not. That, when the biographers finally came to write it all down, would be the story of his life.

'Not this time, Tetterby,' he said, and laid his three-fingered hand on the nightman's shoulder. 'I'm sure there's enough shit to go round.'

'So, Nell, what's it to be?'

Ankle-deep in the mud, Nell tried to focus on the man underneath her. Now that she sensed life in him, it was easier to see the faint rise and fall of his breast; easier to know that he was not flotsam washed up by the storm, but a man with a history of his own. She tried to focus on that, instead of the eleven sets of eyes. They'd never asked her to make a decision before.

'You're wasting time, Nell,' sniped Noah. 'Tell her, Gander.'

Gander was the eldest among them, seventeen years of age and six of those spent sifting the river flats on Murdstone's account.

'It's Nell's choice,' Gander pronounced. 'It's no different to a piece of coal come out of the muck. River rules: sell it, keep it, them who finds it decides it. But listen, Nell, Noah's got one thing right – you got to make your mind up. Once Murdstone wanders onto this stretch, there'll be no deciding either way. You'll lose your chance.'

Nell looked at the great misshapen man. She'd cleared a little mud from his face, revealing fronds of black beard beneath. The man's eyes were swollen, as if he'd been set about with lengths of lead pipe.

'Ain't he suffered enough?' Nell whispered. Then, when it was obvious none had heard her, 'He's already been robbed once. Who are we to rob him again?'

Bursts of chatter broke out among the eleven who

watched. Noah was remonstrating with Gander, claiming they ought to at least take his boots. 'Boots like that, it's sausages all round!' Packrat Jack thought, at least, that it was one in the eye for Mr Murdstone – while Potato Rot, who'd lost his old name when the measles made a mess of his looks, hung his head and said, 'Murdstone'll find out. Murdstone always finds out.'

'It's decided,' said Gander, silencing the crowd with a look. 'What next, Nell?'

Nell hated this feeling. She wasn't good at making decisions. She'd never had to be. Right now, she was back on her knees, trying to wash the sludge from his hair. There was something wrong here too. On either side of the man's head, just above his temples, his skull was raised in two hard protrusions, like wounds upon which the scar tissue had calcified.

What next? What next, indeed. Her mother would have known what to do. And Nell realized, then, that it was those memories which were driving her, right now. She thought of those slippers again, secreted within the straw mattress, and the memory of how her mother had cared for her – back when there was more to the world than the river and its ceaseless mud – coursed through her.

'He needs a place. Somewhere out of the wind. Somewhere we could build a fire.' There was only one place like that that they knew. 'The seaward cave?'

'The seaward cave,' rejoined Gander. 'Right then, Nell. You lead the way.'

It took eight of the eldest to lift the man from the mud. Gander took one shoulder, Packrat Jack the other, and with the others crowded around, a strange convoy of the bedraggled and destitute started wending their way along the river.

They'd known the cave since long before Mr Murdstone first brought Nell, six years old and eyes bright with terror, down onto the mudflats, with the story that her mother was gone and the girl entrusted to Murdstone's care. A mile around the sweep of the river, where the wharfs had been burned back and the riverbank was steep with crooked rock, there was a fissure in the stone wall. It was not, at first sight, much of a cave; inside revealed only a den, fit for children or smugglers. But the incline kept the cavern floor dry, even at high tide – and the angle of the opening, facing as it did the faraway sea beyond the city, meant that any fire lit within was almost entirely obscured from passing rivermen.

Nell approached the cave at a scurry, then heaved herself into the fissure itself. They'd have to hold the man at an angle to get him through – but at least the hollow of the cave was vacant. The ashes of old campfires pockmarked the ground, and in the corner a pile of dried-out driftwood. Kindling for a fire. By rights, it ought to have been handed to Murdstone, then sold on the streets along with every other scrap the river gave up. But Murdstone couldn't get murderous over things he didn't know.

The man was buffeted back and forth as the others bore him into the cave. The fact he didn't stir, even then, gave Nell a singular sad feeling, as if he was already too far gone to be helped. She made sure his head was positioned where the stone gave way to sand, then brushed the hair out of his eyes. She'd never seen a face like this. The eyes were too far apart, the skull shaped like no other. It was more than truncheons that had done this to him; there was swelling here, but underneath that a disfigurement that must have lasted a lifetime. She couldn't even tell how old he was.

Packrat Jack was the best at fires. He stirred one up in a circle of stones. Then Nell, still aware that the others were expecting her to tell them what to do, scampered out of the cave, down to where rocky outcrops caught water in their depressions. At least here she didn't have to live up to their expectations. She filled the weather-beaten pail they kept in the cave with water and ferried it back inside. There, she got to her knees and, stripping out of her ragged shirt, began sponging water onto every inch of flesh she could find.

Gander did the same. Taking a pocket handkerchief – his one token of gentility – from his trouser, he wet the man's bruised lips. Nell hardly noticed, not until she sensed some flickering of movement in him. She'd been flushing the mud out of the shell of an ear – of all the things about him, it was the smallest, almost preternaturally so – when a tiny convulsion worked through his body.

She looked up.

The man's lips were parting, as if asking for more.

In the seaward cave, Murdstone's mudlarks held their breath. Then, 'More,' Nell said, and eleven bedraggled souls watched Gander drip more water into his throat.

The will to live – Nell remembered it well. She remembered how quickly it faded too. Vivid memories streaked across her – how, once upon a time, it had been Nell herself bowed to a patient like this, six years old in the room where she used to live, her mother in the throes of her final fever.

15

'Don't waste your time here, Nell. There's pennies in the pot. Your father's pocket watch. Take it to the river. To Mr Murdstone. He promised he'd—'

Nell had to battle the memory away. The memories of six-year-olds are indistinct things, filled with fabrication and fantasy – but this she knew as gospel: she'd done as her mother asked. That was why she was here, crouching in a riverside cave with the dirty faces of her new family around her. That was why she hadn't been there, in the moment her mother slipped out of the world.

'He's too cold,' said Nell, still stroking the hair on his brow. 'Bring more driftwood. More water. We'll have to warm it.'

Two of the older girls were quick to obey. Soon, a relay had been established – the pail up and down to the rock pools, the boys ferreting around for what scraps of timber they could find. If Murdstone knew, they'd all be quartered; every scrap of firewood had a price on the streets. But Nell continued her work as the others came and went.

His clothes were too wet. They were keeping the fire's warmth at bay. She worked with Gander to roll him, levering one enormous arm out of his greatcoat, then the other, to reveal a dirty workman's shirt and moleskin trousers. At this size, the shirt had to be tailored – and indeed it seemed to have been patched together from older garments – but that was not what drew Nell's eye. She trembled as she peeled back the discoloured fabric, to reveal three puncture wounds in his midriff. 'Get it off him. We need to clean them.' She'd seen it done. They all had. There'd been skirmishes before, with rivermen and other mudlarks. Murdstone would know what to do, but if Murdstone was here, it would be off with his boots, off with his belt, and down to the dolly shop for whatever they were worth.

Nell worked feverishly, daubing yet more water onto his face to reveal what was left of his features. She was still working at the dirt on his neck when Sally-Anne, who'd busied herself at the rock pool, returned to the cave mouth. 'His teeth,' she whispered. 'Nell, dear, step back from him now.'

Nell did not listen. She'd listened to her mother, telling her to leave; since then, she'd grown deaf to pronouncements she didn't judge right.

'Nell, sweetpea, look!' Sally-Anne insisted, more fiercely now.

So Nell did. Now that the man's lips had parted, she could see the enormous teeth within: big, yellowed incisors and molars half the size of a baby's fist. The disfigurement in his jaw made him seem mulish somehow, his jaw jutting forward like a beast of burden.

'And those things on his head,' Potato Rot tremored. By his tone, he'd been wanting to say it from the start. 'I never seen a devil before.'

'He's not a devil,' Nell snapped.

'Devil or not,' said Noah, slinking back into the cave, 'he's a decent pair o' boots.'

'You're not taking his boots!' Nell reared up, upsetting the water pail. 'He's still living. That isn't mudlarking. That's plunder.'

'Pah!' Noah snorted. 'You been in and out of the barges often enough not to care about a little thieving.'

'That's not the same.'

'Look here, Nell, if this old devil's about to drop anyway,

what's the difference if we have full bellies tonight on account of . . .'

A high-pitched whistle soared across the shoreline. Upon hearing it, even Noah – who hadn't yet wrestled a boot off the giant's foot – scrambled out onto the shale. Some distance along the beach, one of the others was waving their arms. Nell reeled down the rocks to find the rest already flocking that way.

'Murdstone,' Noah whispered. 'He's on the beach. You're for it now, Nell. Now's your last chance – own up to those boots, or –'

'It isn't just boots,' Nell replied, trying to stop shaking. 'He's a man.'

'A man with *boots*,' Noah muttered darkly as he left.

There was nobody in the cave now – only the giant, in his fitful rest. Nell lingered at his side. At least there was more colour in him now. But those teeth . . .

She was still holding the giant's hand when Gander appeared, on a whisper of wind, and said, 'Nell, he's going to ask where you got to. If you don't come, you're going to give him up.'

Nell, who felt herself back at her mother's bedside, said, 'Gander, do you think he's a monster?'

'I think there are different types of monsters in the world. And Mr Murdstone's waiting.'

By the time they made it back along the river, Murdstone was already holding court. Along the way they'd ferreted a length of railing out of the mud, the better to show how they'd been spending their time, while Nell wriggled back into her sopping wet shirt.

And there was Murdstone, framed against the city with

the rest all gathered around. His wild white hair, stained by pipe smoke, flew around him like he was the son of the storm itself. He'd shrunk with the years, and leant more heavily on his old driftwood cane, but no matter how much he aged, the sight of him still summoned a strange brew of emotions in Nell. Saviour and captor, sanctuary and prison; she'd never understood that a man could be all those things, with neither one of them contradicting the other. To look at him, he was certainly not monstrous, certainly more human than the creature she'd left in the cave, with his bitter blue eyes and patricianly airs – and yet the way his gaze took each of them in seemed to speak of other, more nuanced monstrosities. The riverbank was Murdstone's domain and the mudlarks his subjects. His were the wrinkled hands that fed them, clothed them, made sure there was a safe corner for them to sleep in at night. In return they owed him: everything.

This morning, the look in his eyes was of epiphany and great expectation.

'Let me tell you a tale,' Murdstone was saying as Nell drew near. Each one of them knew which tale this would be, for Benjamin Murdstone had but one, and he its hero. It was the story of the Seven Trades, the trades by which Benjamin Murdstone had risen from the dirt. 'Picture me now, a rag-gatherer like you: no mother, no father, raised on the charity of London – a charity denied to me by the time I was ten years old. I had nothing, as you have nothing. But I did have the river.' He paused, pitching forward on his driftwood cane. 'It was a morning like this. The dawn after the storm. What were the other boys bringing out of the mire? Pieces of timber, and coals by the bucket. A windowpane and iron hooks. Bounty enough, we all thought. Until I reached down and drew from the dirt the treasure that changed my life. And that treasure was–'

'The ivory sundial,' one of the eleven piped up.

'A gentleman's curiosity,' Murdstone went on, 'but it had fallen to me. That night, selling our wares up and down Blackfriars, I made a trade of that sundial, for a wheelbarrow of my own. With a wheelbarrow, I could ply better trade. Run better roads. It served me, for a time, until – well, you may tell me the rest.'

'The wheelbarrow for a corpse,' somebody said.

'A corpse for a bounty,' someone else went on.

'A bounty for a bookseller's.'

'A rare book for a diamond.'

'A diamond for a bride.'

And here Murdstone reclaimed the telling of his own tale, 'My name for another. Sir Benjamin Murdstone. Seven trades, to lift a man from squalor to the highest station in the realm. It's happened before. It can happen again.'

Nell and Gander settled on the shale, Murdstone propped on a boulder above.

It can happen again, thought Nell – and, for the first time since that figure washed up on the shore, her mind wheeled back to the slippers hidden in her mattress, and all the promises her mother used to make. Murdstone could be monstrous, but he could be inspiration as well – for, if one man could rise from the river, why not another? And if a boy had done it once, then why not a girl?

'How did Mr Murdstone lose everything?' Nell whispered. 'If he climbed that high, why is he here, back on the river?'

Gander's eyes darted around, to make sure no others were preying on him. 'He made a bad trade.'

'What was it?'

And Gander whispered, through gritted teeth, 'He got married.'

'Don't dream of things that cannot happen,' Murdstone pronounced. 'Dream of things that will again. That's why we keep coming to the river. That's why we wait for days like these, when the stars are aligned – not for the rich men in their counting houses, not for the moneylenders and merchants of the Royal Exchange, but for we free folk who grub about on the river, we dreamers who play at pitch-and-toss every day, come sweltering summer or wilds of winter, so that we do not miss our chance. All it takes is one moment. One hand delved into the dirt, to come back with the promise of riches untold.' Murdstone's eyes picked each of them out, from eldest to youngest – until, at last, they fixed upon Nell. 'All we're waiting for, you and I, is for something nobody's seen before to wash up on these beaches. Something so special and unique that its power cannot be denied. And there is every hope it will happen today. Perhaps it's out there, even now, begging for its chance to upend our world.' Murdstone smiled – and it struck Nell, then, that his teeth were perfect and aligned, just like the teeth of the man she'd left lying in the cave; only, unlike the monster's, Murdstone's teeth were false.

'My dears,' he grinned, 'all we have to do is find it.'

2

The Labyrinth of the Mind

Ratcliffe and Beyond, London, November 1861

That touch of water on his lips. He's felt it before. It is
nothing less than the memory of living.

'*Who are you?*' whispers a voice.

A single droplet of water lifts him from the blackness,
restoring him to dreams. In their depths, he starts
thrashing around. He wants to hear that voice again, but
these dreams are too vivid, and soon he is lost in their
twists and turns, their landslides and dead-ends. Now he
stands on the barricades of a city he somehow knows is
called Carthage, and watches as siege engines are hauled
into place. The sandscape is awash with blood. He feels
the eruption as the first boulders crash into the fortifica-
tions, sees men tumbling around him – but he himself
stands rigid, three feet taller than they are and in proportion vaster still. He reaches out to save a spearman from
plunging, and when he sees his hand close around the
grateful soldier it is not the hand of a man, but more like
the paw of a beast, ridged and furred, with wide, yellow
nails.

He lets go in horror, and the spearman falls.

'*Please wake up,*' the voice entreats him, '*I'm here, here—*'

That voice changes everything. The sandscape crumbles, plunging him back into different dreams. Visions rush at him from every side – but, as long as he can hear the voice, he knows there is a string he can follow, to lead him out of his dreams.

A string . . .

The low winter sun shone through low tide and high. It spilled over the palaces and counting houses, the boarding houses and madhouses, its rich, buttery light undimmed by the pillars of black that billowed above Charing Cross. Down on the river, it lit upon the mudlarks as they reached, blindly, into the silt, plucking out bones and coals, scraps of iron – and, more often than not, nothing at all.

But Nell saw so little of it – for instead she stayed at the stranger's side, clasping his hand in the seaward cave.

She'd returned soon after Murdstone left them to fan out along the river. The idea that he'd perished while she was gone had blossomed inside her – and it wasn't long before her feet picked a path, over rock pool and submerged girder, back to the cave. Inside, she crouched at his shoulder. The wounds in his side were hard, livid mounds, raging with heat.

'Aren't you afraid?' Sally-Anne asked. Periodically, one of the others appeared to coax her back to the water.

'Afraid of what?'

'He might wake.'

She pressed the wet rag to his brow. 'He's still in there. I know he is.'

Not one of them understood. She wasn't afraid that he might wake.

She was afraid he might not.

Some new idea seized her. She rose on her knees and, daring to finger the crust around his eyes, started teasing back one of the lids. Dried river mud crumbled at her touch, but then his eye was open – big, dilated and black; inside it, all the infinite depths of his world.

'Who are you?'

'Who are you?'

The voice whispers in the trees above him. He stops, suddenly, and looks into branches heavy with leaf. But he cannot stop long. The sound of hoof-beats thunders behind him. The hue and cry of men and dogs. He staggers on, bouldering into a forest wreathed in mist. Left he turns; then right. Forward he ploughs; then back. It is strange how the whole of the Black Forest devolves down to the few inches in front of your face, the ability to put –

'Please . . .'

This time, he feels breath in his ear. Startled, he crashes to the earth, where great boulders harbour empires of lichen. His body, so vast it shatters roots, has all the breath pounded from it. He has to lie there gasping, the air forming ragged plumes at the end of his muzzle.

His *muzzle* . . .

When he looks up, three trails lead into the outer dark. He knows not which one to take.

'I'm here,' says the voice, and down one of the trails he

sees the mist shifting, making shapes. For one fleeting instant, a giant, lidless eye is staring directly into him.

A curious thing: he feels a tiny hand in his own – though, in truth, there is nothing there.

'You're not finished yet.'

No, he thinks. Not quite.

It took three of them to tempt Nell away, and only then because they promised they'd sit with him in rotation, never leaving him alone. 'But you've got to find forage,' Gander told her. 'If you're out on the streets by nightfall with nothing to sell . . .' He let the thought linger.

In the paling sunlight, she carried her tin kettle to the water's edge. The prize would be a lady's gold locket, hurled into the river by some spiteful lover. In the years since she'd come to the river, she'd dreamed of dredging up something so special: her own ivory sundial, to change her own life. By rights, of course, it would go to Murdstone – 'compensation, girl, for all the good I've done you' – but in her flights of fancy Nell herself was the one who traded it to a better life. Her mind spun back to the slippers secreted at the Water's Edge. How many times had she pictured herself, running – no, *dancing* – away from the river, gliding over the wharfs with those slippers on her feet, out into the west and all the playhouses and palaces where her mother used to stitch?

Dreams like that were foolish enough, but today – when life ebbed and flowed in the seaward cave – they felt more foolish still. Thinking of the stranger brought her back to earth. Two coals would be bounty enough. Mr Murdstone liked his omens; he was fond of saying that a comet had

25

arced across the heavens on the night that he was left, a squalling babe, on the steps of the Foundling Hospital. But the storm of last night had not presaged great treasures on the shore. The others had dredged up the spokes of a cart-wheel, a coil of rope, six twisted copper nails; splendid enough for a night, but not for a lifetime. There'd be no ivory sundial today.

She'd planted a single coal in her kettle when she saw something else cresting the mud, a tiny crab scuttling around it in exuberant circles. It took all her strength to drag whatever it was out of the dirt. The river always put up resistance.

Then she plunged backwards, with the soiled thing in her lap.

What luck to find two bodies in a day? This one was surely dead. She marvelled that the rats hadn't yet taken its eyes. Rats loved to do that to their mortal enemies – the cat. This one had been plump in its lifetime. If they survived long enough, Ratcliffe cats often were.

Nell cleaned it up. It might not set him back on the road to righteousness, but Mr Murdstone would be happy with that.

The sun hovered over her as she picked her way back to the seaward cave. She could hear the halloing of rivermen, somewhere out on the water; chances were, the rest had been onto their untended boats, stealing whatever they could find. The moral definition of 'salvage' was fiercely debated between Thames rivermen and mudlarks.

Inside the cave, Noah was already itching to be back on the water. 'He's a brute, isn't he?' he muttered darkly, bustling off. 'You want to be careful, Nell. What is it

Murdstone reckons? You dine with cannibals, you're bound to get eaten.'

That was what Murdstone said about the rich nobs he'd once been at banquets with. The men who owned merchant armadas. But the man lying in front of her was no cannibal. He was wounded, left for dead, rescued by sheer circumstance – and the hands of a little girl.

This time, when Nell took hold of his hand, she was certain she felt it tense up – like a child, desperate not to let its mother go. Like Nell had been, in the once upon a time.

'I'm right here,' she said. 'I'm waiting.'

And, somewhere – in a dream of fire and smoke – the same words echoed over a desperate man. *I'm right here . . . I'm waiting . . .'*

Nell looked him up and down. At least his breathing was less ragged now. He didn't moan and fit like her mother had done.

Then she saw his feet.

They were huge, livid yellow with bruises and hard callused nails.

But that was not the thing that made her heartsick.

The thing that made her recoil was that they were naked.

Noah was already a hundred yards along the river when she scrambled out of the cave. She didn't have to catch him up to see the boots in his hands. He was swinging them as brazenly as a piece of driftwood. Delighting in his theft, trilling a tune like birdsong as he kicked his way through the shale.

*

'I'd wager you'd rather be on the river, Sir Benjamin.'

There were valid arguments either way, Murdstone conceded. In one scenario, his body put up a bitter complaint as he levered his way through the river silt, relying on the steadfastness of his driftwood cane; in the other, he stood exactly where he stood now: stark naked and shrivelled up, on a dais in a physician's study while Dr Bantam took in every wrinkled crevice.

Benjamin Murdstone had rotted for six of his years in a dank cell in the Marshalsea prison. A little nudity, in the company of a respected physician – a man who owed Murdstone his life, like so many others – would not unsettle him today. He barely condescended to flinch when Bantam took his manhood in the cup of his hand and, first considering the lively weight of the appendage, inspected it for discolouration and boils.

'I can't say it's the old problem, Sir Benjamin. If your days of romancing are over, you can be assured in that regard. These things travel by vice. If the body denies sin, the flesh denies corruption.'

'I'm just so damnably tired. And I haven't been a Knight of the Realm in twenty-one years. I'd thank you to stop reminding me.'

Bantam released his grasp and looked up. 'Our joke, Mr Murdstone. Now, turn if you please.'

Murdstone turned, presenting his mottled posterior for the good doctor's inspection. He put up no resistance when the physician asked him to adopt a pose more suitable for exploration, uttered no complaint when Bantam did what was necessary to ensure the unobstructed flow of his body's waste. 'A little engorgement, perhaps, but nothing considerable for a man of your age. Now, might you —'

The doctor had handed Murdstone a small glass phial, with which Murdstone retired to a corner. These days, it always took much longer than it used to. He hadn't realized, when he was a young man, that one day he would have to push.

Some time later, Bantam swirled the phial around, looking for sediments and silts, then consulted one of the manifold charts on the wall. 'Neither too dark, nor too light. In fact, I might say – a perfect vintage. Have you –' and here he began throwing Murdstone his undergarments, '– considered the obvious?'

Murdstone had always had a quelling eye. He rolled it darkly at the doctor now.

'There's no panacea for age, Sir Benjamin,' Bantam pronounced. 'Grief comes riding for men younger than you. My prescription is clear: a warm bed, a warm fire. Mr Murdstone, isn't it time?'

Murdstone, still half-naked, seethed, 'I never had a mother, Bantam. I'm not looking for one now.'

The doctor put up his hands, acquiescing to the anger.

'I came here to know that my heart wasn't rupturing in my breast. Now you've assured me of that I'll—'

'Oh, Sir Benjamin, I rather think your heart ruptured long ago.'

Murdstone wrenched his driftwood cane from its place by the desk and marched to the door. 'Fine words, coming from you. Or have you so easily forgotten? Eight years old, you were, and thieving from my shop. Who was it who looked at your plight and decided to make something of

you? Who gave you a roof and indulged your love of letters?'
Murdstone was not finished yet; he faltered only because
he had started labouring for breath. He clutched his chest
and, oblivious to the haunted look which had suddenly
coloured Bantam's face, went on, 'If I had no heart, boy,
you'd have been apprenticed to the gutter, like all the rest
– not the Worshipful Society of Apothecaries. You'd do well
to remember that when–'

'Benjamin,' Bantam ventured, moving past all pretence
by dropping the knightly title, 'might I look?' He ventured
near, daring to put his hands to Murdstone's temples –
where, beneath curls of white hair and faded birthmarks,
a vibrant vein had started throbbing.

'Off!' ordered Murdstone.

'Let me listen to your heart,' the physician dared say. 'I'll
bleed you, if I must. Some humours get misaligned.'

Murdstone scoured him with his eyes. The doctor had
already acquired some strange apparatus from his desk; it
hung around his neck, a single metallic disk dangling from
a tube.

'Mr Murdstone?'

Murdstone had conquered his breathing. 'No, boy,' he
muttered darkly, 'I've been bled dry too many times.'

On the Holborn high road, he hailed a hackney carriage
and had it take him to the water. There, with London
Bridge hulking over the Thames, he finally felt composed.
There was no promise in a physician's study; only the
promise of diagnosis and death. Out here, where the river
sparkled, there was nothing *but* promise. The catalyst that
brought about his life's second elevation might already have
been found. It could be anything: a pocket watch, inscribed

with the initials of some gentleman desperate to have it back; a killer's confession, sealed into a bottle and cast into the river's murk; a golden coin, bearing the legend of Julius Caesar. He could have it all back – the townhouse on Hanover Square, the servants to do his bidding – if only the hour was right.

The only thing he couldn't have back was time – and, as soon as he thought about that, the strange tightness returned to his breast; he had to sit, watching some rivermen rescue their barge from the mud, while he remembered how to breathe.

In the legends, there were men who lived for ever. Methuselah lived for nine hundred and sixty-nine honest years. But Benjamin Murdstone's body was full of betrayals. It was the river life that did it. Every year on a river cost a man seven in a pampered Mayfair maisonette.

By the time he reached Ratcliffe, the touch of dusk was in the air. He gathered the crew where he always did, between the storehouses south of the Highway. Last of all came Nell, her freckled face and mousy curls curiously clean of all grime. Balanced on her tin kettle was a drowned cat.

He could feel the anticipation building in his breast – so different from the panic and constriction of Bantam's study. The streets were coming to life as evening approached. Here were the rag-gatherers and the cat's-meat carriers, the rubbish carters and refuse-mongers, the beggars, the barrow boys and bone-men. Here was London, vast, outrageous, free.

'Tell me, what did the river provide?'

31

One after another, the mudlarks set down their baskets, their caps, Nell's tin kettle.

Murdstone saw coals and pieces of pottery, shreds of canvas, chunks of fat tossed overboard from a ship's galley.

He wandered among his wards, still seeking his diamond in the dirt.

Not one of them wanted to catch his eye, but his silence compelled them. 'There has to be more. The storm upturned the river.'

He reached into one of the pails, and came back with a piece of driftwood still rimed in effluent. They'd tried to fill out their finds with stones and cockle shells. But no silver glinted in the bottom of any basket. No ivory sundial hid in the sand.

'Do you want to live like this for ever?' he breathed.

And again he thought: time, time, time – the only resource he had left, and every day it was being wasted.

'Well?' His eyes landed on Nell. Nell, who was the smallest of them all. Nell, who still carried hope and good feelings in her heart. She'd be truthful with him – if not out of gratitude, then out of fear.

'Was there nothing else on the river today, little Nell?'

Nell's head had been hanging. It was easier to lie when somebody could not look through your eyes, directly into your soul. But now she looked up.

Murdstone was not the only one staring at her. Other eyes kept flitting her way, desperate to know what she might say.

'Not a thing, Mr Murdstone. I'm sorry,' she trembled, 'we worked so hard.'

A trade had been made: one lie told, in return for a

stranger's life. But Benjamin Murdstone did not know this, not quite yet, so all he could do was sit back, half-destroyed, as the mudlarks fanned out into the streets to hawk their wares.

Every day, a trade: one more day of his life, for the promise of a better life to come.

But how much life did Benjamin Murdstone truly have left?

*

The gloaming stole like a thief along the river, bringing with it the advancing tide. The sky was clear tonight, its blackness punctuated only by the fires jostling the wharfs.

But slow down now. Sneak a look inside the seaward cave. Sail, like little Nell's voice, into the dreams of a dying man. Old memories, too phantasmagoric to have ever been real, are being unearthed tonight.

Through the knotted passageways of some abandoned monastery, there staggers a man. Left he turns; then right. Forward he ploughs; then back. Some passageways taper into tiny points of nothingness; others open into great overgrown atria. But wherever he turns, the monastery only goes on.

And yet – he knows there must be a way. If only he could hear the voice, it might guide him. It's guided him before, lifted him through the layers of his dreaming. He'd be panicked, trapped, uncertain which way to turn – and there she'd be, his angel on his shoulder, whispering into his ear.

That voice breathed peacefulness into his heart. It beckoned him along the right path.

But it's abandoned him now. He cries out, into an echoing antechamber, but there is no response.

'Hello?' he hollers.

'Are you there?' he cries.

'Please help me . . .' he falters.

But the girl's ghostly voice is gone. Now it's just him and the silence, lost in the labyrinth of the mind.

'Don't go out at night,' her mother used to tell her, 'for at night the devil steps out of men.'

Childhood scares, for a childhood night. Nell's memory of sitting in the upstairs window, her mother bent over her needlework as they waited for her father, was never as vivid as it was with the coming of the winter dark. The others said they scarcely remembered the time before Murdstone. Nell herself clung onto it, with the same faith that the once-upon-a-time Benjamin Murdstone had clung onto his ivory sundial. If she'd forgotten which house it was they used to live in, the memory was no less powerful. She could still hear her mother counting as she ran stitches along a hem. Once, Nell had dreamed of conjuring beauty out of dull fabrics, just as her mother used to do. There was sorcery in stitching. Now, she lugged her tin kettle from door to door, searching for those who wanted cheap coals.

There were regular places she went to. When she dared venture into Bluegate Fields, she could ordinarily offload coals to a boy the others said was sweet on her. The hag who lived above the ironmongery could afford coals from no-one other than a scavenger. But tonight, as darkness hardened, she stood outside the haberdashers at St George in the East and gazed into the window. She'd followed her mother through those doors too many times. On some commission for a lady better than they were, seeking buttons and lace, rolls of thread. A fantasy land for a little girl – until death came knocking, and snuffed the magic out.

She was gazing into the window when she heard the same discordant whistling she'd heard on the river that afternoon. She froze, watching his reflection pass behind her. There was no reason for Noah to be this far away from the corners he usually hawked his finds along Knock Fergus – except, of course, the cobbler's shop at the end of the row.

She turned, just in time to snag him by the sleeve.

'You took those boots,' she said, severely.

In reply, Noah jangled the coins in his pocket. 'You got your thinking all wrong. I was sat at that devil's deathbed nearly an hour. Think of what that hour cost me, out on the river. No, little Nell, I took what's mine by right.'

The measure of a bad soul was how easily he convinced himself he was doing right. 'But when he wakes, he'll need them.'

'Might be they got lost in the river. Could have happened.'

'But it didn't.'

This conversation was boring Noah. He stooped directly to her ear. 'I'll not feather Murdstone's bed tonight. Won't be a single coin in my pocket by the time we reach the Water's Edge. It'll all be in here.' And he gripped his distended belly with the ferocity of an assault. 'You tell a soul, Nella, and he'll know what you've got sleeping in that cave.'

This was how secrets were kept: not by trust, but in fear. She found herself nodding, though every bit of her resisted.

'Come on then,' said Noah, 'you're skinny as a stick. I'll buy you a fish supper.'

Her body cried out for it. There'd be bread at the Water's Edge, and gravy for dipping, but the thought of hot fish ignited corners of her she hadn't known existed.

She was about to go with him, when she thought again of the stranger's hand, tensing in her own.

Then she stepped back.

'Suit yourself, Nella. There's one of us'll be sleeping sound tonight.'

She ran, legs windmilling wildly underneath her, back through the tangle of alleys, back beneath the vast starry vaults from which her mother and father looked down. She was not quite the first up the boarding-house stair, but she caught no-one's eye as she flung herself onto her straw mattress, buried her face and sobbed hot, urgent tears.

They were still coursing out of her as she pulled the paper package out of the mattress innards. Then, alone in the corner – and having first licked her fingers clean – she stroked the contents as gently as her mother once stroked her hair.

The two satin slippers were bound together in soft peach ribbon. Their leather soles untarnished. The darning around their toes perfected by her mother's hand.

She didn't often look at them, except in the dead of night. But now, for some reason she couldn't quite fathom, she needed to *feel* them. She needed to run her fingers along each stitch, knowing that her mother had done the same.

She'd worn them only once.

It was the day her mother had given her a dream.

The attic was filling up now. The whisper went round: Murdstone was in the boarding house below. Then he too appeared, climbing crookedly up the ladder to receive his tithe.

Nobody noticed Nell. That was why it was easy to slide the package back into the mattress. She waited her turn to approach Mr Murdstone, then slunk back to her cot.

'Better tidings tomorrow,' Murdstone moaned, as he beat his way back to the trapdoor. 'But how many tomorrows have we got?'

More than you was the whisper that went round, after Murdstone was gone. Nobody doubted that the old man's passion was undimmed, but all harboured doubts that his body compared.

'You've been crying, little one.'

It was Sally-Anne. She'd come to sit at the bottom of Nell's bed, while they waited for fodder from the boarding house below.

Nell shook her head. 'He took the boots. Noah, when he was playing nurse.'

Sally-Anne shuffled a little closer; then she said, without a hint of malice, 'Sweetpea, that man will be dead before morning.'

Every inch of Nell tightened. 'You don't know that.'

Sally-Anne brushed one of Nell's curls from her eyes, as if to wipe away her tears. 'Sweetpea, there isn't a thing you could do better. Your heart doesn't have to break for him.'

But it did, thought Nell. She wasn't sure why, but it did. The storm had given him to her to protect. She didn't want to walk away – not this time, no matter what anyone said.

'I want my mama,' said Nell.

So did so many who gathered in this attic, but you learned to live without.

See the small child, her face pressed forlornly to the glass . . .

Dusk had deepened to the black of night. From the attic alcoves came the sounds of sleeping bodies, lost in labyrinthine dreams of their own. There wasn't a soul here, not even Noah, who wasn't visited by some devil while they slept. That was why Nell sat at the window in the attic eaves. In her hands: two satin slippers from a time long ago.

She'd waited too long already. She'd realized it, the moment Murdstone had gone. All of her duties dispensed for the day, and still she sat here, praying. But what use was prayer? Sally-Anne said prayers every night. Murdstone prayed for his miracle in the mud. There were angels looking over the good Christian souls of London, but not for those who dwelt in its attics and cellars.

Not for those who clung onto life in the seaward cave.

So she stole among the sleeping bodies, through the attic trapdoor – and off, into the night.

What place was London for a child? The city changed under starlight. By night, every footfall was a peril. The hour of housebreakers and cutpurses was upon her. But by the river she found her courage.

The tide was high, but she knew the river rocks too well to fear it. Sometimes, the water surged around her knees; on the approach to the seaward cave, she plunged to her waist – and thought, for a moment, that she had lost the satin slippers to the tide. Tied by their ribbon around her neck, she wore them like a genteel lady's necklace – and there they remained as she lifted herself from the water and crawled towards the fractured rock.

Inside, the embers still glowed. That was a good sign. She reeled past, dropping at the prostrate figure's side. Her trembling fingers balanced on his breast, long enough that she could feel its stuttering rise and fall. There was still life in him, then. A heart was still beating.

'I'm sorry,' she said. 'I shouldn't have left. But I came back. I'm here now.'

Words she wished she'd said to her mother. At ten years old, there was already so much in life she wanted to take back – so, as if in penance, she untied the ribbon from her neck and settled the slippers in the crook of the stranger's arm. Her mother's token. Sorcery in the stitching. Yes, that had to mean something. It just had to . . .

'I'm here,' she promised. 'It's your Nell. Wake up for me now.'

In a cavernous underworld, where roam the spirits of the dead, the stranger staggers blindly, seeking something, seeking *anything*, just a sliver of light to show him where to go.

Loneliness is both intimate and vast. He'll live it for ever, if he can't find his way out.

And then: '*I'm here,*' says a voice. '*I came back.*'

He whips his beast's head around. Two tunnels open in front of him. Two forks in a road.

'Please,' he utters, 'I don't know which way to go.'

'Open your eyes . . .'

Nell turned back to the fire, crumbling a length of driftwood into the ashes as she sought to bring new life to the flames.

'My mother made them for me,' she said, if only to keep her teeth from chattering. 'There was a seamstress she worked for, somewhere out west. My mother had been an apprentice, once upon a time. That was before she knew my father. And when he got sick, she needed more work. So I went with her, one day, to call on her old mistress. We took the omnibus out west! I'd never seen such things. There are palaces out there. Playhouses and parks. And my mother, she went to the old shop, the one where she'd apprenticed – only it wasn't a tiny shop any more. There were ball gowns hanging in a window. And inside . . .' Nell looked round. She fancied she could hear the stranger's breathing, more laboured now – as if he'd been running, perhaps. She took a rag, doused it in what was left of the water, and mopped his brow. 'My mother's old mistress had started making gowns for the playhouses. There was dancers come to London, all the way from Paris – and when they saw what my mother could do with her thimble and thread, they wanted no other. Come and work for us, they said. So that's what my mother did – stitched their frocks and gowns, and these dainty little slippers, soft enough for dancing . . .' She faltered in the telling, then wondered why she was telling it at all. She'd never told a soul in the attic. None of them carried tokens with them of their former lives. Plenty of scars got carried around, but rarely a hope, rarely a dream. 'There was a day, just weeks before she sent me to the river.' Nell didn't want to say 'died', for there was death enough in the air around her. 'The new playhouse had opened. The Alhambra Circus, that's what it was called. My mother had never taken me before, but I didn't have a father by then, so off I went – to carry her bag, she said, and speak only when I was spoken to, because these were fine ladies, finer than we'd ever be. French ladies – ballerinas, come to dance on the stage.

'I'd never seen a place like that. You dream about palaces, places for kings and queens, but you can't imagine it until you see it. There are other worlds – and there I was, in the middle of one. My mother was taking measurements and holding up fabrics. They *liked* her, those dancers, even though they were so much better than us. And I know she told me not to speak, not to touch – but she didn't scold me when one of those dancers took me up on stage. I suppose it was charity. Yes, that's what it was. The last time there was charity in this life. "But I'll show you how to dance," she told me. And there I was, on a stage, standing on my tiptoes like she told me, then up – up in the air, balanced on her palms like it was *me* flying. *Me . . .*' Was ever a memory as vivid as this one? Pure and absolute; incorruptible, no matter what the depredations since. A memory like that could be tossed into the river's dark waters and never lose its shine.

She had been so caught up in its telling, eyes mesmerized by the rising flames. Now, she turned to the sleeping giant. Her eyes lit upon his blistered lips. 'Wait there,' she said suddenly, 'I'll be back.'

*

'No,' he moans, 'not again, don't leave me again.'

I'll be back.

I'll be back.

I'll be back.

Three words echoing, through the enormity of time.

Nell crashed to her knees, dipping the pail into the water and swirling it to get rid of the worst of the silt. Then, in a tangle of arms and legs, she scrambled back to the rocky crevasse.

He hadn't had a drop to drink all night. That was what it was. He needed water. Something to remind his body it was still alive.

She was warming the water over the flames, skimming off froth and scum, when her thoughts returned to that day at the Alhambra. 'I was so tired I didn't remember the carriage home. I was in the theatre, and then I was being carried up the old stairs, the bed in the corner where it used to be. When she laid me down, I was still wearing those slippers. I think I started bleating, then. I thought I'd be in trouble. I wasn't a thief – not back then.' A momentary shame caught her, for all the devilries she'd had to do since. What would her mother think of her little dancer now? What would she think of everything she'd become? 'But no, she said. They're for *you*, Nell.'

The water was almost ready. For the first time, she could see her reflection in it. She peered at herself, as her mother must have peered that day. 'Mine?' she had said. 'But how can they be mine?' And then her mother had spoken the words she had carried with her ever since. She spoke them out loud, for the very first time: 'They *loved* you, Nell. They said you were a natural. My dancing girl. My ballerina.' Her voice had started fraying, like a poorly stitched hem. Why say all this, to a dying man? Why bring it to mind at all, after so many years of pushing it away, into the edgelands of her thoughts? She hung her head. She did not know. People died in the river every day. There was nothing fair about life. 'My mama said I was to go again, back to the Alhambra Circus, back among the dancers. If they saw me a second time, perhaps there'd be a chance. New dancers had to come from somewhere, she said. Why not the streets of Ratcliffe?' But then: death, and the river. Promises exchanged with Mr Murdstone. 'But if I *had* been a dancer, I wouldn't have been on the river this morning. It wouldn't have been me who found you. It would have been Noah or one of the others, and who knows what they would have done.' She hardened. 'I'll get your boots back. I promise. And when you wake, you can tell me who you are and what happened to you. We can put it right. I know we can —'

The underworld resolves into tunnels of white marble. Landslides retreat at his approach. Dead-ends reveal themselves to be doors. Down some tunnels lies darkness; down others, bright light. He paws his way into that brightness, listening as the voice gets stronger.

'Tell me who you are . . . We can put it right . . .'

Hope springs eternal, in the breasts of beasts and men.

'I'm coming,' he tells her.

And as he starts running, he reaches out his hand.

*

43

The water was almost warm enough. Nell stirred her finger in it, then put it to her lips. You got to know the taste of the river. Wapping water was different from Woolwich, Tower Bridge more bitter than the Executioner's Dock.

A final image raked across her: the last day with her mother, tipping the cup with broth of bone and beetroot to her lips. She'd spilled so much of it, and sobbed for the waste. Afterwards, she'd wondered: if my mother had drunk it up, would she have recovered? Would I have been sent to the river at all? Would I be a dancer, even now, and my mother travelling with me, fitting my gowns?

'Here now, it's ready.'

She turned.

She froze.

The man was no longer lying, derelict, on the cavern floor. Somewhere along the way, he'd picked himself up – and now he was propped against the sloping rock, filling the cave's dark interior. The firelight made a wild fandango as it coursed across him. He'd seemed vast lying down, but not as vast as this. His torso was broad and bulging, his head so heavy it pitched forward, banked in black hair.

His breaths were even more ragged, now that he sat up. One of his leviathan's hands was turned to a fist and used to brace his body on the cold stone floor; the other was pressed to the wounds on his side.

Nell hadn't known she'd be frightened, but apparently it was so; the water was churning in the pail.

From the front, he was less than a man; in profile, more bestial still. And yet, now that she considered him more closely – fighting the urge to run which had, quite unaccountably, taken hold of her – she thought he had the appearance

44

of some creature just being born as well. His eyes were marked not in fury but in caution and terror. They rolled, like a fawn's as it tries to take in the world it's just been instructed it will have to survive.

It wasn't only Nell who was shaking. The stranger was shaking too.

In his hands, her mother's satin slippers seemed fit for a doll.

'Please,' he snorted – and, of course, a face like that couldn't make normal sounds, so the word seemed tortured too. 'Who are you? What do you want?'

3

Down There in the Dark

Off the Ratcliffe Highway, London, November 1861

Perhaps you've known frightened children. Dredge your
memories like mudlarks dredge the river, and you might
even remember a time when you were one yourself. That
oft-forgotten feeling of being tiny and faced with the vastness of the world; as adults, we experience it only when
we gaze at the stars.

Nell tried not to feel small as she stared at the stranger –
but, caught in his bovine glare, it was difficult not to feel
like a fieldmouse.

'Where am I?' the man snorted. 'What is this place?'
With every question, his voice – already so strained, so full
of whispers and cracks – rose in pitch. 'Please – what do
you want?'

With great effort, the stranger lifted himself. Too vast to
stand upright, he seemed, for a moment, to form part of the
wall itself. Then, he lumbered forward. Two great strides
was all it took until he eclipsed Nell. His shadow fell on the
fire, dousing instantly its light. The stench of him, now that
he moved, was overpowering – not just the deep, ripe smells
of the river, but something of the tannery, the stable-yard,
the pure-finders' wagons that rolled up and down Ratcliffe.

His great jaws opened. In that moment, Nell was back in every bedtime tale her mother used to tell. She imagined he might howl, but instead one of his great hands fell to his side, and the place where the daggers had been driven into him. Then, with plumes of breath filling the seaward cave, he pitched forward, into the fissure.

Outside, the tide crashed against the rocks. 'You can't go out there,' Nell gasped, 'not back to the river. I'm the one who found you, washed up on the tide. I'm . . .'

The stranger stood in the opening, his black hair flying in the wind to reveal the calcified protrusions underneath.

'*Nell*,' he said, with a snort like a bull working up its temper. 'You're *Nell*.'

Then he looked back.

Yes, Nell knew fear now. Her eyebrows pinched in trepidation. She hardly dared look at him – except there he was, the world entire, filling up the inner sanctum of the seaward cave.

Frightened children cower and squirm. They shrink into themselves, because children know that the only way to defeat the ogre is to become so tiny that his eyes cannot pick you out. And perhaps that would have been Nell, if only she hadn't seen the satin slippers dangling in the stranger's hand. There they hung, suspended by ribbon from a single monstrous finger.

She'd laid them with him as a token, the relic of one death to ward away another. Something her mother once told her popped, unbidden, into her head: *when you send an act of kindness out into the world, Nell, it will come back and find you again.*

'What did you say?' she whispered.

The stranger only exhaled.

'How do you know my name?'

In front of Nell, the man started swaying, his body twisting around his preposterously sized hips. 'You've been in my head,' he snorted – and Nell realized, then, that it was not a furious snort, but simply the way he spoke. 'What were you doing in my head?'

He shook himself, like a dog labouring out of the river. The act of a man trying to shake some demon out of his thoughts. Perhaps it sent pain ricocheting from his wounds – for he gripped his side again, then sank to the floor in front of the fissure.

'In your . . . head?'

'I heard you calling me.' Strength, fury, fire – whatever it was that had been propelling the giant – seemed to be fading from him now. 'Come this way. Come that. *Open your eyes.*' Then, wrapping his arms around himself, he repeated the one word, '*Nell.*'

Nell had sat like that too, with knees tucked up under the chin and arms wrapped around them, the way a child will cuddle itself when nobody else is there to do the job. Strange how it could make even a behemoth seem fragile and forlorn.

'You were dreaming,' she said, realizing what he meant. 'I talked to you, in case you might hear. I didn't know how deep you were sleeping. How far away.'

'Trapped in dreams,' he said, through teeth too vast for his jaws.

Nell's heart was hammering – but, even if she'd been able to get past him, it was too late to flee. The tide was at its zenith; come morning, they'd find her, like she'd found him, washed up on some distant turn of the river.

If only to keep from trembling, she bowed back to the fire, fanning it to further life. By some strange mercy, the stranger hadn't upended the pail as he crossed the cavern. She set it back among the flames.

'Who did this to you?' she asked.

'I don't remember,' he said, in his rasping, whispery voice. 'Men like these, they always come.'

'But . . . why?'

His hands, gnarled as hooves, came up to touch the prehistoric ridges of his brow. There was Nell's answer: because they saw him for what he was.

'You're frightened,' she realized. She could see it in his big, black eyes. You would not call eyes like that 'doe-like', for there was nothing graceful about this stranger's appearance, but there was something of a fawn's skittishness in them all the same. Something of the prey animal, being hunted.

He whispered, more gently now, 'Where am I, Nell?'

The water in the pail was piping hot. Nell took it from the fire and crossed the cave to place it by his side.

'Ratcliffe,' she said, 'under the Highway.'

'Then the river brought me a distance. How long have I lain here?'

'We found you at dawn.'

A shudder ran through him: exasperation, exhaustion; fear, fury, pain. 'I need to get back.'

'But where?' mouthed Nell.

The stranger bowed his great body over the pail, nostrils flaring as he took in the scent.

'It's just river water. You ought to have drowned in it, but you didn't.' She watched him lift the pail and imbibe.

There, she thought, he couldn't hurt her now, not now he'd drunk from her cup. 'You're safe here. There isn't a soul knows where you are – only me and the other mudlarks. We wouldn't tell a sparrow.'

There was something else she wanted to say, though she scarcely dared. If she asked what came next, it would be the beginning of something. A question like this was like one of Mr Murdstone's trades; it could not be taken back.

'Please – what's your name?'

How do friendships begin? What is the germ of that sacred association? If we are fortunate, we end our lives in a web of cords, each one connecting us to another loving soul. But trace those connections back, and where are they formed?

In one person offering their name, in exchange for another's.

'Minos,' he stuttered.

4

Mr Murdstone's Repose

The Lowood Coach House, London, November 1861

Benjamin Murdstone had lived in finer environs than the back parlour of the Lowood coach house, but he'd lived in much poorer as well. Of all the stations of his life, this room – with its beams fitting snugly together, the armchair, the bedstead and hearth that hardly ever rained black soot – was, perhaps, the least remarkable. Neither low nor high, neither slovenly nor grand; more comfortable than the unnumbered cell in the Marshalsea, but without a hint of the indulgencies that had greeted him in Mayfair. At night, the mice in the skirting kept him awake with their incessant scurrying, but as far as waiting rooms went, this was one he could bear.

Life is full of waiting rooms, he'd once told one of his wards. He'd been a bookseller back then, with a shop of antiquities off the Charing Cross Road. 'The Foundling Hospital was a waiting room. The river, a waiting room. These shelves and counters, they're a waiting room too. Every man's waiting for what happens next.'

'Then you die,' the boy had told him.

'What?'

'Well, Mr Murdstone, if what you say is true, isn't the whole world a waiting room?'

It occurred to Murdstone, now that he was lost in this memory, that that boy had been Bantam. He shook his head with a strange desolation; it seemed like yesterday that Bantam had been knee-high and scaling the shelves of Murdstone & Sons. The years of his life, wasted in waiting.

Just a little longer . . .

He'd been expecting the knock at the door but, nevertheless, it startled him when it came. It was an aspect of old age he hated more than most, this tendency to look backwards and fritter away the hours on moments long gone, as if you could change a thing, as if they still belonged to you. Memory was the curse of a life long lived.

He needed his driftwood cane to cross the chamber. 'One moment,' he called out, reaching for where he'd propped it by the hearth.

As he was levering his way there, he called out for her to enter. Consequently, he was still only paces from the hearth when a key scratched in the lock and the door drew back. There she was, fifteen years old and with all the promise of life still inside her. Marie was the landlord's daughter and earned her keep without sifting through the river mud all year long. Hers was not a profession for which Murdstone had any respect – she would spend her life here, then perish in the same room she'd been sired in; where were the *possibilities* in that? – but he liked the girl enough to have made her a promise: that, when right was restored and Murdstone lionized once more, she would be among his favourite courtiers. The girl had few wits but perhaps she deserved an elevation of her own.

'Did you get them?' Murdstone asked.

Marie had a furtive look about her, but the package was in her hands. 'I believe it's all here.'

Murdstone accepted the package, wrapped in newspaper and string. He'd been sending Marie to the street of Chinese lanterns for the six seasons he'd boarded here, a narrow lane off the Highway where an apothecary dealt in herbs from his native Orient. The apothecary made his living stupefying sailors, but his talents extended much further; the package in Murdstone's hands – of ground horn and bones, dried moulds and powdered roots – had been fortifying him for months. They knew about immortality in the Orient; the apothecary said that one of the emperors of old, having grown weary of his throne, still roamed the continent, cloaked in a vagabond's clothes.

'Marie,' Murdstone began, 'I wonder if you would be good enough to draw me a bath.'

'I'm sorry, Mr Murdstone, I—'

The senses he'd developed on the streets, on the river, in the Marshalsea yard, all told him something was wrong. This was not the apology of someone too tired to carry pails of hot water. He looked at her sharply. He'd been a fool; he'd taken her cowed look for the same docility he'd known in her since the beginning. He hadn't seen the shadows crowding behind her, hadn't drawn in the reek of bodies just out of sight.

She'd brought them to his door.

Too late, he reached out to close it. By then, Marie had already been hustled out of the way and some ox of a man had put his shoulder to the wood. Benjamin Murdstone had taken his beatings across the years of his life – but it was easier to take a beating as a six-year-old scavenger than it was as a septuagenarian. Boys' bodies bounced back; the old were already made out of bruises, blood and broken bones.

Three men loomed behind the first. Murdstone saw them appear as, under the merest touch of his attacker, he fell to the ground. His last hope was to fight back with the driftwood cane, but it exploded out of his hands the moment he crashed down, and now it clattered – head over tip – into the flickering hearth.

There was a fifth man in the doorway. Murdstone recognized him well enough. 'Tetterby,' he whispered. 'Why?'

But he already knew. It was a trade, plain and simple: Murdstone's rejection, for a calamity of his own.

'Give my regards to the river,' Tetterby smiled, before he slunk away.

Murdstone's heart was the Thames in full tumult as the parlour door closed. The package he'd been clinging to had erupted out of his hands and now lay in the corner of his vision; its potions always quietened his heart, but the thought of imbibing them now was a vain and ridiculous hope. Nevertheless, he reached for it; moments later, his wrist was being crushed beneath one of the men's boots, his bones being ground just like the bones of the tigers he had bought.

Murdstone made no sound. This was a lesson of boyhood, never forgotten: don't shout out, don't scream, don't give them the pleasure. The pain moved like a tempest in his body. It continued to wrack him as the first man lowered himself, his knee pressed into Murdstone's breast.

'Do you recognize me, Benjamin?'

Murdstone shook his head; it was about the only part of his body not pinioned in place.

The man reached down and, with thumb and forefinger, prised open Murdstone's eyelid, exposing the full white of his eye.

'Do you remember a man named Elkington?'

Some piece of the mystery resolved in the maelstrom of Murdstone's mind. Of course, Tetterby could not have commissioned these men; the man had no fortune to depend upon, only his barrow and sack-cloths. The only means Tetterby had to repay Murdstone's rejection was by relaying information. He hoped the bastard had done well out of it.

The knee pressed yet harder into his breast.

'Yes,' he gasped, 'yes!'

Elkington, one of the sons of Deptford. That had been another lifetime, when Sir Benjamin stood on top of the world, the colossus who had risen from the river. In the drawing rooms of Mayfair they spoke of Murdstone as prime minister, but that had never been Murdstone's dream. Why waste time in the halls of Westminster, when empires could be constructed in so many different ways? So it was to Louis Elkington and his fleet of merchant clippers that Murdstone had turned for his last and most bombastic trade. A man who had begun his life on the doorstep of the Foundling Hospital would end it as a merchant prince, importing teas and sugar, and all else that came on the routes from the East. The princedom Murdstone had in mind would mean Elkington far extending his reach, but Elkington – seeing in Sir Benjamin's scheme the means to stockpile even more wealth than his father – had been an eager participant in the trade. Nonetheless, he'd been half-ruined in Murdstone's fall from grace; and a man like Elkington – who'd never had to develop characteristics like 'grit' and 'imagination' because he'd been born to his position in life, earned nothing and understood even less – had not the resilience to begin again. Not like Murdstone, who returned to the river.

'We represent his interests,' one of the men said.

'And he's interested in getting his due,' said another.

'Six clippers forfeited. Contracts denied. And yet here you are, Benjamin.'

Murdstone choked out a defence: 'To share in the spoils, you share in the risk. It was a fair trade.'

'Aye,' said the first man, 'and so's this: your life, in return for everything due.'

'I have nothing—'

'You have a roof above you. You have pennies enough to waste on – what is this stuff?' One of the men had torn open Murdstone's package. Ground bone filtered through his fingers like coarse white sand. 'Is Sir Benjamin sickly, or is he just old?'

Without warning, the man pinning him down sprang back. Murdstone clamoured for breath, his arms reaching out as if he had been propelled off some precipice. He got to his knees. He crawled, like a babe. Then he was propped against his bedstead, watching as the interlopers ravaged the room. When they were done – with every fitting smashed, the armchair sundered, the fleece from the floorboards thrown into the fire – the first man returned to Murdstone's side, declared, 'You have until Christmas night', and ended his fear with a single scabby strike directly between his eyes.

It was Marie to whom Murdstone awoke. She'd pulled his head into her lap and was gently cleaning the blood from his whiskers. No amount of delicate sponge-work, however, could wash away the shame.

'I'm sorry, Mr Murdstone. I didn't know who they were. You'll believe me, won't you?'

In silence, Murdstone lifted himself. The tightness in his breast was more vehement than ever.

His driftwood cane was still in the hearth. When he drew it out, its head was a charred black bulb. This he marvelled at while Marie went on, 'I can still come with you, can't I? When you're restored? To be your servant, in a grand house, and do whatever you need?'

Murdstone stared into the cane's charred heart. 'Your father's going to need restitution for his losses in this room.' He had in mind another trade: a promise for the future, in return for a pardon in the now. But when Marie bowed her head – 'Mr Murdstone, he says you'll have to leave' – he knew what he had to do. 'Then I'm sorry, Marie. Our agreement is null and void.'

They'd taken everything he owned. Consequently, when Benjamin Murdstone was ejected from the Lowood coach house, into a midnight world where gas lamps struggled feebly against the winter dark, where moon-cursers ferried unsuspecting strangers by the light of their brands, where the streets vacated by pickpockets were now replete with fallen angels prospecting for gold, he was in possession of nothing but the clothes he was wearing, the boots in which he stood up, and the smoking bulb of his driftwood cane.

He did not want to return to the Water's Edge, but that was where his feet were leading him. It would serve no good for the mudlarks to suspect him fallen low – but Benjamin Murdstone had spent many long winters on the

London streets, and he knew the cold when it was coming on. November, deep November; by morning, Ratcliffe's slag heaps would be bejewelled in white frost. Both kings and vagabonds froze on nights like these.

The downstairs parlours of the Water's Edge were a-bustle, as ever they were. Murdstone ghosted through them, taking to the attic stairs.

In the rafters, the mudlarks stirred at the sound of his footfall. Murdstone watched as each of them came out of their dreams to find him standing there. He started counting them off, one by one: Gander and Sally-Anne, Potato Rot and Packrat Jack; Noah and . . .

'Where's Nell?'

Figures began picking themselves up, rising from the covers like cadavers from the grave. Sally-Anne found the stub of a candle; its rippling halo illuminated the room. Every eye had turned to the bed in the window, where the sackcloth sheeting was thrown back. No small child lay there tonight.

'Where is she?'

Murdstone snatched the candle stub and walked among them. He supposed a part of him ought to be grateful, for here was an empty bed when he was in need, but the mystery of it rankled. He'd had children take flight before. Each child who left the river robbed him of a chance to set straight the course of his life – and tonight, with bruises still blossoming along his ribs, this seemed more pressing than ever.

'Well? She was here this evening. Where is she now?'

Silence can have a curious quality. Sometimes, silence is a vacuum: nothing exists. But sometimes it is a seawall, being pounded by a wrathful tide; waves crash over its turrets, spray arcs over its stones – and somewhere, underneath the surface, the stones meant to keep the sea gods at bay are crumbling, one by one.

His eyes found Noah, rising from the nest of his bed.

'Please, Mr Murdstone,' Noah said, ignorant to the other eyes that begged of him, 'there's something you should know.'

5

The Courage of Others

Off the Ratcliffe Highway, London, November 1861

Minos.

It was a strange name – and yet, by the look of him, it seemed right. A man like this could not be an 'Oliver' or 'Charles'.

'Minos,' Nell said, testing out the edges of the word. 'I like it. I've never met a Minos.' She'd met men with half-names and stolen names, children with names they'd borrowed when they'd lost their own. It was easy to lose your name on the streets of Ratcliffe; folks started hollering at you, based on the canker on your cheek or the time they saw you scrounging for bones in the tannery yard, and suddenly you were called something new. Then your old name faded, and with it the person you used to be. She wondered if Minos was his true name, or perhaps something he'd been given. His face was so unreadable. How did you interpret features like these? The only thing she truly understood was the panic, the pain. 'Minos, where do you live? There must be somebody missing you. Somebody out searching.'

'Nothing like that, Nell,' Minos wheezed. 'Just a lodging house to lay your head. But I've missed work. I'm on the sewer, the Board of Works. They mayn't take me back.' His gnarled hand went, by instinct, to his pocket, only to find it empty. 'I remember now. I threw those men my satchel. I'd just been paid. I thought it might waylay them.' Then his big, black eyes fell on his feet. 'My boots . . .'

Nell's heart performed a little leap. 'The river,' she lied. Something told her she mustn't go on; one lie always spun off into the next, and soon you were tangled in them, like a fly condemned to the spider's web.

'Boots or not,' he breathed, 'I've got to get back.'

But when he tried to lift himself, some fresh pain ricocheted through his body; he gripped the place where the knife wounds festered, crashed against the rock – and, with great effort, lowered himself to the ground.

The effort must have worked some black magic on him. Nell saw a faraway look come into his eyes. 'Minos?'

His head banked towards her, but his eyes seemed to stare straight through.

'You mustn't move. Not tonight. You're weak, Minos.'

'I have to.' His voice seemed distant, as if every reserve of strength he'd had left had been used fighting his way up through dreams.

'Minos, please – let me see.'

She'd been nervous, taking the pail of water to his side, but now she scurried urgently into his shadow. There was an old fable, about a lion and a mouse; it popped into her head as she helped him peel up the patchwork shirt and reveal the livid red welts. The lines the daggers had drawn were still shimmering and raised, but she was surprised to discover their lurid colour was fading. Or perhaps it was just the ill light in the cavern.

'Minos, are you still there?'

He'd closed his eyes. That was the only reason Nell dared touch his brow. She could sense the heat radiating from him even before her fingers felt his clammy, ridged flesh. His wounds might have been in retreat, but fever still persisted – and fever was worse than any wound.

'Nell?' he rasped.

Her body was telling her to back away. Her heart was telling her to stay precisely where she was. 'You need to eat. When did you last eat? I'll bring food, whatever I can find.' She had no idea where she would find it; beg it, steal it, forsake whatever crumbs Mr Murdstone would provide. She had made the promise now; she would worry about the means of it later. 'Crabs. A big, fat eel. You never know what the tide can bring.'

You really didn't, thought Nell – and her hand returned to his brow, this time to wipe a curl of black hair away from his eyes.

He opened them.

'Nell,' he said again, and as he took her in, every shiver in his body seemed to fade.

It had taken every ounce of strength Minos had to pick his way out of whatever dreams had been dogging him. Now, Nell watched as his eyelids grew heavy and closed, like the shutters of the great townhouses her mother once took her to see. She remembered, now, how that had felt: when the shutters in those houses went down, the families within were safe in their own worlds, safe from the London night.

But it seemed different with Minos. Sleep was returning to claim him, but something inside was railing against it.

He closed a hand around her wrist and Nell had the sudden impression of a man floundering in the river, heaving himself onto a raft.

He didn't want to be trapped, realized Nell. Shutters kept out the London night – but what if the thing you were running from was already inside?

'I'll not go anywhere,' she told him. 'I'll be right here.'

But Minos had already slipped away from her. She took hold of his quavering hand.

The manifold rivers of London were in retreat wherever men trod. So many had already been tamed: turned to culverts and canals, then buried for ever in the city beneath the city, the London where Roman legions had once been garrisoned, where plague and fire and mad kings had been variously defeated or endured. The Tyburn was already conquered; the Fleet was on its knees. The Black Ditch, in which Murdstone remembered panning for lost trinkets – up at its source, where the street boys gathered at Rogue's Well – was no more.

But none had tamed the Thames. On nights like this, the scythe it cut through the city made even Benjamin Murdstone feel small, insignificant, unknown. He stood, now, on its swollen bank. In the shadows behind him, Noah braced himself against the cold.

'How far?' Murdstone demanded, gazing out across the black water.

'Ten minutes at low tide,' Noah began. He could still feel the eyes of the others boring into him, though Murdstone had commanded that they stay at the Water's Edge. The look on Gander's face, full of disappointment, reproach, and

not a little spite. 'You can't get there at high. The tide's
too deep.' He'd seen Murdstone lever forward on his driftwood cane. Its charred bulb was not the only sign that
Murdstone had been put through some passion tonight;
out here, there was no knowing the bloody swelling across
his nose, but it had been clear as day at the Water's Edge.
'Mr Murdstone, no!'

The end of the driftwood cane had been driven into the
water, as if Murdstone was commanding the river to part.
But nobody commanded the river, least of all one of its
servants.

Murdstone withdrew the cane and looked back at his
guide. It was impossible to see his face in this watch of the
night, but by the texture of his voice Noah knew a tempest
was brewing inside him. 'Never say no to me, boy.' Then
he looked at the stars above the city, judging the hour by
the wheeling constellations. 'We wait,' he declared.

All of life's a waiting room; he could wait just a little bit
longer.

He awakes to find himself in a hall of glass, each wall
revealing another glass wall behind it – and the infinite
faint reflections of his own face peering back. It takes all
his ailing courage to meet himself face on. Behind him, all
his boundless iterations stretch back. The nearest are iden-
tical; yet, further in, things change. Perhaps his eyes are
deceiving him. Surely it is so. One of the deeper reflections
stands a head taller than him. One deeper than that sports
two spiralling horns.

'Nell?' he whispers.

'Nell?' he cries out.

'*I'm here,*' comes the ghostly voice. '*I'm sitting right here.*'
One of the glass walls shatters and he sees a way through.

Sometimes the thing that gives you strength is the courage of others.

Nell broke her promise in the second hour.

Outside the seaward cave, the tide was receding. It would be some time before the darkness paled, but by Nell's reckoning this was her only chance. He needed sustenance – soon, before he sank too deep to be saved. So it was onto the jet-black river that she ran.

The retreating tide revealed rock pools outside the opening of the cave. Nothing but weeds had been cast into these – but weeds were enough for broth, so she strung some over her shoulder. Then she followed the tide further, past the rocks, onto the freshly revealed mud. Here, by the moon's phantom light, she began searching the shallows. Even the tiniest crab would be something. A great fat eel, almost too bounteous to think about.

She lit first upon a piece of coal. Next upon a tangle of wire. A length of string must have been some fisherman's line, but no pink river trout dangled from its end, nor even a scrap of bait.

She was standing on the water's edge when she saw the dead gull. A gull freshly killed would have been too much to hope for, but even this grisly thing was her prayer being answered. She peeled back the bird's remains – and, just as instinct had told her, saw the crabs underneath.

Disturbed from their banquet, the crabs scattered.

There were four, three half the size of her palm and one plumper yet. It was the plumper one she lunged for. Yet the crab had not survived long enough to reach that size without guile. It darted this way and that in its attempts to reach its mother river.

Nell took off in quick pursuit. In a flurry of grasping hands and stumbling feet, she charted a zigzagging course through the silt.

'Come here!' she cried out. 'Got you!' But her hands kept closing on thin air – and the crab kept scuttling on.

There was almost something joyful about the chase. For a fleeting moment, Nell was able to forget the fevered giant in the cave. She was a girl chasing butterflies in the royal parks; she was with a dear friend, flying kites out on the common.

Then she was on her knees, for the quagmire at the river's edge had taken hold of her. The crab was mere feet ahead. It, too, had ceased its scuttling. To Nell, it seemed to be looking back, its eyestalks revolving to a place directly above her head.

Now was the moment. 'Come on, little one.'

Her fingers were almost upon it when a cane came down and skewered it into the dirt.

Nell twisted. The river mud rimed her eyelashes, but there was no mistaking the figure above, not even in the black of night. His face unusually swollen, he loomed above her with the same air of old: half beloved grandfather, half prison turnkey.

'Mr Murdstone?'

Murdstone drew his driftwood cane from the dirt. As if to reflect the ruin in his eyes, the crab dangled from its tip, bits of its devastated body twitching in its last expense of life.

66

They say that the eyes are the window to the soul. If it is so, poor Nell had looked into two unknowable souls tonight: two sets of eyes opening onto nothing but empty, incalculable depths.

'You have something that belongs to me,' Murdstone declared, with the tone of someone who will not be denied. 'Nella, where is it?'

6

The Sleep of the Dead

Off the Ratcliffe Highway, London, November 1861

'I came to this cave when I was a boy,' marvelled Murdstone
as he heaved his way up the rocks. The idea of Murdstone
as a boy was an aberration; the idea of him in their cave,
even worse. In the story he always told, the story of finding
the ivory sundial, he'd been a boy – but Nell had never
pictured him as anything other than a shrunken version of
the Murdstone in front of her.

He came, now, to the cave's narrow mouth. By the angle
of the rock, there was no sign of the firelight within – but
of woodsmoke there was plenty.

'Come, Nell,' said Murdstone, with a beckoning finger,
'you'll lead on.'

Mr Murdstone exerted a force like gravity, but never had
Nell felt it more keenly than she did as she picked her way
up the rocks. This route which had once been so familiar
felt suddenly treacherous; the path to their sanctuary,
debased and despoiled. Her skin was crawling as she slipped
through the crack in the stone.

Nell had skittered to the farthest edge of the cave by the
time Murdstone angled his way through. Now, here he
stood, his eyes open in rapture as he took in this creature

before him. Minos was still propped against the wall, his great head lolling. His ragged breathing filled the cavern's interior; when he snorted, the woodsmoke shifted it into strange striated patterns. And there, in the cup of his hands, sat the satin slippers, trailing their soft, peach ribbon.

'You kept this from me?' Murdstone whispered.

From some depth she did not know existed, Nell found the courage to say, 'He's not flotsam, Mr Murdstone. He's a living man.'

'Living,' came Noah's whispery voice as he sidled into the cave, 'but hardly a man, Mr Murdstone. Look at him. He had horns.'

Murdstone gritted his teeth as he fell at the giant's side. Laying down the driftwood cane, he dared to lift Minos's strange, protuberant jaw. Every bump and ridge ran under his fingers as he moved upwards, past the man's brow. There, he peeled back hair, to find the calcified protrusions.

'We got you a devil, Mr Murdstone.'

'He's not a devil!' shrieked Nell, starting forward.

Murdstone wheeled around, snatching the driftwood cane and driving her back against the wall as if at a rapier's point. 'Devil or circus freak, you lied, Nella Hart. You suckle at my teat for half your wretched life and repay me with *venom*. What are the rules of the river, Nell?'

'He took his boots,' Nell sobbed, through the tears clouding her eyes. It was not shame but panic that had brought them on. She ought to have grovelled and begged, but instead other words frothed out of her. 'Sold them for the price of a fish supper.'

Murdstone's fury spun in two different directions. He wheeled at Noah, wheeled back at Nell.

69

'You spiteful little *beast*,' Noah exclaimed, 'you've had them all lying for you, every last one. I'm the only one with a truthful bone in my body.'

'And a liar's supper in your gut,' Murdstone seethed, and drove his cane into Noah's belly, so that he doubled over and half his fish supper returned to his gorge. 'Rules of the river, Nell?'

'The river belongs to you,' Nell whispered, cowed at last.

'Bring me ropes,' he said. His eyes were on Nell, but his words were for Noah.

'Ropes, Mr Murdstone?'

'Plenty of barges on this river, boy. *Bring me ropes.*'

Nell hadn't known she'd be afraid without Noah, but apparently it was so. The moment he left, the knowledge that she was alone with Murdstone hardened around her. 'Mr Murdstone,' she ventured, 'his name is—', but then she broke off, for fear of giving anything away. Perhaps it was better that Murdstone knew nothing, not even that the ogre had opened its eyes. *Ogre.* She would have to stop thinking of him like that. His name was Minos and he was a man.

'You were always my favourite, Nell.' Murdstone's voice was heavy with disappointment as he picked his way around Minos, brooding over the feet with yellowed, cankerous claws. 'You fool, this man's wounded.' He'd seen the discolouration on Minos's shirt. 'Nell, what have you done?'

'You don't think I—'

'Somebody stabbed him and threw him in the mire. The river got into his blood. Don't you know what it can do in there? Nell, you damn fool, he needs help – real help, not a little girl to play nursemaid.' His hand returned to Minos's thick brow. 'He's fevered, and you've left him to rot. A man

like this, tossed up on my tide.' His voice rose, and Nell got
the distinct impression of a man trying to drown cats in a sack:
the cats his fury, which kicked and squealed and tried to break
free. 'A man like this comes from *somewhere*. He's not just
some city clerk. Not some ironmonger. He's a rich man's servant
– a charitable man, with so much silver that the only currency
worth anything to him is his own good deeds. Or he belongs
in a menagerie. A man like this doesn't *live*, Nell. He's owned.
That means he's a runaway. There's a trade in it, if I'm right.'

Nell's throat, swollen and raw. 'He's a man.'

'A dying man, if he's man at all.' Murdstone rushed to
the crevice, peered out into the paling world. 'You're to go
to Bantam at once. Bring him to me, before his surgeries
start. If he dismisses you, remind him of the geas I laid on
him when he was small. I lifted that man from the gutter.'
But Nell had only moved closer to Minos's side. *I'm here*,
she wanted to tell him. *I promised I'd stay.* The thought of
catching crabs to make broth seemed so far away. 'Nella,'
Murdstone went on, 'must you make me ask again?'

She could hear footsteps scrambling up the rocks. Noah
had returned, and in his hands a coil of sodden rope.

'You won't hurt him?' Nell dared to ask.

'Hurt him?' Murdstone said, incredulity twitching the
corners of his lips. 'Nell, it's I who shall save this man –
and, by doing so, start a second life.'

Dawn followed Nell along the river, harrying her just like
the tide.

She'd been taken to Bantam before. It was Bantam who'd
saved Potato Rot from the measles; Bantam who attended
the mudlarks in the Water's Edge, to prescribe bed-rest

and honey in hot water. The others said Murdstone liked them to see the doctor, not for the remedies he could provide – for these cost money with which Murdstone was loath to part – but for the promise he inhabited: the promise that, if they doggedly followed Mr Murdstone, they too might rise to positions of respect. Bantam was the very symbol of it, dangled in front of them like a carrot to a donkey.

Strange, then, that Nell's first sight of him was as he emerged from the Courage and Crown on the Holborn high road and reeled, in an inebriate fugue, along the street.

He didn't notice Nell as he tried to thread his key into the lock of his front door. Nell was used to that; sometimes, it helped to be small and overlooked, to matter not at all. It was only as he failed to find the keyhole that he startled at the sight of her. It sobered him in a second.

'Is he dead?' he asked. 'Is this the moment?'

She could see the expectation on his face: Benjamin Murdstone – former mudlark, former inmate, former gentleman and current Lord of the Seaward Cave – had finally accepted his summons to the Ever After, an invitation he had declined on no fewer than seven previous occasions.

When Nell shook her head, she had the impression, somehow, that she was letting him down.

'Then what is it?'

'He says you're sworn to him, Doctor. That you have to come.' For the first time, she found the courage to look him in the eye. 'Dr Bantam, we found a man.'

At least he fed her first. Bantam ministered to the degenerates of Seven Dials, and in return all they had to pay him with were potatoes from their carts, apples, heels of bread;

oatmeal and treacle, when they were feeling particularly thankful. It took remarkably little to fill Nell's belly; the doctor allowed her to eat until discomfort set in.

Then they were back on the river.

In another age, the ride in the hackney carriage would have filled Nell with delight. The Thames glided by, its current moving sluggishly against them. It was said that, in the world's darkest winters, the river froze solid – and that, in these winters, the people of London flocked down to the ice to set up booths and sell their wares. Mr Murdstone spoke of the age they led an elephant onto the river at Blackfriars; a fantasy, Nell thought, but she was sure the frost fairs had been real. What bounty the flats would have given up in a winter like that; a paradise for the scavenging class.

There was still some distance to walk when the carriage could go no further. By now, Gander and the rest had arrived on the silts. Some of them watched as Nell led Bantam on. She was sure Gander tried to catch her eye, but she bowed her head and kept pace with the doctor. Shame both dogged and propelled her every step.

Noah was out mudlarking too. Distant from the rest, he picked his way through the rock pools beyond the seaward cave. There was no day of rest, then, not even for the boy who'd brought Murdstone his wonder.

'It's here,' Nell said, when they approached the narrow crack in the stone.

The doctor looked nervously about him, finding only the barren tide.

'You think you're being tricked,' Nell said; it always disturbed her to realize that even adults could feel like prey,

73

'but you're not being tricked. Mr Murdstone!' she called out. 'Mr Murdstone?'

He appeared at her second insistence. Three hours in the dark had given him a look almost subterranean. Now that he was in the rose-pink light, Nell could see the patterns some bruisers had made of his face in the night. His eyes wore thick red abrasions, his nostrils crusted in crimson.

'Benjamin,' Dr Bantam began, 'what became of—'

'Worry not what became of me. Come in. The dawn's already old.'

Nell tried to fight the sinking feeling as she followed the physician through the crevice in the rock. She watched, through flurrying woodsmoke, as the doctor lowered himself at Minos's side.

They'd bound him by the ankles. Bound him by the wrists. By the embers of the fire she'd cradled, Minos had been transformed from patient to prisoner.

'Oh,' Bantam said, in a voice that suggested he had suddenly embraced sobriety. 'Oh my.' His hands reached out, to finger Minos's wrist and the faintest of pulses that was waiting there. 'And he just washed up on the tide?'

'Stabbed, skewered and thrown in the river,' Murdstone interjected, 'but the rest of these injuries are older, aren't they? He's been carrying them since birth.'

He meant the jutting jaw, the shape of his brow, the way his eyes sat a distance apart.

'They're not injuries,' whispered Nell.

Eyes scoured her. 'Nobody gave you permission to talk, girl.'

The doctor seemed full of admiration as his hands ran over Minos's inert form. When he found the knife wounds, he

hovered over them; when his fingers found the circles of
raised flesh, he lingered longer still. Nell saw his face wrinkle
– an expression that might have intimated disgust in a common
man suggested professional intrigue in the doctor – and,
some moments later, he was ordering her to open the leather
clasp bag he'd brought. Out of it she drew a strange wooden
tube connected by some length of rubber to a dull metal
disc. This he lay upon different parts of the dreaming giant's
breast, his ear pressed to the wood. 'His heart roars,' he
said, recoiling at intervals, 'but his fever . . .'

Now that his intrigue was breeding courage, he began
tracing the swellings of the man's face.

'Have you ever seen anything like it?' Murdstone asked.

'I've attended curiosities, but not like this.' *Deformity* was
not the right word. He'd seen plenty of deformity on the
streets of Seven Dials. Boys were born knock-kneed or
withered; men developed rickets and ended their lives in
the strangest contortions. But this creature was so unutter-
ably strange that he scarcely knew where to begin.

His hands had returned to the nest of Minos's hair.
Beneath the black fronds, he resumed his inspection. Nell
caught herself wondering what dreams were unfolding, even
now, inside that head.

The doctor ceased his caressing. 'Help me turn him,
Benjamin.'

Murdstone seemed uncertain whether he ought to venture
near.

'I can't do it alone,' Bantam went on.

'Help him, Nell,' Murdstone barked.

Bantam's eyes opened fractionally, perhaps sharing some
secret exasperation with Nell.

75

Nell tottered forward, reaching Minos's side.

'Take his shoulder now. I want to listen at his back.'

Nell did not have the strength to help move him, but an extra pair of hands was useful in levering Minos away from the wall. With Nell heaving on his arms, Bantam forced his way behind, lifting up the patchwork shirt to press his listening contraption to the beast's back.

But now Bantam faltered. 'I need light,' he said. His eyes flashed around the cavern. 'Mr Murdstone, a stump from the fire.'

Nell caressed the rough skin of Minos's arm, whispered 'I'm here' in the vain hope it might carry into whatever dream he was weaving, then watched as Murdstone spilled his light over Minos's back. 'A sailor, then,' said Murdstone. 'There are enough of those in the city.'

'I don't think it's a sailor's tattoo, Mr Murdstone.'

Nell lifted herself onto her tiptoes, the better to see the scarred mess of Minos's back. Plenty of sailors wore lattices of scars like this – it was their captains' way of keeping order, out over the endless blue – and plenty of sailors covered themselves in ink to mask the barbarity underneath; but the doctor was right – this was no sailor's tattoo, no depiction of anchors and galleons, nautical stars and shell-backs. The inked scars that dominated Minos's back had been cut into him not by the random fury of a cat-o'-nine-tails, but by a man with a mathematician's precision. They stretched from the blades of his shoulder to the small of his back: a square of intercutting lines, openings and passages between. In its heart, with a single opening running towards the nape of his neck, was a nucleus of knotted flesh.

'A labyrinth,' said Murdstone. Nell had never heard the word, but it sounded strange on Murdstone's tongue, as if he himself was testing out its edges. 'Like at Hampton Court. The Royal Horticulturalists are hosting one in Kensington, even now.'

Bantam remained transfixed. 'It's hardly a garden maze, Benjamin. These scars are deep. There's pain here – great pain.' To Nell's shock, he gripped Murdstone by the wrist and wrenched the flaming brand closer, tracing the lines of the labyrinth with the light. 'The ink is old. It's feathered in his flesh. And this design – I've seen it in Roman tiles.'

'A sailor might tattoo the map of some accursed island onto his flesh,' said Murdstone. 'He might turn himself into its atlas. But –'

Words had failed them both. They failed Nell too. She watched as the flaming brand was returned to the fire, Bantam pinching the bridge of his nose as he thought.

'I don't believe in devils, Benjamin, but this is a most unusual man. I would keep his presence here a secret. No doubt he's running from something. I've seen the like. If men like this don't trade their looks in the circuses, they come to unusual ends. This one's lasted longer than most. Fifty years old? Eighty? How to age a fellow like this?' He paused. 'Listen to me – he's feverish. Send your girl to the river. Bring back water. Boil it, then chill it again. Keep his temperature low – and, by God, rid this place of smoke. Let him breathe clean air. Or as clean as it gets in Ratcliffe.'

'You heard the doctor, Nell,' Murdstone barked. 'The river! And douse this fire!'

Nell was shaking. She tumbled to the cave mouth, though in truth all she wanted was to sit at Minos's side, to comfort him with whispers. Why she felt it so strongly, she hardly knew. It was her words which had pierced the veil of Minos's dreaming – and yet it felt as if something of him had invaded her too. When your heart went out to another, you did not easily summon it back.

The rose gold of dawn had blossomed into low winter sun. The river did not sparkle – for London rivers never did – but, where its waters broke against the opposite wharfs, she saw them capture the crisp winterlight.

Bantam's voice faded behind her. 'I have tinctures that might relieve some of his suffering. I'll have to return with them. But these ropes are too tight, Benjamin. You have him trussed like a hog.' She was skidding down the shale when the last words reached her. 'There's something about the look of him. I wonder if you remember, sir, when I ran errands for you at Murdstone & Sons . . .'

Nell had reached the edge of the river before the others approached. Packrat Jack and Potato Rot were further along the water, but Gander and Sally-Anne drew near.

'Nell? Sweetpea?'

It was Sally-Anne's name for her, the one she used to console her in the night. *Sweetpea*, because there was yet something sweet and innocent in the world. The problem, Nell realized, was that she didn't *want* consoling. She wanted to be the one at the bedside, consoling somebody else. If those dreams of old – that, one day, the slippers might be on her own feet, that she might yet dance, as her mother had told her, at the Alhambra Circus – were not to be, then she could at least have hope here, purpose beyond this endless river. It might have been a cat. A swallow, fallen from its nest. But it wasn't – it was a man, and he would have perished had it not been for her.

She was skimming the scum off the pail when Gander said, 'We tried to stop him, Nell. I promise. But you know Noah – he's never been one to toe the line. He thinks he's better than us. Thinks he can escape this river.'

Nell was about to say, 'We can all escape the river', when Noah's voice sounded from further along the mud: 'He kicked you out too, did he, Nell? Ol' Murdstone's a brigand. You bring him a treasure and he tells you you've robbed him. Well, we'll show him.'

Nell hoisted the pail. There seemed something so natural in the way it swung in her hand; all she had to do was let it swing a little bit further. And no sooner had that thought entered her head, the pail was flying, almost of its own volition. She watched as the frigid water cascaded over Noah's head.

'You're for it now,' roared Noah, once the shock had worn off. 'Murdstone might have let you off a beating, but you'll take a hiding off of me. Get here, Nell!'

Noah was striding forward, still brittle with cold, when Gander threw himself forth. 'There's not one of us wants you here, Noah. *Not one.* Not after you gave up Nell. Take the man's boots, fill your belly, then throw her at Murdstone's mercy? Think you're one of us, do you? Well, we'll see.' Gander looked over each shoulder. 'Anyone want to stand for Noah?'

Not a mudlark moved.

Still quaking, Noah stepped back.

'We don't betray each other,' Gander said. 'River rules. Ain't that right, Nell?'

But Nell was hardly listening. She had already returned to the rock pool. There, something sparkled. She crouched lower, lost her fingers in the dirt, and when she finally pulled them out, a tarnished silver chain was dangling down, half a locket weighing it down like an anchor.

The voices began almost immediately: 'Nell's got the magic touch . . . Another treasure! Hand it here, Nell, let's have a look!' But Nell did not reply.

A silver chain, they all seemed to be saying, what might *that* do for a life?

The same thing an ivory sundial once did, they all replied, in a chorus of silence.

How long had Nell dreamed of this? In those dreams, she would slide a trinket like this into her back pocket, then trade it out on the Highway for something grander. A silver chain would turn into a silken gown; the silken gown would open a door behind which fine young ladies were being considered as dancers; the ladies her mother had once known would recognize the seamstress's daughter, and tell her she had too long been dancing alone. And so would she follow the path Mr Murdstone himself had once pioneered: the rise from the river.

The Alhambra Circus . . .

And yet, as she stood here now, some bitterer truth pervaded her every thought. Why were the other mudlarks cheering? Why could they not see the bitter truth of the river: that sooner or later, whatever the tide gave up would belong to Murdstone; that here, on the river, not even your secrets were your own.

It was sodden, lonesome Noah to whom she looked last. Only he seemed to understand what she was thinking, and this itself was a kind of horror; it meant there was some thread that connected them too, she the keeper of the secret, and he its betrayer. 'Don't you dare, Nell,' he snapped, 'don't you—'

She closed her fist around the chain, drew back her arm, and pitched it as hard as she might into the river.

Sometimes there is strength in being small. They watched as one, as the chain and its dangling locket arced over the water, further and higher than it had any right to go, until it began its steep descent into the river's grey murk.

When it was done, she filled the pail, then turned to tramp back up the shale. Behind her, bodies floundered into the water in search of that which was already lost, but Nell didn't care. She reached the mouth of the seaward cave and angled her way inside. There, the doctor was inspecting the abrasions on Mr Murdstone's face, summoning him back to humanity by lotion and squares of muslin.

'Set it by the fire,' barked Murdstone, 'and back to the river with you.'

She ought to have done as she was bidden, and yet the very act of casting that treasure into the water had brought Nell boldness. She bowed, instead, at Minos's side. 'I'm sorry,' she whispered, 'I won't be far. Don't forget, Minos. Just wake up for me—'

Murdstone, slow to realize she had not already gone, barked out 'River!', and the shock of it propelled Nell to her feet. She skittered, half tumbling, to the mouth of the cave. Yet before she reached the fissure, a shuddering in the corner of her vision brought her to a halt. One of Minos's fingers flexed, then another; the fingers were clenching, forming a fist – and Nell saw, then, what had become of her mother's satin slippers. They were inside the giant's hand, hidden almost entirely, with only the peach ribbon trailing out to reveal they were there at all.

That was enough, she thought. Even if she wasn't at his side, he *knew*.

Nell spent that day on the river, but her heart stayed with Minos all the same.

7

This City of Stories

Let us leave the riverbank now. There are countless tales to be told of the rivermen and their battles with the mudlarks – but London is a fabled city and its streets have yet more stories to spill. There is a dethroned king who drinks cider by night at the Prospect of Whitby public house. In a Hyde Park ditch sleeps a vagabond who would give up his secret fortune to any passer-by with a heart big enough to listen. In this city there are good men and ill, cuckolded killers and mothers on the verge, great men of science and scoundrels of romance – and, in the same moment that Nell caught sight of the peach ribbon trailing from Minos's hands, another story was beginning: a train grinding into Paddington Station, disgorging first a flotilla of railwaymen, clerks, wayfarers and day-trippers; and, latterly – heaving on the suitcase into which she had, two weeks ago, stowed away her life – a young woman with fine black hair, crystalline eyes and a scalded look.

She'd been told London was a storied city; what the storytellers neglected to say was that there was dirt in fables too; that, for every dream foretold, there were a thousand snuffed out. Nobody rhapsodized the wretches in fairy tales; the smog and villainy, the destitution and disease. She hadn't yet left Paddington Station before she'd seen it all.

Outside, London rushed by.

Speak as you will of St Petersburg and Paris, where the streets are alive with magic, but you will not come close to the feeling Sophia had as she hurried past the braying tramps and gentleman thieves outside Paddington Station, bound for the grand white facade of the Great Western Hotel. Inside was an oasis of calm compared to the headiness of London without. She waited among the buzzing concierges until a desk became clear, then approached with the refinement in which she'd been schooled all her life.

'Mrs . . . Chrétien?' the desk clerk began, parroting back the name she'd given, with but one fateful mistake.

'*Miss* Chrétien,' Sophia corrected. She was too slow to stop the desk clerk looking at her hand in search of a wedding band, but the kidskin gloves she was wearing hid her most defining feature.

The desk clerk returned to his books. 'I'm afraid this reservation was cancelled, Miss Chrétien.'

'It was made on account.'

'And cancelled on account as well.' The desk clerk was not an unkind man; there was sympathy in his eyes as he said, 'Perhaps the lady might wish to take a room, regardless?' He had taken a leaf of paper, and onto this he scratched some figures in ink. 'For one of our finest suites.'

Sophia studied the paper. Then she asked, 'And for one of your less exquisite?'

The second figure was hardly less astronomical.

'Then perhaps the lady might need to consider some alternative arrangements?'

Vexation, and not a little humiliation, dogged her to the next hotel, the Imperial. Inside, they recognized her for what she was as well. 'We have had a great many Parisian émigrés staying with us over the years,' said the desk clerk. Well, thought Sophia, émigrés and exiles, they were one and the same. 'And I believe we have the perfect suite for you.'

But when he showed her the numbers he noted down, the look on her face told him all he needed to know. 'Perhaps the lady might look for somewhere a little more to her taste?'

Sophia had not yet learned that peculiarly English habit of demurring to say exactly what you mean, and consequently she was unaware of the derision in the desk clerk's voice as he pointed her to the Victoria on the corner of Lancaster Gate. She was unaware of that clerk's derision, too, when he directed her to the Fitzroy above Cavendish Square, whose doorman was good enough to recommend a little place on Morwell Street, whose proprietress insisted that she *would* let a room to Sophia if only she *could*, but 'I can't be making allowances or the rest would rob me. What I can do, though – what I don't mind doing at *all* for a woman in need – is to put in a word with a man I know, not a stone's throw from here. He often has rooms going, if a lady doesn't mind her quarters a little rough around the edges?'

That was how she ended up standing at the foot of the stark, woodwormed staircase of one of the teetering doss-houses of Seven Dials. Into the darkness ahead of her tramped a squat man whose dark mutterings occasionally gave way to crisp, clear speech. 'This way,' he kept saying, 'I've got just the place for you' – and Sophia, with no place else to go, followed him up, up and up again.

'What do you think?' the man said, in his native Irish brogue. They had emerged into a naked attic room where pale winterlight streamed through dirt caked onto the windows. 'I've dossers chomping for rooms like this, but I like to work on recommendations.'

Sophia decided, then and there, that her journey was to end right here.

Or was that to *begin*?

'Thank you, sir.'

There was the small matter of payment. Sophia had not left her old life behind without learning some guile, so she asked the man to turn aside as she reached into her dark plaid dress and unearthed the pouch from her waist.

To do so meant shedding the kidskin gloves she'd been wearing. They dropped to the floor at her side.

Moments later, when she handed the coins to the man she could now call 'landlord', there was no denying the way he recoiled at her touch. A silver shilling spun out of his grasp, rolling along the floor until it wedged between the floorboards. If only to avoid the sight of Sophia's hand, the landlord stumbled after it like a boy chasing marbles.

Then he returned to her side. By instinct, she had closed her fist, as if to hide the stump of the missing finger which had startled the landlord so much.

'One week,' the landlord stuttered, trying not to stare. 'No excuses.'

Then he was gone.

Sophia's mother had taught her (though in quite different circumstances) that she had to count her blessings – so, alone at last, that was exactly what she did. The room was barren, but there were four solid walls and a pane of glass in the window – and, if there was scurrying in the walls, at least there seemed no place where a rat might scuttle out and study her in the night. Let them make their empires in the brickwork; Sophia was safe at last.

She set down her suitcase, allowing it to fall open – and, by doing so, revealed two silken gowns and the pair of satin slippers that nestled on top, as if in some shimmering nest.

From the palaces of Versailles to the rookery at St Giles, life could lead you on a merry dance. But here she was. Later today, she would dare to call it *home*.

8

A Length of String

Ratcliffe at midnight. A cascade of stars falling over the river. A rich man on some ill-advised nocturnal promenade might find beauty in the lanterns glowing on the wharfs, the ribald sounds of debauchery behind shuttered tavern doors. There would be much to spin stories out of, for those wealthy men concerned with composing histories of London's degenerate class, drifting from doss-house to opium den and back again. When you have a warm bed to go back to, all kinds of romance can be built out of being penniless. But not for dear Nell, sitting alone in the window of the Water's Edge. And not for Minos, stranded in dreams in the seaward cave . . .

Murdstone looked over him now. It had been a long time since he'd spent a night with the river. He'd kept the fire low, remembering Bantam's direction, but it still emanated warmth. If only the brute hadn't slept so fitfully, perhaps Murdstone might have drifted into a slumber of his own. His body was wearing his long hours of wakefulness heavily: joints creaked, muscles groaned.

The giant twitched again. Murdstone, startled from the edge of sleep, crossed the cave to peer over him. He'd seen monstrous things in his time. The menagerie on the Highway held wonders. There were sailors in the hostelries who spoke of savages in uncivilized lands, a place in Covent Garden where they had a two-headed baby pickled in a jar.

But this specimen was something else. Not even the naturalists, who'd spent their last seasons debating man's ancestry in the jungle, would know what to make of this.

'What are you dreaming in there?' Murdstone whispered – and, lifting his driftwood cane, prodded at the man's head.

Murdstone had no way of seeing the tunnels through which a dreaming Minos staggered. He would never see the spiralling passageways, looping stairs and twisting towers through which he fought. Nor would he see the single flicker of colour that the dream-world Minos chased: a fluttering peach ribbon, always just out of reach, leading him through the ruins.

But Benjamin Murdstone had no need to see that strange, distorted landscape to know what the monster dreamed – for, as he was standing there, the brute's lips parted and he whispered a single word.

'Nell?'

Murdstone held his breath. All was silent in the seaward cave.

There was no consolation for Nell in the night. Sally-Anne had come to her bedside, and Gander too; Noah was spending the night skulking in some drinking den in Knock Fergus. The rest eyed her strangely, as if it was Nell herself who'd been washed up, a mystery on the tide. She supposed it was because not one of them could work it out. They all thought something had broken inside her, to want to do that with a silver chain. But Nell knew different.

Now, when she shivered through the depths of night, she didn't even have the comfort of her soft satin slippers. No token of the past for Nell; no dream to light the way into the future. Just the wind in the attic eaves, the frost spreading its fractal patterns on the glass, the sideways looks of the other mudlarks as sleep dragged them under.

'Minos,' she whispered, and imagined the long length of string that tied one to the other. But of course he didn't hear her, and Nell heard nothing in return – not until, in some unknown watch of the night, there were suddenly hands wrenching her from the sleep to which she'd so unwillingly succumbed. 'Up with you, Nell,' a voice was labouring, 'away with you now!' But it was not Minos visiting her in her dreams; it was Mr Murdstone whose hands shook her, Mr Murdstone who clamped his hand over her mouth and said, 'Hush now, Nella, you're to come with me.'

She wriggled like the eels they sometimes caught, feet kicking up a storm in the sheets underneath. 'No!' she screamed, through the fingers that held her. 'Let – me – *go!*'

She sank her teeth into his finger. By instinct, Murdstone let the scrabbling Nell go – and, landing on her feet, she skittered back between the other beds. Some of the others were stirring now. Gander lifted his head. Murdstone, nursing his savaged finger, took up his driftwood cane and levered after her, barking 'Back to bed!' when Sally-Anne started to rise. Soon, he was on top of her again. 'Easy or hard, Nell, the choice is yours.' Then, with all the weight of his body, he propelled her towards the trapdoor.

'What do you want with me?'

'It isn't me who wants you,' Murdstone grunted, and compelled her down, down, down, to crash in a ragged heap on the landing below. 'You're a little liar. He woke, didn't he? You spoke with him.'

She had no words; it was her silence that betrayed her.

'He calls for you in his sleep, girl. *Nell, Nell,* over and over.' He kicked her forward and Nell went, tumbling over her own feet. 'You woke him once, girl, you can wake him again. On with you now!'

The tide was reaching its height, but there was yet a way through the rocks to the seaward cave. Nell flailed in front of Murdstone as they skirted the river's depths, harried onward by both his voice and his cane.

She reached the seaward cave ahead of Murdstone, scrambling skilfully up the shale. Murdstone's voice, carried by the wind, was ordering her to remain outside the crevice, but Nell tumbled through. There would be a few fleeting moments before Murdstone reappeared; the sanctity of that silence was all she wanted.

She fell at his side.

'Minos, it's me. It's Nell.' She fancied she saw him tremor, as he tore through the caul of some deeper level of dreams. 'Mr Murdstone's coming too. Minos, I'm sorry. It wasn't me who told. They've tied you up, but all you have to do is wake. Wake up for me, Minos. Wake up again.'

There was a presence behind her. Footsteps, and a distortion of the light. Next moment, Nell was knocked off her knees by the bulb of Mr Murdstone's cane.

The cavern floor caught hold of her, scouring all the skin

91

from her shins. When she finally lifted herself, it was to see the embers of the fire cast wide. Her shoulder had been smeared in soot and ash. Sparks danced in her hair.

'I told you to wait,' Murdstone said, bustling across the cavern floor. 'Here, clean yourself up.' As Nell was sweeping sparks from her hair, a small leather pouch landed in the detritus around her. 'Bantam brought it. Salts to stir him and ointments for his wounds. Not that he needs those. *Look.*'

If ever there was a symbol of Mr Murdstone, this was it, thought Nell: ointments freely offered to pacify the wounds he'd just inflicted; one hand tender, while the other held the knife. Gander said it was Murdstone's world, kept in perfect balance.

The leather pouch in one fist, Nell crawled back to where Minos was lying. Murdstone had used the tip of his cane to move aside the shackled arms and lift the patchwork shirt. The welts underneath were almost gone.

'How long was he awake?'

Tiny spots of light, like yet more sparks, still floated in Nell's eyes.

'His name is Minos,' she whispered. 'He works on the sewer, the Metropolitan Board of Works.'

'How long?'

'Just for a whisper,' she lied.

'If he was awake for but a whisper, Nell, then why does he ask for you?' The ire was gone from Murdstone's voice now. With the air of a reasonable man, he said, 'I'm trying to help him, Nell. I need to know who he is.'

Nell dared not look up, not if it meant being drawn into Murdstone's quelling eyes. Instead she fingered Minos's arm. 'I was just talking to him, Mr Murdstone. Just talking while he slept. Some of it must have found its way inside.'

'So you conjured him from sleep.'

Nell did shoot a look at him now. Her panic compelled it.

'Conjure him again.'

'Mr Murdstone, I —'

Murdstone bowed around, returning momentarily to the mouth of the cave. 'I'm a patient man, Nell, but I'm old and I'm tired – and I should very much like it if you did as I asked.'

When men spoke like that, there was never any hope of defying them. Murdstone's expectation bred the mudlarks' obedience.

'Minos,' Nell whispered, 'can you hear me now? If you can hear me, give me a sign . . .'

In some underworld abyss, lost for centuries with only the fluttering ribbon to punctuate the gloom, a voice reaches him, so far away it might be imagined.

A sign? he thinks. *What kind of sign?*

He throws back his head and a terrible lowing fills the night.

In the seaward cave, Minos's torn lips parted. The noise that came out of his throat made no word, but it was filled with longing.

'That's it, Nell,' said Murdstone, creeping closer, 'keep going, push a little harder now.'

Nell could feel him above her. She cowered, even as she reached for Minos's hand and closed her fist over one of his fingers. There was the satin, hidden just out of reach. 'You shouldn't have bound him. He's not an animal.'

'You don't know what he is,' said Murdstone, levelly. 'Innocent men don't get thrown in the river.'

'They do,' Nell whispered.

She supposed her defiance ought to have earned her another walloping, but then Murdstone laughed: deep, resonant guffaws which filled the seaward cave. 'There isn't an innocent man alive, Nell. Bring him a little further, girl. He's listening to you now.'

She didn't know if she ought to. It was a butcher's trick: coaxing a piglet from the sty, only to throw him on the chopping block. 'Minos,' she stroked the back of his hand, 'are you there?'

His hand grasped hers.

The rope binding his wrists did not allow them to part, but somehow Nell found her tiny hand swallowed up between his. There it nestled, on a satin cushion.

'Nell?'

His eyes had started opening up. Nell was certain she saw the moment he recognized her as real. Something shifted in his body; he released a breath he'd been holding onto as if it was his last.

It was then that he felt the ropes.

'I'm afraid it was for your own good.' Murdstone's voice rang out. Nell watched as Minos recognized the second figure filling the darkness above her. 'You were fitting in your sleep. I've seen dogs like it. They do themselves injuries.' He paused. 'I'm pleased you've come back to us, sir.' Then he took a step such that his knee drove Nell away from the giant's side, severing her connection with his hand.

'Out with you, Nell, and back to the doss-house. You've done well, my dear. I won't forget it.'

Nell picked herself up. She opened her lips to say, 'Mr Murdstone, I want to stay' – but some wilier part of her caught the words before they flurried out. Instead, she scuttled backwards and vanished through the gap in the rocks.

Outside, the tide had reached the shale. The way along the shore was not yet deep enough to prevent passage, but Nell did not mean to venture back to the Water's Edge. After a few deliberate steps, made only to waylay Mr Murdstone, she stopped, stole back to the fissure – and started to listen.

'You look afraid, sir,' said Murdstone, adopting his most high-born air, 'but you've nothing to fear tonight. It wasn't us who tossed you in the river and left you for dead. Wherever those men are, it's only you and me tonight.'

He'd retreated to a distance, the better to look at the creature as he woke. The fire, obliterated by Nell's tumble, gave off such ill light that it scarcely revealed the stranger's bludgeoned face. Murdstone watched him struggle against the ropes. 'Release me,' the man said, in a guttural, low tone.

'I'll attend to that in just a few moments, sir, if you'll grant me a little patience.' Murdstone had had little cause to speak like this since his return to the river; the mudlarks, and the kinds of men with whom he had latterly dealt (Tetterby sprang to mind), did not respond to tact and diplomacy. For them, only the blunt instruments of order and argument would do. There was no telling what manner of man this was – until he found out, he would have to feel his way. 'I had my physician attend you, while you were at rest. It seems the men who did this to you left you for dead. But you, sir?' Murdstone smiled, timing it to perfection. 'You're as strong as an ox.'

Minos lifted his head. 'Where's Nell?'

'Those welts in your side are almost gone. A man might see miracles in that.' Murdstone paused before he said, 'Who are you, Minos?'

Minos bucked against his bonds. 'Where's Nell?' he asked again, more forcefully now.

'Nell's my ward. You don't need to fret over Nell.' Murdstone worked his way towards the back of the cavern, where the second pouch Bantam had brought was sitting on a ledge. 'You must be famished. Will you eat?' There was half a rooster in the bag, apples and bread. A small jar of honey from the doctor's store. There was brandy as well, but Murdstone decided not to offer this; a monster might be dealt with, but a drunken one might prove more taxing. 'Minos, I've helped you this far. Would you trust me a little further?'

'Trust you?' breathed Minos. 'You have me bound and tied.'

This was something to carefully consider. There was a delicate balance between threat and trust. 'I'll be truthful with you, Mr Minos. I am quite staggered by your appearance. I won't be the first to have said it, and I'm certain you've had your share of foul looks in your life, so forgive me if you perceive any insult in what I'm about to say.' He turned on his heel – drawing a rooster's bone, still festooned with flesh, from the pouch. 'Sir, you have me at a disadvantage. I am . . . apprehensive. I am small and aged, and you would have much to hold over me, had I not taken these precautions.' Murdstone dared to hold up the bone, as if he might feed Minos like a mother bird its chick. 'I daresay you might have done the same, sir, had you met a man who dwarfs you in the way you dwarf me. But that, I imagine, is not a problem you have ever encountered.' Murdstone steeled himself. There was a chance this encounter ended badly – but his was a life of calculated risks, and the difference between victory and failure was only timing. 'Will you trust me, sir?'

Minos's head rocked up and down.

So Murdstone loosened his bonds.

As Minos's wrists came apart, something tumbled from his hands and into his lap; Murdstone might have seen it, if only he hadn't been striding backwards, outside the radius of the stranger's grasp.

Moments later, Murdstone threw him the rooster's bone. A thigh seemed as tiny as a wishbone in his hand, but he set about it ravenously. The flesh was gone in seconds, the crunch of bone signifying both its end – and the birth of some strange frisson in Murdstone's belly.

Even in Seven Dials, they made soup out of bones.

Only dogs ate them whole.

When the wind came, Nell heard nothing at all – but, when it abated, she could hear them clearly, two voices dancing around each other like the bare-knuckle boxers she'd seen outside the drinking houses on the Highway.

'Where did you run from?' Murdstone was saying. 'A man like you would be notorious in London – and yet, until this day, I've neither heard of nor seen you. Somewhere beyond the city, then. You came with a travelling menagerie. Broke free of your master and ran.'

The wind ghosted across her, stealing the first words Minos said. '. . . I don't have a master . . .'

'You must make a living. A man like you would be hungered for by a certain sort of paymaster. You told Nell you were a sewer rat. Is that so?' Murdstone stopped, and Nell detected some pointedness in his tone. 'I'm trying to help you, Minos. People who need help, that's *my* trade. Take Nell, for example – a girl left destitute by her mother; a girl who might have starved, or been sold to much worse, if I hadn't –'

'Nell's mother didn't leave her. Nell couldn't follow where she went.'

After a brooding silence, Murdstone said, 'So you and she did speak,' and Nell pictured his fingers tapping a frantic rhythm on the bulb of his cane. 'What else did she say?'

'She's full of fear,' Minos said. 'So am I.'

'Fear?' said Murdstone, with an air of incredulity. It was the first time, perhaps in her history, that Nell shared her master's sentiment – for the thought of a man like Minos cowering in fear seemed more fantastical than the retreat of the knife wounds in his body, the suggestion of horns upon his scalp. 'What are you afraid of, sir?'

He wakes bound and tied, in a hole in the earth, thought Nell. *Why else? Why else be afraid?*

'Where do you come from?' Murdstone asked again.

'I don't know,' Minos moaned.

'And the tattoo across your back? The inked scars, so deliberately carved into your body? What does it signify, sir? I've seen animals branded. It's been some time since we branded men in this city, but I daresay there are yet corners where men become the possessions of others. Is that it? A mark to name you as another's?'

Now Nell heard silence, thick as treacle.

'Who are you?' Murdstone breathed.

And Minos said, 'I'm just a man. You've no right to—'

'Oh, Mr Minos, you are so very unschooled in telling lies. A competent liar spins stories; a poor one retreats into silence. Your reluctance only stokes the imagination, sir. I knew a man who escaped the Marshalsea once. Perhaps your story's the same? It would explain certain holes in the mystery.'

Nell heard the straining in Minos's voice: 'I told you, sir. I do not know.'

'All men know where they come from. That is not where life's mystery resides. Very few of us know where we're going, but every one of us knows where our story begins.'

Nell supposed Murdstone was about to spin his own story – from the ragged infant on the step of the Foundling Hospital to the hallowed hallways of Hanover Square – but the wind lanced across her again, stealing the next exchange.

'Mr Minos, let me explain my conundrum to you.' Murdstone's voice had sprung back into clarity, and Nell recognized this tone: it was the tone of expectation, the tone that ordered you to bend the world to his bidding. 'You see, my wards – Nell among them – have been tending to you here in this cave for some time, all without my knowledge. Their dishonesty has presented me with a problem. I am a fair man, Mr Minos. I have made *that* my trade too. But the morning you were found, washed up on my beach, should have presented me with a great opportunity on this river. The same storm that ravaged you ought to have brought great treasures to the surface – but, instead of hunting for them, my mudlarks brought you here, and ministered to you. Your presence on this river has cost me dearly. It is, in no short order, your restoration to life that has set me back. Minos, I am going to need restitution.'

Nell held her breath.

'Restitution?'

'I would like to suggest we enter a gentleman's agreement.'

Minos remained silent, but Nell was certain she could hear the way his breathing changed.

'You owe me a debt. Work for me here, on the river, until that debt is paid.'

Minos's voice was pitched somewhere between disbelief and despair when Nell heard him utter, 'So that's it, is it? My life, for your bondage?'

No! she wanted to cry out. Because that wasn't the extent of the pact Mr Murdstone was suggesting; she knew it with her head, her heart, her gut itself. Minos might be of some use on the river – there were always bargemen to intimidate, other mudlarks to frighten off – but mudlarking was about pot luck and nimble hands, not untrammelled power and brute strength. No, there was another reason Murdstone was proffering this pact: he had divined some secret in Minos, something which he would turn to his profit – just as soon as he discovered what it was.

She crept closer still, daring to peep around the edge of the fissure. There, Minos's big, bovine eyes were boring into Mr Murdstone, who lingered just out of sight.

'*No,*' Minos breathed.

Two great plumes of grey billowed from his nostrils as he exhaled the word.

'No?' came Murdstone's voice.

'I can't stay. I won't.'

Nell watched his great hands come down, to tear at the ropes around his knees. She had never seen rope tear, but now she heard the rough rasp of the strands as they ripped apart. First Minos's knees were free; then, moments later, his ankles. Murdstone's shadow was in retreat; it vanished completely as Minos picked himself up. Gone was the unsteadiness he'd displayed upon first waking. Gone, the knife wounds in his breast, the fever that had dogged him through a long day and night. Nell supposed a man of science would put it down to Dr Bantam's tinctures – but Nell had seen the sorts of mixtures street doctors could provide, just laudanum, sugars and syrups. There wasn't a potion in the world that could restore ravaged flesh inside the space of a day, no potion – now she came to think of it – that could resuscitate a man submerged in the river for unnumbered hours.

'Mr Minos, your life is in my debt!' Murdstone announced. Nell watched his shadow gesticulate wildly, puppet theatre against the cavern wall. 'The river claimed your life. I reclaimed it. Your honour compels you, sir, to do the right thing.'

Upright, Minos filled the cavern interior. He shifted around, to cast a shadow of his own.

Nell froze. There was something about this new shadow that unnerved her. In the flesh, Minos was a man – yet in shadow, stretched out of proportion by the lowness of the

101

light, he was something else. His arms rippled with muscularity. His jaw pushed forward like the maw of a beast. His coat-tail flicked behind him, a tail in shadow. And on the sides of his head, the two protrusions seemed more prominent than ever – as if the shadow Minos really was sporting two horns, arcing away from his body like curved butcher's blades.

'The right thing?' said the shadow. The voice that had seemed so frayed and gentle was, at once, full of menace – and in the back of Nell's mind, she heard the echo of Sally-Anne's words: *Nell, sweetpea, look. His teeth!*

'It's a cruel world, Mr Minos. Life is a brutish torment. Those who recognize it stick together. We call them the river rules, sir. When one is in need, the others must rally. What one may lack, the other party provides . . .'

The shadow Minos took a stride forward, and the light in the cavern died. Nell supposed he had trodden in the flames, extinguishing them for ever.

'Sir, hear me out!' Murdstone cried. 'I have only your best interests at heart. A few days, to make certain you are right in body and soul. My physician will attend. The ordeal your body has been through – it would hardly be unexpected if it were to manifest some further ailment. Mr Minos, listen. *Listen!*'

In spite of everything, some element of sympathy erupted in Nell. She threw herself into the gap in the rock. 'Minos, please!'

All fell still in the seaward cave. The darknesses rearranged themselves, Minos still eclipsing Murdstone as he turned around.

His breathing was heavy. She heard a muted rumble –

as of a man struggling for air, or an animal emitting a warning.

'Minos?' said Nell.

He strode towards her. He strode again. He was almost on top of her now, and – though she fought hard to deny it – Nell felt a nascent fear moving through her as well. Her heart was beating hard, as panicked as a baby bird's.

A single monstrous finger reached down. Nell thought: it could thrust me aside, or it could dance gently over my skin; the nail on its end could skewer me to the bone, or touch me like a feather.

Minos stroked the line of her jaw. 'Thank you, little Nell,' he said – and, with those four words, all of the fury that had been coursing out of him moments ago was gone. The deep rumble came again – only, this time, Nell did not think of an animal's burgeoning growl, but the same animal's contented grumble. She stepped back through the crevice, clearing the way for Minos to follow. This he did. Five strides later, he was at the bottom of the rocks, plunging to his knees into the tide.

Along the river, the moon hung beached above the cathedral at St Paul's. Minos walked into its light.

It took some moments before Nell tumbled after him. She had been gazing at him in wonder – for how could a man who, mere hours ago, had been consorting with death, now wade so effortlessly through the river's great swell? – but, before she'd taken three steps, it occurred to her that she could not follow. The river had long ago reached the rocks around the seaward cave. Three dainty steps and it had risen past her knees; another and it would swallow her whole.

'Minos!'

She called it a second time, a third and a fourth, before Minos looked back. He was just a different shape in the blackness now. Beneath the night's starry cascade, she couldn't make out his features, only his mountainous shape as he waded upriver, bound for who knows where.

He did not have horns, she told herself. It had just been a trick of the shadows.

Trapped between Murdstone in the cave and Minos in the water, Nell lifted her tiny hand to wave goodbye.

Out on the water, Minos's hand moved heavenward in reply.

Then he was gone, fading into the black – and Nell was left alone on the shale, with one more farewell carved into her heart.

Volume II

The History of Monsters

9

Second-Hand Myths

*Murdstone & Sons, Reliquary for Antiquities and
Oddities, London, December 1861*

The shop bell rang.

The sign above the door still read 'Murdstone & Sons',
unashamedly holding true to its two defining lies: firstly,
that it still belonged to Benjamin Murdstone, who had
transformed the shop from dusty catacomb to antiquarian
bookseller of high renown; and, secondly, that Murdstone
ever sired any sons at all. There were plenty who said he
had (one or two even tested the supposition in a court of
law), but the truth was that Murdstone's sons were none
but the foundlings, runaways and other ragged boys he had
taken into his tutelage. There had been plenty of those:
scrapegraces found running some con on a street corner,
their natural guile drawing Murdstone's admiration – for
hadn't Benjamin Murdstone once been a child of the streets,
and wasn't he (of all the high-and-mighties in London) the
one to show them the way? In later years, consorting with
merchant mariners and ministers of the Crown, Murdstone
had little time to shepherd the next generation of guttersnipes into Society – but, in his middle years, when
Murdstone & Sons was in its pomp, three dozen had found

their place here. Now there were physicians and philoso-
phers, engineers and economists, apothecaries and
entrepreneurs all across London, each one owing his place
to the moment when Murdstone tapped upon his shoulder
and whispered, '*Come with me.*'

One of them stepped through the doorway now.

It was the first time in thirty years.

Dr Bantam still recognized the smell of the place. That
musty, forgotten feeling – the scent of secrets and treasures
hidden in plain sight. He'd been a scapegrace himself when
he first encountered this shop. Sent in by an older boy,
who swore – above all the logic of the streets – that there
was a certain breed of man who treated books as if they
were *valuable*, he'd been halfway up one of the bookcases
when the plump shopkeeper spied him. Benjamin
Murdstone had looked like a man out of time, even then:
white hair, bitter blue eyes, his clay pipe trailing a thick
fog of tobacco smoke. Bantam had squealed when
Murdstone tried to pull him down. He'd squealed again
when Murdstone, seeing how the boy's grubby fingers had
besmirched a dictionary one hundred years old, took a belt
buckle to his behind. But within a week he'd been learning
his letters in Murdstone's back room, then running errands
in exchange for hot dinners and even, on one memorable
occasion, a hot bath. Bantam's old crowd didn't like the
look of him after that; he was Murdstone's pet now, so
Murdstone's pet he had stayed.

It had been half a lifetime since the shop passed out of
Murdstone's hands, but Bantam was certain that the accoutre-
ments of that earlier epoch survived. He picked his way
between the cabinets where Murdstone had kept his curi-

osities, past a glass case where the crystalline eyes of preserved tawny owls peered out, and around a corner where a statuesque mannequin displayed a nightgown said to have been worn by the good Queen Anne (certification could be provided). Bantam had good reason to doubt its veracity; Murdstone had once turned a tidy fortune off the bearded axe used to remove King Charles's head. He'd sold that axe on three separate occasions, and certification had been provided for each of them too.

Murdstone & Sons' appeal had been its curiosities, but its value had always been its books. Bantam came, now, to the shop's heartland, a tightly packed network of bookcases that reached from floor to ceiling. A shop like this was not vast, but it seemed much vaster by virtue of its innumerable nooks and crannies. To the younger Bantam, it had been almost labyrinthine in design.

Labyrinths, thought Bantam, and his mind flashed back to the scars across the stranger's back. Of all the things about the goliath, it was this that had been seared into his recollection.

It was why he was here.

Footsteps announced the appearance of the shop's new overseer. A man as curious as the oddments sitting in the windows, he had a single glass eye and a nostril that appeared to have been chewed by some scavenging rodent.

'Is the gentleman looking for something in particular?'

Gentleman. They hadn't called Bantam that in the Courage and Crown last night, when they'd brayed at him to inspect a man's boils in return for another drink.

'A book,' he declared.

'A gift, perhaps?' The man sidled closer. 'Yes, now that

Advent has begun, I've had a few of your type come hunting for the perfect present. A token of love is it, sir?'

'A book of stories,' Bantam returned, with his eyes roaming the shelves. He knew precisely the place it used to be. How many times had he taken that book from the shelves – first to get lost in its untold stories, and then to make intimate copies of it, back in the days when Murdstone's coffers relied on a steady stream of forged texts? He brought to mind its red goatskin cover – and its title in faded gold leaf. '*Apocryphal Antiquity*,' he said. 'Open it up, and on the first page . . .' An engraving of a labyrinth. No, he thought, *the* Labyrinth, designed by the artificer Daedalus in an age so ancient it had slipped out of history. 'Sir, do you still keep ledgers, describing each sale?'

The shopkeeper stepped back, his suspicions aroused. 'Who are you, sir?'

'I was a shop boy here, once upon a time. My master kept records of every sale he ever made. If you still have them, perhaps you can help me trace where the book I'm looking for went.'

The man remained impassive, and Bantam knew it was going to take more than a polite enquiry to win him over. That did not matter; he had learned this at Murdstone's knee: there was always a trade to be made. 'I'm a physician,' he said, eyeing the livid spots that drew a crimson ribbon round his collar. 'I could sort your every ailment.'

Murdstone's old ledgers were still in crates in the cellar, birthing wild lichens where the earth's dampness had leached in. Consequently, it was many hours later – in the dankness under the shop floor, with candles guttering to stubs and rats watching from holes in the stonework – that

Bantam opened one of the last surviving books, traced a line of decades-old handwriting and saw the words he had been searching for all night:

'*Apocryphal Antiquity*, to Messrs. Goodman & Sharp, c. Sworders Auction House, 1 September 1842.'

If only the shopkeeper (and his every ailment) hadn't been waiting for Bantam's probing hands on the shopfloor above, his sense of triumph might have been complete.

10

Underworld

London, Above and Below, December 1861

It ought to have taken Nell all day, and that ought to have
earned her a barracking so fierce she would never leave the
Water's Edge again – but, in spite of all we have seen in
this story, good things do happen on the streets of Ratcliffe.
Consequently, it was in the bow of an old waterman's river
wherry that Nell followed the river into the west. Only
when she could see the palaces of Westminster – where few
knew, and even fewer cared, of the existence of mudlarks
and pure-finders, of flushermen and sprat-sellers – did she
ask the waterman to heave to.

'This is the place? Are you sure, girl?'

Nell was never sure. She had slipped beyond the bound-
aries of Ratcliffe so rarely that London was as strange to
her as the sky is to the great fat eels of the river. Yet she
had been sent to Bantam's study only days before, and had
not balked at the task – and, deep inside, she knew that
she had once come this way too, trailing from her mother's
hand. That was why she knew it was possible; that was
why she knew it didn't take silver chains and ivory sundials
to rise from the river. You could do it by the gifts you'd
been given: the sorcery in her mother's stitching. Had she

lived, Nell was sure, her mother would have been courted by princesses. And, if her mother could climb so high, why not Nell? All it would take was for someone to recognize the gift they'd promised she had.

It was those words. The simple act of recounting them to Minos had sent them ricocheting around her head. *They loved you, Nell. They said you were a natural.*

My dancing girl.

My ballerina.

The things you found in the mud went inevitably into Murdstone's hands, but he could never take away the things you nurtured inside. Your memories. Your gifts. Those things were yours for ever.

The waterman was guiding his boat to shore, still waiting expectantly for an answer.

'I think so,' Nell said, but when she looked up at the gilded towers, it was not certainty, only trepidation, that she felt.

'That old goat knows you're out here, does he?'

He meant Murdstone. 'Old goat' was one of the more flattering epithets by which the river-dwellers knew him.

Nell nodded, but it did not convince. 'Here,' he said, and handed her a loop of old tackle he'd skimmed off the surface of the river, 'to satisfy that devil when you get back.'

The waterman had taken pity on Nell before. Along with the tackle, he gave her a heel of bread and hunk of cold sausage, then told her he'd be passing the same way at dusk. Nell – who knew she had to return by the time Murdstone appeared at the storehouses – smiled wanly as she watched him drift off. Then she left the riverbank and, unanchored from all that she knew, bowed into the streets.

At least she had the sausage and bread to fortify her. Something told her there was going to be a long trek ahead.

Nell knew every kink, snarl and dead-end in the warrens of Ratcliffe, but the unfamiliarity of these streets curdled an unease inside her, upsetting her like spoiled milk. The problem with using memory as your street-map was that, too often, it was a deceitful, back-stabbing guide. That day with her mother loomed so large in her memory, but the London through which she walked bore no correlation to the streets she remembered. Sights, smells, sounds – all of it was different.

'Do you know the way to –'

'Can you tell me where to find –'

Hustled out of shops, battled back by brooms, weathering every curse the viperous tongues of London could conjure, Nell spent her morning turned away from every door – for what cared folks for mudlarks, this far from the river?

Until, by some strange fortune, she stepped into Leicester Square – and London opened up.

The square was but a mile through the London labyrinth, but to Nell the voyage had taken half the day. By the time she stepped into its rutted cart tracks, the winter sun was already reaching its zenith. She watched its light fill up the gated gardens, the stables, the fountains, and realized it was only now that the memory she'd brought forth in the cave truly matched the vision in front of her. Yes, she *remembered* this.

She had not known that the simple act of memory would bring her such joy. And who knew that joy could ache like this, deep in the bones?

Here she had stood, clinging to her mother's hand; here,

her mother had crouched and told her how London housed a hundred different worlds, and this was another one, as far removed from the doss-houses of Ratcliffe as the sun was the moon. An echo reached her from across the years: she fancied she could see the impressions her mother's feet had left as she led the younger Nell across the square.

Nell took off in pursuit.

The square itself was busy as the dockside. Bordered by palaces, criss-crossed by carriages, partitioned by grand black railings – such was its magnificence, she might not have been in London at all. Horses snickered. A gentleman marched past, bearing a cane of polished ebony (no drift-wood for him). A lady was helped down from a carriage, her sisters cooing behind her. And it occurred to Nell, now, that there were no rag-gatherers here, no scavengers or houseless poor. They did not know about mudlarks, not in the shadow of . . .

She looked up, just as she had looked up from her mother's side. 'I can't see, Mama,' she'd once said, and so Nell's mother had hoisted her onto her shoulder to gaze at its splendour.

'Is that where we're going?'

'Oh yes, little Nell.'

To eyes used only to the Ratcliffe tenements, the building that dominated the eastern edge of the square seemed a palace plucked from some bedtime tale. As broad as the square itself, its two towers stood taller than any from here to Westminster, its white dome like a cathedral. Nell gazed up and ever upwards. She had been prepared to discover it a fraction of how it had been in her memory, but in reality it was more magnificent still.

'There you are, Nell,' came her mother's voice, from the long ago.

'Are we really to go inside?'

Nell hurried forward.

'Yes, darling,' came her mother's voice.

And there she stopped, in the shadow of the palace. Its doors were opening up, disgorging dowdy-looking footmen and a man of stout significance, who started barking orders at workmen waiting on the square.

Through those doors, Nell had danced.

Through those doors, she would dance again.

'The Alhambra Circus,' she breathed out loud.

*

Twilight over London. Daylight giving way to the deep December dark. They said that the doors never closed at the church of St Anne, but in Modern Times the slums crowded its every side and the latches were locked every afternoon. If there was welcome here by night, it came only in trembling tones emanating through the Judas hole in the wood.

The figure on the edge of the churchyard was not entirely unexpected. The devil has long been known to bide his time at gravesides, patiently waiting his chance to slip within. The children who'd been begging here knew to give him a wide berth. So too did the starlings roosting in the willow boughs above. Only the rats appeared unhindered by his presence, chittering darkly over the burial mounds.

He'd been lurking here some time, where the ground was turned to hummocks by the parish poor, when the priest appeared at the doors. The man was startled when Minos approached. So rapt was he in fortifying God's house that he paid no mind to the creeping unease working its way through his body. It was only the ragged breathing that made him turn. He'd heard those breaths before.

The birdlike man clutched his breast. 'It's you.'

The priest did not bolt the doors when he led Minos within. Minos was used to that. Men were like rabbits; they always gauged their lines of escape.

'It's been some time since you darkened this door. What ails you, sir?'

They sat in the nave, beneath windows where the son of God hung diminished on his cross. The lamplighters must have come out already, for at once spectral light cascaded through the window, illuminating His suffering.

Minos had thought these words so often, but rarely given them voice.

'Sir, I don't know who I am.'

After a silence, the priest said: 'You spoke the same words when you first came to the parish. Yet you found your path, back then. Say it with me.' The priest would have taken hold of the great gnarled hand – but something instinctive, some element of repulsion perhaps, stopped him. 'Your name is Minos. You dwell at the North Marsh Low Lodgings. You are employed by the Metropolitan Board of Works.'

Minos's dark eyes glowered. 'No longer.'

'No longer, sir?'

It seemed impossible for a man of Minos's significant girth to squirm, and yet that was what he did.

'Something befell you,' whispered the priest.

117

'It was some nights ago, after I finished work. Men were hunting me. I looked for sanctuary in the churchyard, but your doors are always locked. So they took to me with knives.' He peeled back his greatcoat, then the patchwork shirt, though – whether in this dim light or the full bright of day – there was nothing left to see. 'Then they threw me in the river.' *My blood feathered the Thames. I slipped out of time and mind.* 'But here I am. It's not natural. Not right.'

The priest was guarded as he said, 'You've told a similar story before.'

'It's not a story.'

'The day you came to London – washed up on the West India Docks, with only a name to call your own. But you seemed to know the city well enough. You knew the Tower and the river.' The priest had gathered some composure since he was startled at the door. 'I don't profess to know what the Lord's plan is for you, sir, but take heart that He does have one. So He does for us all. Why He chooses to cloak your history from you may be a riddle only time can solve.'

Time, thought Minos. He'd had enough time. It had seemed, since the river, that time was all he had. No honest pay any more (though when was pay ever honest in London?); no roof above his head. Just the hedgeback and the gutter, the creeping cold – and time.

'I'm dreaming again.'

Minos had blurted out the words.

'Your old dreams?'

There were so many. He'd already told the priest of those visions he had, of many-headed serpents and winged mares.

But fantasy like that was so easy to dismiss; he would wake, disorientated, to find himself faced with the cold, brutish reality of London once again – and know that one-eyed giants and eagles with the faces of women did not really exist. No, it was the other dreams whose torture stayed with him. 'The older dreams,' he whispered.

'The dreams where you're trapped. Lost. Alone.'

Minos lifted his eyes. 'I'm not alone any more. I hear a voice, guiding me.'

For the first time, the priest's eyes lit up too. Four months had passed since the behemoth shambled up from the sewer where he worked and first presented himself at this door. 'I don't know who I am,' he had said. 'I'm lost.' But, of course, so were so many of God's flock. And now here he was, one of God's most pitiful creatures, starting to hear His voice. There was beauty in this; beauty and truth. To see him was to see one of the devil's infinite hordes; but to hear him speak was to hear a man in the process of being saved.

'And what does He say to you?'

'It isn't your Lord I hear. It's the girl, who found me on the river. It's like a piece of her lodged in me. A thorn in a hand. She guides me through dreams. She saved my life.' He stopped. For the first time, he was shaking. 'Is it real?'

The priest was cautious as he said, 'I think He speaks to us in myriad ways.'

Instinct drove Minos suddenly back to his feet, as if he could slough off this thought like a horse does its halter. 'Not Him,' he said, this time giving vent to his fury. *No, never Him.* The priest had risen too, the better to lift his cassock tails and flee. 'I told you last time. He's your Lord, not mine.'

'Minos,' the priest said, with a searching kind of patience, 'you must be looking for His hand. You did come to His house.'

This was a bitter truth, and it sapped the fury that had been building in him. His shoulders slumped. He said, 'I'm looking for . . . me.' Because that was how it had felt, ever since the river. Ever since Nell's hand, and her voice coaxing him through the ruins of his mind. The knowledge of who he was, where he'd been, what he'd done, was all inside him; he just had to pick his way to the place it was hidden.

Left he turns, then right.

Forward he ploughs, then back.

'Then let Him guide you,' said the priest, not unkindly. 'Accept Him into your life. *He* will show you the way.'

No, thought Minos, there was only one person who could show him – and she resided by the river in Ratcliffe, patron saint of the seaward cave. 'I'm sorry,' he said. 'I don't know why I came.'

Then he was on his feet, taking great strides through the barren nave.

'Why don't you trust Him, sir?'

Minos did not know. So many did. They came here every Sunday, to share in their entreaties. Yet when Minos thought of gods, it was not the divine Creator to whom the priest had devoted his life; not the martyred Son who hung in the window, crowned by thorns. There were many gods, thought Minos, and they were petty, capricious and wild – as creatures with untrammelled power always are. The benevolent Lord this priest worshipped was no god, not as Minos knew the word.

'We are all of us lost,' said the priest, as Minos shambled back through the door.

But Minos didn't listen.

Some of us, he thought, are more lost than others.

Night was not yet here, but the growing winter dark was welcoming to a man like Minos. In winter, few people on the streets of London balked at a man who masked his face behind mountains of scarfs. A face that drew stares in summer could go unnoticed by the long December dark.

That was how he picked his way to the outlands of St Giles, where the jaws of the underworld were hidden behind hoardings and the sound of industry still throbbed underneath him, somehow silent to the milling crowd.

He knew he ought not to venture through. He'd come already, in hope if not expectation, and been dismissed. And yet – if there were no answers from men of God, there could, at least, be the cold, hard comfort of work. It had served him well in the past.

So he bowed through the hoardings and prayed to gods he was sure did not exist.

The chasm in the middle of the yard was ringed in wire, oranges, reds and whites flickering in its depths. On its edges, towers of brick stood like monuments, crowned with scaling ladders and lengths of scaffold. Voices hailed each other, somewhere underneath the earth.

On the windward side of the yard, other lights shone inside a ramshackle lean-to. It was to this door, permanently propped ajar, that Minos tramped.

Inside, a jowly man sat at a desk. The papers he was poring over were stamped by officialdom so many times as to be largely illegible. The soup the man had contrived to spill hadn't helped either. He was feverishly mopping it up when he sensed Minos above. The goliath was too vast to slip inside the lean-to, so it was just his head that craned through the door, appearing as if detached from his body.

'Good Lord, Minos!' the man exclaimed. 'You near frightened me to death. Look – look what you made me do!'

Minos was quite certain the soup had been spilled some time before; some men were born to have accidents, and Beresford Kale was practically an artiste.

'What do you want, Minos?'

'The same thing I wanted yesterday, sir. And the day before that.'

Kale attacked the last smear of soup and set about hanging his papers to dry. 'Am I losing my senses, or have we talked about this? Our position hasn't changed. Nor have the facts of the matter. You vanished, *in absentia*, for two days and nights. Permission was not requested. Permission was not given. Do you see a paper here, stamped with the authority of the Metropolitan Board of Works, granting a leave of absence?'

Minos grunted, 'I just see soup.'

Now, Kale's nostrils flared as well. 'This endeavour is damn near holy, Minos. We're stopping the *miasma*, by God! Transforming the city. Fording the rivers and marshalling the waste this seething mass of mankind pumps out. *Sewage*, my man – it's elemental.' He let out an elaborate sigh, then pegged his last paper up. 'I can't help, sir. The job is gone.'

'You hired two souls to take my place.'

'Aye, and they both turn up when they were told.'

'Wasn't I a good worker, sir?'

'Perhaps, when you graced us with your presence—'

'I worked for the Board six hard months, Mr Kale. I never missed a shift, not until—'

'Yes, Mr Minos – not until you were set about by common cutpurses and hoiked in the river.' Kale picked himself up. 'Show me again, Minos. Show me again what these ruffians did to you.'

Kale had (finally) found his ganger's confidence. Brandishing his pencil like a parrying blade, he battled Minos back into the yard, where the chasm was disgorging a trio of labourers back into the light.

'Have at it then, Mr Minos. Let me *inspect*.'

Minos fumbled with his overcoat buttons to reveal his midriff, its skin tough as tanned hide.

Kale was a short man; he scarcely had to stoop to pursue his inspection. 'There isn't a mark on you. You say you were overpowered and stabbed but seven nights ago? Well, I've never seen a knife wound that leaves the flesh unblemished. Please don't take me for a fool.' Kale used his pencil to direct Minos to roll his shirt back into place. Perhaps it was only because of the labourers eyeing him, but he seemed to be enjoying his bravado. 'Let me tell you what I think happened. I believe you took your pay and drank it away in some den. Whether you staggered in your fugue into the river or not isn't mine to say. What I do say is: you're lying to me, Minos. It pains me to say it, because you carry the burden of an ox – but there's no work for you here.'

Minos lumbered around, head hanging low as he returned to the hoardings. He'd taken but two strides when Kale called out, in valedictory triumph, 'And by the Lord, Minos, buy yourself some new boots – you're walking around like an animal, and winter's already come.'

Minos looked down. His naked, horned feet were discoloured by dirt.

But the truth was, he didn't feel the cold at all.

*

It had been easy to feel brave when she stepped into the waterman's wherry, but somehow every passing hour leached some of that courage away. Now, as the daylight greyed over the Alhambra Circus, Nell wondered why she'd come at all. The square had changed with the gathering dark – and, though the lamplighters were not yet out, the doors to the Alhambra stood open and, from its heart, there spilled a burnt orange glow. Sometimes, figures of shadow appeared in that portal. Sometimes, grand men were welcomed within. But Nell crouched in the heart of the square and watched through wrought-iron railings, wondering how it was you could come so close and yet still be half a world away.

Twilight brought more people to the square. Fine men, with finer ladies on their arms, emerged from the doors of grand hotels, then stepped into waiting carriages to be spirited into the night. Carriages assembled by a place Nell took, by eavesdropping, as Wyld's Great Globe, while street prospectors took up their stations around the statues of nameless kings. To Nell's eye, they looked finer than the women who spent their nights with sailors on the back-streets of Ratcliffe, but the hollow look in their eyes was the same. So too the scent of gin as they whirled past. 'That's one way off the river,' Sally-Anne had once said: a warning, Nell knew, that the only safe path was Murdstone's path; that there were darker things yet than being beholden to him.

Nell looked to the sky. Winter nights came quickly; there might only be an hour left on the river, perhaps two before Murdstone gathered the mudlarks by the storehouses. The closer that moment came, the more the yearning in her heart was matched by a deep, unsettling distress. She'd come this distance, sacrificed a day in the mud, already risked Murdstone's wrath. Was it all to be for nothing? Soon, she would have to turn tail and flee. Then the day would have been spent in idleness and dreaming – and discovering that, when the moment came, she simply didn't dare.

It would have been easier if she'd had the satin slippers in her hands. In her mind's eye, she put them on her feet, then sailed across the rutted tracks of the square, directly through the Alhambra doors. But they were gone for ever now, lost to the giant from the cave, so she would have to do without.

They said you were a natural.

My dancing girl.

My ballerina.

She squirmed through the railings and ran.

Had Nell been less nimble, she would have been trampled three times before she reached the Alhambra doors. But, slippers or not, Nell had dancing feet. Consequently, she had sailed through a forest of legs, sashayed past a spinning cartwheel, and tumbled (inelegant but upright) through marble white arches before she reached the palace.

Nimble feet, however, could not skip past blood and bone.

'On with you now!'

It wasn't only the words that piled into her. So too did a black leather boot, and after that the flagstone floor. Dazed, Nell looked up to discover that she'd made it just inches beyond the threshold. The stern face of a stout, porcine man was looking down. Dressed in a waistcoat, his shirt-sleeves rolled to his elbow, Nell might have mistaken him for any doorman at the drinking dens in Ratcliffe, had it not been for his elaborately waxed moustache.

'There's nothing for you here, girl – so sling your hook, or I'll call a constable.'

Nell lifted herself, trying to disregard the dizziness that came with her tumble. How had it been possible for Minos to survive the river, and yet one little tumble made her feel so sick?

'I'm sorry,' she declared, scrabbling for the words she'd rehearsed all day. 'My mother was a seamstress here. I've come to see the dancers.'

The man's hesitation lasted only a moment. As he pondered, Nell looked past him. The insides of the Alhambra Circus stretched further than she had imagined: a vast hall, hung with burgundy curtains, its two staircases arcing away from it like the horns of a ram. The roof was as far above as the attics of the Water's Edge, further even, with great arches and vaults where clusters of shimmering lights were suspended on wires.

As Nell took it all in, a door opened between the stairs. Two figures emerged, a man in braces escorting a slender woman with a sweep of black hair – but Nell did not linger on them for long; her eyes were drawn to the doors as they slowly closed and the fleeting sight of a cavernous blackness beyond, ringed in galleries and seats.

The auditorium, she thought.

The *stage*.

The doorman's voice brought her back to her senses. 'You're full of horseshit, and no mistake. Seamstress's daughter, with clothes like that? I'll wager you're nobody's daughter. I've seen you begging out on the square. What's your game?'

In the corner of her eye, Nell saw the black-haired woman being escorted their way. At the bottom of the stairs, she stopped to deposit a small set of ivory cards into her companion's hand. These he took with an air of dismissiveness, before shepherding her on.

'My mother,' Nell declared, trying – and failing – to control the tremble in her tone, 'used to bring me here. She was a needleworker. The dancers . . .'

'The Company hasn't even arrived,' snapped the man. 'You're trying your luck.'

No, thought Nell.

No.

Why did that word echo in her so forcefully? Where had she heard it before? It seemed to have an element of magic about it. She straightened her back, told herself she would do what she'd come here to do, no matter what contempt coloured this man's features, and said, 'I want to dance.'

Laughter lit up the man's eyes. It might have spluttered out of him, if only the others hadn't reached the doorway – where Nell was promptly bustled aside so that the black-haired woman could depart. As she passed, the wildflower scent she was wearing washed over Nell. She looked up. If she was not mistaken, the woman was wearing the same chastened look as Nell, as if perhaps she too had been being

127

scoffed at in some inner sanctum. But if that was so, why had she been in the Alhambra's auditorium? What business did she have in there?

'You'll do your dancing on the streets,' the doorman said, knocking Nell backwards. All it took was the tip of his finger to start her stumbling. 'There you go, girl – you're dancing already! Put a cap out. Dance for some pennies. A place like this is for real dancers. Fine ladies, drilled and trained. What were you thinking, girl? London isn't a fairy tale. Look, here, I'll get you started.'

A single tin farthing came hurtling at Nell, striking her directly in the breast.

It was instinct that sent Nell scrambling after it – the instinct of the river, bred into her after four hard years. Later, she would be ashamed at how readily she'd jumped, like a dog performing tricks. By the time she reached it, the door to the Alhambra was closed, and across Leicester Square, twilight was turning towards the early evening dark.

The farthing had landed in a cart track. When Nell's hand darted down to retrieve it, she found that it was not alone. There, smeared in dirt, was one of the ivory cards she'd seen through the Alhambra doors. She picked it up.

Letters: such strange, inscrutable things. How long had it been since she'd had any cause to read? Mr Murdstone had often championed the merits of learning. It was said that, once upon a time, he'd forced his wards to learn their letters by rote, and in that way given them new standing in life. Bantam would have perished on the streets if Mr Murdstone hadn't taught him to read. Yet, in his dotage, all of that had been forgotten; a mudlark was a mudlark, until the river took them under.

But Nell's mother had known letters. Nell's mother had shown her these strange loops and curls.

She tried so hard to remember.

'SOPHIA CHRÉTIEN, Shining Light of the Paris Opera Ballet, Available for TRAINING and TU —'

Her throat was full of false starts and malformed words, but somewhere along the way, the meaning of it became clear.

Nell lifted herself. The humiliation that had burned in her evaporated as she searched for a face in the milling crowd.

The gaslights had started igniting on the sides of the square. One after another, they burst into life.

And there she was: the lady with the cascade of black hair, drawing her scarves around her as she bowed into the dark.

Nell danced after.

It was easy to catch up. The lady was marching with decisive strides, no doubt trying to outpace the coming of night, but Nell was faster. It was what to say when she reached her that stalled Nell. What courage she'd summoned had long since been squandered. For a time, all she could do was scurry in the woman's wake, following her from the square and between the crowded doss-houses beyond. 'Shining Light of the Paris Opera,' thought Nell, wondering what this word 'opera' might mean. There had to be a reason this 'shining light' was striding into seamier streets.

'Pardon me!'

But she did not turn round.

'Miss!'

But Sophia marched on.

'Stop!' yelled Nell, and at last the woman turned.

Behind Sophia, one of the city's lamplighters brought a gas lamp to life. Momentarily blinded by its glare, Nell screwed up her eyes.

'Do you mean me?'

Nell sidestepped the lamp's full glare, to discover Sophia anxiously casting looks into the shadows. No doubt she thought Nell a decoy, luring her into some trap; there were enough gangs that worked like it in Ratcliffe, hunting their marks as efficiently as dogs do a kill. Nell meant to shout out again, to mollify her dread, but something in Sophia's eyes waylaid her. Some familiar quality, echoing through the ages.

And in a second, she was back there, dancing on the Alhambra's stage, sailing above some ballerina's shoulders, feeling like she could fly.

Was it her? she thought. *Were the Fates that kind?* Surely not to a girl who dredged the river. Fate reserved its magic for those born on high, those whose grace and beauty might touch or even change the world. No, destiny was not for gutter rats.

But the pull of that moment was like an anchor to Nell. She felt herself dragged back in time.

'Can I – can I help you?'

She'd been silent too long. Now, Nell teetered forward and said, 'You – dropped – this.'

The only reason Nell could tear herself away from those crystalline eyes was Sophia's hand as it reached out to take the besmirched card. She'd seen injured hands before. In Ratcliffe they were variously withered or ravaged by age, crushed on the dockside or grown cankerous with corns.

To see a riverman relieved of a finger was not unusual, but to see a fine lady – a dancer, no less – with her ring finger severed neatly beneath the knuckle gave her pause.

'There's enough of these trampled into the dirt,' sighed Sophia, in a voice that did not belong to London at all. 'I've been handing them out to the patrons for nights, hoping there's a dilettante among them. Thank you, sweet girl, but a sullied calling card is hardly worth a halfpenny. I have nothing I can give.'

So, then: she thought Nell a beggar. That was what fine people saw when they looked upon her.

They hadn't seen that, once.

They'd seen the seamstress's daughter. They'd borne her aloft.

'I saw you there, in the Alhambra.' Nell started quaking, the second she breathed the words. She had to conquer herself to say, 'You're a teacher. It says so on the card. And – and I want to learn.'

The smile that creased Sophia's face was not the same as the doorman's had been. There was pity in this smile. Tenderness too. She said, 'Girl, I should teach you if I could. You wouldn't be the first dancing girl to come from nothing. But . . .' Here she gave pause, in the way adults will when they are trying to explain the ways of the world to a child, who knows only good from bad, only black from white, and not the infinite shades of sadness in between. 'You saw me at the Alhambra Circus because I'm desperate for work. I imagine you might know how it feels.'

Nell looked her up and down. Perhaps desperation meant two different things, for Sophia was still wearing fine

131

clothes, still cloaked in the warmest lambswool; her face was painted, if Nell was any judge, rouged and lined around the eyes.

'I haven't long, girl, not before I lose the roof over my head. I came to London with so little – only my time. Every hour must make its weight in gold. I'm sorry, girl, but I cannot imagine you might keep that wolf from my door.' She smiled wanly, and Nell got the impression that there was kindness here, kindness being kept at bay. 'So: you want to be a dancer.'

Nell nodded meekly.

'I know that feeling, but the Alhambra Circus – well, if it's any consolation, girl, they sent me away as well. It is hard to begin again, is it not?' Sophia paused. 'Child, I should rather teach you than the debutantes I've been courting. Ungrateful and entitled as only those born to money can be. Not one of their fathers would pay me if they knew how I lived, how little I have left.' She stopped. 'One day, perhaps, we might both be on top of the world. What do you think?'

Nell thought: it's the same dream as Mr Murdstone, isn't it? To rise from the river. To be born so low, and yet die so high.

'I must go,' said Sophia.

She was stepping backwards, out of the gaslight's glare, when Nell called out, 'The card – may I?'

Sophia scraped at the dirt with what was left of her fingers, then returned it to Nell's hand. 'Stay safe tonight,' the dance mistress said, as she retreated into the darkness. 'They told me the London winter would be bitter – but, girl, I had no idea.'

*

The silver lettering above the door read 'Lamb & Flag', but the denizens of these winding lanes knew it by another name: the Bucket of Blood.

There had been some altercation already tonight; the cobbles outside the tavern door were capped by a crystalline landscape of red. Frozen blood shattered beneath Minos's heel as he tramped towards the doorway. There he hunkered down to peer through the window – but the glass itself was frosted, and all he could see were bobbing lantern lights, patrons indistinct as ghosts.

While he was standing there, the door burst open, disgorging two revellers. Minos watched them cartwheel after each other, the air ripe with their invective; then he contorted himself through the door they'd cast open wide.

In the public house, three dozen sets of eyes revolved to take him in.

They'd seen him before, of course – but Minos still heard their mutterings the moment he shambled onto the tavern floor. A few lone faces acknowledged him; in turn, he inclined his head and gave each a gentle snort. Then, he crossed the space that was quickly being made (tables shifted aside, patrons rocking on their stools) to reach the alcove near the hearth. Here sat the tall Clementi cabinet piano whose music, most nights, filled the Lamb & Flag.

There was scarcely enough room for Minos to squat over its stool, but this he did. His enormous hands hovered over the keys. It always occurred to him, in these moments, how each key was once the tooth of an animal – and, as if in sympathy, he fingered the teeth that dominated his jaw.

Then he started to play.

They'd want one of the music hall melodies – he was certain of that. Bouncing rhythms and jaunty chords. He'd have given them what they wanted, if only he could – but the truth was, he wasn't sure how to reach for that kind of music. All he knew were the lilting arpeggios of an older music, the harpsichord played upon piano. And the deeper truth was, he wasn't sure where *this* came from either. It was just what came to his fingers, fat and cumbersome as they were.

Good enough for a few pennies, at any rate.

A few pennies for food.

A few pennies for another night on some ostler's stable floor, while he worked out what was next.

His fingers had danced their way up a single run of music when a vision lanced across him. He'd closed his eyes, the better to feel his way into the melody, and at once he was in the ruin of some forsaken city, the baying of soldiers somewhere behind. In his mind's eye, he stumbled forward; the sharp bite of fire cleaved into his side, and the city was filled with some unutterable howl.

When he opened his eyes, it was to discover that something truly was cleaving into his side; not the halberd of some medieval mercenary, but the prodding finger of Barnaby, who worked the cellars here. A man with chins big enough that perhaps he too belonged in a menagerie, he had often poured Minos a tankard, out of both pity and his own pocket.

'Not tonight, old man,' said Barnaby. 'Him that's keeping bar doesn't think it fits well with what's happening above.'

Minos lifted his head to the rafters.

'I just need a few pennies, Barnaby. They laid me off.'

'Laid you off, is it?'

'I need to scratch something together. I lost my lodgings as well. I won't go begging.' It was because of pride, of course, but there was another reason Minos wouldn't sit on the Strand with an open cap, imploring help from passers-by: few people took pity on a monster.

'There's always the *upstairs*, Minos.'

Both sets of eyes were on the rafters now. Minos snorted, long and low.

'*No*,' he said.

'Him that keeps upstairs has been asking after you. There's more than a few pennies to be made.'

'Aye,' said Minos, 'and a reputation to be made as well. But it's not a reputation I want.'

Minos had lifted himself back to his feet. Patrons tightened around their tables, as if in expectation.

'People look at you and see a brawler, whether you're brawling or not,' said Barnaby, not unkindly. 'You're hungry, my friend. You've no roof over your head. You've no –' Barnaby's eyes grew large at the sight of it, '– boots upon your feet. And it would just be *once*. You needn't do it again. For one night only, upstairs at the Lamb & Flag . . .'

Five scabbed knuckles connected with the black man's face. There was a moment in which he might have stayed standing; then, his mind caught up with what his body was feeling. Knees buckled. Head rolled. Come the end of it, he didn't even have the wherewithal to reach out and break his fall. Moments later, his body was being dragged out of the vice ring while his opponent raised his fists in triumph.

135

In the room above the Lamb & Flag, Minos quaked.

It was a tradition older than any of the men who had come to box here; the Lamb & Flag had been hosting bare-knuckle bouts since their grandfathers' generation. The ring, marked by sailor's rope, bore the stains of all those prior bouts, the blood of fathers and sons making an atlas on the boards.

'This one's been on his feet all night,' said Barnaby. 'If he sees the night through, there's a pot at the counter that would see him warm all winter.' Barnaby rose on his tiptoes, until he reached the ridged concavity that was Minos's ear. 'If you can end it, there'd be half that pot for you. The Flag's never had a man stand all night. There's a reputation to be worried about here as well.' Minos looked round; the brawler in the ring, his face marbled in the blood of his opponents, was drinking from a trough. 'Well? You can't tell me you haven't fought before. Say it to me and I'll show you a liar.'

Minos screwed his eyes shut. Old dreams clawed across him, opening him up. It was as if those claws were slashing at canvas; where the material tore, they revealed faded images underneath. There he was, bound in ropes and dragged at the back of some wagon. There he was again, in a pit with spear-points baiting him from behind cast-iron grilles.

He opened his eyes.

He stepped into the ring.

The brawler was not a diminutive man, but even he was dwarfed by the giant who tramped in to face him. Had Minos been focused, he might have seen the flicker of disquiet that crossed the man's knobbly features – but a

face that has been in this many bouts rarely has the ability
to express itself, so riven by knots and scars is it. As for
Minos, he was being cajoled out of his overcoat and shirt,
the scarves he'd scavenged spooling away until he was bared
to the waist.

In the dark of the ring it was impossible to make out the
scars underpinning the labyrinth tattoo, but the eyes of the
spectators knew, now, that this was no ordinary fighter.
Some had taken him for a sailor, others for the survivor of
some penal colony where the turnkeys had been routed and
old lags held sway. Two hundred years had passed since
the *Batavia* ran aground at the ends of the Earth, and its
survivors turned to barbarians on some God-forsaken island.
But the docks of London were filled with stories like this.
The goliath who'd just stepped into the ring had the look
of somebody who had prospered in a hell just like it. Take
away most men's clothes and they revealed themselves to
be beasts – but the truth was, some men were more beastly
than others.

Minos heard a cavalcade of voices. Wagers were being
placed. Men, braying in anticipation. He did not know at
which point the fight began. There was no battle cry to
signify the start of hostilities. The roar in the room simply
changed timbre – and then his opponent was advancing
forward, feinting back, circling Minos like a scavenger.

The first blow caught Minos in the jaw.

He knew it was coming, of course. The brawler was a
veteran of the vice ring, but that hardly mattered; Minos
had been set upon so many times that the blow seemed
predetermined. He turned his jaw against it, robbing it of
its real heft, and wore what was left of it with a grimace.

137

The brawler had brute strength, and more than an ounce of intelligence. It was little wonder he'd lasted in the ring.

A hush swept over the crowd, as potent as any roar. The expectation of Minos's first blow hung in the air.

Minos rolled his neck, cords of thick muscle flexing. There was a strange scent in the room now, stronger than the sweat and stale beer forming its haze around the men. Fear, thought Minos. The man in front of him was readying for another blow, but fear was flooding his body.

The second blow ought to have been Minos's, but the brawler sensed a hesitation and took his chance. His left fist connected with Minos's temple. A blow like that ought to have caused devastation – and indeed it did, but not to the man on whom it was inflicted; there was the sickening crunch of bone, and the brawler recoiled, nursing a shattered hand.

'Finish him, Minos!' It was Barnaby's voice, but very quickly a chorus formed around him. The crowd had scented something more titillating than blood: they'd sensed the unexpected.

Minos lurched forward.

The brawler knew he was coming. Shaking off the pain in his hand, he brought his other fist back, aimed a sharp jab at the place he judged Minos's kidney to be, then followed it with a punch directly at the artery throbbing in Minos's neck. This worked the crowd into a greater frenzy still. Another flurry of wagers was being placed. Men roared as if they were themselves in the ring, doing battle with a monster.

The brawler's blows kept coming.

It had escaped no man's notice that Minos was yet to land a blow.

It had escaped no man's notice that he was yet to even deal one.

It would have been easier, Minos supposed, if the man's blows really had penetrated him. Then he could have been dragged out of the ring, off to some stable floor for the night. But instead the fists kept coming. Instead, he was buffeted backwards and forwards, left and right. And each time five filthy fingers piled into him, the urge to catch the man's fist, to rip it from his body, to wrestle him back and grind him into the ground grew a little bit stronger in Minos's heart; each time, it took a little more strength to stay as he was: static and reserved, while all the hell in the boxer's body was being unleashed.

'He's toying with him!' somebody guffawed. 'Like a cat with a mouse. Finish him, you dog!'

'Hell,' somebody else grunted, 'he's given up the fight. He hasn't even—'

A fist flew towards Minos, striking him below the calcified protrusion on the left side of his head.

Something in the blow, some element of malice or good fortune, sent a pain like lightning coursing through Minos. He crumpled, his vast body doubling over as he fell. It was only at the last moment that he reached out and stopped himself from hitting the bloodstained boards. He braced himself, while pain lacerated his body.

And as he was braced there, he found himself wrenched out of the ring, wrenched out of the Lamb & Flag, wrenched out of history and thought . . .

Voices whirled around him. '*Please!*' somebody was begging. '*Please, not us!*' A fury such as he had never known rampaged into him, filling every crevice and corner. Heat, wild and unstoppable. '*Eunice*,' somebody was saying, '*Antias!*' He could no longer see the vice ring. Now all he could see was a darkened passageway, tapering to a point. Shadows cartwheeled past, begging for their lives – until, at last, a face materialized from the gloom, and held stalwartly in front of it, a gleaming, wicked blade. '*I've come to stop this*,' said the face. He was handsome as a god.

Another blow, this one to his jaw, brought Minos back to the real world. The roar of the crowd rolled over him like breaking waves.

He was back in the vice ring. The brawler was above.

He'd been lucky so far. He would not be lucky now.

The tangle of darkened passageways, the voices begging for their lives, the wicked blade that had come to kill him – all of it was a tumult in Minos's head as he burst back to his feet. He drew his fists back.

He threw them forward.

His blood beat black. His mind filled with a thousand disordered thoughts. But this was what would end it all. One blow, one death, one victory in the ring.

His fists had almost met the man's frozen face when everything changed.

'*No*,' said Minos.

'*No*,' the voice inside his heart.

At the last second, he lifted onto the tips of his horned toes. The momentum of his blow was too much to stop mid-flight, but now his fists sailed past the man's head, carrying Minos's pirouetting body with them.

'*No*,' he growled again as, in the heart of the caterwauling room, he seized his overcoat and shirt from Barnaby's stupefied hands and fled.

London was frigid, frozen in shadow as it turned towards night. But Minos felt only fire as he stalked its streets. It seemed but seconds after fleeing the Lamb & Flag that he was crashing back through the hoardings in St Giles, circumventing the sewer opening to reach the little lean-to.

Inside, Beresford Kale was ready to depart. Swaddled in a woollen coat, he looked almost childlike as Minos loomed in the door. The terror in his face was childlike too. It only grew more desperate as Minos leant in and, with thumb and forefinger like a great pincer, took hold of Kale's shoulder.

His gaze, desolate and empty. It cut Kale to the quick.

'I want my job back,' Minos breathed.

'I told you, Mr Minos – it's o-out of my hands . . .'

Minos pitched closer, his head dropping on its thick, corded neck until it was but an inch from Kale's own.

'*Give – me – my – job*, Mr Kale.'

Each word tolled, heavy as a funeral bell. They seemed to fill up the little lean-to, then to echo outwards, filling up St Giles, filling up the city, subsuming everything else in Beresford Kale's tiny little life. Kale stood transfixed, like a rabbit to a fox. The blackness in Minos's gaze seemed to glimmer with purpose. To glimmer, perhaps, with dark magic.

And Kale knew, then, that Minos was no degenerate to be dismissed and demeaned. He nodded, like the craven child he was.

'You can start right away, Minos. We'd be – honoured to have you back.'

There was safety in the darkness beneath. London was a dozen different cities, each one built on the ruin of the last, and as Minos allowed the winches to lower him down, he got to thinking that this was where he truly belonged: some relic out of history, a man out of time.

At least, down in the dark, eyes could not take him in. There was no other solitude like this, and it was solitude he craved. Solitude was cleansing. Solitude could heal. Only solitude could help him slough off the fury that had overcome him in the Lamb & Flag.

And that vision. The voices screaming to be saved, and the killer with his blade . . .

The men still toiling down here were few and far between; a lone voice hailed him, but he tramped on, into the deepest recesses. Here, brick tunnels spiralled into each other, then opened into vast underworld cathedrals. The only light in these tunnels came from the whale-fat lantern he carried – but the truth he could tell no man, the truth he would never confide in Beresford Kale, was that he carried it just for show; Minos did not need eyes, down here in the dark. Other senses showed him the way.

In one of the deeper chambers, he stopped. Ahead, the brickwork gave way to the old city beneath London. In time, they would carve a way south from here to meet their brothers taming the banks of the river. There was still a way to go – but there, waiting in the very place he had left it, was his shovel.

Time to take up his burden once again.

He was stepping out of his overcoat when he felt the small bulge in its pocket – and tenderly pulled out two satin slippers, bound together with ribbon. Alone beneath the city, he folded them between his enormous hands.

Hands which, scarcely an hour ago, had been curled into fists.

Hands which had been set on ending a man's life.

Minos opened his palm, protecting the slippers like a baby bird in its nest. No, he thought, they hadn't lost their softness. Six years old, but they'd been treasured and doted upon, as only a child can. As he touched them, he fancied he could feel Nell's yearning rising off their satin – as if she'd imbued the material with not just the longing of her past years, but the love which had come before. It must have been a very special thing to have memories you wanted to cling to, instead of memories – if memories they were – from which you must run.

He lifted the slippers to his gaping nostrils and breathed in their scent. Just the river, he thought. The river and the straw mattress in which they'd been hidden. But mother's love as well, dreams of the past – and a promise for the future.

It didn't seem right he should have them.

'*Nell*,' he whispered, and her name echoed through the old city where he stood.

*

Nell was late returning to the river. Without a waterman to ferry her, she could only pick her own way into the east. And, though she trudged for miles with a sense that something had been lost today, she also carried with her a fledgling hope for the future: the ivory card folded in a pocket, a handful of words promising a trade of her own.

Winter was cruel to a mudlark. It could steal the tides. It dwindled the day. By the time she recognized the sweep of the Ratcliffe river, the stars were already smeared across the rooftops, another day gone. It was only by good fortune that she reached the storehouses before Murdstone appeared. Sally-Anne seemed the only one pleased to see her; she hurried over, Nell's tin kettle at her side, and – having first smothered Nell in kisses – pressed it into her hand. 'I was worried about you. Nell, where did you go? One moment you were on the flats, and the next—'

Nell unspooled the length of tackle the waterman had given her and added it to the oddments in her kettle. Sally-Anne had weighted it with sand, then topped it with coals from her own collection – just a little something to avert Murdstone's ire. 'I just went foraging on my own,' Nell said.

Sally-Anne knew she was lying. Nell knew that she knew. Yet each just looked at the other.

'Just pray that Murdstone doesn't notice how empty your kettle is,' she whispered, at last.

He didn't. When he appeared, his inspection of the mudlarks' finds was cursory at best. There had been something different in Murdstone since he had taken a room at the Water's Edge, a surliness about him this evening that manifested in blatant disregard. He dispatched his wards into the streets to sell everything they'd dredged up, 'before I start selling you.' That last muttered imprecation was one he'd never made before. Things were afoot in the mind of Benjamin Murdstone.

They were afoot in Nell's mind as well. She hadn't carried her tin kettle a hundred paces before footsteps caught up with her.

'We need to talk to you,' said Gander.

'Sweetpea, we're worried,' said Sally-Anne.

'There's nothing to worry about,' Nell answered. And nor was there: Nell could see it all clearly now.

'Nell, there's something amiss in Murdstone. You've seen it more than most. Sally-Anne thinks he's sick. I'm of a mind it's something else – and we'd better pray that it is, because there'll be no Water's Edge for us if he perishes. But you mustn't test him, Nell. There's no knowing what he might do.'

'Winter's here, sweetpea. Can't you feel it?' Sally-Anne reached down and pinched Nell's cheek, numb with cold. 'Don't risk him, Nell.'

It wasn't their admonishment that stung Nell; it was their tenderness, and the fact that it no longer touched her. There was no comfort in the mudlarks, not any more.

'You've got us worried. You've got the rest talking. The silver chain. We need to know you won't do it again.'

'It was a moment of madness,' said Sally-Anne. 'Tell us it was madness, won't you?'

Nell stalked on. 'You don't understand. The silver chain would have made no difference – not to any of us.' Then she stopped, turned and said, 'I'm not staying on the river,' before flouncing on.

Rushing after her, Sally-Anne said, 'Sweetpea, you need to get your feet on the ground. Where would you go? What would you do?'

Nell's hand had darted, instantly, to the paper in her pocket. She wanted to draw it out, to declare herself a dancer, to tell them that she would glide away from them into one of the countless other worlds which existed in the city. But then she remembered Sophia's pitying eyes, and the knowledge that only one thing mattered in London.

From the counting houses to the doss-houses: only coppers and coins could elevate a soul.

'You can't go chasing fairy tales. We don't live in one. We live here, in Ratcliffe, and it's Ratcliffe we'll stay – unless, unless . . .'

'Unless what?'

Gander had caught them up. Softly, he said, 'Unless the winter takes us. Sally-Anne means we're Ratcliffe until we die. Nella, I know it isn't easy. You're younger than I am. You remember how it used to be. I reckon the longer you live, the more those memories fade. If a man lives a thousand years, he probably doesn't even know where he comes from.'

Why did that make Nell think of Minos, all of a sudden?

'Will you do it for us, Nell?' asked Gander.

'Let's get to Christmas, sweetpea. All of us, *together*.'

Their words echoed in her as she took to the streets. They'd left her with coals and the fishing tackle to sell, and of course there would be no shortage of families in need on a wild December night, but before she'd reached the haberdashers at St George in the East, some other compulsion came over her. She'd already returned to the river, to discover the first snow of the season strafing around, when she realized what it was: Gander and Sally-Anne, Potato Rot and Packrat Jack, they'd already given up. They'd limp out their days on the river, until Murdstone either embarked on a new life or lay dead in the sand. Perhaps they'd find him a treasure and, in return for delivering it to his hands, be abandoned to the tide.

Alone among them, only Nell had crouched at the mouth of the seaward cave and heard Minos speak that one magical word:

'*No.*'

At last, she understood why it had felt so powerful. *No.* She'd never thought of the word as bewitching before. She might never see Minos again, but he'd left her with a gift that might forever change her life.

'*No,*' she repeated, as she followed the tide.

In the emptiness of the seaward cave, she brought the remnants of the fire back to life. The flames brought warmth, but they brought hope as well. There'd be little food tonight, but she still had half the heel of bread from the wherryman and this was enough to see her to morning.

No more Water's Edge, she told herself.

No more toiling on Murdstone's account.

Murdstone had found a way off the river. Well, so would Nell. If she was wily, there were places to go mudlarking where Murdstone wouldn't find her. The river went on and on. Then, when next she reached into some rock pool and pulled out some treasure, it wouldn't be to butter Murdstone's bread; she'd take it, in hands washed clean by the river, to the four-fingered woman, and from there she'd glide to the stars.

And all because of that one word she'd heard the ogre say.

'*No.*' She said the word out loud, if only to hear the way it sounded. '*No. NO!*'

The last word's echo was fading when she heard footsteps outside the seaward cave. One after another, they tolled, getting louder, growing closer.

Nell wheeled around. Surely it was too soon for Murdstone to have come looking. Scarcely an hour had passed; she ought still to be on the streets, hawking their finds.

A shadow crossed the crevice. By instinct, Nell reached for one of the rocks that littered the ground. A small, smooth pebble – hardly enough to fend off some brigand, but it would do.

'Who is it?' she cried out. 'Stop!'

'Nell?' came a voice, full of whispers and cracks.

The shadow stepped into the fissure, revealing himself for who he was.

There stood Minos. His black, hooded eyes fell upon her, and he dropped to one knee. Even now, he dwarfed her. She'd forgotten the broken shape of him, the hunted look and great, gnarled hands.

It was those hands he held out to her now.

He opened them up.

Sitting between them were her two satin slippers, still delicately bound in the ribbon her mother had tied.

11

The Book of Untold Tales

*The Street of Hanging Lanterns, off the Limehouse
Causeway, December 1861*

Two ivory dice skittered across the table. Over and over
they turned – until, at last, they landed with seven black
hollows facing up.

Murdstone's heart beat more calmly now. That would do.
He reached out to reclaim the dice, oblivious to the grizzle
of the other men – gnarled sailors, intemperate stevedores,
wretches all – but, before he could send them skittering a
second time, a hand gripped his shoulder.

He froze.

'My money's as good as any other. I won't need credit
by night's end. A promise is worth . . .'

But there was something unexpected about that hand.
The words he'd been about to perform with such vehemence
faded away as he looked up.

There stood Bantam.

The throb of activity in the dark back room went on
regardless. Murdstone had played hazard in much finer
establishments than this, but the sounds of men risking all
at elaborately disguised games of pitch-and-toss was the
same whether you were in Mayfair or the Marshalsea. That

look of being trapped somewhere between epiphany and despair, he'd seen it in the prized salon of a prince and on the street corners off the Limehouse Causeway. This particular gambling den was humbler than most, its tables crowded by dockworkers – but a vampiric man weaved between the tables, looking for cardsharps, and this alone gave the establishment some element of class.

Murdstone left the table and said, 'You're like the reaper, hoving into view like that. If you've come to tell me I'm dying, out with it. I'd sooner know.'

'I daresay you're a few days closer to death than when last we met, but we're all on that road. No, Benjamin, I came because we must talk. I went to Lowood, but they told me you were gone.'

'Excommunicated, no less,' said Murdstone, shaking his head as they came between the tables.

'What happened, Benjamin?'

'Friends from the old times paid me a visit. It seems bad memories linger.' He planted his feet firmly down. 'I'm in pressing need, Bantam. Two pennies must become four. Four must become eight. All of this and more, much more, before Christmas comes. So – out with it. What's so urgent that it's keeping me from the tables?'

Bantam had that excoriating look in his eye; he'd been cultivating this particular expression since he was younger than Nell. It was a look that provoked much ire in Murdstone, a look which said: there are no riches to be made at these tables, and even you know it.

'I may have found your way out of whatever mire this is. Benjamin, we need a place we can speak. I was hoping for your quarters at the Lowood, but if not there, then . . . ?'

Some corners of London bore names redolent of the city that had been lost – you walked with ghosts along the Crutched Friars, you heard the roar of the tourney along the streets of Knightsbridge – but others betrayed a Londoner's pragmatic sense of the world. Narrow Street had earned its name on account of how its potteries and chandlers, its sorting houses and sugar factories, tapered to a vanishing point, the way between them in permanent shadow.

At a certain distance, the darkness was punctuated by orbs of orange light. Murdstone led Bantam there, to bow beneath the lanterns. Here, at the opening of a cut heading north, sat the apothecary Murdstone had so often frequented. At this nocturnal hour, the shop was closed, but the fat wax candle burning in the window was a proclamation that the back den – where sailors were prone to lying stupefied – was open for business.

'Dr Lynn always has quiet corners.' Murdstone's fingers reached for the glass and rapped out a rhythm every sailor knew by heart.

'I've warned you of these places,' said Bantam. He squinted through the glass, and now he scoffed, 'How can you expect me to prepare you properly for the end, if you're paying for these poisons? You call *him* a doctor, now? Do you even ask what he feeds you?'

Murdstone just said, 'I'm a gambling man. You've always known that. But I've found, as I've grown older, that it's more prudent to spread my bets.' He faltered, sensing a shadow through the glass. 'I don't mean to die before I have my due. I'll do whatever I must.' And no sooner had he thought of this, than he was thinking of Elkington's men

151

bursting into his quarters at the Lowood coach house, the feeling of their boots and fists. 'I shall die, at an hour of my choosing, in environs appropriate to my standing in life – which shall not be the river, Doctor; which shall *not* be any lower than at the pinnacle of my years; which *shall* be a bedchamber fit for a duke, with a maid to mop my brow and a boy to feed me grapes, and a friend to hold my hand and tell me that I did well, that you can never – *never* – underestimate a foundling.'

The last words exploded out of him, dragging behind them every breath in his body. Next second, Murdstone was grappling with the doorframe and beating his fists upon the wood.

'You can't beat old age by brute force, Benjamin,' Bantam whispered – and perhaps Murdstone, whose eyes flashed furiously at the words 'old age', would have defied him even then, if only the door hadn't opened up, revealing the apothecary Lynn.

Lynn was a diminutive man, dressed in dark fustian and linens. His complexion betrayed him as the offspring of a Limehouse mother and one of the sons of Canton; there were enough who'd risked their lot settling in Limehouse as Company administrators, but few of them had lasted long. Being between worlds was never an easy endeavour – for a man like Lynn, no chance encounter with an ivory sundial was enough to elevate his standing in life – but it had its advantages too. The niche Lynn had carved out was his alone.

'Mr Murdstone, I must presume it isn't a crib for the night?'

Sailors took cribs in the back parlour here, but Lynn

needed little instruction to guide his visitors to a stark back office. Here, Murdstone looked at Bantam – his face still creased in distaste – across a woodwormed table and said, 'I've never known why you scorn it. A man who spends long nights in the Courage, as you do. We all have our vices, Doctor.'

'It isn't the poppy I object to. I just hope –'

'Why are we here, Doctor?'

Bantam put his clasp bag on the table, then lifted from its innards a parcel of pudding cloth. This he carefully unfurled, revealing the book hidden inside.

Murdstone knew books. The founding of Murdstone & Sons had been by opportunism rather than design, but fate sometimes deals a man a fair hand. Lord knows, it had enough to make up for with Benjamin Murdstone. Murdstone had first learned letters from a man named Wetherill (who, by way of the debtors' prison, had taken an unusual career turn from schoolteacher to scavenger), but the books with which he'd been concerned at Murdstone & Sons were not meant for reading; they were merely commodities like the sugars, silks and teas out of which he'd later sought to make an empire. No, you did not read those books; you bought and you sold – and, sometimes, if you were wily, you rebought and resold again.

The pages of the book Bantam had revealed were not ancient vellum, just rag paper grown yellow with age. By its rivets, Murdstone took it for a hundred years old – he'd handled a copy of *Gulliver* in quite the same condition – but this hardly tallied with the pallor of the goatskin binding. Something about the mismatch unsettled the very idea of the object. It was an inexpert copy, then, styled in such a way that it harked back to an earlier age. And, as soon as Murdstone had made this observation, a strange feeling washed over him. He was not ordinarily given to nostalgia. Nostalgia was a kind of stupefying magic that held you back. But his time at Murdstone & Sons had been one of unrivalled successes, an age when everything he touched was golden and the failures of the future were yet to manifest, and he remembered it vividly now.

'Do you recognize it?'

'It's one of our forgeries.'

Bantam nodded. 'Languishing in some collector's library, gathering dust since the day he realized the fraud. That's the only reason he released it to me. But that's of little import. That my own fingers committed the forgery is merely the thing that brought it to mind. Ever since the seaward cave, it hasn't left me in peace.'

Bantam splayed open the book, a sacrilege had the volume been real. Stretching across its central pages was the same pattern of vertical and horizontal lines that he had last seen stretched across Minos's back: a labyrinth of interconnected passages, and the empty knot in the centre to which the final passage led.

Murdstone drew the book near. 'What is this?' He lifted it to finger the spine. The lettering here was faded, but on the title page the print was bold. '*Apocryphal Antiquity, being the Book of Untold Tales, collected by Anton Castillon.*' He turned the page again. It was nothing more than a collection of writings, and some verbose introduction from the pen of the gentleman who had collated it. Writers were egotists, Murdstone had often observed, and so it was with Castillon. The foreword was little more than a list of

154

his accomplishments and an aggrandizing account of how he had come across each of the seven tales he would chronicle herein. It was difficult to age the book by the man's language – a certain level of pomposity could make a man seem like he belonged to a much earlier time – so Murdstone was intrigued to read Castillon's portentous account of his collection being printed in the same moment 'the Great Comet did Tear across the Heavens'. By Murdstone's reckoning, it made the writing two hundred years old.

'"Being the True and Authentic History of the Treachery of Morgan le Fay at the Battle of Camlann. Being One Man's Exploration Along the Faerie Roads of Olde England. Being the Missing Stanza of the Vita Merlini. Being the Hidden Historie of the Second Ark".' Murdstone stopped. 'Explain yourself, Bantam. I've been clear about my situation. I haven't time to waste reading fairy stories.'

Bantam turned the page. There, at the top of the next leaf, the list of untold tales continued:

'"Being an Authentic Account of the Lie Told by Theseus and the missing Minotaur of Knossos". Read it, Benjamin.'

But Murdstone only closed the book. 'Out with it. You've dragged me from my honest endeavours, so you owe me plain speaking. I didn't teach you to be obtuse.'

'Castillon spent his life on this book, but the stories he spins are much older than him. Read it closely enough and you'll find him an arrogant, spoiled scholar – the forgotten son of some duke, whose lands were bequeathed to his brothers. I suppose it gave him an interest in the neglected end of things. The people history overlooks. There was a second man, by Castillon's measure, who saw the coming of the Great Flood and sought to survive it by building a ship. Only this man didn't hear the voice of God, so his story goes unrecounted. I suppose there was something in my nature that made these stories appeal. Forgotten, over-looked child that I was.' He stopped. 'But I graduated from histories to the medical sciences. I took my apprenticeships and read the treatises of the body. And of these untold tales, I hadn't wasted a moment's thought – not until,' and he flicked through the pages to reveal, once again, the black labyrinth design, 'I saw that savage in the seaward cave.'

Minos. Murdstone would not admit it out loud, but the memory of the brute rising up from his ropes had plagued him in the nights past. Thank God for Nell. The girl seemed to bring some decency out of the brute.

'You know the story of Theseus, of course.'

Murdstone nodded. He had schooled himself in every classic: the Greeks, the Romans, the penny dreadfuls which proliferated across London's streets. One day, scholars would pore over the meaning of Spring-heeled Jack and Varney the Vampyre just as they did Perseus and his slaying of the Gorgon; they'd host literary salons debating the rehabilita-tion of Sweeney Todd.

'The grand artificer, Daedalus, was commissioned to build a prison that could hold the Minotaur. A beast beyond imagination, the offspring of Queen Pasiphae and the Cretan Bull. To keep him, Daedalus built the Labyrinth – and to keep him sated, every year, seven young men and seven maidens were chosen by lot to enter the Labyrinth and meet their fate.'

'You're a fine storyteller, Bantam. The classics' loss has been medicine's gain. And yet—'

'What happened next, Benjamin?'

Murdstone sat back. Every moment spent entertaining this hogwash was a moment lost at the tables. All the moments of his life, running through his hands. 'The years flicker past. Generations of young men and women, served up to the Minotaur. Until—'

'Theseus,' said Bantam.

'There's always a hero, in the old tales. In the real world, it's *you* who has to be the hero. And it isn't some maiden you're saving – you're only saving yourself. It doesn't make quite as fine a tradition.'

'Theseus could no longer see his countrymen devoured, so he made a decision: he would himself enter the Labyrinth, as one of the seven condemned, and slay this Minotaur. And this he did . . . or so the legend would have us believe.' Bantam reached for the book again. '"Being an Authentic Account of the Lie Told by Theseus". This is where Castillon's account diverges. Legend teaches us that Theseus slew the Minotaur in the heart of the maze, and that he led the condemned Athenians back to safety by virtue of a single length of string, gifted to him by his lover Ariadne.'

'She met a cruel fate, in the end. Abandoned by her hero, after all she did for him.'

But Bantam persisted, 'Castillon has it differently. In Castillon's account, Theseus did reach the heart of the Labyrinth, Theseus did fight the Minotaur and lead the Athenians to freedom . . . but he was lying when he told them the Minotaur was dead. Hobbled, perhaps. Indisposed, certainly – for why else did it not rip Theseus limb from limb? But the Minotaur survived. And when, some time later, it came back to its senses, it found the length of string Theseus had followed. And the thinking part of its

157

mind, the part it owed to its human mother, knew then what it must do. For, if a man could follow that string out of the Labyrinth, why might a Minotaur not do the same thing?'

Murdstone had drawn the book back across the table, and now he peered at the woodcut illustrations punctuating the text. Labyrinths in the corner of the page. Knotted string running around the circumference of the writing. He turned the leaf and saw some artist's depiction of the Minotaur emerging from the jaws of the Labyrinth – and now he thought suddenly of how bright the light had seemed on the day they released him from the Marshalsea, how vast London had been after three years inside, how terrifying to have the whole world in front of you and not a clue where to turn. All the possibilities of existence, ranged up against you, begging you to choose.

'Then what?' Murdstone asked.

Bantam stared.

'Castillon has the Minotaur set free. But then what, Bantam? Devastation? Death?'

'*Redemption*,' said Bantam, and turned the page again. 'A shepherd boy found the Minotaur, bloodied and brutalized, in his goat-shed some days later. There he was, sleeping in the straw laid out for the goats. A monster, unable to speak. He ought to have killed the shepherd boy, but he didn't. Nor did he kill the woman who took him in as a labourer on her father's farm. Nor did he kill the priest at whose temple he took sanctuary, when a mob was baying for his blood.' Bantam paused. 'Nor did he kill little Nell, when she found him choked in river mud on the banks of the Thames.'

He had spoken the last words with such solemnity, but by Murdstone's eye he knew he was being scorned.

'The shepherd boy followed the Minotaur, to the end of his days. He chronicled his story, and that story got passed down – until it ends up, right here, in *this* book.' Bantam gripped the tome. 'The Shepherd of Knossos died an old man – but the Minotaur went on living. Generation after generation . . . and, each year, a little less beastly than the last. It's right here, in the shepherd's own words.' And Bantam turned the book, so that he could read it out loud. '"His horns were a little less pointed when I saw him last. His guttural growls seemed almost like words. And, as I bade him farewell for the final time, in the way the light caught his eyes, I thought I saw something human."'

'Hocus pocus,' Murdstone sighed. 'You'd send a man to Bedlam if he spouted a story half as wild. Bantam, you *fool*, you had more sense when you were a child – and children believe in fairies!'

'Benjamin, listen to me —'

'No,' said Murdstone, and rose declaratively to his feet. 'You'll listen to me. Decades may have passed since you worked for me, Bantam, but I still have the better of you. I have real problems, right here, in the real world. If there's an answer for me, it's here in the real world as well. I'll hear no more lunacy, not from one I trained to be better. Not from one I trained to *think*.'

Murdstone was halfway across the apothecary's shop when Bantam called out, 'You saw that tattoo for yourself, Benjamin.'

'Any man can carve a labyrinth into his back, then stain it in black ink.'

'Not all men have the stumps of horns on their heads.'

Murdstone was almost at the door. Bantam made haste to follow.

'Not all men have festering knife wounds one moment, then hardly a scar by the fall of next night. Is it really so hard to believe he might not be human?'

Murdstone turned over his shoulder, his hand still gripping the door. 'Mere moments ago you scoffed at me for daring to believe there might be some merit in this . . .' He opened his other hand, as if to indicate the cluttered shop, its racks of phials, the counter where drawers held powdered horn and strange distillations. 'There you stand, a man of science, unable to believe there might be any worth in tinctures and remedies beyond your Royal Society. Only an Englishman, you say, could ever have dominion over our knowledge of the lungs, the heart, the arteries that sustain us. How is it, Bantam, that one moment you're blind to those possibilities – and yet, the next, you're bringing back gods?' Murdstone was purpling again. His heart, playing another one of its tricks. He conquered it by willpower, rocking his body until it had calmed. 'You ask me to believe that a legend washed up on my river. Forgive me, Bantam – I always thought it was the purpose of science to, one day, do away with gods.'

'You mistake me, Mr Murdstone. You always have. I don't doubt the possibilities of medicine beyond these shores. I doubt the character of a man who would take your money in return for promises and whispers. A man who, damn him, hasn't once set foot beyond the East India Dock!'

Somewhere in the apothecary, a door slammed. No doubt Lynn was listening through the walls.

'It's precisely because I'm a man of science, Benjamin, that I dare to believe. There isn't a man of science in the world who believes we have all the answers. Mr Murdstone, we've barely scratched the surface. We call this the Modern World – and yet we're children, feeling our way in the dark, jumping at shadows, running from ghosts. You remember what that was like, just the same as me.'

Murdstone had been ready to take flight, back to the tables, back to the eternal pitch-and-toss of his life. But he lingered a second longer, and into the silence Bantam said, 'Sailors come back from the edges of the world every year, with stories of things we would scarcely believe a season before. Mermaids. Sirens. Tribes of lost men. They're pulling dragons out of the earth and calling them dinosaurs. They're telling us men were birthed by great apes.' He faltered, before he added, 'I don't believe it's impossible, Benjamin, that you had a treasure beyond imagination in your hands. Your life was built on the legend of a sundial. Well, sir, what if that act was but an opening?'

'Isn't it more likely, Bantam, that he's a runaway from some travelling show? Minos the Great! A brute like that, somebody might have seen the same thing as you. For the promise of a roof over his head, he'd have let them scar him. He'd have let them rename him *Minos*, after . . .'

'The King of Crete, the one whose queen fell in love with the bull.'

Murdstone's silence was not furious this time, but contemplative. Bantam could sense such a change in him that, when he stalked back into the lanterns of Narrow Street, leaving Bantam behind, he was quite taken aback.

161

'Think about the knife wounds, Benjamin. The way he survived the river?'

An hour had been lost to Bantam's lunacy, and Murdstone's place at the hazard table was lost. He had to wait to regain his seat, but even then it seemed as if he wasn't truly in the room. The dice fell out of his hands without any real hope; he lost once, lost twice, lost three times before he scraped a win.

His mind was somewhere else, trapped in Bantam's ramblings.

But those thoughts were like the Labyrinth itself.

The credit he'd been afforded by the keeper of the house hardly rose or fell as midnight approached. That was another night wasted. Another night closer to the end – whether it came at Elkington's hand, or by the treacheries of his own body. By the time he left (and hired some glym-jack to guide him through streets where cutpurses did not lurk), he'd got to thinking that it was all just imaginary anyway, all just phantoms. The money he owed, and the money he'd spent. Leave alone what madness Bantam espoused – there was nothing more mythical in this world than money.

It was just like the book Bantam had brought. A book containing myths, but a myth itself – a myth they had themselves constructed, to gull all those scholarly men who desperately wanted to believe . . .

Murdstone froze. Somewhere, in the darkest recesses of his mind, a light was shining. He'd been stumbling blindly all night, chasing an elusive idea – and now his hands were upon it.

Yes, he thought, as the glym-jack led him back to the river, *that* was the secret, *that* was the feeling he'd been clamouring after. It didn't matter that the book in Bantam's hands had been a forgery; it was not the rag paper and ink, the goatskin and glue, that mattered. You weren't selling a book. What you were selling was only an *idea*.

The idea that it was valuable.

The idea that it was real.

And so it might be with Minos himself.

Murdstone stood on the riverbank, white hair blowing wild in the wind – and, for what felt like the first time, his face broke open in a smile.

'This way, sir,' said the glym-jack, but Murdstone barely acknowledged his existence. 'Sir, let's get off the river. The wind's too strong for an old fox like you.'

But Murdstone bouldered past, barely even using his cane for balance. 'I don't need a guide from here.'

And indeed he did not, because Benjamin Murdstone had seen the way. Whether Anton Castillon had been writing lost history or just plucking fairy tales out of the ether, it mattered not. What mattered was the *idea*, and what he could do with it.

He'd sold forged books before. Why not a forged man? Why not the Minotaur itself?

He supposed he was going to have to track down this Minos after all.

12

The Mudlark and the Monster

Off the Ratcliffe Highway, December 1861

'You came back . . .'

Nell was not certain, at first, whether she ought to take the slippers from Minos's cupped hands. They sat there, on their pedestal of scarred flesh, and seemed like some treasure that did not belong to her. But Minos's eyes were open wide, imploring her. They were hers, and hers alone.

Why, then, did it feel like theft as she pressed them to her heart?

'I didn't think to find you here,' said Minos. 'Not after dark, not in December. I thought to leave them here, where they might be found. Don't you have a place? A roof over your head?'

Nell whispered, 'This is my place. For tonight, at least.' She stopped before she spoke of the next night, and the night after that; she could hold in mind the future two years hence, when she would be gliding on starlight across the Alhambra stage, but the thought of what might happen in a few days still seemed terrifying.

Minos took in the barren cave. Then, like a girl to her doll, his great hand came down to touch her cheek. 'You're freezing.'

However rough and callused his hand, his touch felt gentle as her mother's used to be. He took almost the entirety of her head in his palm. There it remained as she trembled, 'I built a fire.'

'It won't last,' he said – and that was the moment he let go of her, dropping to his knees at the fire's edge instead. In front of him, the flames she'd conjured looked no more potent than candles. She watched as his huge hands reached into the circle of stones, rearranging the pieces of driftwood into a pyramid, to which he then extended his strange, elongated jaw. When he blew into the heart of the fire, it fanned upwards with such majesty that Nell was put in mind of the travelling showmen she'd once seen on the Highway, fire-breathers and jugglers, acrobats and knife-throwers.

'Have you eaten?'

From her pocket, Nell brought the half heel of bread.

'Meagre rations for a winter's night. You'd have better with your Mr Murdstone.' He paused. 'Why aren't you with him, Nell? Wherever he keeps you?'

If only so she didn't have to spill the truth, she blurted out, 'Where have *you* been, Minos? I was worried.' It sounded so facile, but it was true – the mudlark, wracked with concern for the monster. 'I wasn't the one to tell Mr Murdstone you were here. You know that, don't you?'

'I didn't plan to frighten him like I did,' said Minos, and Nell detected a glimmer of guilt as he settled by the fire. 'Has he been good to you since? I had a fear he'd punish you, for the fear I put into him.'

'You didn't mean to. It's not your fault.'

Such innocent words. Minos's mind was already cartwheeling back to the vice ring above the Lamb & Flag, and the way his heart had been roaring when he brought his fists back to devastate the brawler. Worse still, the yearning he'd felt as he hunched into Beresford Kale's lean-to.

'He hasn't punished me.'

'Then why are you here? This is where he keeps you?'

Nell felt suddenly shamefaced. 'There's a lodging house, the Water's Edge. He crams us into its attic. I think he knows the landlady, from long ago. Mr Murdstone knows everyone in Ratcliffe. They say he knew everyone in Mayfair as well, but things were different back then. It was before I was born.' She paused, aware she was not answering the question. 'I won't go back there.'

'Why not? Are they cruel to you, Nell?'

He knew about cruelty, of course. Nell wanted to ask about the knife wounds in his side – but then she remembered they were gone, and as soon as she remembered that, she was thinking about how effortlessly he'd magicked life back into the fire – and after that it was those strange protrusions on his scalp, and the bottomless black of his eyes.

It was hard to articulate, but Nell decided she would try. 'Have you ever felt trapped?'

Minos's eyes glowed with tenderness when he said, 'I have.'

'I don't just mean ropes,' said Nell. 'He doesn't tie us up like he tied you. But he has us in chains all the same. Everything we collect on the river goes to Mr Murdstone. He wants us to find treasures, something to transform his life. But it won't transform *ours*. We're part of the river, so it's by the river we'll stay. Gander and the rest think it's just the way it is. I suppose they think we ought to be

166

grateful. There's blackguard children worse than we are.
There's children bought and sold. I've seen them, up on
the Highway, looking like ghosts. But I have a dream,
Minos. I *know* I can leave the river. My mother . . .'

Nell's voice faded, then. She buried her head.

'You had a mother, once.'

'Don't we all?' croaked Nell. She parted her fingers to
look at Minos. The firelight was there, reflected in the
infinite depths of his eyes – and she realized, suddenly,
that she had no idea what he was thinking; his was a face
too strange to read ordinary human emotions. She thought
there was tenderness in his voice, something like regret
– the kind of regret a good soul had when they saw a
world tipping towards ruin – but she was not sure. 'She
thought Mr Murdstone was a good man. That he'd look
after me. And I suppose he'd say – well, here you are, Nell,
four years later, and still with a beating heart. But what's
the use of a heart that's beating, if it's beating for somebody
else?' There was something about giving voice to feelings
like these that made them real. Buried inside, they could
still be figments of the imagination – but to share them
with another was to set them in stone. Now, her fingers
danced towards her pocket, and from it she drew Sophia
Chrétien's calling card. 'I want to find my own way. If I
find a silver chain, I want it to be mine. The things I find
in the mud, they should change *my* life, not Mr Murdstone's.'

She looked up. The mudlark and the monster, staring
into each other across the dancing flames. *The things I find
in the mud, they should change* my *life*. Those words seemed
to fill up the whole of the seaward cave – for wasn't Minos
also one of those things?

'Can you read?' Nell asked.

Minos nodded, pensively. 'Oh yes.'

'My mother taught me letters, but at the Water's Edge, they don't know words. I've forgotten so much.' She offered up the card. 'Might you?'

The card seemed dainty as a penny in Minos's hand.

'SOPHIA CHRÉTIEN,' he read. 'Shining Light of the Paris Opera Ballet, Available for TRAINING and TUITION for Professionals and Amateurs Alike. DEBUTANTES and DILLETANTES.' He looked up. 'There's an address in St Giles.' It wasn't far from the hoardings where he'd barracked Beresford Kale. 'What is this, Nell?'

So she told him it all, of how she'd gone back to the Alhambra, of how she'd stumbled after Sophia Chrétien.

'And I think it was her, Minos. The same one who danced with me, all that time ago.' She stopped, for the foolishness of it was breaking over her like one of the river's sudden waves. 'Do you believe in chance? In fate?'

Minos snorted sadly. 'I believe life is made up of mysteries. Why mightn't it be her?'

For a time, the idea made Nell feel like she was in flight. But, of course, girls who go flying must always plummet to land.

'I could never go to her, even if I'm right. Because it's riches, isn't it? It's why Mr Murdstone has us searching the river. Rich men don't have to sift through the mud. They can have whatever they like. But if I did find a treasure, Minos – if it *was* for me, not Mr Murdstone, then I could go back to Sophia. I could tell her: here I am.' She'd already gone this far; next moment, the thought that had been niggling at her since the Alhambra simply spilled out. 'In my head, it's her. She's the one who was there, that day with my mother. It's her hands who lifted me up. Only . . .'

Minos bowed his head, imploring her to go on.

'She has all five fingers, in my dream. I can feel them on me, lifting me up. So perhaps it isn't her at all.'

Minos dared to touch the peach ribbon again. The slippers trembled in response. 'What do you know of the ballet, Nell?'

Nell remained silent, unable to betray how little she understood. All that she truly knew was the feeling of it. The warmth of being told, that long-ago night, that she was good.

'They don't dance the ballet, not in London – not yet. But they've been dancing it for hundreds of years in Rome. They dance the ballet in Paris and St Petersburg. Hundreds of years ago, in the old Italian courts, when a noble wanted to outdo his rival, he would hold a pageant – and there'd be music, and dancing . . .' Minos snorted. 'It wasn't like it is now, not back then. They didn't dance in slippers like yours, not until much later.'

Nell had been lost in the wonder of it, but now she said, 'Minos, how do you know?'

'I know lots of things, Nell.' He was thinking of the Clementi cabinet at the Lamb & Flag, and the lilting arpeggios that flowed out of his fingers – but then he was thinking of the fire he'd just summoned, and then he was thinking of capricious gods, of winged mares, of men who needed no stallion underneath them because they were, in part, stallion themselves. Sometimes, it seemed his head was too full; about the only thing he didn't know was where it all came from, what was memory and what was dream.

169

'Here,' said Minos, 'let me show you?'

He would have relented if she'd breathed a word, but instead Nell let Minos guide the first slipper onto her foot. The knots in the ribbon had been pulled too tight for his fingers, so he waited patiently while Nell unpicked them. Then he slipped on the second and helped her to her feet.

'What was it your mother told you?' Minos asked, as he steered Nell out of the seaward cave. *'They said you were a natural. My dancing girl. My ballerina.'*

'You heard every word, didn't you?'

They stepped outside, Nell's tiny hand folded in his gargantuan own. The river had rolled towards the cave since Nell scurried this way, but the half-moon of shale around the cavern entrance remained untouched. Ribbons of white tumbled across the water, obscuring the wharfs beyond. The whole of the river, a flickering miasma of white.

Sometimes snow is beautiful. Sometimes snow is cruel. It was Minos who would later teach her that beauty and cruelty are not opposite to one another, that often they sit in the very same spaces of the human heart. But right now, by some trick of the wind and the steepness of the rocks, the snow did not tumble directly around the seaward cave. The wind whipped a distance around them, and into its calm heart, Minos led Nell.

There they stood, untouched by the winter, untouched by the world.

There they danced.

It would have made a strange sight, if any watermen had been on the river that night. A passing bargeman would have seen a small girl being shown to bend her knees by the ogre beside her. They would have watched as he shifted her feet into position, then put his hands around her waist to encourage her to leap and glide. If their voices had carried far enough, they would have heard her laugh when he turned her around, then laugh again as he – with his bulging, unearthly body – showed her how to raise one leg and pitch the body, extending the arms, the neck, to appear graceful as he danced.

Some time later, the wind changed, and the snow touched Nell. Breathless from the dance, she sat on the shale – and Minos folded his arms around her. The slippers on her feet were scuffed for the first time in their history. Nell fingered their loose threads; she supposed she ought to be heartbroken, but somehow they seemed more real now, as if they had grown into the slippers they were meant to be.

'You'll have to go back to the lodging house,' said Minos – and, in recompense for the sadness of that statement, held her tighter yet. 'You'll freeze on the river.'

'I don't want to, Minos. He doesn't own me.'

'No,' said Minos, and inclined his ridged brow to hers, 'he doesn't. Nobody owns you, Nell. But there's no trap they can build to keep you – not if you're free up here.' And he touched, again, the top of her head. 'Trust me on this, Nell, because you'll freeze out here. It might not happen tonight. It might not happen tomorrow. But the cold will get inside you, and once it puts down roots, you won't know warmth again.' Minos rocked back from her and stood. 'You'll find a way off the river, little one. There's a way out of every prison. Sometimes, it just needs a little patience.'

The tide was too deep for Nell to pick her way back along the river, so it was on Minos's shoulders – like a cherished daughter, or a princess on her palanquin – that Nell returned to Ratcliffe above.

171

The streets were still around the Water's Edge. Even the footpads and shadowmen who owned the night took umbrage at the first breath of winter.

In the shadows of the doorway, Nell said, 'Where will you go?'

Minos knelt to hold her. 'I have a place.' He put his thick lips to the shell of her ear. 'Be brave, little Nell. And keep dancing.'

At least Murdstone wasn't here, thought Nell as she picked her way up through the Water's Edge. Some nights, you'd see him slumped in the common room, contemplating his existence with his face fixed on the flames. Others, he'd be bowed in conversation with one of the tenants from the dormitories below. He'd flash a look if he saw you walk past, and you'd know he was keeping count. But tonight, there was no Murdstone – so it was not fear, just disappointment, that dogged Nell into the attic.

Some of the others were already asleep. Sally-Anne stirred as Nell passed, reaching out a conciliatory hand to take her own. Nell squeezed it back (there was no sense in bad blood), and hurried to the window. There, she looked down through the strafing white. The silhouette of Minos was still tramping away.

Then the snow folded around him and Nell was alone in the attic, secretly stashing both the tarnished slippers and Sophia's calling card in the straw mattress, and wondering, incessantly wondering, how it was that a man so strange, a man who spoke so brokenly but never of himself – who worked in the city beneath London, excavating tunnels and sewers – could possibly know about satin slippers and dancing, and the birth of ballet in the old Italian courts.

She went to sleep that night, certain she would see him again.

13

Two Dreamers Entwined

It was some days later, some days colder, some days bleaker, that Minos returned to Nell's life.

She'd worked hard on the river that day. The others had been anxious not to disturb her – fearing that the next time Nell defied Murdstone, his punishment would be indiscriminate – but, by the time they were gathered at the storehouses, every one could see how hard she'd worked. There were no treasures in her tin kettle, but it did overflow with coals, a bronze key on a length of twine, an old axe head which was certainly worth selling to an ironmonger. December's days were short; Nell's discoveries were a trove. Noah was burning with envy as Murdstone dispatched them into the streets.

And there was Minos, standing between the gas lamps on the approach to Bluegate Fields. Later, he would tell her he'd been following her from the river. Now, he simply shambled out of the darkness and said, 'Nell?'

She startled at her name. 'Minos!'

He knelt, in the slush that still coloured the streets, and dangled her tin kettle from a single finger. 'I know a man who'll take it all.'

And so he did. There was a smithy some way above

Bluegate Fields, and when Minos led Nell into his yard, the blacksmith's raggedy children scattered as if at the approach of a storybook ogre. The blacksmith himself greeted Minos with his own untoward look. 'It's been a time, Minos.'

Minos grunted in acknowledgement, then showed him the kettle. 'Worth a few pennies, at least.'

A blacksmith always had use for coals. The axe head would find a use too. They left, moments later, with the coins in Nell's pocket.

'But how do you know him?'

'He gave me work in his foundry, after I came to London. He's the one sent me to the sewers, when he knew they were looking for hands.' They'd returned to the Highway, where the darkness was hardening. 'I worked hard at the smithy, but he couldn't keep me. Said he'd lose trade, and I suppose he's right. So the sewer was better for me.'

There seemed, to Nell, something inalienably sad about Minos being buried beneath London. 'Mr Murdstone says the sewers will destroy him. He says they'll wall the river. There won't be tides any more, so there won't be mudlarks.' He said a lot more than this when the mood took hold of him, but Nell stopped there. 'I was glad to dance with you that night.'

'That's why I'm here,' said Minos.

'To dance again?'

Minos's great head lolled. 'The Alhambra Circus isn't so far from the yard where I work. After what you said, I've been tramping there every night.' He looked down the long barrel of the Highway. 'It's better that you just come. If you trust me?'

'Trust you, Minos?'

This time, his shoulders rolled. 'I'm afraid it's a long way. We could sit on an omnibus, but people would stare. There might be trouble. There'll come a day you could sail the buried rivers, but until then . . .' He knelt again, offering his shoulder as he had to wade through the river on the night that they danced. 'If it's not uncomfortable?'

Nell touched the great hump of his shoulder. 'People will stare at this too.'

But Minos only snorted, 'They'll blink and we'll be gone.'

And so Nell was borne aloft again, to sail along the Highway seven feet from the ground. The gas lamps blinded her when she swooped into their halos; the snow, when it came, made miniature storms around her face; but London, seen from on high, was so different from below.

For the second time in her short life, Nella Hart flew.

She was flying still when Minos's loping stride came to a halt, and she looked up at the dizzying array of lights.

For an hour they had followed the river west. Now, beneath Blackfriars – and the beaches where Murdstone was known to have larked in the mud himself, in some bygone age – she could pause and see the vast nightscape: London, aglow with oranges, yellows and reds, all of it flickering like a magic lantern behind the strafing white.

'Time to come down, little Nell. It's on your feet from here.'

The last time she'd seen it, twilight was drawing near; tonight, Leicester Square was bejewelled in gaslights and ice. Every iron railing seemed hewn out of crystal. Each rutted track, frozen hard. By the tumult in the square and the snickering of agitated horses, the winter kept neither fine gentlemen nor street prospector at bay. Songs were being sung. Carriages waited at the hotels to either set down or pick up their guests.

And there was the Alhambra Circus, a stark white palace ringed in gaslights like the stars which were missing from the sky.

Nell and Minos waited some distance away, each of them dwarfed by its wonder. The Alhambra was open tonight. Figures clad in black gathered at doors flung open wide, then slipped, one after the other, into a portal of light.

A doorway to another world, thought Nell.

She thought she heard music.

Minos breathed in the bitter December air, smacking his lips as if tasting its vintage. 'We may have to wait a little time.'

'For what?' Nell asked, eyes shimmering with expectation.

'It won't be long,' Minos replied, and in the peculiar wrinkling of his lips, Nell thought she detected his own crooked smile.

Minos was right; it wasn't long at all. In fact, it was already happening. Behind them, a convoy of three carriages wheeled past, slush spraying from their horses' hooves as they came. 'This way, Nell,' Minos snorted, and lumbered forward, following the trails the carriages left in their wake.

There was a second entrance to the Alhambra, hidden between gaslights on the Charing Cross Road. Here, the carriages had come to a halt, forming a half-moon around the doors. By the time Minos and Nell approached, hand in great hand, the first carriage door had opened – and out of it stepped a man dressed in black. It took Nell a moment to understand he was a servant, and that the real thing Minos wanted her to see was still inside. Something buzzed inside her; there had been such a dearth of it in her life that she did not, at first, recognize it as excitement. She strained on Minos's hand, drawing him closer to the carriages.

At once, the horses started shifting.

She'd seen horses like this, up on the Highway. They spooked at some sudden noise, or were filled with fear at the approach of the man who'd beaten them into submission. The horse in front of her, sleek and black, rolled its head, trying desperately to see beyond its blinkers. Its nostrils flared; it whickered in unease. Fear like that spread quickly. The horse at its side began to prance from side to side – and, moments later, the disquiet reached the horses harnessed to the other carriages.

'Whoa, whoa!' one of the coachmen was calling – but it was not this, in the end, that stilled the spooked horses. Their whickering stopped only when Minos reined back on Nell's hand, compelling her to slink several strides further away.

Now that the horses were stilled, the coachmen returned to the business at hand. As they reached into the carriages to guide their residents out, Nell said, 'What happened? Was it us?'

'Quiet, little one. Here they come.'

'But Minos, those horses were scared of—'

She was about to say 'you', but then she saw the ladies stepping out of the first carriage. Tall, lithe and elegant – but they held her attention for only a moment, because behind them came a man whose arms were laden with three beautiful gowns. It was this man to whom every other paid deference. An attendant similar in stature – and similarly laden with silks – emerged from each of the other carriages; they were the ones who hustled into the Alhambra first, protecting their wares from the ragged snow before the Company followed.

Nell was rapt. Memory flowed through her, as amorphous as a dream – and she was certain, suddenly, that this was the same back door through which she had once followed her mother.

She was still staring when she heard Minos say, 'Do you know what you saw?'

'Dancers!'

'The Neva Ballet. All the way from St Petersburg.' Minos crouched. 'As far as I've ever wandered, Nell, if I could only keep it in mind. I heard whisper of them on the square one evening. I thought you'd want to see.'

The dancers and footmen were vanishing into the Alhambra now, enveloped by the light. Behind them, the door closed – sealing the Company within; sealing in the wonder, sealing in the joy.

'I haven't always been a sewer slave, Nell. I've lived in a lot of places. I've taken all manner of work. You have to, when you look like this.' He lifted back his hood, to grin – she was certain he was grinning – at her with crumpled lips.

Nell was not mistaken; in the same moment the hood peeled back, the horses at the carriages, whose coachmen were now readying to leave, grew restless again.

'I was a footman, once, at a court in Rome. When they danced at court, they danced the ballet.'

179

Nell was not sure how a man from an Italian court washed up on a London river, but somehow, in Minos's broken brogue, it seemed to make sense. 'What was it like?'

'I can scarcely remember. Just like I scarcely remember tending the gardens at the monastery where they took me in. Just like I scarcely remember the whaling ship where they had me with a harpoon in my hand. Or the black forest where I wintered, roping the fallen trees. I know I must look strange to you, Nell—'

'You don't!' she said, clambering up close, like a child who has disappointed her father and is suddenly desperate for reassurance.

'But it runs deeper than that. When you look like this, it isn't just flesh. It reaches the bones. The head and the heart. I'm not like you, Nell. Look at you, down there —' His finger extended to touch her, at exactly the place where her heart was beating its wild rhythm, '— ten years old, but when you're fifty, sixty, seventy, you'll be able to bring this day to mind. There it will be, archived away in that great library in your head. You'll be wandering those passages and you'll pluck a book from the shelf, and there'll be your memory, perfectly preserved.' He paused. 'But not for me, Nell. In my head, those books are in different languages. Pages torn out. Books turned to dust and mould.'

Nell, who'd never visited a library – nor knew how to imagine what one was really like – strained to understand. 'Don't you *remember*, Minos?'

'I dream,' he replied. 'I know I was at sea before I came to London. I do remember that. But before then?' He shook his head. By now, the horses and their carriages were wheeling away. The back entrance of the Alhambra Circus was empty as the dawn. 'They're vague things. They shift across me sometimes, when I sleep. But it's like it isn't real, not any more. Where does dreaming end and memory begin?' He paused and, taking her by the hand, began to lead her back to the pastures of Leicester Square. 'That's why you should treasure those slippers, Nell. Everyone needs a token, to remember who they were, back at the beginning – before all of this,' and he opened his arms, as if to encompass not only the square but the vastness of life itself, 'got in the way.'

'Minos, why *don't* you have a token? It isn't fair. It isn't right. You should –'

Minos lifted a finger to his lips. 'Look, little friend – they're coming.'

Nell saw it too: the knot of people underneath the gas lamps in front of the Alhambra was thickening. Some were already streaming into the palace's inner sanctum. Yet more carriages appeared on the square to deposit their passengers, then creaked off into the winter dark.

'I wish I could see it,' said Nell. 'Just for one breath.'

'Maybe you can.'

He'd said it a second time, perhaps a third, by the time she looked up.

'What do you mean?' asked Nell, but Minos had already taken down his hood.

'Wait for the moment,' he rumbled – and one of those fathomless eyes closed in a wink.

A convoy of new carriages had arrived in front of the Alhambra. Nell watched as Minos shambled towards them.

He did not have to step into the light before the horses sensed he was there. She'd seen this at the back of the palace – but at least, back there, Minos's reticence had kept their panic in check. Now, he had no such compunction. Whatever scent he carried reached the horses. The first turned its head frantically; the second, unable to see beyond its blinkers, whickered as if beset by wild animals.

From one carriage to another, the panic spread. A woman crashed out of the first as the horses tried to take off. The second was heaved sideways by horses trying to bolt.

One of the horses reared.

Minos stepped into the gas lamps in front of the Alhambra. By now, horses on the other side of the square were sensing the panic of their brethren. Despite the roars of its driver, one of the carriages took off. Mere moments later, with its horses bolting in different directions, the carriage crashed to the earth. Somebody screamed. Attendants in black began coursing out of the Alhambra to corral the chaos.

Minos was almost gone. Nell caught sight of him, striding past the last gas lamp and into the shadows beyond. The moment darkness took him, he looked over his shoulder. A sea of panicking coachmen separated them, but Nell was certain she knew what he was saying. 'Go – go while you can!'

So that was what she did.

Over the square, past the toppled carriage, between the snaking bodies of passers-by. More carriages were approaching now, but their drivers had the good sense to linger at a distance, where their horses had not yet spooked. Nell reached the front of the Alhambra while the theatre attendants were still streaming out. A rotund man in braces had seized his opportunity to direct affairs. Some distressed patron was sobbing; her dress had been destroyed, her evening ruined. Nell did not care. She was already at the doors. She was already slipping through.

The warmth hit her like a wave. She had never felt anything like it. The walls themselves must have housed furnaces, for it was like she was walking into the heart of a fire.

It was busier than it had been that day she tried to come here. Men in frock coats marched across the hall, taking to the stairs with their paramours on their arms. Sometimes, faces turned to the doors – and the hullabaloo of whatever was happening without – but the guests, bedecked in fineries more elegant than Nell had dared to imagine, all seemed to be drawn in the same direction. Nell tracked them up the sweeping stairs, into galleries above. Then, they vanished.

She didn't know she was shaking. A faintness had come over her. Perhaps it was the heat that was prickling her skin, or perhaps it was just the effect of this place where she was standing, this place a river girl had no business to be. She tried to take a step, but she faltered. She felt like a foal. A fool, as well. What was she doing here?

Dreaming . . .

There was still a hullabaloo outside. Still a hope she might see them dance. She scuttled forward, acutely aware of how different she looked to the fine ladies gracing this establishment, and reached the foot of the stairs.

Then she started to climb.

Somebody had seen her; she was certain of that. A shrill voice called out, but it was only one of the guests; the Alhambra's attendants were all on the square, consoling ladies with ruined frocks and gentlemen entombed inside their fallen coaches. She reached the first landing without being accosted. Then she reached the second. Something drove her on again, until she was scrambling up to the third, and highest, gallery. Here, a pair of guests were stepping through a marble arch: another portal, thought Nell, to yet another world. Well, she'd come this far. She gambolled after them – bursting through velveteen curtains into the heart of the Alhambra itself.

She'd come so high.

She hadn't realized how it would feel.

In the heart of the Alhambra was a vast circular chamber, and gazing down on it galleries that reached into the dome above. Clusters of tallow candles illuminated the boxes on the galleries below – but, up here, open rows of seats looked down upon the circular stage three fathoms underneath. Was it really down there, she wondered, that she'd been led onto the stage? Was this the place her mother had sewn hems while she flew in arms?

The seats were already peppered with guests: lordly and saintly, as any must be who spent their evenings here. Nell wended her way between them, ignoring a litany of reproachful looks as she reached the wooden balustrade and peered over the edge.

The dizzying feeling was almost overpowering. The stage, lit up by another constellation of candles, seemed to be at the bottom of some great well. Nell had felt small before, but not like this.

'You!' a voice cried.

'Pickpocket!' somebody else shouted out.

The cries dogged her as she scuttled along the row. She supposed she should have expected it. To a certain Londoner, there were only two sorts of people: the elegant, and the unwashed. Scrub Nell up, put her in one of their frocks, teach her deportment and manners – and they'd still smell the river on her. It didn't matter; she'd known it couldn't last long. She only hoped it might last a little longer, long enough for the galleries to fall silent as the dancers trooped out onto stage below.

Perhaps, if the commotion on the square had not been mysteriously reignited by the return of a certain cowled figure, an attendant might more easily have been summoned – and Nell ejected back to the streets. But, unbeknownst to Nell, the square's equestrian panic went on. Coachmen blamed it on the weather. Animals could sense a coming storm, they said; in elder times you'd think it an omen, but we've forgotten the old lore, in this Modern World. So they marshalled their resources and corralled the frightened beasts, while inside the Alhambra, Nell scurried from gallery to gallery, seeking out an unseen corner, cramming herself beneath the seats so that she might last just a little longer, just long enough to know, in her heart, that there really was a world beyond the river.

Some time later . . .

The Alhambra was filled with lights. A reverential hush spread from gallery to gallery. Nell, who had been holding herself in a tight ball beneath the seats for too long, feared the silence might give her away – but then there was music, music far below. She reached out, to part the tail of the gown the lady above her was wearing, and angled herself so that she might see through the balustrade.

Geometry defeated her; from here, she could see nothing. To be able to gaze upon the stage, she was going to have

185

to creep closer; to press herself against the railings, or somehow contort her face through.

The gentle susurration of applause welled up from the galleries below. That had to mean something. A sense of panic flushed through her; this was it, this was the moment, and here she was, unable to see the very thing she'd come here to discover.

To begin the day on the river and end it in the Alhambra was already beyond imagination – but how sweet would be the pain of being here and yet not seeing a thing?

Like a mouse out of its hole, Nell emerged. The balustrade was only two feet in front of her. She crawled towards it, seizing the railings in her fists. Then her face was between the bars, and all the Alhambra's great auditorium unfolded in front of her eyes.

The music of the piano had started softly, but now it was soaring. Nell had not known music before, only the caterwauling that spilled out of the inns of Ratcliffe. She had not known, until the sounds of violins sailed in above tinkling piano keys, that music could be like snowfall. She did not know, until the first blast of horns, that music could conjure storms.

And here were the dancers.

They came out of the arches between the lowest stalls, gliding out to the circular stage as if they, too, were untroubled by gravity. It was the music that gave them magic, Nell thought. Here they came, each one flying on the other one's heels.

They said you were a natural.

They loved *you, Nell.*

A hand grabbed her by the ankle.

186

'Got you!'

The dancing did not stop. The music did not fade into silence. The rest of the auditorium remained bewitched – but Nell was wrenched out of it now. Heaved back through the balustrade, she found herself flipped onto her back by a dark, moustachioed man.

The Alhambra's attendant took her by the scruff of the neck (he slapped her once too) and hoisted her up. 'Pockets,' he snarled, 'empty them!' She was too panicked to resist, too panicked to feel the devastation when the coins she'd taken from the blacksmith tumbled into the attendant's hands. 'We get sneakthieves in here sometimes, gentlemen,' the attendant said, dragging her back through the startled spectators, then towards the velveteen curtains. 'They come to a sticky end soon enough. They don't last long. Too old for saving, too young for a noose. But it gets them in the end.' With Nell's legs kicking madly underneath her, he barrelled her through the curtains and onto the gallery at the top of the stairs. Here, Nell was cast to the ground. 'There'll be a constable along soon enough, boy.' *Boy*, he said – and, not for the first time, Nell was grateful for her short, ragged hair; to be a girl could be a terrible thing. 'Come on now, down with you.'

'*No*,' she said, and sank her teeth into the man's fleshy palm.

A few precious seconds was all she'd earned, but a few precious seconds was all it would take. Before the first blossom of pain had faded from the man's hand, she threw herself at the stairs, tumbling from one landing to another. By the time she reached the bottom, the man had drawn the attention of the attendants milling at the doors. A flotilla

187

turned to face her – but Nell was already hurtling onward, already bursting back onto the snow-white square.

Her eyes sought out the figure she was certain would be waiting – but he was not by the railings, and he was not by the lights; he was not to the left, nor to the right – and what few horses remained stood contentedly with their masters, not one of them spooked.

'There you are,' came a voice, simmering with fury. 'You'll pay for—'

She turned. Another attendant had marched out of the Alhambra doors. His hand was drawing back now, whether to strike or seize her, she did not know. Nor would she ever find out – because, at that moment, Minos's own hand came swooping down. 'She's with me,' he uttered, and stepped between them.

'She's for the constables, sir, a pickpocket and a sneak.'

Minos had already drawn her to his side. There she huddled, swaddled up behind his brawny forearm.

'*She's – with – me*,' he rasped, each word as deep and resonant as church bells.

Even Nell was startled then. There was a timbre in his voice, something that did not seem like the Minos she'd come to know. She felt a tremor moving through his body, like something inside him was being wound up, then simply held there, throbbing with promise, pent-up with potential.

'Minos?'

She craned her face upwards, but Minos's gaze was on the theatre attendant, the echo of his words still heavy in the air. It was not just the violence in his tone – because, protective as it was, violence was certainly there; it was the way those three words were pitched, somewhere between certainty and chaos, the way Minos seemed to know beyond all doubt that he would be obeyed; that to be denied was to break nature's laws.

She begged the attendant with her eyes, but she needn't have bothered. He too could sense the promise in Minos. Opening his arms in acquiescence, he shuddered back into the shelter of the Alhambra, just as Minos hustled Nell away, back through the gaslights, back to the outer darkness of the square, back to the bitter snowscape of Charing Cross and the river beyond.

Some time later, beneath the bridge at Blackfriars, with two hot potatoes in their laps and a miniature cairn of roast chestnuts in between them, Nell and Minos watched a loose barge drifting past. The warmth that was spreading through her was enough to have battled back the fear – yes, she would admit that she'd been afraid – that had coursed through her on the square. Watching Minos tear through the tough potato skin with his tombstone teeth was even enough to raise a smile. And yet, as she watched him tossing chestnuts into the air, then cracking them between his incisors as he caught them, she remembered the first feeling she'd had upon approaching him on the river. The shapeless terror of reaching into his jaws, Noah's voice goading her on.

'You wouldn't have hurt that man, would you?'

Beyond the arches of the bridge, rags of snow danced like spirits – but here all was serene.

'When he was trying to snatch me, I thought—'

'He shouldn't have been touching you, Nell.' Minos threw another chestnut, then plucked it out of the air with a satisfying crunch. 'What you saw in the Alhambra – was it everything you'd dreamed?'

189

Nell thought she would never forget it, just like she'd never forgotten the first time. Sometimes, memories got lodged in the back roads of your mind. While so many others faded away, the ones that changed you were the ones that you kept. 'Next time,' she said, daring to believe there would be one, 'I'll walk in there as a dancer.' She reached into her pocket, drew out Sophia Chrétien's card. Most nights, she pushed it into her mattress, to nestle with the slippers in a nest of straw; but some mornings, she took it with her, to carry the promise of it wherever she roamed. 'Just one treasure, and I'll run. One silver chain. By the time Murdstone knows, I'll be gone. One trade, to change my life.'

'Something you found on the river . . .'

There was a faraway wistfulness to Minos's tone.

'What about you, Minos? Don't you have a dream?'

Minos snorted, 'My dreams have changed of late. It's ever since the river. Ever since your seaward cave.' Lifting his hand, he stroked her hoar-frosted hair. 'There's a church I sometimes visit. I tried to tell him there, but he didn't understand. He said it came from his Lord, but he's wrong. It came from you, Nell. Every night, I'm hunted through ruins and temples. Every night, through forests and dark crypts, through cities I don't know, mountains I can't conquer – and, every night, with no idea where to turn. I'm locked in some cellar. I'm trapped in mirrored walls. I know I'll never get out. The fear of it dogs my every step.' He paused. With his arm around her, he peered into Nell's eyes, and she into his. 'And then the seaward cave, and a little voice telling me: *come this way, I've got you now . . .*'

'My voice,' said Nell, with a tremble that was both wonder and pride.

'I've started hearing it, even when you're not with me. I follow your call, and I know I'll find the way.' He paused, and shook his head – as if to rid himself of some other thought, some needless emotion. 'I've been lost so long, Nell. Lost in this body, lost in this head – never quite knowing where I come from, never quite certain where I'm going. Drifting – because what else is there? But I don't feel adrift any more – not since you drew me from the river and showed me the way. That's why I brought you here tonight. I wanted to help you. I owe you a debt.' He tightened his hold on her. His heart was a roaring furnace; for a time, it wasn't winter at all. 'You asked me why I don't have a token – something to keep my own hopes alive, something to shine a light wherever I'm going. But I do, Nell. You're my token. And I'll find a way to repay you, even if it's the last thing I do.'

Volume III

The Labours of London

14

The Bleak Midwinter

Off the Ratcliffe Highway, Christmas 1861

All across London, the snow comes down.

In the rolling fields of Richmond Park, where the red deer play, it lies in fields of pristine white. Over the gardens of St James, it falls in flakes as fat as a small child's fist, obscuring even the grand edifice of Buckingham Palace. On the rooftops of Hanover Square, where once lived London's only knight who rose from the river, it grows crisp and even, undisturbed but for the prints of foraging sparrows and chats.

But in the rookery of St Giles, where carters, street-sellers and the houseless poor still ply their trade, it does not settle in fairy-tale drifts. Along the streets of the Devil's Acre, the snow has hardly touched the cobbles before it is churned to slush by cartwheel and boot. Down the North Marsh lanes, the white has never been pristine; here it is marred by hoof tracks and trotters, trails of steaming manure. Only the children of ministers and merchant princes have white Christmases in London; for the rest of us, its colours are grey, black and brown.

So, while you sit at your hearth-fire with this book in your hand, spare a thought for old Benjamin Murdstone as he levers himself from one office of the Metropolitan Board of Works to another, asking men who do not care whether he is guttersnipe or lord if they know the whereabouts of a deformed brute named Minos; take pity on the good doctor Bantam, who tramps to the studies of learned scholars, his copy of *Apocryphal Antiquity* in hand; and give your prayers, most of all, to little Nell – who, at the end of every dwindling day, carries her tin kettle to St George in the East, there to meet (though none may know it) her one true friend on this Earth.

'You should come and see the rest,' she said tonight, December three weeks old and the midwinter dark already closing its fist over the city. 'Sally-Anne's worried. She sat on the end of my bed, and told me there were bad people in Ratcliffe. But if they saw you, Minos, if they *knew* you . . .'

Minos hushed her with one of those whinnying snorts. Tonight, they sat together on the leeward side of the church house, where the graves wore crowns of white. He'd brought her mutton and milk. Yesterday, a string of sausages which he'd roasted black in a fire. Nell never asked where Minos got the food from, though she was certain his pay would not stretch to meat and milk every single night. She tried not to think of that strange, commanding voice he'd used on Leicester Square. Perhaps he'd put the same fear into a butcher, or perhaps he was merely a thief; there were enough of those in Ratcliffe, and only a shred of them without any goodness in their hearts.

'If not all of them, Minos, then Sally-Anne. Gander. Packrat Jack's got a good heart. Most of them have.'

'I can't,' Minos breathed, sucking mutton grease from his fingers.

'They'd understand.'

Nell hated it when the silence went on too long; it meant she was losing him, that he was drifting further into the tangle of tunnels of which he dreamed.

'Sally-Anne says I'm getting rounder. That I'm not just skin and bone. Winter's been here a month already – real winter, when there's rag-men freezing on the Highway.' Nell had seen it more than once: on the deepest of December nights, the difference between life and death could be as infinitesimal as a lambswool cloak. 'They wonder why it is. There isn't enough goodness in Mr Murdstone's gravy to put fat on bones. So they'll think I'm stealing. But if they met you, it might be different. They'd know you for what you are and —' Minos's eyes had flashed up at her. 'I meant they'd know you for my friend. Their friend too, if you'd let them.'

That silence came again. She listened to the deep rise and fall of his breath. 'Is there time for another story, Minos?'

He shifted, as if to ready himself. He sniffed the air, in that way he always did. To Nell it was just London smog and woodsmoke, the eternal rot of the river, but Minos always detected something she could not. Perhaps it was fanciful, but it seemed to Nell that he was scenting the passage of time. Some men could read it in the heavens; Minos seemed to scent it on the wind.

'Aye, I reckon so. What will it be?'

'Something I haven't heard before.'

'There's plenty of those.'

'You decide, Minos. Something that . . . something that's like you were really there.'

Were there any stories that weren't? He'd told her so many across the nights since they danced on the riverside – and Nell always felt as if she had been transported to some other place, some other time. She'd been there, in the long-ago Italian courts when they first danced the ballet. She'd been there, in the hold of a hundreds-year-old whaler as they navigated the ice floes of the northern wastes. She'd been there, in desert kingdoms and jungle ruins; at the sides of paupers and princes, in palaces and prisons. And in those worlds, she'd trekked with the desert caravans, been taken into the confidences of kings, schemed her way out of traps set by adventurers and brigands.

'Something for Christmas,' she ventured. 'There must be stories like those.'

'Oh, but Christmas is hardly old enough for the best tales. Winter is more ancient than Christmas, Nell.'

'But I like Christmas. If there was an age without Christmas, I don't want to know it.' Half of her Christmases had been spent in the Water's Edge – but she still remembered those precious Christmas Eves with her mother and father, the joy of presents left in the hearth. 'Don't you know a Christmas story, Minos?'

Minos scented the air again. 'Oh, but I do,' he rumbled, looking upwards, 'and it begins on a night much like this one. The sky, pregnant with the promise of more snow to come.' His arm tightened around her. 'And a lonesome traveller, on the road too long. Look at him, Nell. He's a pack on his back and a cloak wrapped around him. But he's tired, tired beyond measure. He needs shelter. He needs succour. And this mountain road is lonely, only forests on every side. Until . . .'

'Until what?' begged Nell.

'Until he comes to a crest and looks into the valley below. And what do you think he sees?'

Nell had no answer, but she rose eagerly onto her knees and implored him with a look.

'Christmas lights . . .'

15

Two Huntsmen

From London to Oxford and Back Again, Christmas 1861

So, then, this was the place.

Christmas night: those two words, which induced such delight in the good children of Knightsbridge, had been stirring dread in Murdstone as December grew old. Now he could see it, hoving into view like one of the merchant ships he'd once waited for on the dockside – only, instead of bringing him the wares on which he intended to build his empire, it brought the fear which had been discomfiting him each night. Christmas night – what a night to lose one's head. The Tudor kings would have been proud.

Now he stood among rutted tracks on the edges of St Giles, where the snow lay blooded around the doss-houses and market squares. He'd known these streets well, once upon a time; if the look of them had changed in the generation since, the feeling was the same. He sheltered in the lee of one of the doss-houses and wondered if it was one of the very same he'd slept in, on his rise from the river. Likely old places: you started out thinking they were luxurious, when what you'd had before was the street; then, when your fortunes changed, so did your tolerance for bedbugs, rodents and lice. You had to keep moving. Change was the fundamental substance of life.

The problem came when you found yourself back at the beginning, when you had to perform the same changes for a second time. How could you feel triumphant at the roughspun of a dormitory bed when you'd once lounged in silks? How to feel kingly eating indescribable meats, when you'd once dined on songbirds and pineapple tart?

The hoardings he was approaching hadn't been here in the older times. Nor had the yards beyond. A city like London, Murdstone had long ago surmised, was like the river: forever in flux, constantly reshaping its banks. Only dead cities ever stayed still. So it was with what went on underneath his feet: sewers branching out from yards just like this. Murdstone had suffered more than most with the reefs of foul air that rose from the Thames, but the Metropolitan Board of Works' quest to enslave London's rivers, to have them purge the city of its foul, seemed to him like Prometheus stealing fire from the gods: an act of wild hubris, man reckoning with forces far beyond his ken. And no sooner had he thought of proud, boastful Prometheus scaling the heights of Olympus to bring back fire, his mind turned again to the reason he had come here: Minos, the man Bantam said was a myth. He'd tramped to seven different sites already, but at last the trail had led him here.

'Minos?' said the officious man presiding over the yard. Murdstone had known men like this in his past endeavours. Promoted one rung above their abilities, they spent their lives constantly battling their own ineffectuality instead of advancing their cause. 'Who's asking?'

The man had introduced himself as Beresford Kale, an imperious, knightly name directly at odds with his jowly appearance.

'Benjamin Murdstone,' he said. 'I'm the one who pulled him from the river.'

Kale, who had been bobbing in and out of his lean-to, gave Murdstone an incredulous look. 'You mean to say he was telling the truth?'

Murdstone merely shrugged.

'Here's a man, tolerated at this site only because of his industry,' Kale proclaimed. 'It's been six months since that savage took up a shovel on the Board's account, and I'll be clear: there was many a soul here who railed at his joining Our Endeavour at all.' These last words he spoke with such self-importance Murdstone might have thought him a priest. 'But for six months we suffered him – always muttering to himself, always lost in some dark thought. You'd have thought he'd come back from India, with a brood on him like that. But he was a solid worker, so we learned to ignore the whispers under the breath. Learned to forget, even, that look he'd get in his eyes – like he's never really belonged in this world. But then? Then, one day, he's just not here, and it's like the Great Stink lifting again. All that tension, all that melancholy – just gone! With industry like his, he left us in sore need, but if that was the price we had to pay, so be it. Until,' and here Kale shook his head ruefully, 'he saunters back in and takes back his job. Threatens me, no less, unless it's given. And now you stand here, telling me all that horseshit he spouted was true? Tossed in the river, stuck with knives, and yet survived? It makes no sense.'

'Nevertheless,' said Murdstone – and, letting the word linger, he gravitated to the chasm in the middle of the yard.

Scaling ladders, ropes and pulleys plunged into the darkness beneath. A lone figure passed by, visible only by their lantern glow.

'He's down there now?'

Kale declared, 'I couldn't let you venture there, sir. It isn't safe.'

Murdstone continued to stare. There had been a time when he would have looked upon the men toiling in the dark as fellow adventurers, each charting their own course through life. Now, he saw only clodpolls, stuck in their eternal loops, like pigeons pecking for grain in the park. You needed imagination to rise from the river, but you needed even vaster reserves to do it again. When you'd been a god, it was crippling to walk among mortals.

'Of course it isn't safe. You're opening the earth. You're bricking up rivers.'

Kale said, 'It's part of the Grand Design. Mr Bazalgette sees all.'

Salmon used to leap and dart in the Tyburn. Before the Fleet was poisoned, it teemed with life. 'Their currents still run,' marvelled Murdstone. 'What makes you think you can conquer the tide?'

Kale looked up, at a sky heavy with cloud. 'Engineering, my man. The Grand Design.'

Murdstone thought: they're all fools; Canute couldn't hold back the tide, and nor could common man.

'Send for him,' he proclaimed.

Kale faltered. 'Send for him, sir? The man's at work. He has hours of toil in front of him – more than that, to make up for the wrong he did. I can no more send for him than I can summon the spirits.'

Murdstone was about to hoist himself onto the scaling ladder when Kale reached for his arm.

'What do you want of him, sir?'

'The man is in my debt.'

'One debt prefigures another,' Kale announced, 'and I'd thank you to leave this yard.'

For a moment, Murdstone weighed up the idea of denouncing Kale, then rolling regardless over the edge. In the end, it wasn't Kale, nor any fear of the dark, that stopped him; it was another old story: Orpheus, and his descent into the Underworld. Ever since Bantam, those stories had been impinging upon him: boyhood tales, which now he was being asked to believe.

He had retreated to the gap in the hoardings when he looked back, to find Beresford Kale quelling him with his eye. But Murdstone had been upbraided by ministers and kings; the idea that he might feel some discomfort from a sewer rat was fanciful beyond measure. Instead, he called out, 'What do you know of him, Kale?'

Kale contemplated before he replied: 'There's some men who keep their life's stories secret because they're fools. Others because there's wickedness in them, and they daren't let it show. But talk to the gangers here, and they'll tell you he talks of having been a whaler. A servant. A monk. Anything that pops into his head on any given day. So I'll tell you what I think, Mr Murdstone, and pray he doesn't hear: there's some men who keep their silence because their lives are secret, even to themselves.'

There was nothing as unnatural, Murdstone thought as he pushed back through the hoardings, as a man who didn't know himself.

But whatever Minos's history was, it would belong to Murdstone soon. A life's story, falsified or not, could be just the commodity he was searching for. All this time, he'd dreamed of unearthing his second sundial. Not in his wildest flights of fancy had he thought that treasure might be as intangible as a life story. But here it was. He would turn it to profit if it was the last thing he did.

He looked down. Somewhere beneath him, Minos was building walls against the tide. But he couldn't stay down there for ever.

All Murdstone had to do was wait.

Then a hand clasped his shoulder – and everything changed.

Step away, now, from the street corner where Benjamin Murdstone is about to parlay with brigands and thieves. Soar across London's rooftops and way into the west, over farms and frozen downs . . .

In the same moment that Benjamin Murdstone felt five filthy fingers on his shoulder, the good doctor Bantam was taking his first steps into the frozen spectacle of steeples and spires that was Oxford in winter. A city like this conjured fairy tales at Christmas, but not to Bantam, whose head was buried in a hastily scrawled map, searching for the address he'd been handed two days before.

He'd made a journey to this city in his younger days, an acolyte to a surgeon who – just like Murdstone – had enjoyed the company of lesser men. There was always much to learn in the field of medicine – but, for all he'd learned about the body's vertebrae and bile, the thing Bantam had absorbed, above all others, was that he would never truly gain the respect of Great Men. He could deal in bloodletting and antimony on the streets of Seven Dials and be considered a saint – but, no matter what knowledge he accrued or feats he performed, to the scholars of a city like this, he would always be a street quack. And he got to thinking, now – as he came upon the same river whose waters, many miles downstream, tantalized Mr Murdstone with treasures in the mud – that this was the one thing Murdstone had never been able to teach him: how to start the day as one thing and, by fall of night, have become another; how to begin your life at the Foundling Hospital, and one day look out of your Mayfair townhouse, a knight courted in the corridors of power, and think nothing of it.

He'd wondered, often, if it was a kind of villainy to change one's life.

Only snakes shed their skins.

And then came this story, of the Minotaur born half-beast and his slow road to becoming a man . . .

The address was upon him now: an old smithy, at the heart of whatever hamlet this used to be. Even fairy-tale cities grew grey with the coming of industry, and Oxford had been no different. The scholars here still studied in their Elizabethan towers, but along the river construction sites proliferated like the trees of an ill-kept forest.

He knocked on the door.

The man who appeared had evidently been expecting another. He had about him the look of a water rat, shrewd yet startled.

'Professor Briggs?'

The name had been given to him by a junior scholar at King's College – who had, at the end of three fruitless days spent knocking on doors, taken pity on Bantam. 'Men in universities don't want to reach too far,' he had said, with a disconsolate shake of the head. This was news to Bantam, who had always been told learned men wanted to plumb the meaning of existence, to one day walk hand in glove with God. 'There's a comfort in knowing what you know. Their view of Divinity hasn't changed since the days of the Tudor kings. Their views on Antiquity are older still. Oh, there are some who'll enjoy a tussle over the finer points of Perseus's journey. You'll find a few high-born souls sparring over their translations of Herodotus. But they're not interested in looking *further*. No, sir, you won't find the man you're looking for in a university cloister. But such men do exist . . .'

As there were backstreet doctors, so too (it transpired) were there backstreet scholars: classicists – or at least one classicist – banished from the profession. Asa Briggs had the air of the archive about him, but so too the air of disrepute. His academic stoop spoke of his time devoted to study – but his waxen flesh and unkempt robes revealed him as a man who had not been cosseted by a university college. Shorter than Bantam by a head's height, he peered up the long beak of his nose.

'You'll have to forgive me,' Bantam began, 'but the sky is turning towards darkness and I've come a long way. If I may, I'll get straight to the point.'

Briggs looked past Bantam, as if trying to decide if this was some ruse.

'If you're from the college,' he said, in a high, nasal tone, 'I'll refer you to my letter. My symposiums infringe on nothing. A private gathering of students might irritate the know-nothings of the colleges, but it breaks no bounds. They talk at will in the inns of this city, sir, and none may prohibit *that*. What difference if they come to my humble abode to discuss the *Metamorphoses*? Hardly a matter for interdiction, sir.'

Bantam opened his greatcoat. He'd been holding the book, wrapped in muslin, against his breast. Now he opened it up.

'I'm not from the colleges, sir. What your quarrels are, I neither know nor care. But your name was given to me as somebody who might be able to shed some light upon this.' He watched as Briggs's eyes took in *Apocryphal Antiquity* with a spasm that hovered somewhere between indignation and delight. 'Might I come in, Professor? I should dearly like a little of your time.'

Many erudite gentlemen kept studies inside their homes, but Briggs appeared the kind of man who kept a home inside his study. As soon as he stepped through the door, Bantam was put in mind of a barnyard which had been abandoned, then reclaimed by thistles and thorns – only, in place of rampant foliage, here were books and oddments. Out of Briggs's principal study they spilled, growing in disordered stacks up and down the hall, filling every alcove, narrowing every stair, bursting like cankers out of cabinets and drawers.

Briggs had led him to a shadowy nook, hemmed in by yet more bookshelves, before Bantam handed over the volume. A book could get lost for ever in a place like this; lose sight of it, thought Bantam, and it would turn native, off to run wild among its brethren on the shelves.

As Bantam settled in one of the nook's threadbare chairs,

Briggs began turning the book in his hands. He could see, of course, that it was fake. A man like this would have an expert eye. And yet there was still some marvel in him as he turned the pages.

'You're not the first to whom I brought this book. I traipsed from one end of London to another, but there wasn't a man who'd speak of it. But I was told you lead private study here. I was told you debate books the colleges won't mention.'

Briggs's eyes narrowed. 'Tread carefully with your words, sir. What you describe might easily suggest sedition. I've had my livelihood ruined, my reputation tarnished for ever – and all because I thought to broaden the mind. Men have been quartered for their interest in a certain sort of book. Women have been burned. You might say that's all in the past, but that isn't how it felt when they ejected me from Oriel College.'

Bantam saw, now, an air of boastfulness and self-glory in the man. The colleges of Oxford had long given homes to those advocating radical thought. In their cloisters men had sought to reimagine the House of God itself. It therefore seemed faintly hysterical that a scholar might find himself ejected for entertaining myths untold by ordinary scholars. Better, perhaps, to imagine there was some disgrace in Briggs's past; the man certainly had the air of one who was intimate with ignominy.

'So they threw you out.'

'Have you ever been called a quack, Mr Bantam?'

Bantam, who had so far declined to describe his profession, only nodded.

'They study Spenser in the colleges. They know their

Herodotus! Whole symposiums devoted to Euripides. But they cry sacrilege if you dare suggest there might be some simple human truth derived from stories which have slipped off the edge of our maps.' Briggs shuffled around the room. 'A man has to get his bread from somewhere. So I teach privately where I can. There are always students intrigued by the tales that go untold. I am a practised mesmerist, and there is often work for me in this. I am an accomplished lyrist, and this too has been known to spin gold.'

'A lyrist, sir?'

Briggs cleared away two towers of books, revealing a small stringed instrument sitting between two rivets in the wall.

'The lyre, sir. Just as Orpheus played to soothe his way through the Underworld. I daresay I could lull you to sleep right now, should I wish. Just as the satyr used to do to young men out frolicking in their forests.' Briggs's lip curled, a look that only hardened Bantam's suspicion that some indiscretion had compelled him out of the college. 'But then, of course, I should never get to learn what might bring somebody to my doorstep with this copy of Castillon in his hands.'

So here it was, thought Bantam. He'd receive a better reception with Briggs than he had with Murdstone, at any rate.

'What do you know,' breathed Bantam, 'about the Minotaur of Knossos?'

Murdstone hadn't seen them as he took up his vantage by the doss-house wall, but somehow he'd known they were there. Elkington's footmen: he'd seen them often across the past days. Sitting up on the wharf as he gathered his wards on the mudflats. Eyes ogling him across a crowded tavern floor. It came as no surprise to Murdstone that a wealthy man with a talent for grudges might expend income on a little light intimidation – but it didn't keep him from tensing when he felt their fingers digging into his flesh.

Two men stood, one at each of his shoulders. The first said, 'You're a long way from home, Benjamin.' The second gave that manner of guttural grunting that only a man employed to take and deliver beatings can: somewhere between an infant's laughter and the braying of an ass.

Murdstone tried to step forward, but the hand was reining him in. 'It isn't Christmas night – not yet . . .'

'Our benefactor thought you might need a little encouragement.'

And Murdstone seethed, 'I've never needed encouragement, gentlemen. Your benefactor understands this.'

'The problem, Benjamin, is that you've been being observed – and our lord isn't satisfied. What efforts have you made towards restitution? You've been seen in gambling dens – but what use are pennies? You've had your wards ferreting around the river – and yet, what treasures are unearthed? You might as well have been praying.'

'I learned prayer was useless when I was a boy.' Murdstone tore free of them now. He limped forward a single stride, before turning on his driftwood cane and saying, 'I'm glad I chanced across you today, gentlemen. Because you're wrong. You say I'm no closer to making restitution than I was when you first cornered me in my lodgings – lodgings from which, I'm sure you're aware, I was summarily ejected. But I must thank you for that, because it set me on a course for greater things. Had you not visited that night, I might still be festering in the Lowood coach house – but instead I have been presented with an opportunity.' He looked them up and down. Due, no doubt, to the fact he had been speaking with words longer than one syllable, their faces were creased in confusion. 'Let's not wait for Christmas night, my fellows. I should like an audience with your benefactor before then. In fact, I should like to go to him right now.'

Louis Elkington, named after the old Sun King of France (his mother having spent her formative years in Versailles), had lived in grander environs when Murdstone last had his acquaintance. The townhouse they approached on the outermost edge of Farringdon Within was not lacking in substance – but compared to the Deptford palace he'd once owned, it was a paltry affair. Still, everything's relative, thought Murdstone as he allowed himself to be manhandled through the railings, then to a tradesman's entrance at the townhouse posterior. Elkington liked to bemoan that his fall from grace had been as precipitous as Murdstone's own, but Murdstone had not been cushioned by family allowance; they'd both lost palaces, both lost futures, but only one had ended up on the river with mud beneath his fingernails.

Though they left him in a small receiving hall, he wasn't kept waiting for long. Elkington had evidently retained – or thereafter reclaimed – some of his household staff, because a maid who waddled by took alarm at his appearance, while another shared a secret look and promised him a package to take on his departure. 'An egg custard, wasn't it, Mr

Murdstone?' Evidently, he'd made quite an impression on her in his earlier days. For Murdstone's part, he couldn't remember a line on the woman's blanched face.

'On with you,' came a voice, one of the footmen returning to drag him onward.

But Murdstone didn't need dragging. He'd walked into enough meetings with merchants. When lords met commoners they saw only scoundrels and simpletons, and those opinions hardly changed, no matter what riches you brought into their lives. You had to win them over every time.

The place was hardly a throne room. Hardly even the drawing room of old, where Murdstone had last convinced him to expend his family's fortune in anticipation of an empire. Nor was Elkington the same man as back then. His russet hair had paled to grey and his jowls grown in direct proportion to the sinking of his eyes. The man had the faintly cadaverous air of a Ratcliffe rag-gatherer, offset only by his finely tailored suit. Dress a wraith in evening wear, however, and he remained a wraith. The heirloom ring he wore was loose on his finger, but the man could not have been undernourished, not in a household like this. His family had boxed him away, but they had hardly impoverished him; he was simply the wound they'd cauterized, lest its infection taint the rest of their riches.

Elkington had pointedly not looked up when his footman announced, 'Mr Murdstone of the River!' Instead, he set about arranging his desk, an ornate piece salvaged from the captain's retreat on one of the old clippers. Murdstone supposed it was meant to lend the room an air of importance, yet to his mind it showed only a man mired in the past – for here stood an admiral without a fleet, a captain becalmed. It mattered not that the townhouse was comfortable and grand; Elkington had been marooned here all the same.

'Your stench is your herald,' Elkington finally said, arranging the last of his trinkets. A ship in a bottle – it was all so damnably predictable. 'So let's keep this brief. I shall need what's left of the day to air out my quarters.' Only now did he look up. 'By God, Murdstone, you're like a dog – you age seven years every summer. They used to call you handsome.'

Murdstone decided not to give him the pleasure of a reaction – for, upon seeing this faded visage, his instincts had unexpectedly turned towards pity. The river was always going to take its toll on Murdstone's body, but something far more invidious had drained the life from Elkington. Here stood a man whose every earthly need was catered for; it could only be his soul that was famished.

'You can imagine my surprise to learn you'd returned to the river, Benjamin. When that little man who collects night-soil begged a word of me, I had scant desire to invite him in. I used to break bread with lords of the realm. Was I really to pour port for a shit stirrer? And then those two little words: *Benjamin . . . Murdstone . . .*

'I had a mind to see you dragged before me, while I was carving my goose. There I'd be, picking at its carcass with you bloodied at my feet – and all my family gathered around.' His words had the air of exultation about them, but they stopped abruptly. 'I knew you couldn't make good on your debts, Benjamin – yet I'm a sporting soul, and every man deserves a chance. So why are you standing before me, instead of playing pitch-and-toss in one of your grubby little gambling dens? Why are you not hunting treasure on your fetid river?'

Murdstone took a breath. There was, he realized now, something energizing about this moment. It had been so long since he proposed a trade as wild as this. No trade was ever made equally; no butcher accepted one dead hog in payment for another. The art was in trading something lesser for something greater, and this was where a man's wiles were best employed. Murdstone's life had been built on trades like those – but the difference was, he'd always had *something* to play with. A wily man could make an ivory sundial worth more than it appeared. It was the moneylender's secret: that an English pound was worth everything to one man, and yet nothing to another.

But Murdstone had never tried to sell a myth before.

He'd never asked for his life, in exchange for a legend.

'Mr Elkington,' he began, and filled his breast with all the conviction he could not feel, 'I am here to make you an offer.'

As soon as he was finished, Murdstone stepped back. If the words 'Minotaur' and 'Knossos' had felt ungainly on his tongue, he did not show it. To make a trade did not require absolute conviction, but it certainly required its imitation.

'The path from this point is clear,' he concluded. 'Myth brought back to the world, with you and I the men to do it.'

Murdstone would not characterize the look that came across Elkington's face as 'despair'. It was more like a fatherly weariness – which vexed him further, for Elkington was some years his junior and had surely acquired less wisdom in his mollycoddled life. The last time he'd stood before him, he had been full of grandeur – but now he felt like a street-corner penitent, asking not only for a few crumbs of sustenance, but for a little *faith*.

'You've had a month, Benjamin. The moon has waxed and waned. Your tides have turned a hundred times. And now you stand before me, reeking of your river, and instruct me to believe in a myth.' Elkington hesitated, but when Murdstone moved to fill the silence, he vehemently said, 'You sold me some rank shit before, Benjamin, and I ate it up. But didn't I deserve more than *this*? It is either a failure of your imagination, sir, or an insult pointedly made. You *ruined* me. I want restitution, not ridicule.'

'I didn't instruct you to believe it, sir.'

'You stood there, Benjamin, and spun it like I was a child at his governess's knee!'

Governess, thought Murdstone, incapable of hiding his disdain. Children who grew up with governesses did not really grow up. They remained on their governess's lap long after the old dear was taken; they were sipping syrup from her silver spoon even as they died.

'The facts are these: the brute exists, and so does the legend. These things I can demonstrate. Sir, I don't care for the veracity of the story. A treasure washed up on my river, and I intend to grasp it with both hands. We live in an age when men are desperate for wonders. Let's serve them one – let us make mankind believe in a myth.'

No doubt Elkington would have barracked him once more – but, at that moment, the door burst open, revealing a startled servant and a lady in dark crimson fineries. The lady cast her scathing eyes, first at her husband, and then at Murdstone. She had always had a devastated look about her – a certain sort of merchant nobility often did – but it had grown more crevassed since Murdstone last saw her. In the days since, Clara Elkington had been known to say that she had always seen through Benjamin Murdstone – that he had been a fraud from the beginning, that a ragamuffin never really left the river – but that was not the way Murdstone remembered it. He remembered her hand under the dining table, and the way she brightened in his presence, most of all.

'What is he doing here?' she demanded, eyes squarely on her husband.

'Clara, you intrude upon a private meeting.'

'*No*,' she snapped, and Murdstone thought: well, this was new; she'd never stabbed at her husband before. Somewhere along the way, she'd got the better of him, and now to denigrate him within earshot of others was *de rigueur*. '*No*, Louis. The man who robbed us has been invited back into our home. The man who left our sons to grow up without an ounce of pride. Without a station in life. He's standing right *there*, and I demand to know why.'

'Perhaps I might be permitted to address this,' Murdstone chimed in – but the waspish way Clara turned on him quickly disabused him of the notion.

'You'll do nothing but stand there, until you're escorted out of this house,' she announced, and Murdstone – sensing there would soon be some resolution in the matter – opened his palms, inviting her to continue. 'He's come with a proposition. Well, hasn't he?'

'Clara, I am hearing him out. I haven't lain down and asked him to ravish me.'

'No, not this time,' she snapped.

Murdstone watched, with an anthropologist's detached interest, as both husband and wife realized some Rubicon had been crossed. Clara's scornful look softened as soon as the words left her lips – and, if she did not stretch as far as contriteness, at least she betrayed some awareness that she had goaded him too far. As for Elkington, he rose assuredly from behind his desk, wearing the look of a watched pot. Husbands and wives, thought Murdstone, were truly deplorable creatures. He'd found that out, once upon a time – but how much more gratifying was it to watch as an outsider? Here was the living example of the world's worst trade: in exchange for the privilege of not dying alone, a life could be spent in permanent rancour.

'Enough,' Elkington began. 'Clara, hear my words. Benjamin has attended us today at my instruction – because, albeit at an hour far beyond that which is reasonable, he has determined to fulfil our contract. Isn't that so, *Benjamin*?'

The last word was pronounced so that it contained all the conspiracy of the occasion. In reply, Murdstone mutely nodded.

'And what is he *asking* for, that he might settle the scales?' Clara began, not yet ready to flounce out of the fight – not until some minor victory was won. 'If he comes for merchant ships, you may tell him that you have none. If he comes begging for capital, then he must go begging on the streets. I will not write to your father on his account, and–'

'I don't need capital,' Murdstone interjected, though he was sure that time would come. 'I need some assistance. The employ of some of your men, if it can be allowed.'

Clara said, 'Men *are* money. You know this. Who is to pay for their time?'

'I am, a thousand times over, if I have the right of this endeavour.' Murdstone turned his gaze back to Elkington, and realized, as he surveyed the room, that all three of them were lost, all three of them stumbling in the dark, uncertain what was next. You spent your life like that, taking one wrong turn after another, losing yourself further with every ill decision. It took a moment like this to see that there might be a way out; what you needed was a map, and for the first time in an age, Murdstone felt as if he held one. 'A band of your footmen, at a time of my choosing, for but a few short hours. If I'm wrong, if I can't turn this treasure to a profit that benefits us all, then you may throw me in the river – and I should welcome it.' He looked from husband to wife, then back again. 'I'm not asking for anything you can't lose. A little help, and a little more time.'

Silence, vast as the seas, filled the drawing room. Questions were being asked, then answered, without a word being said, all the nuances, passions (and, yes, the contractual disputes) of a marriage being played out in imperceptible shudders and stares.

Elkington glared.

'I told you you had until Christmas night. Even at my worst, I have always been a man of my word – so allow me to maintain that tradition. You'll have your men, Mr Murdstone, but in return I shall know, by Christmas night, whether this story of yours is a bait meant to fool me, or whether there really is a second act in the story of Benjamin Murdstone.' He hesitated, and Murdstone observed that, in spite of all he had lost, his passion for drama had been preserved. 'Either way, Benjamin, in blood or in wealth, restitution will be mine.'

'Here,' said Briggs, 'look.'

In the moments since Bantam made his enquiry, Briggs had unearthed from some bookshelf a small statue cast in clay. Bantam took it immediately for what it was. Though its monstrosity was faded by the years, the sculptor had somehow rendered the Minotaur in perfect form. A square bull's head sat upon shoulders that rippled with cords of muscle; the body, though nominally belonging to a man, was as preposterously proportioned as any portrait of Perseus. But it was not his mighty horns or brutish jaws that unnerved Bantam; it was the way his eyes were rendered – either by degradation or design – as empty sockets in his head. Dark, vacant concavities which ought to have opened onto a man's soul – but opened instead onto nothing at all.

'He's beautiful, isn't he? He's the work of an old Habsburg sculptor, who studied with de Vries. I won't say how this fell into my possession. A story like that is too delicate for strangers. But take a look at him, sir. *Study* him. What do you see?'

Bantam was still staring at those empty eyes. 'I see a beast.'

It was the answer Briggs had been plumbing for. 'It's what everyone sees, but I wondered if you – you who've read your Castillon – might see differently.' All of a sudden, he turned his wrist, closing his fist over the Minotaur's head and horns. 'Now – now what do you see?'

A torso with thick, defined muscle; arms that bulged, and fists that clenched.

220

But only a man, thought Bantam. As absurdly realized as any of the busts in the British Museum – but still a man.

Briggs smiled condescendingly as he peeled back each finger. 'One moment a monster,' he said, 'one moment a man,' and he obscured the Minotaur's visage over and over, transforming him with every flick of the wrist. 'They damned him in legend. Well, it's always easy to damn a man who's different, isn't it? We learn to do it almost the moment we can walk. But it always seemed unjust, to me, that the Minotaur was condemned. Ask any scholar, and you'll find: every hero we rhapsodize in stories, every victory they won or labour they achieved, was done in defiance of the evil they'd perpetrated, somewhere in their past. Heracles, and his twelve labours? Penance for slaying his own children. Daedalus, who constructed the Labyrinth? Sir, he dashed his own nephew to death on the rocks beneath the Acropolis. Antiquity was no age of heroes and villains. An age like that could never resonate through time. No, this was an age when no man was purely a hero, no man purely a rogue. How familiar are you with your classics, Mr Bantam?'

Bantam's mind strayed back to those long summers spent servicing the shelves of Murdstone & Sons. 'Heroes abandon their lovers,' he said. 'Fathers devour their children.'

'People are deceived, betrayed, tricked, undone – but the people who've wronged them might be heroes by story's end. They've taken the head off the Hydra, or rescued their lover from the abyss. I like to think the Greeks knew a little about this sorry old business of *being alive*. That's something we've forgotten in Modern Times. We Englishmen remain a puritanical breed. Being good or bad isn't a human choice. Being good *and* bad – that's the human condition.'

'And the Minotaur—'

'Born half a man, but in legend wholly a beast. Doesn't there seem an injustice in it? Heracles got to atone for his crimes. Even Kronos, who feasted upon his children, was released from the Abyss of Tartarus and made a king. But not so the Minotaur. No, in legend, the Minotaur is just another Hydra. He's Scylla or Charybdis. Just a monster to be vanquished in service of some hero's journey.'

'You mean to say they were blind to the part of him that was man.'

'I mean to say the people of the ancient world made a choice: rather than look for the man in the Minotaur, they chose to see only the monster. They constructed their prison for him. They made him a legend. And, for ever after, that's what he was: born to a woman, and yet belittled as beast. The mythographers were a cowardly lot. Just storytellers, trying to make sense of a world too complex to be distilled in mere words. I suppose you can have some pity for that. The world has grown more complex yet. But when it came to chronicling these stories for the ages, the Minotaur presented them with the thorniest of problems. To look him in the eye and see him for anything other than a base beast must have been like peering into a looking glass. They would have had to acknowledge the monstrosity in all of us. Being good *and* bad, Mr Bantam. Being man and beast.' He faltered, for another thought had stolen upon him. 'I suppose, in the modern parlance, they'd call it: half angel from on high, half monkey from the jungle. The truth can be an uncomfortable companion. They didn't dare to see it, so when Hesiod and the others came along to start setting these stories down, they spun a different story instead.

'You must remember – these stories go back to our very beginnings. They chronicle an age long before manuscripts and paper, before vellum and stone tablets – before, even, the written word. You might think you can imagine the world back then, Mr Bantam, but your Modern mind could hardly envisage a world so incomparable to our own. But try as you might. Picture a world replete with stories: told around fires, told at festivals and games, spun in songs and verse and passed from cradle to grave.' He paused. 'Then, one day, along come men with letters and ink. New, learned men who say they can trap those stories, pin them down and bind them for ever. In this world, it's practically sorcery. Stories change, but words do not. The page petrifies a story, Mr Bantam. Now it lasts for evermore.'

Bantam interjected, 'So those men got to *decide*. Which stories would last through all of Creation, and which would fade away.' He stopped, and into the pensive silence that followed said, 'Hesiod and his ilk didn't just record stories. They *directed* them as well.'

The scholar smiled; it was always a boon when a student came to some understanding on his own. 'I believe there was a time when the Minotaur was more pitiable than monstrous. A baby is not born into the world to commit great evils. Few of us would look into a crib and say: there lies a regicide, quietly suckling his thumb. The story Castillon tells, I feel certain, is the elder one, the one that sits more snugly in the mythos. And yet, when it came to fixing the story in time and mind . . .'

Bantam snorted, 'It was the mythographers who slew the Minotaur, not Theseus.'

'Easier to kill the monster than accept you might be the

same kind. And so it was told, generation after generation: Theseus smote the Minotaur, right there in the heart of the Labyrinth.' At once, Briggs stopped. He had seen the way Bantam was still studying the sculpture, the way one of his fingers traced the base of each horn, then probed the protuberant bovine jaw. 'It isn't often a visitor comes to me and sits there, rapt in untold tales. You have a purpose, sir. I can smell it on you. If you aren't sent by the colleges, then who are you sent by?'

'I fear it is too fanciful, even for a man steeped in this lore.'

'It isn't just Castillon, is it? What did you find?'

Bantam said, 'I'm a physician. I came across a . . .' he faltered before saying 'man', though that was what he said. 'A giant, by any reckoning. Brigands had tossed him in the river after sticking him with knives. But he washed up on the shore and shook away the fever. Wounds that had been festering at dawn were but scars by nightfall, then gone altogether. Beneath his hair, two stumps of bone, as if . . .' Why did it seem so preposterous to speak of it, when he'd seen it with his own eyes? 'I've seen monstrosities. I've treated men who've made tragedies of their bodies. But none like this.'

The measure of Briggs's breathing had changed. 'Tell me, as you inspected this man, did you find —'

But Bantam already knew what he was saying. He plucked *Apocryphal Antiquity* from Briggs's hands and opened it up. There, scored in black, was the same labyrinthine design he'd seen carved into Minos's back.

'Every corner's the same. It's what brought me to the book. It's what brought me to you.'

Briggs's eyes danced across the page. This time, Bantam was not mistaken; they were dancing in delight.

'There's a question you haven't asked me. One pertinent to this matter.' He could barely tear his eyes from the page, but by force of will he looked up. 'Do you really think you're the first, Dr Bantam?'

There was another room, more deeply cluttered than the last; it took Bantam some moments to realize that Briggs had led him into his bedchamber, for the place was a veritable nest of papers, books and candle-stubs. Soon, Briggs had entered a wardrobe slumped against the chimneybreast, ferreted through cloaks and blankets, and emerged with a small wooden trunk in his hands.

It was a thing meant for travelling, a dull wooden box with a clasp to keep it locked. Inside lay only more books. Briggs lifted the first. Only – this was not like the books Bantam used to bind for Murdstone. The covers were pieces of engraved wood; the pages within, animal skin turned brittle with age. 'This codex is beyond value,' Briggs began, lifting it to the fading window light.

'Where does it come from?'

'There are many treasures in the Bodleian Library. But there have been several fewer since the college denounced me,' Briggs smiled. 'Come, see . . .'

So Bantam did.

His grasp of Latin was rudimentary – a physician knew only what he must – but he did not need to be fluent to understand. Indeed, he hardly needed any language at all – for there, decorating every margin, intruding upon the lettering with its horns and wild jaws, was the Minotaur.

He read the first leaf. He read the second. By the third,

his head was full. Briggs had already removed a second book from the trunk, a smaller thing bound in dogskin from some centuries later. He dangled it in front of Bantam, like bait on a line.

'How many?' Bantam breathed.

'Stories. Sightings. Moments when a man has thought himself turned mad for the thing he's encountered. I told you already, Doctor: you are not the first to come across this creature. For how else does an untold tale survive, unless that story goes on?' Briggs paused. 'The Minotaur continues his quest, then. He is more man, now, than monster. And yet –'

'Still monstrous,' whispered Bantam, scouring the vellum in disbelief, as stories cascaded past him, as hundreds-year-old horrors unfolded again. 'I told my associate they were drawing dragons out of the dirt and calling them dinosaurs. That the Modern World still yields wonders. That if something survived of the Ancient it would not, perhaps, be beyond belief. And yet, now that I see it . . .' He looked up and, for the first time that day, his face was etched in alarm. 'There's a girl. She's the one who drew him out of the river. She spoke to him in dreams. He listened to her; he followed where she went.'

Briggs's features hardened. He went to the window, looked out upon the winter world beyond. Perhaps some corner of his imagination was playing tricks on him. Perhaps he fancied the Minotaur was waiting out there, right now, his horns tearing holes in the sky.

'Listen to me, Doctor. We have stood in this room, you and I, and spoken of the man belied in favour of the beast. We have talked, together, of the humanity forgotten behind that monstrous visage. But do not forget: while he exists, he is not yet man. While he persists, that piece of him he has spent centuries seeking to overcome is still living. It's still in his head. Still in his heart. Read the codices, Bantam. Drag yourself through my books. If you need to know the fates of those who already crossed his path, the shreds of it are all here – well, for those who *survived*.' Briggs heaved a great sigh. 'Bantam, do you care for this girl?'

'I scarcely know her. She's one of the river children. The motherless mudlarks.' And yet he was fond of her; he had to admit that. A piece of his heart ran with all of Murdstone's wards – but Nell, who'd turned nursemaid for no reason other than charity and love, most of all.

'Whatever else this creature is,' Briggs went on, 'the blood of his father still beats in his veins. One moment a man, one moment a monster. And, whether you care for this girl or not, Dr Bantam, for as long as this connection lasts between them, her life is not her own. She's a pig in the butcher's yard. She's made the very same mistake as Hesiod and the others, who saw only half of the creature, who could never envisage the whole. I'm afraid your friend is in the most terrible danger, Doctor. They don't write "misplaced pity" on a pauper's grave – but it's the thing that will kill her, when the beast comes out to play.'

16

The Yule Tide

Off the Ratcliffe Highway, Christmas 1861

'What are you dreaming of, Nell?'

Nell sat in the window of the Water's Edge, watching the ghostly street below. No snow was falling on Christmas Eve, but Ratcliffe sat under a dirty white cowl. They'd be wassailing in the west; behind the doors of every good family, fires would be crackling, hot wine being served. Gander said he used to know a family who brought a tree into the house and festooned it with wax angels and paper dolls. And if Nell had never had a Christmas quite as ostentatious as this, she still remembered the parcels in the hearth, the extra log saved for the fire; the feeling of Christmas night. Sally-Anne shuffled closer and said, 'Nell?'

She'd seen Minos tonight. Her belly was full on account of him. She'd been warmed by the wild beating of his heart. In Minos's aura, she never felt cold. Never alone. But it was the moment they parted that was gnawing at her. She'd taken from him for nights on end. Grown to depend on his hulking shadow and those stories he'd tell (how did a man's imagination conjure wonders like this, mothers with heads of writhing snakes and a golden, winged ram?). And yet, for too long now, her hands had been empty of anything to give in return. No gift for Minos, not even on Christmas Eve.

He'd taken her to the Alhambra.

Stoked her dream.

'Sally-Anne,' she said, 'I'm going to need your help.'

Midwinter's night had passed, the world begun its slow crawl towards spring. Across London, church bells pealed in celebration of all the centuries since Christ saved Man.

But he had not saved those who dwelt on the river. Elsewhere in London, gifts were exchanged, tables bedecked in feasts – but, on the river, the tides still came and went. It was Murdstone's mantra of years gone by: if the tide was ignored for even a day, the river would choose that day to cast some treasure onto the shore. So instead they toiled on: Christmas Day, just another day to commune with the mud.

'Fewer barges on the water,' Packrat Jack muttered darkly. 'Fewer coals, fewer bits of scrap, fewer of Mr Murdstone's treasures. It's the worst day to be a mudlark.'

'Aye, but Mr Murdstone needs us out of the way, of course,' said Potato Rot slyly.

'Why's that?'

'Well, he'll need to organize our Christmas feast.'

Two seabirds, tussling over the carcass of some crab, scattered at the explosion of groans and laughter that echoed across the waterfront. There were second helpings on Christmas Day, but never a feast; never a Christmas goose, nor even a rooftop pigeon.

'He might surprise us,' Sally-Anne said. 'Nell might find him another treasure yet. Mightn't you, Nell?'

But it wasn't a treasure for Murdstone Nell had in mind. It was a gift for Minos – the only gift that mattered.

Midday on the river, but Nell was nowhere to be found. Nor was Sally-Anne. Instead, they stood outside the cobbler's shop at St George in the East, gazing through their reflections to the giant pair of boots on a plinth beyond.

'I keep coming back thinking they'd be gone, but every time – there they are. I wanted to sneak in and take them back.' Nell looked up at Sally-Anne's flushed face. 'But I didn't do it. I just didn't have the courage.'

Sally-Anne wrapped her arms around herself as she said, 'You found him, then. That's where you go, after we leave the river every day. I've been telling Gander you're a good girl. That you wouldn't take risks.' She shuddered. 'Oh, Nell. It doesn't matter that he's not a monster. He's a man.'

'I thought you might help me. I was here two days ago and . . .' She'd heard it, plain as day, as the cobbler spoke with some customer outside his shop: he was going to his sister's for Christmas night, a widower crying out for the family hearth. 'Sally-Anne, let me show you.'

Nell took her by the hand and led her into the dark lane between shops. Here, where rats raised their winter young on leather scraps, a window sat in the brickwork two yards above Nell's head.

'I think I could prise it open. See,' she said, and took a piece of flint she'd unearthed out of her tin kettle, 'I've got everything I need. I just need help to reach it. Those boots belonged to Minos. By rights they're his. So I wouldn't be *stealing*. I'd be putting right a wrong.'

'Oh Nell, they'd hang you for less.' Sally-Anne bent low, until she was looking into Nell's eyes. 'I don't know what to do, sweetpea. There's no talking reason to you. There hasn't been, ever since that man washed up on the river. You don't know him, Nell.'

'I do,' she whispered.

'Then tell me one thing about him. Tell me where he comes from. Tell me what he's been doing all of his life. Tell me what happened, that he got tossed in the river.'

Nell drew her fingers, which had been entwined with Sally-Anne's, sharply away. 'Then I'll do it another way,' she declared.

Before Sally-Anne could say a word, Nell burst back onto the high road. She drew the flint back, prepared to pitch it into the heart of the cobbler's window – and she would have done just that, if Sally-Anne hadn't seen the madness from the corner of her eye.

'*Nell!*' she cried out, her own hand darting out to stop the flint's flight.

'I thought you might understand.'

'You're not six years old anymore, sweetpea, you're –'

'Stop calling me *sweetpea*!'

'– going to be seen. You're going to be beaten. Ask Mr Murdstone, Nella – ask *him* what a prison cell is like. You're ten years old. You have a whole life to live. Don't throw it away for someone you barely know.' Sally-Anne's voice had broken. 'Nella, please, it's Christmas Day. We'll go back to the river. We'll sell what we find. And then we'll be at the

Water's Edge, and there'll be Christmas night, all of us together, the way it's meant to be.'

Nell shook her head with such ferocity that the world in front of her turned to a blur. 'I won't come. I won't come unless you help me.'

So Sally-Anne turned back to the lane between the shop-fronts. 'Nell, you bloody fool – you'll get us both hanged.'

But there was the window, daring them to try.

Night fell quickly, just like the tide. Murdstone did not gather his wards by the storehouses, not on Christmas night – there was always a goose somewhere, for Benjamin Murdstone – so instead the mudlarks took themselves to the streets as soon as the light waned. Nell, who had hidden the salvaged boots in the seaward cave, was late in taking them to the churchyard. As she approached, she got to wondering if Minos had given up on her – but no, there he waited, hidden by the age-old graves.

His overcoat was filled with gifts aplenty, but Nell stopped him before he laid them out, strangely nervous as she pressed the boots into his hands.

'It's not a real gift. I know that. They're already *yours*. But here they are – and, and,' she felt foolish saying it; she hadn't said it in so long, 'Happy Christmas, Minos. Happy Christmas.'

His great arms enfolded her in his stable-yard stench. Sally-Anne was a fool, thought Nell, as his warmth enveloped her body. You didn't know a person by documenting their history or charting their path; you knew them by the feeling they gave you when you sat in their company. That feeling, it was the untold story of who they were.

232

'Did you find your treasure today, Nell?'

He asked the same thing every evening. Over the passing weeks it had achieved the quality of ritual.

And, as if to conclude that ritual, Nell hung her head.

'Coals, sold along the Highway. Just pennies, for Murdstone's pot.'

Sometimes, when Minos breathed, you could tell his dissatisfaction. His breath plumed. 'Then I don't believe in Christmas,' he snorted. 'I *won't*. Children in their Knightsbridge nurseries get their miracles. Why not mudlarks? If there really was a god in the river, he'd have thrown something up. A Roman coin. That silver chain you tossed in – sent back on the tide. *Second chances.*' He'd been working himself into something of a fury as he spoke, but by measured breath he calmed down.

A god in the river, thought Nell. Sometimes, it was like there was a riddle in the things Minos said – though she was quite certain he didn't know it. If you lived by the wharf-sides, you got to know that there were all manner of gods in the four corners of the world – but Nell had only ever heard two men speak of gods in the river: Minos, and Murdstone himself.

'I dreamed about it.'

Nell felt the thrum of his heart. 'Dreamed, Minos?'

'Christmas night, you'd find your treasure in the river – and I'd carry you, on my shoulders, to that address in St Giles, and see you through the door. Sophia's student. A mudlark no more.'

Not a dream of the night, then; just an idle wish of the day. Nell felt inordinately sad at that. She had thought, for a moment, that something had driven out those dreams of dark, looping tunnels, that phantasmagoria of many-headed serpents and man-eating birds that peopled his nights.

'How do you think *she's* spending her Christmas, Minos?'

This was a dream Nell had indulged through the long Christmas Day. If the rest had seen her dancing from rock pool to rock pool, imagining she was one of the dancers trooping out on the Alhambra stage, they had overlooked it as Nell's childish excess. But it had sustained her on the river, and the image returned to her now. 'Perhaps there's a ball,' said Nell, 'in one of the townhouses. That's a likely thing for rich nobs to do. People like Mr Murdstone once was, they'd bedeck their halls, wouldn't they? And after the banquet there'd be music and singing, and a place cleared for dancing. You can't imagine the sorts of houses they live in, Minos.'

Minos softly snorted, and Nell remembered that, in the stories he sometimes told, there were palaces more extravagant than any in London. But those were places he'd dredged out of his imagination, weren't they? Those places weren't real.

'I like to think Sophia's there, Minos – she's gone to the home of one of her students, and she's dancing with them.'

After a time, Minos said, 'Well, if Sophia's dancing – even if it's only up here,' and his finger touched the edge of Nell's begrimed head, 'perhaps you should too. You'll need to be ready, Nell. When you find that treasure, when I take you there, you'll need to be practised. You won't want to squander a chance like that.'

Was it fantasy, or was it real? Expectation, or just hope? In this moment, Nell didn't mind. She had hold of Minos's hand, and now she was being drawn to her feet – and now, though the only music was the winter wind through the gravesides, she was preparing to dance.

'Wait!' she cried out.

Then she was reaching for the gift she'd brought with her, angling the boots onto his feet.

'They still fit you,' she said, with some modicum of pride.

'Thank you, Nell.'

Nell was about to slide back into his arms, but something in that 'thank you' didn't seem right. 'It wasn't just me,' she blurted out. 'I told one of the girls. Sally-Anne. She's the one who helped me get back your boots.' Nell was distinctly aware of his deep black eyes taking her in. 'They're good people, Minos. I know it. If they met you, you'd know it too. And Minos, I—' Why did she hesitate, even now? 'I want you to meet them. If I'm to dance this Christmas – well, Minos, maybe they should too.'

Somewhere in the parish, bells had started ringing.

Nell tumbled up the stairs at the Water's Edge. She knew, already, that Murdstone was in the attic; she could hear him summoning each of the mudlarks in turn, wishing them happy Christmas even as he collected his tithe. The old man was constant as the river. She felt for the coins in her pocket, scant pickings for a day's work, then heaved herself up through the attic trap.

He had the smell of spirits about him. He so often did. As the last of the coins left Nell's hand, Murdstone took her by the wrist. 'Is there anything you need to tell me, Nell?'

At first, words failed Nell. Then, in faltering fits and starts, she said, 'Happy Christmas, Mr Murdstone.'

She never got the chance to learn whether it was what he expected. In that instant, he let go of her wrist and made for the trapdoor. 'There's food below. Make sure you get your fill. The river will be waiting by morning.'

Silence smothered the attic, until the last of Murdstone's footsteps faded away. Then, at once, the mudlarks started scrambling. Evidently Potato Rot was the most famished; the prospect of a stew brimming with bone and fat propelled him to the trapdoor with ungainly haste. He was almost through when Nell called out, 'Stop!'

As one, the mudlarks turned.

'Come on, sweetpea,' Sally-Anne said, uncomfortable with this secret they shared. 'It's Christmas night. Let's be together.'

'Together,' said Nell. 'But not here, Sally-Anne. You're invited – every last one of you.' And her eyes took in Noah, skulking behind the rest.

'What's going on, Nella?' Gander began.

'I want you to meet someone. He's waiting for you. He's bringing food. He's my friend.'

'Your – friend?' one of the mudlarks piped up.

Nell looked for comfort in Sally-Anne's eyes, but even she seemed to be imploring her to pipe down. 'We're all hungry, Nell. It's cold out there. But here are our beds and here's our banquet. It isn't much but it's ours.'

'Then eat it,' Nell said. 'But there'll be more where Minos waits. Christmas night isn't over until the church bells peal – and I know where I want to be. Please,' she said, more softly now. 'Because tomorrow it's as far away from Christmas as it can ever be. Who knows what happens in a year? And I think – I think—' She was losing her way,

taking one wrong turn after another, like wandering Ratcliffe
in the blizzarding white. In the end, it was only by fixing
on the image of Minos that she could find her way. 'I think
we deserve something more.'

The tide was coming in.

The wind was taunting every fire Minos brought to life.
Seven of them, arranged outside the seaward cave. He
pounced on each, cupping his enormous hands around the
stones, rearranging driftwood and coals. Above one, Nell's
tin kettle simmered. Above others, fat sausages on skewers.
But if the tide advanced much further, it would be in vain;
Nell might let him ferry her on his shoulders through the
river, but what hope was there of the other mudlarks permit-
ting themselves to be the burden of a beast?

Then, by some imperceptible change in the wind, he
knew they were coming.

He lifted his face to the rush of air. Perhaps faint voices.
Perhaps a scent. Perhaps just an age-old instinct that told
him when people were out *searching*. He stared along the
great sweep of the river, where the wharfs dazzled with
lantern light – and, occasionally, the raucous sounds of
celebration were borne above his head, like the ghosts of
the parties being held across Ratcliffe.

A party like his own.

Here they came.

They'd seen the fires from a distance, but it wasn't until
they could feel their flickering warmth that Nell saw Minos.
There he stood, a black silhouette wreathed in rags of snow.

The mudlarks gathered behind her, seemingly unable

to cross the line of fires without her direction. And here they all were: Gander and Sally-Anne, whose hand suddenly took Nell's own; Potato Rot, Packrat Jack, Noah and all of the rest. Each one looked up at the risen giant.

'It's just us, Minos,' Nell said – sensing, perhaps, his reluctance as he shambled forward.

They'd last seen him lying recumbent in the seaward cave – but how much more unnerving was it to see him looming above them, a monster pressed into the shape of a man? You could not gauge a sleeping man's girth. His jaws seemed so much vaster; his shoulders so much broader than they had lying down.

'Minos, meet the mudlarks.' Nell let go of Sally-Anne and crossed the fires. 'They're the ones who helped bring you out of the river. They carried you into the cave. They . . .'

Nell noticed, with alarm, that Minos's unknowable eyes had found Noah at the back of the crowd. For his part, Noah thrust his hands into his pockets, refused to look up.

'Noah, this is Minos.'

Nell realized he was shaking. The cold was gnawing at them all, but this was not the trembling of winter's touch.

Noah opened his lips to acknowledge Minos, but in the end it was Minos who spoke. 'I've been hungry too,' he said, his stilted words filling the air. 'It was only boots. It wasn't you who threw me in the river.'

The silence returned, as a look like wonder coloured Noah's features.

'Come and see.'

The mudlarks watched, balanced on the line that separated

238

apprehension and astonishment, as Minos swept Nell into his arms and turned to shamble back across the shale. Lit up from below, she waved wildly, urging them to follow. Then she was gone, in the arms of the monster, into the seaward cave.

The mudlarks looked from one to the other. 'For Nell,' said Gander – and he was the first over the fires. Then, one by one, driven by hunger or curiosity or merely the common good, the others hurried after.

Through the crevice, the smells exploded. Not just sausages, Gander saw, but apples baked in coals, rich faggots piled up on a table of stones. Nell's tin kettle steamed, not with river water but with black, bitter tea. Somebody had toasted slabs of dark bread. A pot of honey glistened like some treasure. And all around them, hanging from cracks in the cavern roof: Christmas wreaths of holly and fir, ripe red berries and fluttering ribbon.

Nell rushed into Sally-Anne's arms the moment she and Gander came through the fissure. 'Isn't it wonderful?' she cried. 'It's – Christmas!'

Not a Ratcliffe Christmas, that was for sure. Not Christmas in the Water's Edge. 'I'll bet Mr Murdstone never had a Christmas like this, not even on Hanover Square,' beamed Nell, as the rest crowded into the cavern.

'But where does it all come from?' whispered Potato Rot.

Twelve mudlarks looked at Minos. There he was, bowed at a low-burning fire, pulling hot potatoes out of the embers. It took him some time to understand he was being studied. But then, his leathery hands hardly seeming to feel the fire as he pulled each potato out, he lifted his protuberant jaw and said the only two words he could think of, the only two words that could make sense of such an otherworldly occasion.

'Happy Christmas.'

And, 'Happy Christmas,' they ventured in return.

Come, join the fray . . .

They say there is not magic in the Modern World. Well, let them tell that to a family of famished mudlarks, presented with their very first Christmas feast. Let them say there is no wonder to twelve children starved of fantasy, as they gaze around their secret den and find it dressed up like the nursery of some Kensington townhouse. Try saying there is no such thing as enchantment to Packrat Jack as his face grows sticky with honey; to Sally-Anne, as she gets to play mother, dishing up baked apples and sugar; to Potato Rot as he warms his toes in front of embers stoked up for exactly this reason.

Say it to Nell, who watches her friend's courage grow, bit by bit, as the others ask him of his life before the river, of his work in the tunnels beneath London, of all the cities and countries, the times and places, he has been in his long, varied life.

'But where do you come from?' Potato Rot asked.

'How did you get all *this*?'

'How did you really survive the river?'

Questions, questions, questions: such dangerous, slippery things.

'I was a sailor, before I came to London.' This much he remembered. 'I don't sleep in lodgings any more. I work and I toil.' And, as for the river, 'By good fortune, and a small girl's grace.'

'A story!' Nell declared, when bellies were growing full and hearts grown warm. 'Minos tells the best tales.'

Silence settled across the seaward cave. There had been enough stories in the Water's Edge over the years. Sally-Anne had spun them for Nell and the rest, back at the beginning. And yet, wasn't there something special about sitting here with the lumbering giant, expecting a tale from some other place, some other time?

'Any tale, Minos, any tale at all!'

The mudlarks watched as Minos settled at the back of the seaward cave.

What story was this to be? Minos knew so many, though their origins were as indistinct as the music that flowed from his fingers at the Lamb & Flag. Stories curdled at the back of his mind. They pillaged each other for plots and spare parts, so ravenously that it was difficult to know where one tale ended and another began. But wasn't that just storytelling? He had a dim impression, somewhere at the back of his mind, that he'd earned his supper, once upon a time, by telling tales on nights just like this.

But never to an audience of mudlarks.

Never to Nell.

'There once was a traveller, who came to a city—'

'What city?' piped up Potato Rot, whose heart had grown bold now his belly was full.

'This was the city of Paris. But the Paris I'll tell you of was not the Paris that exists today. The brightest, boldest city in the world was, back then, a chaos of rutted tracks and barracks for armies. But it was yet a city of kings, the beating heart of the old world. And the traveller who came to its gates, just as summer was reaching its height, did

241

not come freely. No,' said Minos – and, unless Nell was mistaken, a strange dewiness came over his eyes – 'he came in the back of a wagon, trussed up like a hog, accused of a crime he did not commit . . .'

'Not this story!' Nell exclaimed. She was not sure why, but some dark frisson had come over her. 'A happier story. Aren't they the best?' She faltered as she said it; she was suddenly not sure if she was right. The best stories ended in happiness – but along the way, didn't there have to be peril and darkness, tragedy enough to bring tears to the eye?

'Give us a story where there's a hero,' said Packrat Jack.

'And a villain,' said Potato Rot. 'That's what the best tales are made of – heroes and villains.'

'The hero has to go on his quest,' said Gander, his interest piqued.

'Yes, he has to go to the tower, to rescue a maiden.'

'Or to a fortress, to slay a wicked king.'

'But he kills him, and makes his way home, and then – then there's only good, and all the wickedness is banished.'

The wicked and the good, thought Nell. Yes, that was the heart of every story.

'I think I know just the tale,' said Minos. A sudden inspiration had come upon him, though by the furrows on his face Nell knew that he was still hunting for the story, still turning left, turning right through the back roads of his mind. 'Yes, yes,' he ventured, with the smile rising on his ungodly features. 'This is the tale of a king, lost far from home. A king who'd been at war, but now that war was done. And all that he wanted was to make his way home – home to . . . to Ithaca! – and the wife and son he'd left behind. But for ten long years would he roam, and one by one his crewmates were devoured by one-eyed giants, or tricked by poison flowers or . . .'

The mudlarks, rapt at first, had started shrinking towards each other. No, thought Nell, nor was this the tale for a Christmas night – wherever it had come from, however it might end. Now that she heard Minos speak of the witch goddess who turned the king's men into swine, she flurried to her feet and said, 'I know something better than stories. Minos?'

Minos stopped his telling.

In Nell's hands, drawn out of her raggedy waistband, were the two satin slippers. She'd slipped them, in hope, out of the mattress as she coaxed the others from the Water's Edge.

'Yes,' said Minos, his own eyes lighting up in wonder, just as they had when he recalled the story of Ithaca's lost king. 'Yes!'

If the other mudlarks ogled the treasure Nell was holding, she did not notice; besides, what kind of a miracle were satin slippers when they shared the seaward cave with Minos himself? 'And now you have dancing shoes too,' she said, and nudged his enormous leather boots.

'I think, perhaps, I might dance in my footprints tonight.'

Out of them he stepped, revealing his sprawling, horned feet. Then he took Nell's hand and led her out into the midnight white.

Outside, the world was a glorious whirlwind. The tide, which had reached its height as they luxuriated within, had started to recede. Snow settled on the mud it left behind, making crystalline fields of the slurry they'd be searching in only a few short hours.

'Shall we show them?' asked Minos.

With her small hand grasping Minos, Nell entered the ring of low fires.

'Imagine what Sophia Chrétien would say, if she could see you now.'

And she danced.

She supposed it was graceless. She supposed the beautiful ladies her mother had stitched for had soared on the music, just like they did at the Alhambra Circus. She supposed the students Sophia taught did not take partners who towered over them, nor shatter shale as they danced. In all likelihood, they were like spirits, light as the air. But did *they* laugh as heartily as Nell, when their partner scooped them off the ground and whirled them in a circle, as if to make them one with the snowflakes? Did they feel the very world melt away, as the land that had taunted them for so long became something *other* – no longer the river to which they were yoked, but the river down which they might sail away, to a bigger, better life? Did they forget that they were motherless, all because of a dancer's touch? Did they forget that they were condemned? Did they realize, when balanced on high, that nothing else mattered, nothing but this feeling of freedom, nothing but this hope of deliverance?

Did they understand that, in the bleakest midwinter, there was still joy?

'Come on!' Nell cried. 'Join us, join in!'

They had orchestras in the Alhambra, but on the river the only music was the sound of the tide, the shanties being sung in far-flung taverns, the wassailing of the mudlarks as they rushed onto the shale.

But never was a music hall finer. No palace ballroom

could ever compare. Minos was about to sweep Nell back into his arms, but she resisted his draw so that she could watch the other mudlarks dance. Ungainly dance, unordered dance – dance without rhythm, dance without instruction, dance without care. She thought it was the most beautiful thing she had ever seen. They crashed together like waves. They scissored and laughed and came apart. One partner pirouetted from another, finding themselves by chance in another's arms.

Not one of them left out. All of them together, making a stage of the shore.

Then it struck Nell: there was something wrong about this image. It wasn't the beauty, set against the bleakness; it wasn't that, for a moment, everything seemed right with the world.

There was something missing.

No – *someone* missing.

Twelve had come to the river. For as long as Nell danced in Minos's arms, one of the mudlarks ought to have been dancing alone. And yet, as she scoured the shore, she saw no solitary dancer.

Only moments before, Nell's heart had been soaring. Now it was falling, falling into the dark.

She started counting them off, one by one. Here was Gander, and in his arms Sally-Anne. Here was Potato Rot. There, Packrat Jack. She named them all, though already she knew whose name would be missing. He'd betrayed her once already, sold a dying man's boots for a fried fish supper – but she'd thought: Christmas night, fat sausages on sticks, hot tea and friendship, stories and dance; how could past treacheries matter on a night such as this?

245

Nell scrambled across the shale, clawed her way back to the seaward cave. Inside, the air was thick with grease and soot. Yes, she thought, a second deceit had surely been too enticing – but there the boots sat, in the very spot where Minos had left them.

She crashed back onto the shore. Strange, but the cold was touching her now. Gone was the night's magic, and in its place just the sting of the winter dark. So too could she see the snow for what it truly was: there was no enchantment in it, not any longer; the flakes that had beguiled her were only the bitter shards that would rime the river by morning, making it impossible for a mudlark to do their work.

Across the shale, the dancing continued. Not one of them had noticed. Not one of them understood.

Nell supposed it was she who would have to tell them, and by doing so end their night's magic. It was this that hurt her most of all. She would have liked to remember this as a perfect moment, a Christmas crystallized in time, something she could come back to whenever life got hard – but if he hadn't run away with the boots, he'd run away for some other reason, and there was only one she could think of. It would ruin them all.

'Noah!' she cried, into the whirling white. 'Noah!'

17

Each Man a Monster

Off the Ratcliffe Highway, Christmas Night 1861

'The river,' cried Sally-Anne, 'what if the river took him?'

The tide was almost obscured by the shifting white veil, but Nell watched as the mudlarks cantered towards it, recoiling with horror as they plunged into its frigid waters. Noah's name was being torn out of every mouth: upriver it went, downriver it went, over the rocks and wharfs, into the frozen heart of Ratcliffe. But it would not stop him, nor summon him back – for Nell knew, with a certainty she could not describe, that he had not danced himself into the river, nor grown disoriented in the white and somehow got lost. 'Noah!' Gander was bellowing, but it was all in vain. He was not coming back.

She scrambled down the shale, until she reached Minos. For the first time, Nell thought she could truly read his expression. He was frightened. Bewildered. Betrayed, she thought, as he dropped to his haunches and cupped her cheeks with one enormous hand.

'Nell?'

'I think he's gone to find Mr Murdstone,' she stuttered. 'I thought it would be different on Christmas night – that it didn't matter about the boots, or, or . . .'

'It's a trap,' breathed Minos.

'No!' she sobbed, and tried to cling onto him – but Minos was already standing, and Nell already staggering back onto the shale. She landed hard, the wind beaten out of her, and there she would have stayed, if only Sally-Anne hadn't picked her up. 'Minos, I want to come,' she called out. If he heard her, he did not look down. He was already striding backwards, then turning to bound over the guttering fires. One great stride turned into a second; with the third, he launched himself along the shore like something animal. The bound he took was surely greater than any man might have achieved. He vanished, momentarily, in the swirling white, then reappeared, fainter now as the veil closed around him.

'Get off me,' Nell said, and squirmed out of Sally-Anne's grasp. She staggered forward, shouting his name – but, in the end, it was only her cries that followed Minos as he charged downriver.

Her friend was already too far gone.

A *trap*.

He was in the jaws of a trap.

Minos had known, the moment Nell cried out the name, that a trap was being sprung. It wasn't only animals that knew when they were being hunted; a man could develop intuition every bit as powerful. Now, though the snow kept closing and unclosing its fist around him, every sense told him he was being tracked – not just by Nell, but by others as well. Men would beach their riverboats and stagger through the tide to apprehend him. City guards would stream off the wharfs, armed with halberds and spears.

He didn't know when, and he didn't know where, but he'd been here before. He'd felt the chains and ropes. That story he'd tried to spin, of the shackled man being taken by cart into Paris – he didn't know where it had come from, but he knew it wasn't imagination.

'Minos!'

Somewhere ahead of him, the Thames began its long arc south. The lights of a wharf he hardly recognized glimmered above, crowding the tops of the sandstone cliffs. Nell's voice was tinier now, and that was as it should have been. *Think*, he told himself. All he had to do was *think*. Yet somehow, it seemed the most difficult thing to do. There was another part of him, one that wanted nothing to do with consideration and thought. It was the part, he realized now, which had told him to tear apart the brawler in the vice ring above the Lamb & Flag. Its fury frightened him so much more than any trap Murdstone could spring. And he realized, then, that this was what he was running from: running, in vain, from the compulsions of his own heart.

It was only *thought* that could slow his breathing. Only by thinking could he conquer the thunder in his veins. He stopped at the cliff-side, taking his bearings by the sights, the sounds, the scents that reached him through the snow. And he realized, then, that he ought to leave the river. If he took to the streets, perhaps he could find his way. There were yet sanctuaries in the city where a man could go unseen. Christmas night in a sewer – it was as fitting a way to spend it as any.

Onward he goes.

Left he turns; then right.

Forward he ploughs; then back.

He had hardly risen to the wharf-side when the figure emerged from the shadows. Between the storehouses that crowded the wharf, the snow was not as all-consuming as it was on the river. Consequently, when Benjamin Murdstone revealed himself, Minos was able to see him for what he was: just a small, crooked man. That secret part of him said: swat him aside, go to the sewer; they won't find you there, not in the tunnels you built for yourself. But the thinking part of him wrestled the feeling away. He realized, now, that Murdstone was not alone. Noah was standing in the shadows behind.

Minos strode forward, a feint meant to test the man's mettle. Murdstone skittered, near dropped his cane.

'I merely want to talk.' Murdstone opened his palms, as if to say he posed no threat. A lie, of course. Minos could smell a lie; that was an instinct too. 'Sir, I think you would agree that we began our association in unfortunate circumstances. I have realized, on reflection, how blunt and heavy-handed I was, with you just recovering from your ordeal in the river. I'll make this plain, Mr Minos: I was wrong. I haven't said as much very often in my life. The fact of the matter is, I've rarely had to. But I was wrong that day on the river, and I'm here to put it right.'

Minos lifted his nose to the air. The blackness was in his blood again. He tried to calm himself by breathing deeply, but there were other voices sailing towards him now, whether real or imagined he could not say. *'Lycias, don't fight him! Lycias, play dead!'* He whipped his head around, as if he might see drunken sailors reeling along the wharf-side. But no – the voice was within him, just as it had been that day in the Lamb & Flag.

The voice was within him, but the panic was real.

'What do you want with me? I'm nothing to you. I don't owe you my life.'

'You misunderstand me, Minos. I've been searching for you for some time, just so that I can say these words. Sir, I believe I can help you. I know how you live – in the lice-infested lodging houses, the hedgerows and gutters, the sheltered lees underneath the London Bridge. And I know how you work – existing only in darkness, hiding away where no man might see. But I can change all that. You might consider it the craft of my life: to lift a man from his sorry beginnings to a higher station. No, I am not here to possess you, Minos. I am here to present a business proposition. A trade, if you will: my time for yours, that we both might live out our days in the safety, the surety, the comfort we deserve.'

Now there was silence on the wharf-side. Murdstone's face remained impassive, barely shifting as Minos lumbered forward. One step he came, then two steps, then three, the flat of his nose flexing as he drew in each breath – and an untold scent which came on the wind.

'Tell me, Mr Murdstone,' he said – and all of his trembling had stopped now, as every muscle in his body turned rigid with anticipation, 'what kind of business proposition needs six soldiers hiding in the shadows?'

Sally-Anne was begging her to slow down, screaming for her to stop, but Nell was fleeter of foot. She sallied along the riverbank, searching for the impressions his horned feet had left in the snow. When she found one, she rampaged on; when she found another, she knew she was growing close. Over and over she cried his name – but now the cold was starting to bite, and now her voice turned towards begging. 'Minos! Minos – please! This way! It's me.' She could hardly hear her own words, so quickly were they swallowed by the snow. 'I'm your token. I'm your Nell.'

It was Nell's voice that softened the fever rising through Minos. He supposed she was still on the river – but he dared not turn, for the silhouettes behind Murdstone were already revealing themselves as men. He'd summoned them with his words, robbed them of their chance to surprise. They were younger than Murdstone, bigger too, in heavy leather greatcoats with truncheons and lengths of piping in hand. Three had coils of rope slung over their shoulders – but none of them were cattlemen, none of them ship-wrights.

Those ropes had a different purpose.

'Stop!'

It took some moments for Minos to understand the order had not been for him. The men seemed to do as Murdstone bade, but not without hesitation. Minos sensed them brist-ling, like dogs called off a scent.

'You have me at a disadvantage, sir,' Murdstone stam-mered, as he tried to seize back the conversation. 'You will forgive me, perhaps, if I came here with a little insurance. I still remember the river cave, Minos – you wanted to do me a violence, perhaps would have done, if only my ward hadn't intervened.'

At the word 'violence', Minos froze. 'I don't want violence. Not then. Not now.' *Violence.* The word blew through him like a gale, filling up his insides, upsetting his balance, leaving his body in disarray.

He didn't *want* violence.

Did he?

'These men are here to guarantee my safety. They're not a threat to you. Come with me, Minos. I would like to talk.'

'And if I don't?'

Minos was right; the men really were like dogs. Now, like dogs, they disobeyed their master. It was the work of seconds for them to encircle him. Six of them, each one bigger than the last. He started shaking. It was probably enough. How many had there been on the riverbank? He closed his eyes and tried to remember.

Closed his eyes . . .

He remembered the riverbank, yes, but he remembered so much more. These images were just fleeting, like the recollections of dreams: here he was on a sun-swept beach, with men dragging him to a grave they had dug in the sand; here he was in a stone prison cell, guards leering through the bars as a key turned in a lock; here he was, being driven at knifepoint to a bonfire in some lonely monastery grounds.

He opened his eyes. 'Please don't do this,' he whispered.

But they had already begun.

Nell might have reeled past, drawn from one vortex of white to another, if only she hadn't heard the hue and cry above. She stopped in the lee of one of the low sandstone cliffs. Lamps were burning at their peak, but it was not this that drew her. It was voices raised in anger – and, among them, Mr Murdstone himself.

253

The satin slippers were shredded around her feet, shredded like a dream. She tore them off, sticking them into her waistband as she took to the cliff path. The way was steep enough that she had to use her hands, heaving at tussocks of coarse grass so that she could scramble above. Up here, where the wharf met the street, Minos stood surrounded. Six men corralled him. Two were unspooling rope. In the centre of the ring they made, Minos cowered. His shoulders were hunched, his arms raised up as if to deflect the blows he was certain would come.

'Stop!' she screamed, bewildered to discover she was singing in chorus with Murdstone, on the other side of the fray. 'Minos, this way . . . Minos!'

He turned, revealing his face to Nell. His black eyes did not, at first, understand that she was real. He took a step in her direction, but his attackers took this as their cue, driving him back, tightening their circle.

She called again, but it was no use. By now, some other compulsion had come over her. She bounded forward, naked feet skidding wildly on the hard-packed ice. She was coming for him. She would lead him from it by hand. This time, words were not enough. This time, it wasn't a dream.

She was almost at the circle when one of the men planted his foot in her path, sending her sprawling onto the street. There, bloodied by the fall, she lay gasping.

Everything was distant; everything out of reach. Then, with one deep breath, the world returned, a riot of noise and colour. Nell picked herself up. One of the slippers had fallen when she crashed to earth, but she made no lunge for it now. She looked up, only to find Minos with the men packed hard around him. Two were holding his arms. Two

254

others, heaving his head back, exposing a neck corded with muscle.

His black eyes found her.

Nell would never be certain what happened next. There was already such violence on the wharf-side, so why it was that moment – with Minos staring at her so forlornly – that she pictured the snow discoloured by torrents of black blood, the fires of devastated lanterns rushing up the storehouse walls, a man dragging himself over the cliff-side, looking for the sanctuary of the frozen river, she did not know. But here it was, as vivid as anything she had seen in the waking world. She could smell the smoke. Feel the prickling heat. Sense the untold terror.

It was all there in Minos's black eyes, the reflection of some future yet to come.

'*No*,' she said, out loud, for all to hear.

The men binding Minos paid her no attention; to them, it was nought but the final exhortation of a beggar girl to leave her friend alone. But Minos understood. Nell watched the rigidity ebb out of his body.

'Then run,' she told him. *Run*.

And she thought she understood, then, what had happened that night on the riverbank: how cutpurses had come about him, to stick him with knives; and how, even as they dragged him to the water, he had listened to that little voice saying *no*. Because he could kill them all, thought Nell. She'd seen the possibility in him outside the Alhambra. She'd seen it when Murdstone first tried to possess him, in the cave. She saw that possibility more starkly right now.

But he didn't need to fight. He could still run.

He opened his arms. Perhaps the men thought he was

already bound, but it was not the case. The ropes sloughed off him. The men staggered back. Minos turned, no longer a cornered animal, and bounded past Nell, back to the cliff edge, back to the river. One moment he was hanging there; the next, gone to the silvery white maelstrom of Christmas night.

*

He'd been holding her by the scruff of the neck, so fiercely she could feel where his fingers gouged into her flesh. Now, he thrust her downward, bloodying her again as she broke her fall.

Nell looked up. Murdstone had harried her some distance along the river, to a place where a tavern of dropsical appearance squatted over the water, its forefront held in place by timbers, struts and lichens as old as London. She'd seen this place before. Gander said that, in times gone by, they staked smugglers to the narrow stone stairs that led from the river to the doss-houses above. The thought took hold of her that this was what Murdstone meant to do to her. But no; soon, she found herself hoisted into the stench of the tavern itself. Across the crowded floor she was driven, through vagabonds tunelessly attacking Christmas hymns, around a corner where one man held spirited conversation with his unconscious companion, and into a booth at the tavern's uttermost end. Here, cocooned by windows thick with condensation, sat the good doctor Bantam.

The doctor's eyes radiated alarm as he took in the bloody grazes which coloured Nell's cheek. He had pinned open her eye with forefinger and thumb, seemingly to inspect for other damage, when he said, 'You were supposed to bring the man, Benjamin, not the girl. I suppose something went wrong.'

'Elkington's footmen were over-zealous. I could have brought him in by commerce alone, if they'd had an ounce more caution.' As Murdstone sat, Nell saw the way his pains ricocheted around his body; the winter was gnawing at him, the same as it gnawed at them all. He filled a tin tankard from the jug Bantam had already acquired: deep amber, cloudy as the river. 'But the trade isn't concluded yet. It's just forestalled.' There was another tin cup on the table; he filled it and thrust it at Nell. 'Drink, girl. It will warm you through. Bantam, there's stew on the other tables. Tell them to bring whatever they have.'

Bantam glowered at the man, as if to say: I'm your physician, not your servant. And yet there was an older power at play here: once Benjamin Murdstone's lackey, always Benjamin Murdstone's lackey. He finished tidying Nell's face, a handkerchief dipped in beer as his tincture, and was swallowed up by the crowd.

'Drink,' Murdstone said – and, when Nell picked at her split lip instead of lifting the tankard, went on, 'This is what he's been teaching you, is it? *Disobedience?* Nella, you never had a wayward bone in your body before that beast washed ashore. You were enough to warm an old man's heart. He's brought out some wildness in you. But I'm telling you to drink. Human bodies don't last. They need nourishing. It's been a tempestuous night.'

'He's not a beast.'

Murdstone stared at her, as brooding as Minos himself. 'Oh, but I beg to differ.'

257

It was at this opportune moment that Bantam reappeared. Bantam made an honourable physician, but a foul butler. His hands were smeared in the stew he was delivering; the bread he'd brought was crammed into pockets and consequently covered with lint.

Murdstone appraised her. 'She isn't hungry,' he deduced. 'The beast fed them tonight.'

'I told you – he isn't a beast.'

Murdstone looked sidelong at Bantam, as if to offer him the floor. Bantam only reluctantly took it up; he'd felt less jittery telling a woman her husband was going to die. 'Nell, you're young but you're not naive. You've seen the seamier sides of Ratcliffe, but I want you to understand this, and to take it as gospel. There are sides seamier still.' He folded his hands, as if feigning a patience he did not feel. 'Nella, what has your Minos told you of where he comes from, of who he *is*?'

Their eyes were boring into her; their silence, which they let stretch out, a weapon.

'He has a gentle heart. I've seen it. I've felt it.'

'She'd do well in the courts of Westminster,' Murdstone murmured. 'When a question is presented, Nell, it is your duty to answer it. What has he told you?'

This time, Nell tried to use her own silence as a weapon – but the blade was dull; the hilt had no heft. 'You've seen him,' she ventured, when silence was no longer enough. 'It isn't just his body that's different. It's his soul as well. He isn't like you and me. We remember where we've been, what we've done. Minos's memories fade –'

Murdstone's fist shook the table, spilling beer, spilling stew. 'You should have come to me.'

'Why?' spat Nell, rearing up in her seat. 'So you could go after him with ropes? With truncheons and pipes?'

'*Down!*' Murdstone thundered, loud enough that some of the wassailers were momentarily chastened.

Nell sank again.

'Why do you care? What do you want with him?' She wanted to say, 'I'm not *yours*' – but the words rang hollow, because of course she was. 'He's been kind to me. He's only a man. There are kind men, aren't there?' And she managed to tear her eyes from the table to take in the doctor. 'You're telling me he's a monster, but I know what monsters are. I'm sitting with one right now.'

'Nell,' said Bantam, 'you must open your heart to what I'm about to say to you. A little time ago I visited with a scholar who shed some light on this man who washed up on our river. This man who remembers little of where he came from, or how he's spent the long years of his life. This man who stands a head taller than the greatest men in London; who tears ropes like string; whose scars healed in unholy time . . .'

'Who bounded away from me tonight like no man I have seen.'

Bantam sighed. 'It was the scarring on his back that started this. That particular design, so distinctive it could mean but one thing. Nell, my sweet, this world is full of wonders – but there was a world before this one, and in that world were beasts more beautiful and terrifying yet . . .'

Nell did not, at first, care to listen to this story he spun. For a time, it was easy enough to retreat into herself – to get lost, as Minos did, in the landscapes of the mind.

And yet . . .

There was a world before this one, said Bantam. A world remembered not in the bones of the dragons they dig out of the earth, but in stories of gods and monsters and the men who were but pawns in their games. This, he said, was an age beyond our understanding, as strange to our eyes as our own world would be to the men who live many centuries hence – when, finally, the ends of the Earth have been reached, and everywhere man has trodden goes his civilization with him: when the railways loop the continents, when every indigent race has been bred into humility, when industry pockmarks the land. 'No, Nell, their world of gods and monsters is almost unfathomable to my eyes. And yet some relics survive . . .' He told her of the fortress Acropolis, and how it still stands on the hilltops above Athens. He told her of the great Lion Gate in the unearthed ruins of the Peloponnese, seat of Perseus, the ancient king. 'Learned men go on expeditions to discover the remnants of that lost world.'

Murdstone leered across the table. 'But there are more relics than mere pottery, girl.'

'There is a story,' said Bantam, 'not fit for a girl to hear. Of a beast, born to a queen, too monstrous to be a part of mankind. A beast that would not be tamed. A beast that demanded sacrifice and blood. An artificer was employed to build a prison so impenetrable that the beast might never be freed. They named it the Labyrinth. Nell, do you know what it means?'

She shook her head.

'You've seen it, girl.' Murdstone's fingers flicked up and down, as if to describe its shape. 'On the beast's back, carved there long ago and inked in black.'

'To placate the beast, boys and girls were sent into the

Labyrinth each year to be devoured.' Nell shuddered; at once, the tavern seemed quieter, the air between them less opaque. Bantam's words compelled her to listen; they would no longer be ignored. 'Until a warrior named Theseus decided: no more. That the barbarity had already been too long. Theseus took an oath, that he would himself enter the Labyrinth – and end this beast for good.'

Murdstone shook his head, gave a rueful smile. 'But the best laid plans come to nought.'

'Theseus fought his way to the Labyrinth's heart. By the token of a lover, he found his way out again. But he did not slay this beast, this Minotaur. The Minotaur awoke, and in him was the glimmer of something he had not encountered before.'

'What was it?' Nell whispered.

'A memory,' Bantam replied. 'The memory that, though he was born a monstrosity, half of him was human. It was that memory, that little candle flame, that lifted him from his deathbed. That memory that compelled him to follow the string Theseus had left behind, and in that way escape his prison. That memory, Nell, that he carried with him into his new life. And I believe he carries that memory in him still – though perhaps the centuries have been too long for him to remember it. Perhaps,' he said, more slowly now, tempting Nell to understand, 'the centuries have been too long for him to remember anything at all. He may seem gentle to you, Nell, and I am certain he has been courteous and kind. But tell me you've seen no wildness in him. Tell me you've seen no monstrosity.'

Nell wanted to, but something choked the words as they came to her lips.

'You're not the first he's befriended,' said Bantam. 'The scholar I met with keeps an archive, writings from across the centuries of man. The fevered scribbles of those who crossed paths with this Minotaur.'

Murdstone murmured, 'The ones who survived,' but Bantam tried to smother the words as he carried on: 'They're fragments, Nell, but the picture they paint is not of a man given to gentility.' The leather clasp bag was at his side. Out of it he drew his scrawled notes. 'I can tell you stories of a barbarian creature who massacred whole villages in the ancient Macedon. I can show you the account of a horned man fighting in the Colosseum of Rome. I can show you a shambling brute brought before the Virgin Queen as a prize, held in a menagerie for courtiers to gawk over. I can show you that same shambling brute two hundred years later, a ship-hand on a whaler, scourging the northern waters . . .'

The cup, which Nell had been clinging to so tightly, burst out of her hands, spilling its contents across the table.

'It's different men,' she stammered, 'it has to be—'

'All of them with that same tattoo?' Murdstone breathed. 'The Labyrinth, carved into his back? No, girl. Some gaoler did it as a gift to the ages. It's like the mark of Cain.'

Bantam paused, for he had sensed the faltering loyalty in Nell. 'I don't tell you this to distress you, Nella. But it's for your own good, now. You must sever your connection with this man. Whatever it is that draws you to him, you have to kill it tonight.'

Murdstone pitched forward. 'I made a promise to your mother, girl. I told her I'd see you safe.'

Nell spat, 'You don't know what a *promise* is. All you know about are trades!'

Murdstone might have brought his hand back to strike her, if only Bantam hadn't taken him by the wrist. The touch redirected his fury. 'A trade *is* a promise. It's time you learned it. And you *will* help me, Nell, because you made a promise to your mother as well. If you don't remember, I can recite it for you.'

Nell stared at him, rigid as bone. Then, just as Murdstone's lips parted, she said, 'To stay out of trouble and do as Mr Murdstone says.'

The silence would have been suffocating, if only the drunk wassailers hadn't been reaching the zenith of some song.

'Where does he sleep, Nell?'

'I don't know.'

'Then where do you meet?'

'He won't go there again. Not after tonight. Not now he knows you're coming. He thinks it was me who put him in this trap. I saw it in his eyes, before he started running. He thinks I'd sell him to you, but I wouldn't. I *won't*. I'm leaving the river anyway, Mr Murdstone. I'm ten years old. I'm not a child.'

Murdstone threw himself back. Then, his fury spent, he hoisted himself onto his feet. One unutterable bark across the tavern floor later, Noah appeared. He barely had the decency to look shamefaced. He just stood there as Murdstone gave him his orders, then took Nell by twisted ear and dragged her across the tavern floor.

Into the night he kicked her, up the stone stairs and through the doss-houses crowding the wharfs. Over Ratcliffe, the midnight bells were pealing. Christmas, dead and waiting to be buried. Nell staggered with his fist in the small of her back. 'You're poison,' she said, over and again. 'You took his boots and he forgave you. He gave you sausages on a stick. You were to be a part of it.'

'Shut your mouth, Nell.'

'Murdstone won't look after you, not when he has what he wants. You think he'll take you with him. One day you'll be a knight of the realm. Well, it isn't so. It isn't warmth. It isn't love. It's only a trade.'

Noah reared back. 'I said *shut your mouth*!'

Too late, he decided to shut it for her. His open palm came down to cover her face.

Nell tried to squirm free, but Noah's hand was too fast. It filled her up. All she could do was breathe him in. The muffled words she cried out were not her begging him to stop, only her telling him that there was only one beast on the streets of Ratcliffe – and he was right here, taking out his hatred on a ten-year-old child.

Some echo of her words must have reached Noah. He thrust her down, kneading his hand as if it was he who'd been taking the beating.

'You think you're different to the rest of us, Nell.' For the first time, she wasn't sure whether he was snarling or about to sob. The latter seemed unthinkable, and yet she heard it in his voice. 'Warmth and love? What right have you to—'

'*No*,' said Nell, suddenly.

'No?' Noah whispered, tightening his stance. '*No*, Nell?'

Too late, Noah realized she had been shrieking the word at a place directly behind his head. He turned over his shoulder – but there was not time to recognize the great shadow falling over him; there was only time to feel himself ripped off the cobbles, for his legs to kick madly underneath him, for the breath to be squeezed out of him as two great hands lifted him up – and then, with the crunch of cracking ribs, cast him back down.

Were it not for the snow and ice, the fall would surely have broken his back. His eyes were full of stars. He rolled, reaching for a store-room wall, but the hands had taken him by the legs. They were tearing off his boots, and very likely his feet along with them. That was when it made sense. *Boots*. He heard Nell crying, 'Minos, please; Minos, *no!*', but this time her words had not penetrated the madman's mind.

Noah could believe this Minotaur story now. History was littered with the bodies of his quarry; now there would be another one, right here on the streets of Ratcliffe.

Nell leapt up, wrapping herself around Minos's arm. 'They're only boots,' she sobbed, 'only boots!'

'The boots never mattered.' Nell had never heard him mangling his words quite as much, like the deaf girl who sold flowers up on the Highway. 'It's you, Nell. He shouldn't have been touching you.'

The fleeting distraction Nell had provided meant Noah could slip forward. Now his boot popped off his foot; then came his trousers, torn to pieces under Minos's touch. In the end, it was only by squirming out of them altogether that Noah wriggled free.

He'd escaped his father like this, once upon a time. That was why he knew not to look back. Wasn't there an old story about that? *Look back and be damned.* He vanished between the storehouses, didn't stop running until he made the Water's Edge.

Nell looked at Minos. The great man's breast was heaving. He touched her cheek.

She tried not to flinch. How could a hand that had been a weapon but moments ago now be the thing to console her? And yet console her it did. As her panic ebbed away, so did the fever in Minos. 'I'm sorry, Nell. I know it wasn't you who set them on me.' He snorted back what Nell could only imagine were tears, though no cascade made its way down his cheeks. 'I told you once before, men like these always come . . .' His words petered away for a second time, until he found the courage to go on. 'I came to say goodbye. I can't stay, not now.'

'Minos, you—'

'But I couldn't leave, not without this.' He had reached into his greatcoat, and from its innards produced the satin slipper which had slipped into the wharf-side snow. He'd trodden on it, then, before he took flight – and, in that way, rescued it from the gutter. 'You need your token, Nell.'

He had already pushed it into her hands when Nell said, 'Don't you need yours?'

There was something like fury building in him – fury, or was it shame? The two things could be so akin. He shambled across the street, disappearing into shadow.

Nell tumbled after.

'Don't go,' she begged him, 'please don't.'

His head hung low, rolling from side to side like a mistreated carthorse. 'I have to.'

She sprang up, if only to trail from his arm. 'But not tonight.'

There was little hope of safety in the seaward cave. The other mudlarks must have scattered, back to their forevers in the Water's Edge, but the cavern was the first place

Murdstone would go hunting. So instead it was to the churchyard that Minos took Nell.

It was a simple thing for Minos to break the bolts and usher Nell within. No candles had been burning in the windows of the nave, so they were sure to be alone. Beyond the chancel, a corner was cloaked in shadow; here they settled, Minos's greatcoat as a bed. Nell heard the steady thrum of his heart radiating outwards, the warmth of his body like a blanket.

There were so many things she wanted to ask him.

Where will you go, Minos?

What will you do?

Was it like this before, when you had to run away?

Perhaps it ended like this every time: each new parish, each new beginning, moving inexorably towards its end. She held onto his arm. What might it be like, to know that nothing was for ever, to know that nothing could last?

'Where will you go?' she finally whispered.

'Upriver,' he said, 'or down,' more wistfully now, as if there was no point in wondering where life might lead. 'Somewhere without people, for a time. I should like that. There are so many people in the world, Nell. Do you ever feel them watching you? *Waiting?*'

No, thought Nell. It wasn't like that for a mudlark. The river could swallow Nell whole, and the ripples she'd have left in the world would last but seconds. By season's end, they wouldn't mention her name on the mudflats. By the time another had passed, her name would be gone. Her life, like a castle built of sand, reduced to nothing by time's endless tide.

'I don't want you to forget me.'

Minos peered down, stroking the hair from her eyes.

'You'll go somewhere and soon enough you'll go somewhere else – and everything before it will fade away, like silt in the river. After a little while, you won't remember Ratcliffe. Washing up on the tide will be like a dream. And me? I'll be gone too.' It wouldn't happen at once. He'd see her, as if at a distance – only that distance would grow longer with every season, until she was but a blur on the horizon; like the dying of a candle-flame, like the memory of a mother.

She wondered if she would forget him too.

'I won't try and stop you,' Nell said, nestling closer. 'It's what Mr Murdstone wants. That I should take you to him, like a Judas goat at market. They told me a story tonight. They say you're not really a man. That there was a queen who lived long ago, a queen who gave birth to a beast – a Minotaur, that needed blood and sacrifice and . . .' If Nell felt the strange shifts in Minos's body, she did not react. She was clinging to him too tightly, and perhaps that was why he felt so rigid. 'They locked him up, this Minotaur, and sent boys and girls for him to slaughter – until he escaped and started roaming the world, and, and . . .' She sighed. 'I wish you hadn't grabbed Noah. He'll tell everyone he was going to die. You might have been able to stay, if only you hadn't.'

Nell looked up, afraid Minos was lost again, lost in his thinking.

'Take me with you,' she whispered, though she already knew he would tell her 'no'. In the end, he didn't use words. He tightened his hold on her, and closed his heavy, ridged eyes.

It had been nice to have a friend, for a time.

Nell tried to stay awake that Christmas night, yet because she was ten years old, the fight was beyond her. Soon, she had drifted into sleep, lulled there by the sonorous beating of his heart – and, hours later, when she woke in the cold grey light of the nave, it was to find herself alone again, bound to return to her motherless Ratcliffe and all of the orphans at the Water's Edge.

It was the first day of the rest of her life.

18

The Eighth Great Trade

From the Mind of a Monster, Across All Time

Dreams, dreams, dreams – but what else is there, down here in the dark?

He opens his eyes.

No church any longer. No St George in the East. He lifts himself, only to discover no girl in the crook of his arm; indeed, hardly an arm at all, just a rippling appendage of muscle and hair. No nave in front of him, no chancel in which he's made a nest. Only a sanctum of dark stone, the dais in its centre both altar and bedstead, and in the walls the same carving over and again. He doesn't know much, but he knows what this is: the labrys, the two-headed axe; they came for him with weapons like these, when they drove him into the dark. Of all the things he remembers: this most of all.

The only light here comes from the embers of the fires he stokes. Little cauldrons, where one dark archway opens to another; enough to see by, enough to blacken the walls, enough to fill his Palace with soot and smoke. He'll have to do his rounds, rousing each one back to life. His hands can hold nothing so delicate as a flint, so there is never a hope of reviving a fire once its ashes are cold. Great tracts of his Palace are in forever darkness now. He knows his way through

270

those sightless tracts by touch and scent, but any Guest who comes upon his Palace would turn to madness if they strayed too far. His Palace is wide and his Palace is deep and his Palace is the world for ever and ever. His Guests will need light, if they are to have any hope of finding him at all.

Underneath his hoofed feet, a carpet of bone fractures and shifts. Sometimes, a herd of goats, a braying ass, a sounder of boars, are driven down the Long Stair, which rises from the uttermost end of his Palace to a great Door above. This is the bounty his Palace provides, frequent enough to sustain him, rare enough that the aching emptiness within him has never truly been satisfied. This feeling is beyond hunger. It is the permanent state of being. Aching and empty, empty and in need.

A sound echoes through the Palace. That is the way of things here; the archways amplify sound. He stops feeding the fire, cocks his head, heavy with two curled horns. It is the tiniest of sounds, like the scampering of the rats he sometimes hears: the turning of a key in a lock, at the top of the Long Stair.

Now his heart is aflame.

His Guests have arrived.

Why do they scream already? Why is the scent that floods his Palace so ripe with sweat and shit? He turns towards the sound, following the spiral of passageways as the scents fill him up. Oh yes, this is hunger now.

Onward he goes. Left he turns, then right. Forward he ploughs; then back. It is strange how the whole of his Palace devolves down to the few inches in front of his face, the ability to put one foot in front of another.

Sometimes, an eruption of voices reaches him. Unfathomable howls, formless and wild – but these are not mere animals stampeding through his Palace. He is no dumb brute; he can tell the difference between animal and man, between beast and mortal human. 'Eunice,' somebody is saying, 'Antias, come!' And next moment, 'When you find him, Lycias, don't fight him! You play dead, Lycias. Play dead, do you see?'

Through one arch and then another; over a landslide of stone, the relic of some skirmish of the past; up spiralling stairs and back again. He is still in the Palace's heart, but his Guests will arrive soon enough. They cannot help it. The man who built this Palace was ingenious beyond measure; the walls compel them to move ever deeper.

He cannot wait to meet them.

He will reveal his Palace to them.

Welcome them to its innermost heart.

His blood is beating black. The emptiness inside him is vast, vaster than the Palace itself. It is devouring him from within. Soon, it will have eaten him whole. He needs to fill it. Hunger can run deeper than the gut. This is his very soul, crying out.

Something else is crying out too. A terrible lowing fills the Palace. He does not know, at first, that it is him. His body and soul have joined in chorus. Crying out for his Guests.

Come to me! Come to me!

But if they will not come?

Well, damn them, he will go and fetch them.

The walls burst past, blurring in the edges of his vision. Archways and dead-ends and ravines. It is the hunger driving him now, just like the wind that filled the sails of the ships on the harbour he still remembers. That hunger obscures all other thought. He wants to find them. He wants to hold them.

He wants to feel their bones shatter in his embrace.

He wants to feast on their flesh while they writhe in his arms.

To taste the warm cascade of iron-rich blood.

It is what his Palace was made for, and he is its priest.

He is going too quickly now, for their scent is too strong in every breath that he takes. His senses are in overload; he has become that which he is meant to be. He rounds a corner, and ahead of him shadows dash. The roar that rips out of him is itself godly: it is his herald. And here he comes . . .

'Please!' somebody is begging, in the Forever Dark ahead. 'Please, not us!'

He springs forward, soaring on his hunger, and stops only when a figure materializes from the gloom.

There is no fear on this one; or, if there is, he masks it well. Handsome as a god he is, broad and shimmering in sweat, his body defined by muscle more divine than any mortal man's. In one hand he holds the dwindling stub of a ball of string.

In the other, a blade that is already flashing forward.

'I've come to stop this,' he declares.

His Palace has not known battle like this.

Its arteries tear open, and out pours the blood.

What was it that propelled Minos up and out of that dream? Not little Nell, for she lay curled in the crook of his arm, thumb in her mouth like a lonesome babe. Not her gently coaxing voice, telling him which tunnel to follow, which stairway to climb. His body was shaking, and Nell shaking with it. But here he was, back in the waking world.

The church was a blur. It was just a dream, he told himself. Only a dream. And yet the hunger which had coloured that dream had somehow erupted, with him, into the barren nave. The emptiness was inside him, asking to be filled.

Dreams had echoes, didn't they? You dreamed that a loved one had died and it dogged you through the days. That was all this was.

He closed his eyes. A voice whispered in his ear: *'You're fiercer than your father was. By the gods, look at you.'* There came a sharp grunt, and the sound of metal striking bone. By an instinct he did not understand, Minos reached up to touch his temple. Why was it suddenly so painful? Was it just the echo of that dream? *'You should know, before I kill you, that I was the one who slew your father . . .'*

Panic drove Minos to open his eyes. It was all still here: the nave, the church, the snow swirling past stained glass.

But the voice continued:

'Oh yes, I caught up with him on the fields of Marathon. It was me who dragged him back to Athens, by way of old Hecale's hut. It was me who raised the altar and slit his throat. A bull like that is meant for the gods. And now I'll send them his son . . .'

'No!' Minos screamed, his voice filling the church.

In his arms, Nell shook – but, by some mercy, she did not wake.

He looked down at her: his anchor, his ballast, his token. She was the one who could blot out the voice. Even bloodied at Murdstone's hands, she looked so innocent; he extended a single finger, to touch the graze on her cheek.

'Bandits I've killed. Their bodies rot on the long road

*through Attica. The great sow of Corinth, dead at my hands.
But you – you'll be my legend . . .'*

'Not if I kill you first,' seethed Minos.

Too late, he realized he had uttered the words out loud.
No longer did he stand in the Palace of his dreams; now
he sat with his arm curled around a little girl, staring at
her beautiful but blemished face, telling her he'd kill her.

Minos tore away the arm in which Nell was still slum-
bering, rolling into the greatcoat he'd spread out. Her feet
scrabbled, but she did not wake.

Not if I kill you first . . .

Hot fire exploded in his midriff. It was the same place
the footpads had stabbed him, but somehow the pain reached
deeper. He was already tumbling away from the sleeping
Nell – but there was no outrunning the pain. He lifted the
patchwork shirt, as if he might see blood streaming out of
the place a sword had plunged into him – but there was
no mark upon him, only his old, leathery hide.

It was only the story Murdstone had spun; it had crept
insidiously into his thoughts, corrupting him as he dreamed.

He shook himself. The voice was no more, but the hunger,
the emptiness was real.

Not if I kill you first . . .

He looked again at Nell and knew, then, that his decision
had been right. He would run tonight, run while she was
sleeping, run and never look back. By morning he would
be miles away. By New Year, the other side of forever. And
he would take whatever had corrupted him, whatever forced
its way out of him in visions and voices and those six unutterable words, with him.

The sides of his head were throbbing again. He reached

up, daring to thread his fingers through his hair. Perhaps it was just the dream again, but this time something felt different; something felt changed at his touch.

He reached the door of the church, stepped out into the whirlwind of night. The glass in the windows was barnacled by frost, the reflections they showed already bent out of shape. All the same, Minos stood in their glare and peeled back the mats of black hair that framed his face. Now he saw why such heat and pain blossomed at his temples. The calcified protrusions were riven with cracks, and those cracks crimson with blood. He told himself that he'd been beaten, somewhere on the dockside. In the confusion of ropes, he'd taken blows.

But not like this, he thought.

They hadn't hit him like this.

He tried not to think of it as he lumbered over the churchyard wall and made for the Highway. Follow it east, follow it west, the direction hardly mattered. It was the horizon he was aiming for. He tried not to think, as well, of Nell waking to realize he had gone. No doubt she would sob at finding herself abandoned. Partings of the ways always hurt more without goodbye.

But she had been wrong in one thing.

She had said he would forget her. That every echo of her would fade as the memory of their time together disintegrated. But, whatever foul tricks his mind played, Minos did not mean to forget. When you have found goodness in this world, it is your duty to hold onto it, to summon it back whenever the world shows you its worst. So, no; once he had reached his horizon, he would find a man who could carve her name into his flesh, dig out the scars and stain them in black that she might always be with him. 'Nell', inscribed on him until the day he died, just like –

He hurried down the Highway, where only dogs and vagabonds dared tread.

– just like the Labyrinth, scored across his shoulders.

Who had carved it into him?

Whoever it was, he realized now, it had been at his command.

But why?

As a token, he thought.

Something to make him remember . . .

The pain in his temples reached a new zenith. Then, just as suddenly as it had blossomed, it faded away. He stopped, dropping to his knees at a ditch-side. There was only the vaguest of reflections to be seen in the ice here, but again he scraped back his hair. The crimson fractures on his scalp had faded, just like the welts in his side, but there was no doubting it now: the protrusions had changed in shape, like swellings that had not gone down.

The voice scythed into him again:

'*Oh, now you see. Now you see the truth of it. You let it slip out, when you beat that boy. By the gods, you'd been hiding it for so long, covering it with every good deed, that you'd almost forgotten. But once a monster . . .*'

The voice kept crowing as London dwindled behind him, as the last of the wharfs petered out and only scrub country remained. He had to keep telling himself that he was doing this for Nell, that every step he took was another step towards keeping her safe. That was the promise he'd made, and every step its fulfilment.

He simply hadn't understood, until this night, that what he was keeping her safe from might be himself.

Yet she would wake at dawn and have no choice but to return to the river. And then?

He supposed she'd go on searching. Day in, day out, looking for her miracle in the mud. Perhaps she'd find it. Perhaps she'd train and dance, after all. One day, Nell Hart would glide across the Alhambra stage.

Or perhaps it would be like Gander and Sally-Anne had said. His memory wasn't so malformed that he couldn't bring her words back to mind. *'We're part of the river, so it's by the river we'll stay. Gander and the rest think it's just the way it is.'*

Minos stopped. Behind him, London was but a shadow. In there, countless thousands of lives went on. People were dying. Others gave birth, renewed lost loves, or struck out on adventures of their own. The cat's-meat carriers, the barrow boys and bone-men, the ministers and merchant princes – every one of them followed the same trajectory of a life, from nothing, through London, and back again. There were too many to waste a heartbeat on, for the world kept turning.

But then there was Nell.

No promise would be fulfilled by sending her back to the river. That was a fool's definition of duty. But to stay at her side, as men came hunting, as dreams coursed forth into the waking world – as his body itself betrayed some secret he did not yet understand – where was the promise in that?

Minos closed his eyes. If only there was someone to tell him where to go, which fork in the road to travel: forward or back, left or right. But here he stood, alone, and losing himself further with every step.

No voice in his head now, neither Nell nor some sneering swordsman.

It was, he realized, the saddest thing in all of Creation.

He would have to listen to himself.

In the Water's Edge, sleep had not come to Sally-Anne. Long past the midnight hour, she sat upon Nell's empty bed, looking down at the street below.

'She isn't coming,' crowed Noah. He had returned to the attic some hours before, denuded of trousers and to the scornful eyes of all who remained. Gander had meant to set about him with fists, but it seemed somebody had already done that. 'You can forget about Nell. She isn't one of us. She's gone with him, and good riddance.' He picked himself up. 'Don't you lot see? Murdstone can keep us on this river, or he can help us out of it – just like he did for the doctor. But Nell? Nell won't play Mr Murdstone's game. So I say it's good she's gone – off to the monster, and be damned with it!'

That was enough for Gander. He reared out of bed, tumbling across the room to show Noah what they really thought of him. One treachery was too many; the legacy Noah left was an insult to them all. 'I might not be Minos, but I can give you hiding enough. It's you who isn't one of us. If anything's happened to Nell, you'll be the one wearing it, Noah! You'll be the —'

'*Hush!*' Sally-Anne exclaimed. Some of the other mudlarks were scrabbling back in their bedcovers, foreseeing the fight to come, but now they turned their attention to Sally-Anne.

At the window, something had caught her attention. Soon, the other mudlarks were crowding her shoulder.

It was not Nell that they saw.

It was Minos.

Gander looked back. 'He's here for you then, Noah. Here for you and whatever you've done to poor Nell.'

Noah picked his way, like a beaten dog too frightened to abandon its pack, to the window. 'It's him who took her, you fools. Not me.'

Minos. There he stood, almost as tall as the gas lamp whose weak flame fluttered at his side. Eleven faces watched as he craned his neck upwards. Then, out came one enormous, gnarled hand, beckoning them to come down.

'Something's happened to Nell,' Sally-Anne whispered.

In a second she had wrapped a sack-cloth around her. Then she was scrambling down the ladder and through the crooked hallways, out into the night.

'Where is she?' she demanded, as conviction carried her to Minos's side. 'Noah says you ripped her out of his arms. But he's lying, isn't he? You wouldn't hurt a hair on her head.' She paused, but only long enough to take breath. 'So *where*?'

'Nell's safe,' Minos said. Then, with words half-formed, 'And she's going to be safer. I've come to see him.' He inclined his head to the Water's Edge, as if scenting something on the wind. 'He's here, isn't he? The man called Murdstone. Nell's keeper.'

Murdstone's quarters were on the second storey. Sally-Anne knew he was inside, for the only souls haunting the common rooms were those who had succumbed to sleep before staggering for their dormitory beds.

The hallway was narrow enough that, after Sally-Anne had knocked, she had to contort her way back past Minos. Some of the other mudlarks had appeared now, to watch from the shadowed recesses further along the hall. They were watching when the door drew back. They were watching when Minos thrust his foot inside, so that it could not close again. They were watching, with hands clasped tight, as Murdstone took in the terrible visage of Minos filling the doorway above.

'Let me in,' said Minos, flatly. Then, when Murdstone did not immediately step back, he pitched forward and said, with words echoing as if in some cavernous hall, '*Let – me – in.*'

Murdstone teetered backwards, revealing quarters so cramped that Minos could barely force his way through.

'You're not going to touch a hair on her head,' Minos began. 'Do you understand?'

Murdstone's eyes darted, but there was nothing to see. In that moment, he was back in the seaward cave, smothered by the stranger's shadow; only, this time, there was no little girl to bring the bastard to heel. 'Where is she?' he stammered.

'I've heard your fable, Murdstone.'

Somehow, Murdstone found the wherewithal to say, 'Aye, sir, and I've heard yours.'

Minos was becalmed, but for no more than a moment. Across the backs of his eyes, a vision burst: the Palace of his dreams, its looping stairways and sudden falls, the Forever Dark between the rings of fire. *You – you'll be my legend . . .*

He looked at Murdstone, feeling the hunger within.

Not if I kill you first.

'Seven trades,' Minos rasped, if only to drive back that bastard voice. 'Seven trades to change your life. A sundial for a wheelbarrow. A barrow for a corpse . . .'

'I know my life, sir,' Murdstone roared back. In the hallway without, Sally-Anne reached for Gander's hand – for this was not courage they could hear in Murdstone, but the last, desperate feints of a man about to be murdered. 'The question is – do you?'

The blood ought to have come next. Sally-Anne and Gander ought to have seen its torrents rushing through the door. And yet there was only silence, until Minos said, 'There's a hole, gouged out of her mattress. You're to go there now and bring back what you find.' He stepped back, revealing a small passage to the hallway. Out of it Murdstone appeared, as diminished as a man on his deathbed.

Upon seeing the mudlarks gathered there, his eyes flared. 'Go,' he ordered, and Sally-Anne did as she was bidden.

It was some moments later, Murdstone trying to corral the demons in his breast, that Sally-Anne reappeared and passed Murdstone the crumpled leaf she'd found. This Murdstone studied – a feat which would have taken seconds, if only he'd been able to stop his hand shaking. So did his body betray him, this close to the end.

'SOPHIA CHRÉTIEN,' he read. 'Shining Light of the Paris Opera Ballet, Available for TRAINING and TUITION.' He looked up. 'Out!' he bawled at the gawking mudlarks. 'It's the river at dawn. Out, out!' Then, when their scattering footsteps had faded, he said, 'What's the meaning of it? You come here to kill and instead—'

'I've come to stop this,' said Minos, and in the ruins of his mind a god grinned wickedly as he said the same thing.

'With paper?'

The yearning exploded inside Minos. It burned with the white-hot heat of a star. The engorged protrusions at his temples prickled, like a wound knitting itself back together. He bowed his head, pulled back his hair, revealed the changes wrought in him to Murdstone. And those words he'd spoken to the priest, in an age that now seemed so long ago, echoed in his mind. *'I don't know who I am.'*

Better, he thought, to stop this with paper than a blade.

'Your life, Mr Murdstone, made out of seven trades. Well, I'm here to make your eighth. You're to find Nell tomorrow. She'll go to your river. But it's the last time she'll dirty her hands there. It's the last time she'll ferret in the mud for trinkets to change your life. By New Year, you'll take her to the address on this paper, and pay for her to start again. She'll live a life where she's safe and warm, where she's trained to do better than she did the day before – where she might, one day, live in love and comfort, not at some cruel man's mercy, not from one day to the next. Neither of us will ever see her again, Mr Murdstone. She won't look back.'

Murdstone contemplated both the shred of paper and the beast who presented it. The protrusions beneath his scalp seemed so much more pointed than they had in the seaward cave. Like a foal's horns, beginning to bud – only this creature, standing before him, was no foal. 'I've made bad trades in my life, Mr Minos, but this feels more like a threat.'

Minos drew his head back up. 'You haven't heard what I'll proffer in return.'

283

At once, Murdstone's hand stopped shaking. *This* was interesting. The paper that described Nell's future fluttered to a stop. He looked at Minos and said, 'Yes?'

And Minos rasped, 'I don't know what you want with me, Mr Murdstone, or why you've come hunting. But I know the legends you've been spinning. And I know the dreams that plague me every night. So here I am. I'll give you what you want, if you'll give me mine in return. Take me away from Nell, neither you nor I to lay eyes on the girl ever again – and I'm yours, for whatever it is you have in mind.' He paused, nostrils flaring as he took a long, laboured breath. 'Here I am, Mr Murdstone: your eighth great trade.'

Volume IV

The Heart of the Labyrinth

19

The Ballerina and the Beast

*From Ratcliffe to St Giles, and the Long Road South,
January 1862*

How does a life change? Sometimes, at our own command.
We wake up and decide we will do battle with the morning,
so that by nightfall we sleep not in the gutter, but in silken
sheets, with a hearth-fire to warm us and handmaids to do
our bidding.

But other times, lives change for reasons we cannot
comprehend. Gods roll their dice. A minister makes new
laws. Somewhere, the rain lingers too long and the wheat
in a farmer's field grows spoiled, so that the grain does not
get milled, so that the bread does not get baked, so that,
somewhere else, a young man goes hungry and sets out on
a career of thuggery and housebreaking instead. The chains
of cause and consequence stretch in a lattice across the
world, so complex that we can never trace them back to
their beginning. Instead, we call it Fate.

So it was for Sophia Chrétien, on the morning Benjamin
Murdstone came to her door.

There were no students to come on New Year's Day, so
of course Sophia's heart started racing the moment fists
rapped at her door – and of course she took the poker from

the hearth before she ventured near. She'd told the other tenants that they were not to admit guests without summoning her first, but evidently none had listened. In London, as in Paris, one man's fear mattered nothing to another. They thought, of course, that she was keeping a boudoir here – she had seen them look with scorn at the girls who came in and out, heard the whispers every time she stepped out on a night-time foray – and no amount of explanation could subvert a suspicion once it was already aroused. 'These are my dancing girls,' she was wont to say – but the English had a talent for euphemism the French did not, and every protestation only entrenched them further. In the end, she had done as the English did: just let it rain.

But this was no dancing girl's knock. She balanced one hand over the poker and called out, 'Who is it?'

'My name's Murdstone,' came the reply. 'I come with a proposition.'

Proposition. Words like that would only embolden the suspicions of this house. Sophia thought suddenly of those early days in Paris, where the ballet had felt like a market and half the patrons only there in case their eyes fell upon some girl they admired. Backstage had too often been a brothel; the *foyer de la danse* a hall where futures were either made or squandered, all according to the lasciviousness in some gentleman's eye. And didn't Sophia Chrétien know about that? She flexed the tip of her phantom finger, if only to remind herself that she was no longer one of the *petits rats*. She was in London now. She had changed.

She opened the door.

It was a strange man who stood there, with a bulbous, charred cane in one hand and one of her ivory calling cards in the other. By his appearance she took him for a street-seller, by his ripe scent a vagabond hardly surviving the winter, but something in his demeanour spoke of fallen grandeur. There was a patricianly air in the way he addressed her – as if he had no doubts that he would be obeyed. There had been men like that in Paris too.

'Mrs Chrétien, I presume?'

She closed her hand, as if to hide the phantom finger. 'Miss Chrétien,' she corrected him. It was then that she knew he was not like the men in the *foyer de la danse*, for no sense of opportunity entered his eyes when she told him she was unwed. 'I see you have one of my cards.'

Smeared in dirt it was, dried and crumpled. Somebody had been hanging onto that old card for weeks.

'And I have a girl for you. Professionals and amateurs alike, it says right here. Well, this one's nimble, this one's fleet of foot – but if she's danced in her life, it's only to slip away from some rag-boy on the streets. You may have to work to turn her into a dancer.'

Sophia sensed that the man would brook no rejection. Nor was she in a position to give one. No doubt rumour of her 'dancing girls' had already made it back to the man who owned these hovels. One day he would come to drive her out of here, shouting about scandal and sedition – but, if she had money, she would be safe enough.

'There's many a poor girl turned to the stage.' So went the story of almost all the *petits rats* at the Paris Opera Ballet. Sophia alone might have scaled the Company's heights, but she was not the only one to begin with dirt begriming her fingers and calluses on her feet. 'But why this girl? Who is she to you?'

'She's in my care, since her mother passed. It's this she wants, so it's this she'll have. You don't need any more explanation than that.' Murdstone paused. 'There'll be a fee, of course.'

Now it came to it.

'Well, sir, you see my surroundings. I can afford little charity.'

Murdstone took in the room that was at once Sophia's home and rehearsal hall. 'The Paris Opera Ballet, it says here.' He brandished the card. Was he judging her, she thought, for reaching such heights and then falling so low? Or was his an admiring eye? 'It would surprise you to know that I often had cause to visit Paris. I attended the Opera myself. Well, a gentleman does anything to entertain his wife. Marie Taglioni danced for us, back in her pomp – but, by the looks of you, that was before your time.'

Sophia might have taken this Murdstone as a charlatan until he spoke about Marie Taglioni. Hers was a name that shone brighter than any in the ballet's firmament. When Sophia was a girl, and first being drilled by those over-bearing instructors at the Opera Ballet, the rumour was that, in faraway St Petersburg, a patron was so bewitched by Marie's talent that he bought a pair of her ballet shoes, cooked and garnished them, and made them the centrepiece of his meal. Twenty years ago, Sophia had dreamed that the same fate might one day befall a pair of her own slippers. Girlhood dreams: so much safer than the dreams of a woman grown.

'From the Paris Opera to the rookery of St Giles,' said Murdstone.

He was taunting her, probing a story Sophia did not mean to tell. Instead, she remained silent, until finally Murdstone added, 'She'll need board.'

'Board?' Sophia asked.

'Paid for, of course. A man named Elkington will be footing the bills. He'll pay promptly, for as long as the arrangement lasts.'

Sophia faltered. She had long ago said she would never believe in manna from heaven – what did the English say? *Once bitten, twice shy?* – and yet here it was.

'And how long will that be?'

This was the first time Murdstone seemed to have any doubts. He waved his fingers airily, to brush the question away. 'I'll deliver her at dawn. Treat it like life, Miss Chrétien: take it one day at a time.'

Nell did not know it was the last day of her old life when she trudged to the river the following morning. She did not know, until she saw Mr Murdstone's beckoning hand, that the carriage on the wharf-side was meant for her. Not until she had picked her way up the riverbank did she understand something strange was afoot. Call it fate, call it happenstance, call it an Act of God – but, when Nell felt the carriage door closing behind her, one life ended and another began.

The sounds of the city had changed by the time they reached St Giles. The calls of seabirds faded away and, in their place, the cry of street-patterers and a vagrant's howl. When the carriage came to a stop and she dared peep out, she could hardly see the snows which had smothered the city days before. What snowbanks remained were

291

filthy mounds. Instead, a tangle of streets exploded with colour. Courts and cobbled rows wended in every direction, seven passages exploding out of a square where the street-corner gin-drinkers already abounded. Some street priest was decrying their sinfulness, while the squawking of lovebirds could be heard deeper down the row. The smells of freshly baked bread and night-soil vied for dominance in the air.

She was not very far, she decided, from the Alhambra Circus – but it would not do to think about that now; to bring it to mind only brought back visions of Minos, and she'd tried so hard not to weep for him.

Besides, Murdstone had settled his gaze on her. At last, he broke his silence.

'Take it.'

He had produced a package from beneath his seat. When Nell peeled back the newspapers, her mouth turned suddenly dry. Something here did not make sense. She fumbled to hide its contents, then faltered – for why was she hiding that of which Murdstone already knew?

Inside the newspaper were her two satin slippers, now so dirtied they were hardly recognizable as the delicate things her mother had stitched. She'd crammed them back into her mattress after Christmas night, and there they'd remained – or so she had thought.

'But what—'

'They belong to you, don't they?' Murdstone said, refusing to look her in the eye. 'I'll give you credit for that, Nell – I never took you for a deceitful one, not until these past weeks. You hid it well. A month ago, I'd have had you selling these at dusk. But,' he shrugged, and kicked open the carriage door, 'times change. Out with you, Nell. Out and don't come back. It's the black door. She's waiting.'

Whether it was the promise of a new life, or the boot in her backside, that propelled Nell out of the carriage, it was impossible to say. But soon she was standing in the heart of the bustling Seven Dials as the horseman drove the carriage away. The street-sellers were singing, the houseless poor were milling – and ahead of her, through the parting throng, stood a narrow black door.

Minos watched as the door drew back and the woman crouched down to study Nell's face. Sophia Chrétien: he knew her only in the hazy descriptions Nell had given, the fine lady ghosting through the Alhambra halls. From this distance he could see neither her crystalline eyes, nor the stump of a finger on her delicate left hand. But something in the way she welcomed Nell extinguished the last remaining nerves in his breast. Nell looked stiff in her embrace, but surely not with unwillingness; no, it was bewilderment that would be dogging her today.

Uncertainty for the future was a terrible thing – but how much more unnerving was uncertainty about the past?

Between the spoil heaps of Seven Dials, he reached up and threaded his fingers into his matted black hair. The flesh above his temples might not have been riven with cracks any more, for a week had passed since the lacerating pain of Christmas night, but he could feel some jaggedness underneath, the same jaggedness as broken bone.

And the dreams since, hadn't they been more disquieting too?

Only when the carriage stuttered past and someone issued his name did he turn away from Nell. The horses snickered, unsettled at his approach, but the coachman had the better of them; by gentle words, and the liberal use of his stick, he cajoled them back into obedience. Besides, they were happier once Minos was inside. Once he'd settled, his great girth unsettling the carriage's balance, he looked back down the street. The black door was closed, Nell vanished into her new life. He was glad to have seen it done. He looked at Murdstone and said, 'Thank you.'

Murdstone weighed up the words. 'A trade doesn't demand thanks, so let us leave it at that.'

It did not escape Minos's notice that, as he spoke, Murdstone's eyes had lifted, again, to those places on the edge of his skull. He turned his head, as if to occlude them – but there was no hiding from his monstrosity, and nor had there ever been. You could pretend for a time, in the company of a good soul like Nell, but most men did not deny the evidence of their own eyes.

'Are you afraid of me, Mr Murdstone?' There was fear enough in this carriage, but Minos was not sure whether it rose out of him or from his captor. 'I'll let you bind me, if you must.'

There were chains at his side – Elkington's men had demanded it – but Murdstone quietly swept them into the trunk beneath his seat. 'Ropes and chains, Mr Minos, are not what bind us. You're bound by a promise now. I think we both agree on that?'

The carriage had started to move. On it went, through the hurly-burly of Seven Dials.

'Won't you at least tell me where we go?'

Murdstone inclined his head graciously and said, 'Mr Minos, your palace awaits.'

Nell felt Sophia's arms fold around her before she found the wherewithal to speak. The black door had fallen closed, condemning them to the darkness at the bottom of the building's stair, but Nell breathed in the scent of blossoms and carbolic, felt the butterfly touch of Sophia's black hair, and wondered at how quickly the world could change. Scarcely an hour ago: her hands in the river. Now, Sophia Chrétien was whispering into her ear, 'It's *you*. Of all the souls in the city, I hardly believed it might be you.'

Nell whispered, 'I don't know why I'm here.'

For a dream fulfilled, chirped a little voice inside her head.

But she dared not listen, not even as Sophia said, 'Come, let me show you.' So instead she just followed her up and further up: round every twist in the crooked stair, past closed doors where families variously squabbled, slept and survived, and to a door at the very top.

Nell had dwelt in attics before, but when Sophia turned a key in the lock and ushered her through, she understood that this was not to be like the Water's Edge. The darkness of the stairwell vanished completely as she crossed the threshold. Across one wall, broad windows let in the cold winter sun. There was little else in the room. A simple bedstead sat in the corner, a sheepskin rug kept the draughts at bay – but, aside from that, only the hooks on the wall and the gowns that hung from them. Hidden in their tails was a suitcase of worn leather, a travelling trunk fit more for a sailor than a lady.

It was the first time Nell had seen her in the light of day. Sophia Chrétien was small, banked in black hair, with eyes wintry and blue. There seemed, to Nell, a strange distance in them – as if she was being studied from far away – yet, when Sophia spoke, that distance dwindled to a vanishing point. Nell had heard countless languages on the streets of Ratcliffe, too many to know by heart, so she did not immediately understand Sophia was born in the slums of Paris. That knowledge would come later, along with so much else. 'You look frightened, my dear. But there is little need. Do I look so terrible?'

By instinct, Nell shook her head – but, if it wasn't fear that she was feeling, it was something perilously close. She clung to the package in her hands, for only that seemed to bring her any calm. An hour ago, she'd been on the river, eyes roaming the rock pools for the tell-tale sign of a trinket. Now she stood on the precipice of a dream fulfilled. She dared not let her mind stray too far ahead. To do so was surely to risk getting lost in a fantasy – lost in a dream, just like Minos.

Minos . . .

He had to be at the heart of it. It was only Minos who knew about the advertisement she'd found. But days had passed, a new year dawned, and she'd seen nothing of her friend. He was gone from her, as surely as the river.

'They tell me your name is Nell, that you're a seamstress's daughter, that you dream of dance.'

Nell floundered to reply and, in the end, said nothing.

'You were there, that night at the Alhambra Circus. It

was *you*, wasn't it, who cantered up to me with my calling card in your hand? It was you who declared: "I want to learn".'

'There's been some mistake,' Nell stammered. 'Mr – Mr Murdstone . . .'

'Must think dearly of you, to give you a chance in life.'

So, then. She'd been fooled by some lie. Tricked into some deceit. Benjamin Murdstone barely thought dearly of himself; the only thing he nourished each night was his own ambition. Nell felt certain he would gladly have traded his left hand, just so that his right might prosper. 'No,' she whispered. 'No.'

But of course Sophia did not understand. 'Let me see you,' she said, and returned to her knees. From here, she could look clearly upon Nell's face. 'We must get you washed up, Miss Hart. A dancer does not need the grime of the river besmirching her.' She touched Nell with a finger, to dislodge some piece of weed encrusted just beneath her ear. 'Well, it is a dancer you dreamed of becoming, is it not? Don't forget: I saw *you* as well, that night at the Alhambra. Both of us there, petitioning for a second chance . . .'

Nell found that language had deserted her.

'May I?' Sophia began, and lifted each of the satin slippers from Nell's hands.

She held them to the light. She turned them in her hands. She ran a finger inside each, hovering on the stitches Nell's mother had made. 'These are good slippers, Nell. They're supple and soft, but they hold their shape. They're made to last.' She caressed the scuffs that marred the soles, then the places where the river had discoloured the satin. As Nell watched, shame coursed through her;

297

she'd kept them perfect for so long. But Sophia's eyes were full of wonder as she reached for Nell's foot and slid the first slipper on. 'Where did you get these slippers, Nella?'

'My m-mother made them.' The words were little more than tiny breaths.

'Then your mother was a very talented seamstress. I should have been proud to dance in slippers like these —'

'I think you did!' Nell blurted out. And then she couldn't stop the tide. She told Sophia of how her mother had started stitching for the stage; of that web of old connections that had drawn her, in her poverty, to the dressmaker off Covent Garden, and the doors of the Alhambra Circus. Of those few, fleeting moments when Nell herself had been borne aloft. 'And I woke up at home, and my mother told me . . .'

They loved *you, Nell.*

They said you were a natural.

'My dancing girl,' she whispered out loud.

Sophia had left Nell's side. She stared, perhaps dreaming herself, through the attic window, and all of St Giles unfolding underneath. 'I do remember,' she said. 'We did come to London, five summers ago. There was a girl,' and for a time she lost herself in dreaming again, burying herself in its back-roads just as assuredly as Minos used to do, 'a tiny little thing. I led her onto stage.'

River children rarely cried, but Nell cried now. That memory had been inside her, parched and starved for so long. Sophia's words were like rain falling on that barren land. Its monochromes exploded to full colour. She fell, as if from the galleries above, straight onto the stage at the

Alhambra Circus, straight into the arms that had held her
aloft.

Sophia turned to her.

'My sweet girl, life has been cruel since then, has it
not?'

As Nell dried her tears, and the room reconstituted itself
in front of her, she chanced to look at Sophia's brutalized
hand. And it seemed to her, then, that Sophia had not been
speaking for Nell alone: that if life had been cruel to one,
it had been just as cruel to another. For how else did the
prima ballerina of the Paris Opera Ballet, a star whose light
ought to have charted its path through the heavens, find
herself in a grubby St Giles garret, grateful to be teaching
river children how to dance?

'I don't know if I can dance,' she ventured, with broken
voice. 'I'm a river girl.'

'Nell, every dancer who ever graced the stage began
where you are now. Do you think I come from so very
much? Do you think children are born to dance, like foals
are born and take their first steps? No, my girl. You learn
and you learn again, and in that way you rise up.' Sophia
braced her by the shoulders. 'It's how a penniless child
becomes a princess.'

Nell had heard similar fables, and been drawn into similar
promises, before – for hadn't Mr Murdstone charted the
same course in his life, from penury to opulence, and from
opulence back into penury again? At least to dance did not
mean dredging the dirt of the river. In dance, you might
look for a treasure inside yourself, not have to seek it in
the tidal mud. There seemed to be potential in that.
Something more hopeful, perhaps. Mr Murdstone offered

up his future to raw chance; Sophia, to discipline and talent hard-won.

'Have you danced, Nell, since that day?'

All Nell could think about was that evening on the river with Minos. But then she remembered: Christmas night, and stepping into his arms at St George in the East; rushing out of the seaward cave, fanning out across the shale with all the other mudlarks cavorting around. An audience of fine ladies and gentlemen might not have paid to come and watch a dance like that, but did that matter? It had still been *dance*, had it not? To feel light and free? To know, with your entire heart, that you could manifest joy, even in the bleakest surrounds?

'Just on the river, with all the rest. I have –' she caught and corrected herself, '– I *had* a friend. He showed me how. But it wasn't like you. It wasn't like the Alhambra.'

Sophia took Nell's hand, lifted it above her head – and, with a simple flick of the wrist, turned her around. 'Then I'll give you your first instruction. Miss Hart: rid yourself of any shame. So you danced on the river, in your naked feet – and the only music the seabirds overhead? What shame is there in that? Nell, one day – once I have drilled you until your body is supple and lithe, once you can stand on the points of your toes and pirouette, glide and sail like a swan – you will return to that night on the river, and think it the finest, the purest you ever danced.'

Nell came to a stop. There was something she wanted to say, though she was not certain how to give it voice. 'Is it true, then? Are you going to . . . train me?'

And Sophia said: 'There will be tuition aplenty, and a place for you here, if you work hard. I haven't long been in London, and perhaps you think my *studio* is not very grand. But things are beginning, Miss Hart. The stars,' and she looked up, as if to find them in her rafters, 'are about to align. And if our chance reacquaintance can teach us anything, perhaps it can teach us this: there is a place among those stars for both of us, if only things go according to plan.'

'*Is he dead?*'
   '*I think – I think he's dead.*'
   '*Then leave him, Lycias. Anthylla, let's go.*'
   But, '*No,*' said the god. '*Gather your courage, friends. This is not finished. There are too many of us scattered in the dark . . .*'

Minos broke free of the dream, only to rear up into the roof of the carriage. Somewhere ahead, horses startled. There was startling in the carriage too: not just Murdstone, but the three footmen who'd been instructed aboard at the townhouse in Farringdon Within. By their skittish appearances, Minos had taken them for the same footmen who'd tried to encircle him on Christmas night – but now, with the dreaming world still fading into the real, he imagined them like the swordsman marching through the Palace dark. He reached again for the protrusions beneath his hair. '*Watch for his horns,*' someone had been sobbing, '*he'll gore you with his horns!*'

But no, he told himself. They were not horns. Only in his dreams was his head laden so. In the waking world, it was just the shape his long-forgotten birth had given him. That story Murdstone had spun for Nell was like a sickness, and like a sickness it spread.

'Water,' he gasped, and soon a skin was being pressed

301

into his hands, its waters upended into jaws better fit for a trough. At least it revived him. The shock of the cold drove away those dreaming voices as well, for it was they – not the voices of the footmen – that seemed to be filling the carriage.

Now that he was back to his senses, he pawed at the cloth curtains, parting them to reveal the landscape beyond. So, then, he'd slept for some time: twilight was here, and soon the full pitch of night. The city had diminished behind them some hours ago. Now, south through some flat fenland they travelled. The dark inclines of downs rose above, tinged in pink by the day's last light.

His reflection, imposed over that landscape, showed no Minotaur, only a man. He bowed his head, trying to discern the changes of his skull – and convinced himself, for the first time, that it had all been some trick of his fever, that the dreams had not truly come to life but only deceived him into believing it so. He fixed on his own eyes, and their infinite reflections. 'I don't know who I am,' he'd said to the priest – but that had been wrong, hadn't it? All along, he'd been saying the wrong thing. 'I don't *want* to know' – that was where real honesty lay.

But now, he supposed, he was on his way to find out.

'Mr Murdstone, where are we going?'

When Murdstone did not reply, Minos drew his head back from the window. He had not noticed, until now, how Murdstone was wringing his hands, nor how he concentrated on each breath. His complexion was wan, his eyes yellowed in the lamplight. Even the footmen had sensed some blight about him; Minos could see it in their shadowed looks.

'Mr Murdstone, you're sick.'

Murdstone's eyes took an aeon to find him, as if he too was rising through the layers of some dream. Minos thought he recognized this. It had been the same in the seaward cave, as he staggered towards Nell's voice.

By degrees, Murdstone conquered his breathing. 'You don't need to fear for me, Mr Minos. The roads are not kind to a man of a certain vintage, that's all.' The effort it was taking to enunciate each word was written in the crevices of his face. 'Of course, there's every reason to believe that you, my friend, are older still. But we'll find that out when we reach Amberstone.'

Amberstone. It was the first time Minos had heard the word. 'What is this place?'

Some camber in the road sent a quiver through the carriage. The footmen rode it like sailors leaning into a wave; Murdstone's body revolted, riddled with sudden pains.

'I work at the mercy of a man named Elkington. An associate, from older times. But, if he's to give me what I need, he must believe in you. He needs proof. There was a time when my word was enough for that man, but I'm afraid that age – like so many you've lived through – is lost. Before he commits more capital to this endeavour, he wants to know who you are, Minos – as do we all. As, I'm led to believe, do you.' He grunted again, as the carriage rode the edges of some ditch. 'Amberstone House is his family's retreat. My physician will meet us there. A learned man – he should be most interested to read the pattern of your skull. He attended you on the river, though you were lost in dreams. He is on his own errand now, rounding up another. A man who's followed your history. A mesmerist by trade.'

'A mesmerist?'

'A man who can tease some meaning from your addled mind.'

Perhaps there really would be an answer, thought Minos. Perhaps somebody else could pick their way to whatever lay in his heart, where he, Minos, only got lost among the switchbacks and dead-ends.

'And if there's no meaning to be found?'

The moment for reply did not come, for at once the carriage slowed. Up ahead, the coachman was drawing the horses around. Minos felt them leaving the rutted track behind. 'We're here,' came the halloing cry, and in moments Elkington's footmen were marshalling Minos onto the thick marsh grass at the edge of the road.

But this was not Amberstone House, whose name conjured up such prosperity and grandeur. This was only a coaching inn, a building of sprawling stone sitting in a dell at the side of the track, fires alive in its windows. Outside, barns and stables littered the yard, a team of young boys stripping horses before corralling them to their stalls. A certain boy, rapt by Minos's appearance, was already gesticulating wildly to encourage the coachman on.

Murdstone was the last to lever himself out to meet the gathering dark. As the coach creaked away, he leant upon his driftwood cane, trying to shake every knot out of his body. There would be no further journeying tonight; to travel by winter was to travel slowly, in fits and starts. 'It will be a stable floor for you, Mr Minos,' he said, as the burning lights of the inn drew his eye. 'But I suspect there's no feather bed waiting for me either.'

'We'll stand a guard,' one of the footmen began.

'Listen out for him. This one talks in his sleep. Remember all that he says.'

'And should he run?'

Murdstone looked at the beast: if things went according to design, his last ever ward. 'Do you plan on running, Minos?'

Minos gazed into the darknesses beyond the inn. The pitted road, the moonlit downs, the drovers' roads leading who knew where. He could throw himself along any one of them. He could brush these men aside, set out on his own, and not a soul could stop him. He'd felt that power in his hands already. It was the hunger of that creature in the Palace. It was the yearning of the dockside.

But if he ran, he might never know.

I don't know who I am.

He snorted sadly. 'I go where you go, Mr Murdstone.'

Murdstone was hobbling away as he said, 'Listen to him, boys. Our Minotaur has this in common with your employer: he understands the cost of a forsaken contract.' He stopped. He looked back. He inclined his head, in understanding. 'And there's a little girl depending on him to live up to every word.'

As the same darkness drew over London, that girl was learning a lesson that the good children of Belgrave Square had known all their lives: that the weariness of day's end does not have to come with blistered fingers and aching bones; that exhaustion can itself be elating, when your day has been spent in a dream.

There had been plenty of hard work – Nell had brought water from the Great Earl pump, collected groceries and delivered manifold messages on tiny ivory cards – but, between times: the dancing.

It was different from dancing with Minos. In fact, so little of it really felt like dancing at all. Miss Chrétien showed Nell 'posture' and 'poise' and dictated to her where her feet should go and for how long. Dancing, it turned out, was a kind of mathematics – and for Nell, who had never spent an afternoon in the ragged school while some teacher narrated the importance of numbers, it was inordinately difficult. 'My tutors taught me that dance does not only happen here,' Sophia said, and clasped Nell devilishly by the foot. 'It happens *here*,' she said, and caressed Nell's temple, 'and *here*,' she added, with a hand over Nell's heart. 'And *here* and *here*,' as her hands found every corner of Nell's body, rearranging her by minute degrees so that elegance prevailed. 'Is it hurting, dear Nell?'

Nell did not like to admit that it was, but nor did she like to lie.

'I'll let you into a secret, Nell. There isn't a night I danced in the Salle Le Peletier that I didn't hurt. They would sit in their boxes and watch me glide across the stage, but had they seen me hours later, lying crooked in the bathhouse while the steam restored me, they would have thought me an old harridan, broken by age. And me, hardly twenty-four years old.'

There was much in this that Nell did not understand. It was on the tip of her tongue to ask: if you danced in palaces, if you sailed across the stage while so many garlanded gentlemen gazed on, why are you here, in the bosom of Seven Dials? Why are you teaching a beggar girl how to dance? But asking the question would be like the sewage that coloured the river: something fresh, tainted for ever. If there was a reason, Nell did not want to know it – not now. Let her live in a dream, just a little longer.

They danced until dark. They danced until Nell felt the burning white heat of exhaustion. It was with some shame that she sat, then, and ate the baked potatoes that one of Sophia's associates delivered to her door. Dripping across their fluffy white interior was butter enough for every mudlark at the Water's Edge. There was milk from a jug, richer than anything Nell had ever tasted. Roast nuts, sweetened with honey; apples, preserved in a jar; all of the luxuries she had only dreamed of in the Water's Edge.

She thought of the mudlarks now, and realized not one of them would be eating; by now, they might have left the river, but surely Mr Murdstone was marshalling them at the storehouses and sending them to the streets.

Sophia must have noticed some feebleness coming over Nell. She had been speaking of their tasks for tomorrow, of 'an appointment on Belgrave Square, a Society dancer – she has only an ounce of your love for it, Nell, but her father has ambition for her, so dance she must' – but, upon seeing the ghostliness of her face, she stopped and said, 'Rest, Nell. Sore bodies mend more swiftly than sore hearts.' And Nell watched as she folded her palm over the missing finger of her left hand.

Then she rose to her feet, her body lifting gracefully from the boards where she sat. 'You may accompany me tomorrow, Nell – though they must not know you started today as a rag-girl, so we will have to begin at a dressmaker's shop.'

The idea roused Nell, if only for the memory of her mother. 'But Miss Chrétien, I can't possibly –'

Sophia raised her hand. 'I can't possibly take a student to Belgrave Square dressed as you are. And my reputation must spread, Nell, if I'm ever to return.'

'To Paris?'

She knelt, like a mother to a child. 'Not Paris, child. Never again will I dance at the Salle Le Peletier. But there are other theatres, other companies that might one day have need for a woman like me.'

Nell whispered, 'That's why you were at the Alhambra Circus.'

'You're clever, girl. That counts for much in ballet. Let me tell you, Nell: if you had been among the *petits rats* desperately milling at the Opera House in Paris, you would have risen from the flock. We would have stood shoulder to shoulder, you and I, on our way to the top. You're light on your feet. Nimble and quick. That's a trifle more than can be said for some of my students. More than might be said for some of the corps de ballet I once knew. Tomorrow you'll begin to understand where those things can take you. But I'm afraid I must go alone tonight.'

It was only now that Nell understood Sophia was preparing to leave. Her eyes darted, suddenly, to the windows, the hard darkness that had smothered St Giles, and she wondered: am I to be sent out into it? To wait among the street prospectors and gin-hawkers, until Sophia returns? The Ratcliffe nightscape had always unnerved her, though she knew its every shadow. What place was St Giles for a child?

Sophia had seen the look on Nell's face. With a smile, she said: 'You're to stay here, Nell. I shan't be long. Not all the nights in Creation could turn this girl into a dancer.

308

But try I must. Just rest,' she whispered, 'I'll be back soon.'
Then, when she was already at the door, she said, 'There
is but one more thing.'

Nell, who still could not comprehend a lady like Sophia
willing to leave a river girl here alone, said, 'Yes?'

'If a knock comes at this door, do not answer it. If a man
hails me from the street below, do not let him see you at
the window. Don't call out. Don't peer back. This is my
tower. *Our* tower, now. None may come here, without my
say.'

Nell was startled. 'Sophia, is there something to be afraid
of?'

'Not for rag-girls like us,' Sophia declared, and turned
on her heel as she vanished from sight.

Rag-girls like us? Surely Sophia was condescending to
her. Sophia Chrétien was no more a rag-girl than Murdstone
a mudlark.

Unless, thought Nell, those things existed in the heart,
and you carried them with you until the end of your days.

Like the monster inside a man.

Like this story of the Minotaur, inside Minos.

The last thing Nell heard was a key turning in the lock.
Then, though Sophia had counselled her against it, she
peeped around the window-frame and watched her go.

Night came on. The sounds of St Giles were so different
from Ratcliffe, the hullabaloo from the street below hardly
fading as the hours marched past. It did not do to wonder
why Sophia feared so much some interloper, not when Nell
still felt an interloper herself. Instead, she wondered at her
surrounds. Nell had spent unending nights in an attic, but
none like this, where the hearth-fire still radiated warmth

enough to put her to sleep, where there was food left on a plate because her belly could take no more. She washed herself again in the basin Sophia had set aside, taking delight in the lather that came from the bar of soap. Then she took a blanket and sat in the hearth-glow, the satin slippers curled in her lap.

She wondered what Sally-Anne would say, if she could see her now. No doubt she would tell her: you don't *know*, Nell. Who she is, why she wants you, why a lady might have fallen so low as to invite mudlarks to her parlour. *'Tell me one thing about her. Tell me what happened, that somebody cut off her finger. Tell me why she fears so much for a simple knock at the door.'*

They'd said the same about Minos. But here was that sensation again: that you didn't have to sit with another soul and listen to their long chronicle just to know them. You knew them by the feeling that filled you up when you breathed them in. And right now that feeling was: who even needed to dream of dancing, when there was the warmth of a fire, and food on your plate, and a lady who – no matter what her story – had told you you were *good*?

Minos had said that too.

She wondered where he was now. On his odyssey back into solitude, she supposed. Searching for sanctuary, some-where far away. She gazed down across St Giles. The snow was in retreat across London, but perhaps it still marred the lonely roads Minos travelled. It would be cold on the river tonight. Frigid at the Water's Edge. But Nell didn't have to worry about that – because, for the first time in her life, she was one of the lucky ones, watching from the window, the heat of a hearth-fire prickling at her back.

Tonight, she got to curl up in a chair and step outside of the story.

There were people out there who had to live it.

Murdstone had been wrong: there was, indeed, a bed of feathers waiting for him in the coaching inn. But neither feathers, nor the attention of the inn girls, would soothe him tonight. Ragged sleep was not the sole preserve of the ogre in the stable-yard; every hour, Murdstone either flurried up from sleep or felt some hag sitting on his chest, tightening its hold. Minos had been right: it was the privations of the road, echoing in his body. No doubt Bantam would have bled him, or had him chewing coca; Lynn would have brewed some tincture and told him to imbibe it after dark. But it was like bailing water from a sinking ship. One day, the water would be too much.

There were voices outside the door, fingertips jostling at the handle. Murdstone was drawing the bedcovers around him when two of Elkington's footmen burst within. The first said, 'He's dreaming, Mr Murdstone. We thought you ought to know.'

Something to focus the mind – that would be better than any tincture a doctor could provide. 'Give me a moment,' he uttered.

It was after they'd gone, and he was dressing himself for the winter night, that he realized there was blood in the seat of his drawers. Chinese silk: they'd been with him since Mayfair, but now the grime of the ages was wearing an altogether different hue.

So, then, his body continued to betray him. He stayed with the feeling for some time, marvelling at the stain on his fingers. Then he buttoned himself up and went to the window. No matter – the body betrays all of us in the end. There was still time for all he desired and deserved. The brute was his now. At Amberstone House, if this man Bantam sought had any true talent, they would open his mind, tease out of it all the beast had sought to bury. Then Murdstone would know. Then, Minos himself. By the time they returned to the townhouse at Farringdon Within, Murdstone would be able to prove he was in possession of a relic far greater than any sitting on some dais at the British Museum, being clucked over by scholars as if the old kings still lived. Elkington's capital would be released, and Murdstone's vision brought to life.

He closed his eyes and pictured:

He stands at the doors to the Labyrinth: the Labyrinth he has built by Royal Commission. They called this place Regent's Park, but that will be its name no longer – for here, designed by some latter-day Daedalus, are the acres of tunnels and looping stairs, underworld halls and overgrown atria, that house the last remaining legend on Earth. Now, they come from far and wide to see him. Not gods and heroes, as in days of old, but scholars and barons, the sons of merchant princes with money to squander: all of them, fancying themselves Theseus as they venture into the Labyrinth to meet the Minotaur. Their riches flow into Murdstone's own; their wonder buoys him up. 'You, Benjamin Murdstone, were like Icarus: you began life a river whelp, but flew too close to the sun, and came crashing back to the tide. But now, sir? Now, you are soaring high again, on wings that never melt. What a life you have lived, to bring magic back to the world.'

Once a Monster

The Oxford colleges send their dons. The Egyptian princes send their sons. Greek lords, who claim ancestry with Perseus and Andromeda, Jason and Medea, come to confront this creature who – with memories resurgent – can tell them of the world that was lost. Each one of them pays him a ransom. Each one of them pays him respect.

Murdstone's aches relented a little, the longer he indulged in this scheming. Yes, he would take this creature and show the world a legend. Draw kings and queens, royal surgeons and scientists into the fantasy he'd spin. Upset the historians, tantalize the poets, stoke the terrors of a generation – and ride the tide until it washed him up in the comfort of a Mayfair townhouse, and a reputation that would long outlast his mortal form.

The last great act of a great man. The legend of the Minotaur would continue into the ever after, but so too would the legend of Benjamin Murdstone: the knight who rose from the river, and died with a smile upon his face.

'Just a little longer,' he told his ailing body. If a beast could endure the torment of centuries (knives in his side, preening demigods sent to slay him), Benjamin Murdstone could endure another few years. If this was to be the endgame of his life, he would play it like a master.

The footmen stood anxiously by as Murdstone hoisted himself into the stable. The first thing he noticed was the unease of the horses. A pair of roan geldings snorted at each other, while in some further stall one of the ostlers struggled to pacify his mare. 'They've been at it all night. Spooking at every little sound.' The footman led Murdstone to the stall where Minos was spread out. There he lay, his body carving a deep depression in the hay.

Looking at him here, it was easy to think him more animal than man. His body was bent into a crooked shape; his naked feet scrabbled every time some whispered imprecation left his lips. Murdstone knew a frightened man when he saw one. Holding this in mind, he opened the stall doors and bowed his head to listen.

It was like no language Murdstone knew, nor any he'd heard on the streets of Ratcliffe. A good Christian man might have said he was speaking in tongues – at least until Murdstone heard the whispered plea, '*Phaedra!*'

'Mr Murdstone, perhaps you should step away.'

He would ignore that voice. The beast knew the pact he had entered.

Murdstone reached down, to part the brute's hair. It would take the doctor to be certain, but to Murdstone's eye the protrusions truly had grown, changed in shape, hanging heavier on his head. Perhaps it was only the madness that came over men as they reached the end of their own lives, as they grappled for magic and meaning to carry them into the dark – but he wondered, now, why he had ever doubted what Minos was at all. Why he had ever entertained the selling of a fraud. It was the old sensation: you didn't have to sit with another soul and listen to their long chronicle just to know them. You knew them by the feeling that filled you up when you breathed them in. And right now that feeling was: terror, miscreation, bridled rage.

'*Phaedra? Phaedra!*'

Murdstone rocked backwards. He'd heard that name 'Phaedra' before. You couldn't found a place like Murdstone & Sons without absorbing a little of the classics. *Phaedra.*

314

She'd been the younger daughter of Knossos, one of the princesses of Crete. Sister to Ariadne, who'd unlocked the doors to the Labyrinth.

Sister to the Minotaur. Half-sister to a beast.

Murdstone focused on Minos, as he twitched and turned through his dreams.

'What's happening to him, sir?' asked one of the footmen.

Murdstone thought to prise open the creature's eye, as if he was opening the trap to some oubliette and peering at the fitful denizen within.

But something – some nascent fear, perhaps – stayed his hand.

It was as if another door had been unlocked – a door in the deepest recesses of the creature's mind. Out of it were rushing all of the memories he'd long ago forgotten, like the last condemned Athenians scrambling back up the Labyrinth stair.

'Ready the horses,' he told the footmen, 'for we leave at first light.'

20

Onward He Goes

Through Time and Mind, January 1862

'We're here, sir,' said the coachman, and drew the horses down.

Dr Bantam looked up from the books in which he had been losing himself, then tucked them neatly inside the travelling case at his feet. Across the carriage, Asa Briggs's blanched face bore the look of a man who, lost at sea, finally spies dry land. The disgraced professor, it turned out, did not travel well; the road across the downs was coloured by the stops they had made, Bantam dispensing coca leaf every time.

Bantam helped him out of the carriage, into the bracing air of evening's approach.

Amberstone House: once the seat of noblemen, now the seat of men who bought their nobility. The manor hung above them, a fortress of brick two hundred years old and rescued from the disrepair of an earlier age. The approach to the doors ran over a bridge which spanned the manor's moat. In its waters rippled the reflections of the manifold turrets crowning the building. A commoner would have called it a castle, but the architects of old knew precisely how much ostentation would inspire envy in a king and had targeted their designs appropriately.

Even so, it was the grandest building in which Bantam would ever set foot. He left the coach behind and, lending his shoulder to Briggs – who took too long to rediscover the proper use of his feet – began the approach.

Tenancy of the manor had first been recorded in the Domesday Book, granted by the Conqueror to some faithful lord – but, after hundreds of years of ruin, it had been rebuilt by a baron who later lost it in a game of cards to a lawyer of Lincoln's Inn. From that lawyer's hands it had made its way into the Elkington family hoard. By the looks on their faces, the resident staff – content to spend their winters in idle stewardship of the property – were ill-at-ease in welcoming yet more strangers. A sour-faced grounds-keeper attended them at the door, and might have sent them away with a flea in the ear if only Murdstone hadn't been waiting.

Murdstone had his own blanched look about him; Bantam followed him deeper into the manor.

'Elkington's family permit him but two weeks at the manor each summer – so, by rights, we oughtn't be here at all. But it was this or Farringdon Within – and the man is a slave, these days, to the caprices of his wife. Imprison a monster on her premises? Coax from him the truth of who he is? She wouldn't hear of it.' Murdstone paused. 'Elkington's to arrive inside a week. We have until then to prove what we must.'

They had reached the foot of a staircase that swept up and ever upwards, but Murdstone had to steady himself before taking the first step. The protests of his body were too many; Bantam could see every pain lighting up his body.

317

'It's the travelling,' Murdstone snapped, when Bantam tried to lend him his arm. 'I'm not built for it.' Three steps up, he laboured for breath. 'It feels different beyond London, does it not? A man's soul gets trapped in the city. It's like I left it behind. But we'll go back there, Bantam. I've seen it now. We'll take a Minotaur back to London. They'll enter our Labyrinth to meet him – and there they'll find him, not quite a monster, but not quite a man . . . And you and I, Bantam, we'll grow fat on the glory of it. We'll build him Labyrinths in Paris and Rome. We'll send him back to Athens and Crete to show them what we found. Who'll care for lions in the Zoological Gardens when they see this? Who'll care for dinosaurs in the dirt?' He faltered, for another step demanded another breath. 'But I need Elkington's capital first. I need to prove to him the glory of this endeavour. And the beast, he needs to know as well –'

'He came willingly, then?' came the wheedling voice of Asa Briggs.

He'd been climbing the stairs behind them. Now, both Murdstone and Bantam looked back.

'He knows the meaning of a trade,' Murdstone began.

Briggs shook his head. 'You stand there, sir, and speak of enterprise and riches. You look to a life built on the promises of monsters. But open my books, and I'll show you centuries of promises – and every one of them broken. I'll show you the good Christian souls, taught to believe in forgiveness, who joined Lycias and Anthylla, Antias and Eunice, the children of Celeus, as his victims. Sir, I've spent my life in his study. If he rests above us, right now, then he rests there not because of a treaty you made. Daedalus

318

had such ingenuity he could make a grown man fly – but not even the Labyrinth he designed could hold the Minotaur, not in the end. It would be an act of enormous hubris, Mr Murdstone, to believe you've built a better Labyrinth out of words.' He paused, glowering darkly. 'The gods of old always frowned upon man's hubris. Hubris destroyed better men than we sorry three.'

For a time, Murdstone was silent. Bantam believed it was because he was focusing on his breathing, but in truth he was only suppressing his wrath. 'Remind your scholar, Doctor, that he is here at my invitation. That he is part of no enterprise. That any fee agreed upon is to be paid at my edict, or not at all.' At this point, Murdstone decided he had no need for a translator. He turned his obdurate eyes upon Briggs. 'They've spoken to me of hubris all my life, sir. Hubris, for a foundling boy to want to learn his letters. Hubris, for a mudlark to sign his name on a deed of property. Hubris, for a man stripped of his life's work to refuse to die in the sewer.' On the last word, his voice had risen with such violent inflection that Bantam reached, again, to take his arm. Murdstone shook him away and said, 'So I *will* have my Labyrinth, sir, and I *will* have my Minotaur in its heart, drawing the eye of the world. And when I leave this world, as soon I shall, they will not speak of me as the knight who rose from the river and returned to perish on its tide – but as the man who brought myth to the Modern World. The man who rediscovered magic. You're here for your knowledge of this creature. You're here as a mesmerist, to plumb the back rooms of his mind. But one more word, sir, to dissuade me from my course, and you can be gone from this manor and miss the moment to which your own life has been inevitably leading. Do I make myself understood?'

Minos had not meant to sleep, but the more he ran from it, the stronger the beast that chased him. For a day and night, now, he'd been enclosed in these walls, confronted with a palatial four-post bed and its mountain of eiderdowns. For a man who'd for so long slept in the cavities of sewers, it was like a banquet prepared for a starving man.

So sometimes he slept, and sometimes the visions came . . .

The footmen remained outside the door. Oftentimes, he heard them tramping back and forth; others, relieving each other from their post. Consequently, he paid it little mind when other, stranger voices were heard in the hallway. Murdstone had left him a bucket of water and he was on his knees, dousing his head – to banish the temptation, to keep himself from sleep – when he heard a key turn in the lock. Moments later –

A vision lances across him. Here he stands in the Palace dark, the same sound startling the silence. A key has been turned. A door is creaking open. Footsteps clatter, and now the whispered pleas. His head, heavy with horns, rolls in their direction. This is it, he thinks. His Guests have arrived . . .

– Murdstone reappeared.

The water that was beading his eyelashes obscured, momentarily, the men who were flanking him. Minos had seen neither before, though something in the depths of his subconscious called to mind the taller of the two, who stood with a leather clasp bag at his side. The second was more diminutive, with the waxen complexion of a man given to the night. It was this man who was most fearful; whether it was scent or simple feeling that told Minos this, he didn't know. He waited, in silence, until one of them spoke.

'Minos, you'd do well to thank the gentleman on my left. Dr Bantam is an old ward of mine. He attended you on the riverside, when those welts still burned in your side.' The door closed behind them, and Minos had another flash of some ancient feeling: doors locking, that meant something too. 'Of course, those welts are long gone. No remedy my ward could provide could ever have banished them so quickly – so perhaps you have little to thank him for, after all. Your body, sir, is beyond our reckoning.' Murdstone shuffled closer, whatever trepidation he was feeling countered by the urgency to show Bantam. 'May I?' he asked, and Minos bowed his head to relent. Then it was Murdstone's hands that peeled back the matted hair; Murdstone's hands that revealed the pointed protrusions underneath.

Bantam bowed to the inspection. 'It's many nights since I inspected him, and yet . . .' The doctor paused. It would have been easier to deny it – that is what the rational mind demanded he do – but the evidence before him was plain. The protrusions had grown from his skull, but not with the quality of swelling. The cracks in the calcified flesh were like land baked dry. 'Did you hurt yourself, sir? Were you attacked?'

'Attacked, but not injured,' said Minos, remembering the wharf-side.

'Then what became of you?'

Minos was about to speak when he saw the faltering look on the other man's face.

'The answer's in the old books. In the nature of the beast. Remember your Castillon, Doctor.'

Bantam nodded.

'What does he mean?' barked Murdstone.

'The beast escaped his prison, and went into the world.' Minos watched the diminutive man inch closer, a look like yearning in his eyes. 'To shed his monstrosity, he touched lives, did good. He learned sympathy. Learned language. Tilled the land, or stood on battlements to protect his fellow men. Somewhere along the way, he lost his horns, began to seem more man than beast. And yet . . . One moment a man,' he repeated, and it seemed that these words echoed in Bantam, 'one moment the Minotaur. Tell me, sir, what did you do, on the night your body changed?'

But it was Murdstone who replied: 'He savaged one of my mudlarks, the boy I sent with Nell.'

'Savage him?' Minos reared up – and all the men skittered backwards. '*Savage* him, sir? It was him on top of Nell. His hands all over her.'

Some strange frisson was working its way through the second man. He stammered as he said, 'But you felt it, didn't you? The hunger? Did you dream of blood, if only in those few scant moments? Did you want him dead, for what he was doing to the girl?'

Minos was silent. He was silent, still, when Murdstone said, 'Answer Mr Briggs, sir. It is what you came for. I would hold you at your word.'

'Yes,' Minos whispered – and, as he did so, some distant echo, as of a maiden screaming, blew across him.

'There is a new science,' Bantam had begun. 'Phrenology.

It permits us, by measurements of the skull, to prove the degeneracy in a man.'

'Oh, but not for a Minotaur,' whispered Briggs, in reverence. 'Not here.' He stumbled closer, checking every step. 'I didn't dream I'd get the chance. *Minos*, they say. So you took your step-father's name. It wasn't your first, of course. There were others, along the way. Severin, many hundreds of years ago. Madoc, in a time earlier still. Asterion – yes, that was the name your mother gave you, on the night you were born . . .'

Minos stammered, 'My m-mother. I don't remember my–' But perhaps he did, for here was a feeling like no other: the soft cocoon of love, unconditional and absolute. He had no idea where the feeling came from; the closest he got was a memory of Nell – but he quickly banished her from his mind. She was not here now. He was right to have driven her away. That was the thought he would cling onto: that she was warm and safe, and back in London being indulged in a dream. 'What do you want with me?'

'Mr Briggs is a scholarly man. He is here at my request,' said Murdstone, 'as a man who might fathom the mystery you present.'

'What need have I to fathom monstrosity, when I hold this blade in my hand?'

Minos's head rolled suddenly, seeking out the boastful voice. But no fourth figure stood in the corners of the suite; no preening god prepared to do battle. He shook himself again – but too forcefully, it seemed, for some fearfulness had erupted in Murdstone and his companions. He lifted his hands, as if to show them he meant no harm.

It was then that he saw the knife.

So, then, it wasn't some god come into the Palace of his dreams to kill him. It was the same doctor who'd tended him on the riverside. The doctor, he remembered now, for whom Nell had been sent.

Nor was it a sword, as he'd seen flashing towards him while he slept. In Bantam's hand was just a small scalpel blade, currently being unfurled from the cloth roll of scissors, tweezers and other prying instruments he kept.

Murdstone must have seen some fury in Minos's eyes, for now he too opened his palms – as if to suggest that men wielding knives might be saints, after all.

'Why?' Minos whispered, eyeing the knife.

'You made a trade with me, sir. Your life, for hers. *I'm yours*, you said, *for whatever you have in mind.* Well, here I am.' Murdstone took a breath. 'I mean you no harm, Minos –'

'A strange thing to say, when you're about to put a knife to my throat.'

'– but, before we ask Mr Briggs to cut open your memories, it would, perhaps, be wise of us to see this wonder of your body once again. My benefactor will want to know how thorough we've been.' Murdstone nodded towards Bantam. 'You're in good hands, Minos. Your body's been through worse, has it not?'

A sword at his throat, biting into thick skeins of muscle.

A volley of arrows, peppering his back.

For a time, Bantam set the blade aside. Instead, his hands roamed across Minos's body, tracing the odd contours of his jaw, taking a ruler to the points risen out of his skull. A notebook was being filled with measurements. Observations in a hurried scrawl. 'Are you ready, sir?'

Sir. Had anyone ever used the word with less sincerity than these three men who came to prove him a beast?

The blade bit into the flesh just below his knee. Though the incision was deep, it spilled little blood – for, within moments, Bantam had bound the wound with tight muslin cloth, then turned his attention to the other leg. This second cut was more jagged, but it wasn't pain that rushed through Minos. It was yearning. It was fury. It was a whisper of that sensation he'd had in the Lamb & Flag.

When he uttered that sacred word '*No*', the men in the room thought he was telling them to stop, that their experiment with his body had gone far enough. They retreated at his bidding, but came again by fall of night, and again at dawn – to unpeel muslins, take measurements and ponder, to let more blood and carve more notches in the hide. Every time, when they heard that word, they slowed their approach, told him they were treating his wounds with tenderness, reminded him of Mr Murdstone's Eight Great Trade. But every time they misunderstood.

That 'no' he uttered hadn't been meant for them at all.

It was the only word he had to reason with the monster inside.

*

If three days could so totally change a world, what might life look like by the first breath of summer?

Three days on the river rolled sluggishly by, but three days in Miss Chrétien's quarters passed in mere moments. On the fourth morning, Nell woke before dawn and realized that, somewhere along the way, the old river feeling had left her. It wasn't the dread – not exactly, for she had never truly dreaded the river; what use was there in dreading the certainties of the tide? But something had shifted inside her, something much less tangible than the scent of coal tar in her hair. No, it wasn't dread that had gone; it was, she decided, the sense she'd had of *belonging* to the river. And if the idea that she might belong here – where Sophia was fixing her hair in a small hand mirror – had not yet taken hold, the sense that she was no longer a mudlark was startling, liberating – and, at times, shameful as well. For when she pictured Gander and Sally-Anne leading the others through the mud, there seemed something unfair about the currant bun with which she was presented each morning; the first moment Sophia took her to the confectioners on Earlham Yard and introduced her to the singular delight of a chocolate mouse, its sweetness mingled with sorrow that her good fortune could not be shared. 'That's what makes you good,' said Sophia – when Nell, too knotted for dancing, confessed what she was thinking. 'But don't lose your heart in sorrow for others, not when you've had so much in your own short life. You're allowed to dream. Once you start finding shame in that, you'll already be lost.'

She tried to do as Sophia had said, and threw herself into her new life in St Giles. Every morning there was water to fetch from the pump, groceries to buy, the chamber pot to dispose of and letters to deliver – but it was by dancing that Nell would now define her life. On the first day, trotting after Sophia in a dress of wool challis – very likely the most uncomfortable thing she had ever worn – she had sat in the salon of a townhouse in Berkeley Square, trying not to marvel at walls steeped in oil paintings, at hearths that roared, at the very idea that a girl might have grown up with cooks to bring her supper and maids to plait her hair. On the second day, to a garden overlooking the river they had gone – but it was some time into the dancing, watching Sophia instruct a merchant's daughter in the demure way to pivot and turn, that it occurred to Nell that these same waters would soon roll past Gander and Sally-Anne, Potato Rot and Packrat Jack. There was much to learn from watching Sophia teach, but in these houses Nell's energy was given to flightiness and feeling unsettled, conquering the knowledge that she did not truly belong. Better were the afternoons where Sophia welcomed girls into her garret in St Giles and instructed them there. Sometimes, Nell would be sent on errands, but others she was invited to stand in the corner, to watch or mimic the patterns through which Sophia led her girls. 'It's instruction for you both,' Sophia would say. 'You must observe, Nell – and you,' she went on, turning to her student, 'must learn to be observed. Should you reach the stage, you shall be being observed for the rest of your life. For good and ill, wherever this dancing life leads.'

It became clear to Nell that there were two kinds of families drawn to Sophia's study: the grand and eloquent, who summoned Sophia to teach their daughters to dance as Society expected; and those who dwelt a rung down Society's ladder, desperate to trade their way to the top. For a certain sort of lady, to dance was much the same as mudlarking: by prospecting at masquerades, they sought to unearth a treasure, or at least make a trade that bettered their lives. No ivory sundial would do for these ladies; only a husband, who might give them children to live better

327

lives than they. Each generation, trading itself for the next. For the first time, Nell thought of what Gander had once said of Mr Murdstone: '*He got married.*' Life, which had seemed so simple on the river, was in truth filled with infinite landslides and dead-ends. And no sooner had she thought of that, she was picturing those dreams Minos had described, the lattice of ink and scars across his back. The Labyrinth, in that story from long ago.

And if that was what life was, just loops and switchbacks, dead-ends and cave-ins, with every soul trying to pick their way through – and either escape or reach the Labyrinth's heart – then what might these days with Sophia be for Nell? It was hard to think of them as for ever. But so was it hard to imagine she might be back on the river by the first breath of spring.

It occurred to Nell that many of the young ladies who attended Sophia's quarters were picking their way towards dead-ends of their own – for, though Sophia never said it, many of them were certainly being indulged. Some father or sweetheart had come across the same ivory calling card as Nell and sent their loved one here, to make a fantasy come true. She got to know where talent lay: not in the poise or performance, for both those things could be taught, but in the head and the heart. And she understood, too, the value of courage – which, it turned out, was not to be reserved for those times when you were confronted with a villain, but could be vital in simply leaning into a turn, or daring to take somebody else in your arms. 'It's not the courage to step out onto a theatre's stage that you're chasing,' Sophia told one of her students. 'It's the courage to be yourself, unfailingly yourself, in the full gaze of others.'

Those girls who came, not dreaming of the stage, but of capturing the eye of some suitor when the season began, did not seem to inspire Sophia as her other students did. 'It matters little how light on their feet they are, nor how well they keep their balance. They're dancing to be *seen*,' Sophia scoffed, as – late at night – she arranged Nell's limbs and led her around their quarters.

'Isn't everyone dancing to be seen?' Nell asked, for Sophia too often spoke in riddles.

'Oh, but no,' Sophia smiled, and lifted Nell past the windows so that, for a fleeting moment, it seemed as if she was soaring above St Giles. 'There were four thousand eyes watching me when I danced the sylph in *La Sylphide*. They took in every corner of my body. But Nell,' and she set her down in the heart of the room, 'I wasn't dancing for them. I was dancing for *this*.' She pressed her hand to Nell's breast. 'Have you ever done something just for you, Nella? Something everybody else thought foolish, something they called rash and dangerous, but something that simply had to be done, because your heart called out for it – because to deny it would have been to deny being *you*?'

Nell saw herself casting the silver chain back into the river that had just disgorged it. She saw herself steadfast at Minos's side, while the others tried to cajole her back to the water.

'Then you already know, Nell, what it means to be a dancer.'

Sophia was about to glide with her, again, around the room, when Nell – faltering as she took her hand – said, 'Miss Chrétien, your finger . . .'

'Not yet, Nell,' Sophia said – and, seizing Nell, threw

her into the dance. It was not as wild tonight as it had been on the river, it was not as unbridled and untamed, but every bit of it came from the heart. They would not, Nell later decided, understand it at the Water's Edge – but she refused to feel ashamed of that.

Life kept changing. One world faded, while another was born.

They wouldn't understand it at the Water's Edge, but Minos assuredly would.

*

He is still sleeping, sprawled in a nest of shredded blankets, when they come. Three men to corral him, and yet more standing guard. He awakes, to find a loop of rope has already been thrown around his ankles, that another is being fitted, like a horse's bridle, around his jaws. He would tell them to stop, if only he had words. But he has never spoken a word in his life, nor even formed one in the ruined chaos of his mind, so his protest comes in howls and roars – the sounds that, in the months to come, will reverberate through the hallways of the king, echoing in rumour across Crete and the oceans beyond.

Out into the hallway they force him. Spears to pierce his hide, makhaira blades to threaten and cajole. When he resists, they swipe at him. When he snarls, they cut into his shoulders. Beyond them, a woman is screaming – but not out of fear. She is screaming for them to stop. But stop they do not. He tries to turn to her, for he has some sense she might help – and, when they stop him, the sadness, the panic, the rage that erupts in him is too much to comprehend. He bows his head,

*gores the guard on one flank, eviscerates the guard on the
other. It takes a mob to subdue him. Roped and beaten, he is
dragged face-down along the stones. Then down, down, down
they go, down into a crypt where a marble door he does not
recognize is standing open.*

Beyond it, stairs plunge into the darkness beneath Knossos.

'Is he awake?'

A voice, reaching out from beyond this dream.

'They heard him roaring in the scullery below.' *Murdstone's
voice, calculating and sly.* 'We'll be making our own meals
from here on, gentlemen. Elkington's house staff are gone.
They wouldn't stay a second longer. Not now they realize
what we have.'

Minos opened his eyes. It had been but a dream.
Guardsmen had not come to bind him and drive him out;
only a physician, a scholar, a mudlark.

Why, then, did he feel as cornered as he had in his dream?

They had, about them, the same wariness that they always
wore when they came into this room. They had come often
in the passing days: to deliver him sustenance, then take
their knives to his legs, his shoulders, and finally his midriff;
to measure him as he healed, to ask questions about every
scar. 'Your body's an atlas,' the physician had begun. 'Your
foot was broken. Do you remember when you fell? There's
crookedness in your spine – but I've never seen a back set
and healed. Every rib, shattered. Is none of it in here?' he
said, prising open an eye to peer inside.

Their knives were kinder than their questions. Sometimes,
he heard them gathered beyond the locked door. They kept
their conversations low, not knowing that he could hear
every word. 'The body records every barbarity,' Bantam

said. 'Dig up a Roman legionnaire and a good physician could tell you how he was killed. Find one of the old plague pits and you can read their stories in their bodies. But as for the mind . . .'

'The mind buries what the body betrays. But what is buried, gentlemen, can always be unearthed.'

That was the voice of the scholar, and it was the scholar who came to him now. He'd been the most fearful, back at the beginning – but, across the days, his confidence had grown. Now it seemed to match his curiosity. Bantam and Murdstone accompanied him to the door, but it was the scholar who sat at the hearthside and invited Minos to sit before him. Like a traitor, thought Minos, being brought before a king.

'Memory's a fickle thing, isn't it, Minos? It plays games with us. A man could never hold in mind the whole chronicle of his life, so some piece of us must choose what to cling onto and what to hide away. But it's all a part of us. Every little thing we did. Every thought we've had, every word we've spoken, every feeling we ever felt – that's what makes us who we are, whether we remember it or not.' He paused. 'What *do* you remember, Minos?'

'I remember being at sea,' he said. 'London on the horizon, shrouded in fog.'

'And before that?'

There were fragments. He'd told Nell, easily enough. Rome, when she'd asked him about dancing. The monastery and the frozen north. But that was all they were: just fragments, as oblique as his labyrinthine dreams. Somehow, recounting the things he'd told Nell seemed more perilous, here in this chamber. So he sank back into silence, until finally the voice of Murdstone called out, 'Do you *want* to know, Minos? Who you really are? Not just some sewer worker. Not just some brute with a malformed mind.'

Minos turned over his shoulder. Beyond Murdstone, the footmen – sensing their inmate's sudden move – marshalled themselves. Murdstone turned to them and said, 'Stand down, you fools. Don't you understand this yet? Our guest is here of his own volition. Should he change his mind, he will leave – and none of us will stop him. It isn't your truncheons keeping him here. It isn't that pepper-box revolver, or your falchion blade. They might make you feel safe, but only the way a lost child's ragdoll brings him comfort. Something to cuddle, in the long, lonely night.' By now, he had turned back to Minos. 'No, the only thing keeping him here is a promise. This world is built out of them. Go back to London, and you'll find a city built, not out of bricks and stone, but out of promises and oaths. I promise I'll give you a ha'penny for a candle. I promise I'll bring you water. But there are bigger promises at play – aren't there, Minos? What else is it, but a promise, that stops a man from marching into another man's house and taking all he owns? What else but a promise that keeps London's streets from turning to rivers of blood? Without promises, we'd be butchers. It's promises that tamed the world. Promises that turned beasts into men.'

Beasts into men. No doubt those words had been chosen for their effect; they sliced into Minos more fiercely than any of the physician's blades.

'Our scholarly friend here is a studied mesmerist. He believes he can lead you back, through the doors your mind has closed. Will you follow him, Minos?'

Minos's head rolled, as heavy as if it really was burdened with horns, back to the scholar.

'What must I do?' he asked.

That was when they began.

*

London in thaw. The gutters of St Giles were awash with snowmelt. As Nell dodged through the carters and street-sweepers, bound for the stationers on Mercantile Lane, her mind flashed momentarily to the river. No doubt its banks would be swollen, the mud more treacherous and yielding little to desperate hands. But Sophia had told her to put away her shame, so that was what she would do. She tried not to think of Sally-Anne as she splashed through the water pooling in every cart track; she thought instead of the new leather shoes she was wearing ('you've been a rag-girl too long, Nella'), and how she would polish them tonight while Miss Chrétien was off teaching some lord's daughter how to dance.

The stationer was expecting her, for she'd presented herself here two days earlier. A curmudgeonly man, he had had the measure of Nell in an instant – but today he broached a smile. 'She's keeping you scrubbed, then, is she? Next, she'll be chopping that hair. Handmaids to ladies can't go round looking like boys. They need turning out. Now, you can't be as beautiful as her – but she'll want you prettifying, you can count on it.'

He was still grinning when he handed Nell the package. As she'd been instructed, she furled back the newspaper wrapping to check the small ivory cards: 'SOPHIA CHRÉTIEN,

Shining Light of the Paris Opera Ballet, Available for TRAINING and TUITION.'

'I'm not her handmaid,' she protested. 'I'm her student.'

It was meant to be a defiant proclamation, but defiant proclamations were not often met with laughter. 'Do you know who she *is*, girl?'

Nell was furiously bundling up the cards again when he went on, 'That a lady like that washes up in a squalid place like this is a miracle. That she might turn some river girl to her apprentice would be a miracle too many.'

'Sophia was a rag-girl once.'

The stationer looked dubious at this. 'Like a caterpillar to a butterfly, then. Trust me, girl. There's no place for motherless rag-girls where she's going.'

Nell was purpling by the time she reached the shop door; fury, humiliation, the righteous need to call him a liar – all of it frothed around inside her.

The tingling suspicion that he was telling the truth.

It was hard to suppress those feelings as she picked her way back to their quarters. So consumed was she, damning herself for falling headlong into some fantasy, that she didn't see the post-cart as it rolled past, raining great arcs of filthy snowmelt around her. Nor did she notice the street priest harrying some derelict down the street, screaming after her that the Reform Society would wash away her sins. Buffeted first by the derelict, then by the priest, she fell at last upon her posterior, where the frigid filth embraced her.

It embraced the package she was carrying too. Try as she might, Nell could not stop it from bursting out of her arms. By the time she rescued it, it was sodden through. So too was Nell's new idea of life.

But at least the hand of some stranger was reaching out to help her aloft; there were yet good people on the streets of St Giles.

'Here, love, let me.'

It was only the post-boy, his barrow ditched by the edge of the track. He had the look of a mudlark about him too, thought Nell, as he set her back on her feet and started dusting her down. She supposed he'd seen it in her, and for that reason taken pity, but today the sympathy stung.

'That looks like a new dress. There's some mistress won't be happy with you for that.'

The fear of it echoed in Nell. She hadn't yet thought of Sophia as waspish or cruel, but there had been days when Mr Murdstone was not a villain, days when he played the part of grandfather to perfection; you never really knew what was lurking under the surface.

'Well, let's hope one of these impresses her.' The post-boy took two letters from his satchel and delivered them to Nell's hands. 'First's a local letter, but see – this one's from Paris.' There was an address written in cursive hand, and a stamp so different from the penny blacks on the letters that normally came. 'Listen here, is it true she used to be a ballerina? Her, up there that keeps you? I talked to a man reckons they fancied her a queen in the theatres. It isn't often you get a queen in Seven Dials.'

Nell's heart was turning somersaults as she carried the sodden package up the narrow stairs. If any of the other tenants had listened out, they would have heard her whispering apologies, over and again, casting them in slightly different hues every time. Only the perfect apology would do. If she was going to be sent away, it would not be for

lack of contrition. She would make Miss Chrétien understand; she would beg, or steal, to replace what she had
ruined.

The door at the top of the long stair was sitting open
when Nell approached, the half-formed entreaty on her lips.
Sophia was already shepherding her morning's student out
of the door – not quite a hopeless case, this one; Sophia
said she would have made a fine member of any corps de
ballet, if only her father hadn't been intent on finding her
a husband – but, the moment she saw Nell, she bustled the
dancer on her way, swept Nell into the salon and said,
'What happened, dear girl?'

'I'm sorry,' Nell said, but that was all – for the words
she'd been rehearsing had vanished from her head. 'I was
out on the street and, and–'

Sophia took stock of the situation in a second. Perhaps
that was her dancer's poise too.

'We must pin and dry them, Nell.' She had already taken
the box and, opening it up, carried its contents to the
hearthside. 'Fetch strings. We shall hang them like washerwomen at the river.'

Nell wasn't certain if washerwomen had ever used the
filth-ridden rivers of London, but she leapt to Sophia's
service, grateful that she had not immediately been sent
away. Then, as they dangled sodden cards above the fire
like bunting, the panic began to bleed out of her. It was
strange how easily emotion could erupt out of your heart.
Every passion was locked up inside its own prison, until it
grew too strong and forced its way out.

Minos, she thought again. She would have liked to have
seen him now.

'Miss Chrétien, I almost forgot.'

Letters came each day, so Nell thought nothing of it as Sophia plucked them from her grasp. If she saw the way Sophia's eyes narrowed at the sight of the Parisian hand, she was too focused on hanging the last of the cards to wonder why. If she saw the fleeting panic, the momentary alarm, it was nothing compared to the panic she had felt some moments before, so she let it ghost by. Perhaps it was the feeling of relief coursing through her that made it difficult to perceive the deepening creases of Sophia's brow – but, when she tore the unopened letter in two, then in two again, then scattered the scraps in the kindling basket by the edge of the fire, Nell at last turned and stared.

'Sophia, is something wrong?'

The letter's remnants were still fluttering down – but shredding it seemed to have restored the colour to Sophia's face. 'Some letters are welcome,' she said. 'Some letters are not. We get to choose which ones we read, dear heart.' Then she inclined her head and faltered not one second as she opened the second missive.

This time the effect on her was startling. Where the first had made hollows of her eyes, this seemed to ignite them. Her eyes scoured the page, turning it and reading it twice. Then, the most beautiful thing: Sophia was smiling, as Nell had rarely seen her smile before.

'What is it?' Nell wondered. 'Sophia, what happened?'

Sophia dropped to her knees, folded Nell in arms. She was still braced there, breathing in the wildflower scent of her collar, when Sophia said, 'We may not need to worry about these calling cards after all. Nell, my dear: look.'

338

Sophia retreated from the embrace, just enough for the letter to unfold between them.

Nell did not have to focus for long before the same sense of exultation rushed through her – for there, at the head of the page, in print so clear even an ill-educated mudlark could read it, were the words 'ALHAMBRA CIRCUS'.

'You asked me what happened, little one,' said Sophia. Then, with a smile so luminous it could itself have filled the stage at the Alhambra Circus, she added, 'The stars, Nella: they're about to align.'

*

'What do you see?'

Those words: he'd heard them a hundred times already.

'Open your eyes.'

But they were already open.

'Where are you, Mr Minos?'

Minos reared up from the bed where they had instructed him to lounge, the fug of opiate smoke like a reef around his head. At the bedside, the scholar Briggs startled out of his chair, then found his composure and encouraged Minos to return to his position. 'I am not a stage illusionist, sir. There is no trick being perpetrated upon you. You're safe here.'

It didn't feel safe. The world itself was an unsafe place, but here most of all. He looked around. Only the scholar remained; the rest, he could sense, lurked beyond the doors. He was shaking as he lay back down. 'It's like standing on a cliff edge,' he trembled, 'trying to find the courage to throw yourself off.'

'Perhaps it isn't courage you need,' Briggs began. 'Perhaps it's trust.'

Minos's eyes rolled madly in their orbits. 'Trust?'

'When was the last time you trusted another soul, Minos?'

'*Nell.*'

'Leave aside the girl. There were others, weren't there? She isn't the first who took your hand. Not the first who nursed you, or gave you warmth. Close your eyes, Minos.'

This he did.

'Where are you?'

Only in the infinite blackness.

'When you open them again, fix your gaze on the light alone. Say not a word. Only breathe.' The moment lingered, as Minos swam through the dark. 'Open your eyes, sir.'

The shutters in the room had been fastened. Vast velvet curtains drawn, to extinguish the last slivers of daylight. Alone in the room, only one light flickered. While he had been lost in the blackness, Briggs had placed a single candle at the foot of his bed. Minos focused on it now. As he watched, its dancing seemed to grow: more rhythmic, more vibrant. Somewhere along the way, he stopped focusing on the light itself; now he was being drawn to some place beyond it, an infinite distance away.

He had been clinging to the bedsheets – but now his fists unfurled, and now he was falling, plunging, plummeting into the light.

'Minos, I want you to look backwards. To a time before Nell. Before the brigands who threw you into the river. Before the sewer and the smithy. Before . . . London.'

He was silent, still gazing through the candle-flame.

'*Before*,' said Briggs.

'I can't see it,' Minos whispered – but of course he could. There were different shapes in the candlelight now.

He is standing at the taffrail, with ten braying bodies behind him and only an endless grey-blue expanse in front. Becalmed for days, they are telling him. Their hold filled with endless barrels of saltpetre, bound for auction in a distant land – but every day at sea is another day unpaid, every day another one of worsening hunger, drought, madness. 'Captain should never have brought you aboard,' says one. 'Don't matter how strong a man is, how hard he works, when he's carrying a curse,' says another. 'No, we don't need to draw lots to know who the unlucky one is. He's standing right in front of us. Look, lads, he's not even going to fight back . . .'

'Stay there, Minos. Be with him.'

He plunges from the taffrail, plunges past the hull of the ship, plunges towards the welcoming water. And as he nears the surface, in the split second before he crashes through, he sees his reflection looking back. It is him, he knows. The water has distorted his features, so that his eyes seem bigger, set further apart, so that his snout (for, yes, these are not the jaws of a human being) appears broader than it ought – but a man can always recognize himself.

Can't he?

'What do you see?'

Briggs's voice came from so far away, like the voice a god sends down to his chosen one on Earth.

'I'm sprawled across driftwood. Taken by the ocean. In and out of sleep.'

'Good,' whispered Briggs, soothingly now, 'that's good,

Minos. So tell me, as you drift there, with all the empty
fathoms underneath you and the endless leagues around –
that man on the driftwood, what is *he* dreaming?'

Something in the idea startled Minos. He lifted himself,
started seeing the candle-flame for what it was once more.

'Just sail with him,' said Briggs. 'Sail down *into* him. Do
you remember what it felt like, there on the ocean?'

Minos felt himself falling, falling back into his mind.

'It goes ever on.'

*Left he paddles; then right. Forward he floats; then back. It
is strange how the whole of Creation devolves down to the few
inches in front of his face, the ability to cling to the driftwood
for one moment more.*

'You're lying there with him. You *are* him. Trail your
fingers in the waters. Lift your face to the heat of the sun.
Now, Minos, close your eyes again.' He did so. 'Put yourself
where you once were.' He did so. 'Sink into his dreams,
Minos – and tell me what you see . . .'

Murdstone did not know he had been holding his breath
until the moment the pressure grew too strong. Then, with
the sound of a child's croup cough, he fell against the
hallway wall.

'They'll *hear*,' Bantam said – and, taking advantage of
his master's momentary weakness, shepherded him to one
of the neighbouring bedchambers. 'Running water,' he said,
attending a sink basin. 'These Elkingtons don't know the
meaning of want.'

The tin cup of ice-cold water was the restorative
Murdstone needed. 'It's the travelling,' he croaked, reaching
for his cane. 'I still feel its echo.'

Bantam glowered, 'You've been at rest for days. You've eaten well. You've slept.'

'I don't sleep, not any longer. Not now I'm this close.'

Murdstone had meant to pick his way back to the hall, to listen again to the unspooling of history through the walls, but it seemed as if the room was listing. The driftwood cane was not enough; Bantam had to guide him back to the bed. 'How long has it been since you visited my study, Benjamin, and refused to let me listen to your heart?'

This time, Murdstone glowered.

'Winter has reached its depths. Now it fades away.' Bantam had to steel himself for what he said next: 'As do you, sir. But . . . let me do what I can. The opiates I procured for our guest – they might bring you some comfort.'

Murdstone rose, propelled not by the strength of his body but the doggedness of his mind. 'I won't end my life in a fugue. I'm not ready yet.'

He was almost at the door when Bantam barked out, 'Your obstinacy will kill you.'

Murdstone dragged himself back to the hallway; for the first time, he could hear sobbing, sobbing coming from the chamber where Briggs sat with the beast. 'If it's obstinacy that has carried me this far, let me be obstinate a little further.' The older man had found some new vigour, but perhaps it would not last long; sometimes, in its last throes of life, the body won a momentary reprieve. 'Bantam, those places on his head, they always bore the echoes of horns. Since the wharf-side they've started budding once more. If what Briggs believes is true, might we coax him further? Better, perhaps, that he has the true look of the beast when we put him in his prison? What a spectacle that would make. What terror it would provoke. Yes, Bantam, terror would sell this thing. Men go to freak-shows for less. They watch tigers prowling in a cage. Imagine what they would pay for *this*.'

'If that's what you want, he would have to visit some evil upon us.'

Murdstone near thrilled at the prospect. 'But Elkington couldn't deny us then. To arrive at Amberstone House, and see the horned devil striding among us. His family's hoard would be open to us, were it so.' The sounds coming from beyond the door were brimming with emotion. Whispers, sobs, a man retching as if his body was rejecting some poison. 'I thought I'd have to sell a fraud. Piece him together from story and superstition, break him into the act of it like a horse. But I'm glad I'm to be no showman.' At last, he smiled. How long had it been since a smile graced his face? 'Listen to him, Doctor. He's on his way now.'

'On his way, sir?'

'Being hunted,' said Murdstone, 'through the labyrinth of his mind.'

*

'Wish me luck,' Sophia had said. 'The stars will align,' she'd proclaimed. But the star that shone in her was burning too fiercely, or so it seemed to Nell – as if it was masking some trepidation underneath – and throughout the afternoon, as they danced, she could not keep her mind from straying to the sound of that envelope tearing, and the ghostly look which had crossed Sophia's face as she took in the Parisian hand.

344

Sophia had gone with the twilight, off to answer her summons to the Alhambra Circus, and Nell with the same instructions of every evening ringing in her ears: to answer the door to no man, to brook nobody calling her name from Seven Dials below. If the instructions had, on nights past, seemed unnerving to Nell, they had always been eclipsed by the wonder of four walls, of food in her belly, a warming pan at her toes. On this night, however, she could not keep her eyes from straying to the kindling basket, the ghost of some voice calling out from the fragmented letter.

Betrayal came in many forms. Nell tried to ignore its calling as one hour bled into the next, but the night-time summoned devils and, with each passing bell, temptation grew. Sophia had given no explicit instruction to leave the shreds untouched, but there was still a feeling of deceit as Nell dirtied her fingers among the coals, fishing out each piece. It was certainly not as wicked as Noah robbing Minos of his boots, nor of Noah turning tattle-tail as they danced on Christmas night, but some element was surely the same. Or perhaps this was simply what being a civilized girl did to you: on the river she would have thought nothing of gathering up the scraps some other threw away; here, even the tiniest things could be a deceit.

But she wanted to know.

She needed it.

Her life here, scant days old, seemed like the ice that formed on the rock pools in winter: precarious and thin, to be shattered at the merest touch. If it wasn't going to last, she would know it; if, one day, she would have to be a rag-girl again, she would better do it forewarned. Lives changed and changed back again at the world's most mercurial whims.

From the river to Society and back to the tide; from the slums of Paris to the Opera Ballet, and back into destitution. Nobody knew the future, thought Nell, but if she could only *see* . . .

Sophia had done her best to destroy the letter, but she'd done so unopened and, consequently, portions of it remained in scraps of envelope, easier to stitch back into a whole. The edges she found, and laid out like a jigsaw puzzle she remembered sitting in front of the fire to complete with her mother. So far, she thought, so simple. But it was when she came to the heart of the letter that she stumbled. Perhaps she could piece this thing together by following the loops and curls of each severed word, but she would never be able to read it, never be able to understand what it was that made Sophia fear it so.

Of course, she should have known from the start: a letter coming from Paris was bound to be written in French.

It was a disconsolate Nell who painstakingly followed the fractures until the letter was whole again. Laid out in front of the fire, she traced each bludgeoned word – but, out of all of them, she recognized only one: 'Sophia', written in ornate script at the top. At the bottom, this word 'Georges' must have been a name as well – but what he wrote to her, why ten simple lines provoked such dread, Nell would never know.

A foot outside the door.

A key in the lock.

Nell burst upwards, like a rat startled from its hiding. So lost in the letter was she that she had not heard the tread on the stairs. Now she heard Sophia's voice – 'I'm back, dear Nell' – and the same panic of being apprehended on the riverside, Murdstone looming above, blossomed inside her. She grabbed the letter's scraps by the handful, tossed them into the fire – where smoke and hot air turned them to a fountain, and the papers burned bright before settling as ash.

The last scraps were still aflame when the door opened and Sophia whirled in. It seemed to Nell that she had been dancing ever since the Alhambra Circus – for, though the tails of her dresses were marked in snowmelt, she came into the room as if gliding on air. Of all the returns Nell had expected, none had been like this: before breathing a word, Sophia sailed around the room, plucking each of the drying ivory cards from their strings, and promptly depositing each in the fire. There, like the scraps of the letter she'd just condemned, they vanished into the chimneybreast in so many flurries of ash.

'Sophia, don't you need those –'

A finger touched Nell's lips, inviting her silence. 'Nella, my dear, there has been a change in circumstance.' She left Nell and continued to chart a path around the room, collecting more drying cards for the fire. 'I told you, did I not, how lives can change? Well, we are setting sail into great change now – and sooner than I had hoped. Have you heard, Nell, of the Neva Ballet?'

'Miss Chrétien, I saw them!' The thrill that gripped Nell was near as vivid as it had been on that winter night, Minos at her side at the back of the Circus. 'They were arriving at the Alhambra, ready for their first show. That was the night I . . .' *Sneaked inside*, she wanted to tell her. *Saw them in the lights.*

But before the words had left her lips, she saw the strange

347

look that had suddenly diminished Sophia. Though her eyes still brimmed with anticipation, they had narrowed in bewilderment as well – for there, lying in the hearth where she had been throwing the dirtied cards, was the scrap of a letter written in French, a letter she had not cared to read, a letter she had thought destroyed.

'Nell?' Sophia began.

She crouched down to lift the fragment. There it balanced on the tip of her finger, with that one word 'Georges' glaring out.

Her broken words:

'You read my letter.'

Did she say it with an air of accusation? Was it resignation, disappointment, or worse? Nell floundered as she said, 'I didn't. I – couldn't. I was frightened. Every night when you leave – *don't answer the door, if someone calls your name* – and the look, the look when I brought that letter. I've lived out there. I'm a Ratcliffe girl. The motherless mudlarks. I know what's out there. I know the desperate things they do. And I – I wanted to know.' Nell was trembling, trying above all things not to cry – but the feeling, now, was of the ice splintering beneath her, the frigid waters dragging her down. 'I'm sorry,' she breathed. 'I shouldn't have. But you've a secret and I wanted to know if I'm safe.'

How strange: she'd never thought of safety before. In Ratcliffe, you knew that you weren't, so you didn't let it prey on you. It was the illusion of sanctuary that had unsettled her most.

Sophia blew the last fragment from the tip of her finger, until it was caught by the fire. Then she said, with no little tenderness, 'I don't blame you, Nell. When I was a rag-girl,

I wouldn't have dreamed of something like this. But you're more fearless than I ever was. I should have seen that in you.'

'Will you send me away, Sophia?'

Nell had known she had to ask it. She was grateful when the words rushed out of her, more grateful still when Sophia shook her head and said, 'No, Nell. Not like this. The future is opening its doors, to you and I. And yet—'

'Then is it safe, Sophia? Are *you* safe?' Nell looked around her. 'If you were safe, you wouldn't be here. You already rose from your river. If you were safe, you'd be in Paris, dancing on the stage. The . . . Salle Le Peletier. So that means you ran away. You left everything behind and just ran.'

Sophia lifted her hand, splaying each finger to reveal the place where the fourth should have been. 'I left everything, Nell, so that I could begin again. My family, my friends, my livelihood. My—'

'Your . . . finger,' Nell breathed.

'It is a long story, Nell, and in the past. Tomorrow is the future. It's down *that* road we must walk. Never look back, little one. It will drag you under, like it does so many. They open their minds to what once was and get lost in it. It devours them. But Nell, the Neva Ballet is in great need. They approach the end of their run, yet sickness runs rampant through the Company. London, it seems, is a city of disease. Their principal, their dance master, too many of their corps de ballet – few of them are on their feet. I didn't think I would dance again. Damaged dancers are worth so little. But dance I shall – and, Nell, I am in sore need of an assistant.'

'Me?' Nell whispered.

Sophia touched her cheek.

'But the letter, Sophia. The knocks at the door. Don't

show yourself at the window, don't listen to my name . . . *Georges*,' Nell said, hoping she was saying it as she must. 'Who is he?'

There was a moment in which Nell feared Sophia wouldn't answer. Perhaps she had goaded her too far. Perhaps she would snatch back this offer just made.

But then Sophia stretched out her arm, to marvel at her butchered finger once again.

'Oh Nell,' she said, 'I forget what it's like to be a child. For all your worldliness, there are yet things you do not see.' She bowed down, braced Nell by the shoulders, and looked her in the eye. 'He was my fairy tale. He was my treasure. But he was my nightmare as well: my Bluebeard, my gaoler. One moment a man, one moment a monster.' She paused, if only to take a deep breath. 'He was my husband, Nell – until the night I set myself free.'

*

Darkness gathered over Amberstone House. Hours flickered by. But in that ill-lit room, in the recesses of that malformed mind, time had no meaning.

Onward he goes.

Left he turns.

Then right.

Each dream nestled inside another.

Men inside his memory, with memories of their own.

Men inside *those* memories, with yet more memories of their own.

Back Minos goes.

Back to the beginning . . .

*A heaving dock. The year of 1689. 'This one's got brawn,'
says a ship-hand, accompanying his captain through the crowd,
'if you can stomach the look of him. That's a face not even a
mother could love. But he'll be good with a harpoon in his
hand.' And he is. So good that he puts the other sailors to
shame. One of them comes for him in his cabin, meaning to
put an end to their humiliation. The only way they'll kill him
is to kill him in his sleep. It is their good fortune, not his, that
their plot is exposed before it can be carried out. Minos is
worth as much to this vessel as six common men; whatever
monstrosities he carries, a captain cannot argue with capital.*

'And what does that man remember, when he closes his
eyes at night? What does he dream, on those northern seas?'

*Shackled in chains, caged like a tiger, another dock in another
land. London, the year of 1582. Elizabeth Tudor sits upon the
throne. They tell him he is to be a gift for a queen, and he has
been dragged before queens before, so this he understands. Yet
they take him instead to the Tower, where beasts have been
imprisoned for centuries, dragged back from wherever England's
great explorers go. Lions strut boastfully along the parapets.
An African elephant sways sullenly in the shadows. He senses
their lonesomeness as he is deposited among them. 'I'm a man,'
he bawls at his keepers, but they only scoff, 'Half a man,
perhaps.' And they are right – for, in the metallic shine of the
bars which cage him, he can see his reflection. Distorted by the
bar's curve, it nonetheless reveals him for what he is. Men are
not shaped like this. Men do not have thick hides of fur running
from their neck and over their shoulders.*

'And that man,' said Briggs, 'he too must dream.'

'But is he a man?' whispered Minos.

'Even animals dream . . .'

Dream he does. In the year 1488, he has found solace in isolation: the goats he herds in the remote Genoan hillsides do not look at him any more suspiciously than they do every other man. So rarely does he venture into Genoa, he wonders if he will ever have to speak to man again. He might live out his days here, shepherding one generation of goats to the next – and that is all that he thinks of, until the day a messenger arrives from faraway Milan. 'I was told I'd find you in these hills. The goat man, they said – but, by His Holiness, I hadn't thought they meant it as literal. You have the look of your animals, sir.' He does; he cannot deny it. Even his head is shaped as if it once carried horns. 'I come with an invitation. My master, Bergonzio di Botta, has need of a man like you.'

'I never heard the name.' That voice hardly sounds like him; indeed, it hardly sounds like a voice at all.

'The dance master, sir?'

In reply, he only looks at his goats.

'A wedding is being arranged. My master is tasked with its celebration. He has need of a man like you. A man of,' and here he pauses, unsure whether his words will inspire intrigue or anger, 'a special appearance.'

'Appearance?'

'Well, sir.' He has brought little with him, but perhaps Minos should not be surprised that, of the few objects in his pack, there resides a hand mirror.

Into it he looks . . .

'And what do you see?'

On the other side of the door, Murdstone heard him lowing. He looked askance at Bantam, who hovered by his side. Elkington's footmen milled. Blades had been unsheathed.

Truncheons raised. 'I've seen stage illusionists,' said Murdstone. 'I've sat in seance parlours while mediums held forth that they were speaking with the dead. All just tricks. Sleights of hand and suggestion. A man might tell you anything in a trance.' His eyes were pulled back to the door, beyond which Minos had started speaking again. 'But the stories he spills, they're not ones Briggs is leading him into. It's not a trap. It's just . . .'

Like the river bursting its banks, he thought.

Like the walls of the Labyrinth, being pulled down.

'Stay with him, Minos. What does he do, the goatherd? Does he answer the calling?'

'He goes to the pageants – to stand mute and be fawned over, like he's part of the decorations.'

'And after that,' said Briggs, 'he lays down his head, he drifts into sleep, his dreams stir up times even earlier still . . .'

The year of 1228, there or thereabouts. News of the world hardly reaches him, living in this black forest as he does. But this year famine sweeps the land. Crops wither in fields. Mothers lead their least favourite children to the forests to abandon them there. And that is where the rumours of his devilry begin. 'There's a beast-man living in the forest,' they start saying. 'It's he who brings the blight.' So they come after him with pitchforks and spears, gangs of men heady with violence and hope. When they spring their ambush, he is not ready. But he is bigger than them, stronger than them. He screams the word 'No!', but they will not take no for an answer. Nor, it seems, will that piece of him that wants to fight back, that sees blood as his birth-right.

353

'There's blood,' said Minos, and on the other side of the doors Murdstone gripped his cane. 'Blood on my hands . . .'

He has killed two men before the voice gets the better of him. 'No,' it tells him, and that one word changes the world. He realizes what he has done and, exposed to the horror of it, flees into deeper wilds. Murderer, *they call him.* Monster. *And they are right – for, when he reaches the banks of some river and finds his reflection, it is to discover his face more bestial than it was the last time he saw it, the stubs of horns regrown on his head.*

His screaming echoes through the forests. They will speak of it for generations to come.

'Leave him there,' said Briggs, 'let him find sanctuary. Follow him to his woodland den. Tell me, Minos – what does *he* dream?'

Another cage. Another aeon. How far back, who can say? Only a single shackle holds him now; iron chains bind one leg to a stake driven into the earth. Through bars like a portcullis he can hear the roar of a crowd. It crashes over him like a wave.

Then, a figure appears at his side. A boy has scuttled in from some hidden door. Deftly, he unfastens the chains, then vanishes through the same portal that disgorged him.

The portcullis starts rising. He shambles forward, into the light.

Now he stands in the heart of some dusty expanse, with galleries surrounding every side: a colosseum – the Colosseum, *he remembers – with its every seat swarmed. At his appearance, their cries grow more frenzied yet. A sound like this is surely herald to the end of the world.*

Then it grows louder.

On the other side of the arena, a second portcullis is rising. Out of it bursts a chariot, two blinkered horses heaving a carriage of bronze and gold. The chariot describes an arc around him. He turns on the spot, following its path. And, because he is so focused on the two gladiators who leap from the carriage, he hardly notices the multitude of other gates rising around the arena's periphery. It is only by the fervour of the crowd that he understands ten, twenty, thirty will be ranged against him.

So there is blood, and there is shattered bone. Their ropes will not bind him. Their blades, though they pierce his flesh, will not puncture his heart. Some work in teams, but teams are easily sundered. Others die heroes' deaths, to the ecstasy of those who look on. And it is as he grinds one into the earth, where already the sand has turned into a crimson mire, that he sees his own face staring back at him, from the silver of the dead man's shield.

It is an animal's face.

It is heavy with horns.

In the bedchamber, Minos lifted himself. He opened his eyes. 'I don't want to stay,' he writhed. 'I want to be – *me* . . .'

'Oh, but this is you, Minos. You're getting to the centre of it now. Wending your way to the heart of who you are. Tell me, what is he thinking, in the heat of the Colosseum? As he stands there, taking another gladiator's life? What does he feel?'

'He's frightened,' shook Minos. '*I'm* frightened.'

'Yes, yes, and—'

'There's another one coming for him now.'

He sweeps around to face him. This one is bigger than any. In his hands, a two-headed axe: the labrys, Minos thinks; yes, he's seen this before. He's seen the look on the man's face

355

*as well: the look of triumph and disaster, of worship and fear.
'I've come to stop this,' he says as he sweeps the axe down.*

'He's heard those words before, hasn't he?'

'I don't know,' Minos gasped.

'Yes, you do, sir; yes, you do. That's the reason you're afraid. That's what you were thinking, as you faced him in the Colosseum. That's what made you pause and—'

The axe cleaves into him, reaching deeper than bone. The howl of his agony incites the crowd to further riot. Somewhere up above, an emperor is lifting his thumb in the air: his instruction for a death.

'What is he thinking?' Briggs demanded, more insistent now. 'Those words, that face – they sent him spiralling back in time. They opened some memory. The gladiator reminded him of something, did it not? Of *someone.*'

'Yes,' said Minos, with a breathless agony, 'yes.'

'Who?'

Silence. Outside the door, Murdstone bowed his head. In the chamber, Briggs reached out, as if to pluck some unspoken idea from the air.

'Theseus,' said Minos.

He opened his eyes.

21

Bolder by Night

'It doesn't take much, Nell, for a dream to turn sour.'

The fire burned low in the St Giles garret. Nell's slippers were arranged by the hearth. Across them, another tale was being spun: not nearly as ancient as those Minos used to spin for her, but just as ghostly all the same.

'The wealthy are different, Nell, in different parts of the world. They satisfy themselves or build their hoards in so many different ways. But the poor? The poor are the same, the whole world over. They're hungry and they're houseless. They're pockmarked with disease. They're broken by labours no mortal man should suffer. And wherever they live they have the very same desire, buried in their hearts: that, one day, by God-given fortune or the toils of their own hands, they won't live in the same destitution to which they were born.' Sophia paused. 'And that was me, once upon a time. That was my parents. Born and raised in that whirlpool, without a moment to profit or dream for the time they spent keeping warm, the hours they spent putting food in their bellies.

'Until I was born, and they spied a way out.'

'The ballet,' Nell whispered.

'There were men who scoured the city for dancers like me. Young girls, to train – just as young men got swept up to be soldiers. I am not too proud to think they chose me for my talent. I learned, later, that what they were looking for were good, pliant girls – girls who might either glide across the stage, or else fill the foyer on those nights when the *abonnés* came round. The *abonnés*, Nell – the patrons of the Opera, the men who keep its fortunes alive. There was a need for girls who might light up the stage, but there was greater need for girls who might light up when the *abonnés* came round. Do I need to explain myself further?'

Nell shook her head. She was ten years old; she knew that there were different ways men forced women to dance.

'But me? I soared above the girls with whom I was instructed. I didn't need one of the *abonnés* taking a shine to me, just so that I could be gifted a contract. I wasn't long one of the *petits rats*. No, Nell, I won my part in the corps by talent alone. So, while the other girls peopled the foyer and the patrons crawled around them, I was being garlanded on the stage. I was being written about. Painted. Admired. I needed to be no man's mistress. And if, one day, I chose to take a suitor, it would be because I wanted it, not because some man's eye had lit upon me in the foyer, and a promise had been made to the Opera in return for my hand.

'And then . . .'

'Georges,' Nell said.

'A gentleman,' said Sophia. 'Descended – though none might say it, in France – from an old line of kings. A man as different, or so I thought, to the rest of the *abonnés* as the sun from the Earth. A refined man; an equestrian, an antiquarian, a man of the theatres and courts. Georges was not like the others. He did not keep mistresses at the Salle Le Peletier. But then he saw me dance in *La Gypsy*. He saw me sail through *La Sylphide*. And, in want of a wife as he was, he let it be known that he should like to meet.

'Well, Nell, I had already seen the way girls were swallowed up by the *abonnés*. Their value to the Opera is in how happy those men might be kept. But there was something different about Georges. Something *more*. So I went on walks with him – along our own river – and I accompanied him to the theatres, where I was to see how others spent their lives on a stage. And, after we had spent many such evenings together, and Georges had listened, as a certain man will, to the challenges I faced with my pointe-work – which, Nell, is when you stand just *so* –' and she left the hearthside momentarily, to rise sylph-like onto the tips of her toes, '– I discovered that he had paid a visit to my parents, to ask for my hand in marriage. And because things felt as if they could not go wrong in my life – because I had risen so successfully from the whirlpool that takes girls like me under – I married him. Suddenly, my family lived in comfort. My father, who was old before his time, could rest. My mother, whose doggedness had seen us through life, was indulged.' Sophia flexed the stump of her finger again. 'And I thought the story of my life would be without twist and turn. That I would dance until I could dance no longer, and then retire to raise a family who would never know the squalor to which I was born.

'But everything changes, Nell. And men reveal themselves once they have what they want . . .'

Nell shuddered at the telling; she had known one such man in her life. But there were others, weren't there? Gentle men, timid men; men who brought you food in the depths of winter and danced with you on the riverside, caring not for what the passing rivermen might see. If wickedness existed, then kindness did too. That was the thought she clung onto as Sophia continued.

'What happened, Sophia?'

'It is an ordinary story, dear Nell. They do not spin ballet out of stories like this. Georges believed he had given me the world. But, because he was a man who got what he wanted in life, it did not occur to him that, once what he wanted had changed, the world might not change with him. That, when he had married his ballerina – and decided, after all, that what he wanted was somebody who did not take to the stage every evening, somebody who did not receive bouquets from admirers, somebody whom others might have adored – he could not simply remake her as he saw fit. Because what was I without dancing? *Who* was I, if he took that from me? There are certain men, Nell, who demand that the world bends to them.'

'So you ran away?'

'Too many times, dear Nell. Took off my wedding band and left it on the armoire for him to discover when he came home from his soirees.' She stroked her savaged hand again, and a shudder ran through Nell – for her imagination was a bloody kaleidoscope, imagining how this man must have wrested her finger away. 'I went to stay with my mother and father, but of course they lived at Georges' indulgence – so

360

my husband came to fetch me back. I ran to a cousin, and stayed there some weeks – but a carriage came to take me home. He sent his footmen to the theatres where I worked. His bouquets arrived on the eve of each performance, so that the world thought him my hero; and yet, bit by bit, that grand home in Versailles was becoming my prison. Five, six, seven times, I tried to leave. Five, six, seven times, I found myself brought back. Concessions were made: I might dance for one season more; I might dance in Paris, but never travel to Rome; I might dance, but dance only – never share a celebration with the corps de ballet after our evening was done; never take dinner with the directors and instructors. And eventually, Nell: I might dance, but only when he was watching.'

Nell had thought there was only courage in Sophia, but at this last recollection her voice caught in her throat – and Nell understood there had been fear and anger here all along. And the moment she saw this, she was back outside the Alhambra with Minos; or she was in the seaward cave, that time Murdstone tried to tell him he was *his*. It bristled inside Minos too, didn't it? Just beneath the surface. This anger. This fire. He'd shown Nell nothing but gentleness and timidity, but the fire was there too.

Maybe it was there in everyone. It was there in Murdstone, whose silent furies had always pockmarked her days. And perhaps, Nell thought, it was in her as well. Hadn't it burst out of her when she cast that silver chain back into the river? Wasn't there a storm inside her too that might one day be unleashed?

'You can't own someone,' Nell whispered.

'There are men who try.' When Sophia wiped her eye, a

tear beaded on the stump of her missing finger. 'You cannot wear a wedding ring when you dance the ballet, Nell. It is an adornment of the world beyond the stage. So every night, I would leave my wedding band on the armoire by our bedside – and every night, when I came home, he would make a show of placing it upon my finger. As they say in London: *with this ring, I thee wed.*' Sophia mimed it for Nell; there was a thrill to its pantomime, but there was some frisson of horror too. The way Sophia put the ring on her finger, it might have been ropes around her wrists. And this made her think of Minos too. How was it that all thoughts looped back there?

She thought of the way the ropes had torn when he strained against them, and some terrible notion struck her. There was more than one way to break free. 'Your finger, Sophia!'

'Oh, Nell,' said Sophia, sensing this new trepidation, 'it is not so fearful as it sounds. But it came to me with the clarity of the northern stars. Because every time I tried to leave and was summoned back, every time I returned from the stage and he led me to the armoire, it was the ring on my finger that renewed his hold on me. That ring didn't just tell the world that I was his, that – quite without knowing it – I had forfeited the right to be my own. It told *him* the very same thing. I could not stop him from sliding it back over my finger. Not unless –'

'Oh, Sophia. You did it to yourself.'

Nell could almost hear the sickening crunch. She could feel the rush of revulsion that Sophia must have felt. The hot blossoming of pain. And yet, for some reason she could not fathom, she could not tear her eyes from the place where the finger had once been. Sophia was still speaking – 'and left it there, on the armoire, for him to find, so there could never be a shackle to hold me again' – but Nell hardly heard. Because Nell was thinking of escape. Of what it meant to change a life.

'Sophia, the letter . . .' She stalled. 'He wants you to return?'

'I told you when I ripped that letter apart, dear heart: we get to choose which missives we read. I'm beyond Georges now. I don't have to listen to his orders. The ties that bound us are gone.' Sophia touched Nell's hand, the stump of her finger coming to rest on her palm. 'All of this is finished. That's why I destroyed that letter. Because, if you let it, the past will come back to devour you. Better, sweet girl, that it stays where it can't touch us. The past is like a cancer, Nell. It corrupts. It lances us with its claws and tries to drag us back. But you and I are going to live here, right here and now, in our own beautiful lives. In the morning, you will accompany me to the Alhambra – and I shall introduce you to the magic of *Giselle*, and the Wills. And as for the past? Well, let it stay buried. It can't hurt us, unless we set it free.'

'*Theseus.*'

Even as the word left his lips, the moment crystallized in Minos's mind. Its edges hardened; its sounds, scents, textures grew distinct. He saw the prince's face contort. Felt the bite of the sword in his side. Around his head erupted a chaos of crying as, steadfast until now, a dozen Athenians scattered into the Forever Dark. He could feel the warm cascade of blood matting the fur on his shoulder – but, most of all, he could feel the rampant hunger, the desperate yearning which had been suppressed within him for so long. He let out a cry, and in the bedchamber the candle guttered into blackness.

'St-stay with the moment,' Briggs was stammering.

Minos sensed movement in the room; the scholar was trying to relight the candle, but his hands kept fumbling the match. '*No*,' he said. '*No*,' and '*No*' again.

'You've reached it, Minos. You're in the heart of the Labyrinth.' A match flared, but it did not last long; Briggs cursed when the flame reached his fingers, then cast it aside and fumbled for another.

'The story,' said Minos, and the shifting air in the room told Briggs that he was rising, 'you're the one spinning it, spinning it in my mind. It isn't real. It can't be real. You're the one who put me there.'

'Oh no, Minos. Your mother put you there. Your step-father, the Cretan king. Daedalus built it to keep you. But, by God, you couldn't be kept.' Another match was struck. In its light, Briggs saw Minos up close. The darkness had cloaked his movement; now his face was but inches from Briggs's own. Up close, every knot and ridge was clear. How had untold generations ever mistaken those eyes for the eyes of a man? 'Tell me how it happened. Tell me how Theseus left you for dead.'

'*No*,' gasped Minos.

'How you woke and followed Ariadne's string.'

'*No*,' he gasped again.

'What was it like, to feel the first breath of day? Where did you go, sir? What did you see?' He stopped. Some compulsion he would never understand – for, though he did not know it, these were the last few seconds of his life, tumbling past – told him to reach up and finger the man's hair, searching for the place where the horns which had gored so many had started bursting forth. 'Or did you not have the capacity to think, back when you sported true horns upon this head? Were you animal in mind as well as body? Just fear and hunger and brute instinct? One wonders,' he marvelled, 'at what point a Minotaur becomes a man.'

'*NO!*' Minos thundered.

Scant hours ago, Briggs had warned Benjamin Murdstone against the dangers of hubris. The greatest artificer in antiquity had failed to imprison this beast. The promises of monsters were worth less than those from lawyers and fools. And yet, here he stood rapt, even as Minos's breath enveloped him, even as Minos – unable to bear these thoughts, nor to listen any longer – brought back his hand and swatted him aside.

Even as he flew backwards to crash against the marble hearth.

The body of a Minotaur might recover from daggers and swords, but the body of a man is a more fragile thing. Bones stay broken. Lungs rupture and burst.

Lycias and Anthylla. Antias and Eunice. The children of Celeus. All his countless victims, from the Labyrinth to London. Now there would be another name to add to the chronicle.

It was, Briggs decided as he tasted blood on his lips, a most fitting end.

Outside the door, Murdstone shrieked for the footmen to approach. They too had heard that single word tolling, '*No – no – NO!*', until at last it was accompanied by the crashing of flesh against stone. That Murdstone had to bellow for them at all betrayed the fear bred into them on the wharf-side. They turned, hands hovering over their weapons – but that was all. So slow were they in reaching the door that it was Murdstone whose fist closed over the handle; Murdstone who was wrenched off-balance when the door opened up, revealing Minos standing stricken in the ailing light.

Briggs sprawled across the hearth behind him, blood frothing at his lips.

'Sir,' Murdstone ventured. *'Sir!'*

Minos drew back his hand, as if he might scythe his way through Murdstone as well. Then he stopped. To Murdstone's eye, he seemed to be staring straight through him – not to the footmen (who, woken from their torpor, were brandishing weapons at last), but to some distance beyond: through timber and brick; through night and day; through what was real and what was imagined.

Murdstone looked for some sign of horns breaking through flesh, of the haggardness of the beast returning to the man's body. So far, he could see nothing. But there was animal here, of that he was certain; animal in Minos's darting eyes.

'Let me through.' Bantam's voice punctured the silence. Only he had the spirit to step towards the beast. 'He needs me,' he declared, then snapped his fingers in front of Minos's eyes, demanding attention. 'What have you done to him, sir? *Let me through.*'

That look in Minos's eyes, it was as much fear as fury. Bantam took advantage of his momentary hesitation to contort past. There, in the bedchamber, he dropped at

Briggs's side. If the man had any breath left in him, it was his last. As his eyes sought Bantam out, they flickered for the final time. 'He's dead. The scholar's dead. Minos, why —'

Minos wheeled around, as if taking in the room for the first time. 'No,' he whispered.

'Sir, we must talk!' Murdstone seethed. *'Sir!'* He had meant for Minos to sink back into the room, to retreat into some corner like a scolded child while the footmen rolled through – but instead he stepped forward, barrelling Murdstone back into the hallway. Arrayed around him, the footmen lifted their weapons.

'What have you done?'

Bantam's voice seemed suddenly small and far away – for, as Murdstone picked himself up from the wall, the footmen started barking orders. 'Stay where you are!' one demanded. 'Not one more step!' came another. But if Minos heard a word, he paid it no mind. Striding forward, his great hands braced the walls. An old painting, oil on canvas, fell from its hook to be trampled at his feet. *'Sir!'* Murdstone exclaimed, but Minos did not stop. 'Where are you going? We can talk. We can still talk —'

'Talk?' breathed Bantam, somewhere behind. 'Talk? But this is what you wanted, isn't it, Benjamin? To drive him to it. To coax him out.' He gave his own mournful howl. 'There were better ways, sir – better ways!'

'Bantam, you fool, did I teach you nothing? You don't command the tide. You simply sail with it. And here he is, Bantam, right here . . .'

The footmen were falling back with each stride Minos took; the wall they made, of truncheons and knives, was no wall at all – just another tide, retreating at his advance.

'Put your weapons down!' Bantam called out, lifting himself from the body to return to the hall. 'By God, put them down, before it's a massacre!'

He had to say it again before the footmen acknowledged him. Even then, something compelled them to resist. They held to their weapons faster; each tightened against another's shoulder, blocking the hallway ahead. It wasn't until Bantam screamed it a third time, rupturing some blood vessel in his own throat, that his words penetrated their fear. Truncheons clattered to the floor. A blade went back into its sheath. The footmen fanned out, pressed themselves to the walls, palms open and petitioning peace.

The look Murdstone gave Bantam was a gorgon's stare. 'Don't fail me now,' he seethed, then turned to plead with the stumbling giant. 'Minos,' he began, faltering in his footsteps, 'Minos, stop. I can help you.' He stressed the last words, because here, he was certain, lay the answer. 'Let me help you. It's what we're here for. It's what I do.'

For the first time, Minos turned over his shoulder.

'You? Help . . . me?'

There was doubt in those words. There was suspicion. Murdstone could hear both things simmering just under the surface. But he was not mistaken: there was some element of hope as well. The past was rushing out to consume Minos; all he needed was a buoy. A drowning man does not care whether an angel or devil casts him a rope.

'It's part of our trade, sir,' Murdstone ventured, more tenderly now. 'I wouldn't leave you in want. What happened in there was misfortune, that's all. Briggs was a disgraced scholar – he scarcely had the intellect to know what he was doing. I can see that. Others will too. Minos, we're one in this endeav–'

Too late, Murdstone saw what was about to happen. He'd taken his chance to win the monster's confidence; one of the footmen took his chance too. That sibilant whisper was the sound of his blade being unsheathed. But this time there was no hesitation, no warning, no threat. He brandished the blade with two hands, driving it up and under Minos's arm, metal screeching against bone as it sheared off his ribs.

Minos's howl lit up Amberstone House. Bantam rushed back to the horror of Briggs's body. Murdstone cowered from the thunder unleashed. Along the hall, the other footmen took flight. They did not see Minos as he reached around, grappling with the man who attacked him. Only Murdstone watched as Minos barrelled him against the wall – where at once his back was broken, where the gore of his shattered face discoloured the hanging portraits, where the sword he'd thought would make him a hero clattered onto a body blooded and broken, never to be held in loving arms again.

'I can help you,' Mr Murdstone had said.

But no: there was only one person who could help Minos now.

He started to run.

The blade is inside him. Its tip touches bone. His whole body is on fire, and the god above him leaning down. All of his life is flashing before him now, just as it will flash before him many thousands of years into the future: a coruscating cascade of everything he has ever been and everything he has ever done.

Did I deserve this?

Did I deserve this, just for being born?

'Come away from him,' said Murdstone. 'There's no saving him now.'

The smell of gore, so potent and ripe. A body comprised of unnatural angles. Mis-hung portraits, in oils and blood. Bantam did not weep over the patients of Seven Dials, and he would not weep for Briggs – the only one among them to truly know the hell into which they were wading – but he brimmed with feeling for the footman in the hallway. He arranged his arms, his legs, tried to make some sense of a body treated like kindling. Behind every body lay a life. 'You wanted it,' he said, and (though it could never be so) he felt the fury rising in him, just as it had done in Minos. Over his shoulder he turned. 'Benjamin, you bloody fool. It's what you wanted!' He stopped. 'Say something. You stand there like it's on *his* hands. Well, it isn't – it's on yours.' His voice cracked. He closed the man's eyes. 'It's on ours.'

'I didn't want death,' Murdstone breathed, lost in some labyrinthine thought. 'They'll call him a murderer now. Send thief-takers to bring him in. Briggs would have told us: they've done it before. But it didn't end well for them back then, and this century's no different.' He stopped. 'They'll hang him, but he won't be hanged.'

'Then what?' snapped Bantam.

Murdstone was still.

'*Then what?*'

370

'I must think, you dog.' He limped along the hallway, back to where the broken Briggs lay. 'Newgate wouldn't hold him. The colonies, perhaps. But he wouldn't let them take him.' He took a guttering breath. 'I wanted the beast out of him. I didn't want them dead. You must see that, Bantam. It presents more problem than opportunity. I have always been a careful man.'

Sometimes, a man says something so unlikely it seems he is standing in some shadowy, second world. Two men are speaking, but neither one with the other. *Problem?* thought Bantam. *Opportunity? Careful?*

'I'm finished with you, Murdstone.' He drew himself up, marched past his old master and collected his clasp bag from Briggs's side. 'There's no geas on me any longer. My debt to you is done, a hundred times over. I'm grateful you lifted me from the streets, sir, but I won't hang for you. I didn't counsel this.' He had been marching back, but hovered now over the footman's corpse. 'There was another way. There had to be. Minos came to you. You could have made this happen.'

'I still can.'

But Bantam was marching away.

'*I still can!*' Murdstone roared. He heaved himself after Bantam, each breath growing more ragged as he reached the top of the manor house stairs. 'Stop right there,' he wheezed. 'You don't walk away from me, sir. You're in the thick of this. You're here, in the Labyrinth with me. We either come through and live out the rest of our years as lords, or we hang together. There is no middle road, Bantam. The gutter, or the stars. My side, right now – or the noose.'

Bantam was already halfway down the stairs. At this last,

he turned. The fury had been rising in him above, but the flames were suddenly doused; now all he felt was an empty, preternatural calm.

And he thought he understood, then, why it was that Minos, lost in his fugue, had reached for that one little word.

'No,' he said, and turned to march on.

The night was vast. The skies empty and full of stars. Minos was a league from Amberstone, in the scrub country beneath the downs, before he dared to look back. The coach track, turned to a mire by the snowmelt, bore the deep depressions of his tracks. They could follow him, then, just like he'd followed that length of string. But so far he had not sensed the stampede of horses, nor heard the calling of his name. Even so, he dared not close his eyes, for every time that he did *he saw him coming, Theseus and his blade.* Or he was being *wrestled from his bedcovers in the fortress of Knossos, bound in ropes, dragged down to the open Labyrinth door.* He found shelter in the lee of the trees that bordered the track. The place beneath his arm was raging with heat, the wound already begrimed in dirt. There was yet snow between the tree roots, and this he packed onto the lesion.

But the pain in his breast was eclipsed by the burning in his skull. He reached up, to finger those calcified places under his hair, and was certain – though how much could fear change a man's perception? – that they were more protuberant yet.

His fingers drew back, sticky with blood. Something was cresting the surface, breaking through all that had held it in: just like memory.

The hair on the back of his hand, beaded in crimson.

Funny, he thought, he'd never had hair there before, not coarse like that.

In truth, you would call it *fur*.

Just a dream, he told himself. Just a fever. The wildness of the night.

But of course he knew.

The wildness wasn't out there at all.

It was rushing directly out of his heart: all the thousands of years of his history, clamouring to make themselves heard.

*

So there it stood: the Alhambra Circus.

Nell reached the heart of the square, not yet ten minutes from the rookery where she'd awoken, and stared at its towers and great white dome. If it looked more ordinary by day than it had against the black of night, when its lights spilled out and its heart hummed with soft music, that did nothing to diminish her wonder as, hand folded inside Sophia's, she made the approach. The first hours of morning had been spent in preparation – which, Nell discovered, had meant yet more grooming; words like 'deportment' and 'grace' meant nothing to Nell, but they were of great significance to Sophia – but at least that meant she was near unrecognizable as the rag-girl who'd stolen inside on that wild December night. She did not suppose she would feel as if she *belonged* here, even trailing from Sophia's arm, but at least she would not be harried out by zealous ushers. Then she could take in the wonder without any fear.

The man who greeted them had little time for Nell, because every reserve of obsequiousness he had was spent in fawning over Sophia; Nell thought she would not have betrayed such emotion even had her mother been summoned back from the dead. As the man led them deeper into the palace, he seemed to be both congratulating Sophia on her appointment and eulogizing the Alhambra's good luck. 'Because this run might have been forfeit without you. And closing nights, as you know, are the ones that last longest in memory. Our patrons might have deserted us in droves!' He smiled, folding his hands. 'Until, of course, it was recalled that, some weeks ago, a lady of some inestimable pedigree came to petition at our doors. A garlanded baller-ina, teaching Society dances from her garret in St Giles? My directors had just cause to believe it a ruse – quite an uncommon one, granted, but there is more deviousness in Seven Dials than in the halls of Westminster, madam, and perhaps they can be forgiven for seeing a fraud where there was only . . .' He bowed so deeply Nell thought he would topple onto his head. 'Majesty,' he declared.

Flattery did not seem to wreathe its magic around Sophia, but perhaps flattery was an art that held no power over those with real talent.

'I was grateful to receive your letter. And the Company are prepared?'

'The Neva's pride has been dented, but they are consum-mate show-people; they know that reputations are at stake. Understudies may take prime roles, but what of the roles they then vacate, when there are none to follow? I'm afraid they have found London a midden this winter. Three of the corps didn't make it to opening night, and since then . . .'

He mimed as if bubbles were bursting all around his head. 'A lady of your pedigree must, of course, be able to slide into any role. But at such short notice, with no knowledge of the Company itself? You have your detractors in the Company, madam. But M. Kolpakova said he had seen you in *La Sylphide* – and that, if this was truly a chance, they should grasp it as a dying man does the hand of his lover.'

'Three nights left,' said Sophia, 'and the next performance nigh.'

Nell skipped between them, desperate to keep up.

'With princes and lords in our auditorium – though none may yet know it.'

Sophia nodded. 'They shall have the spectacle they came for.'

Sophia was getting ahead again. Nell hurried in her wake. Soon, they had reached the end of a long hall – and the man who had greeted them was opening a door, then standing back to permit Sophia to float through. Nell faltered before following; these next steps were surely not for her. But then Sophia looked back, and the weight of expectation drew Nell towards her, as forceful as gravity.

Together they emerged onto the empty Alhambra stage.

Nell had seen it from above, but how much more cavernous was it from below, with every seat and stall empty? She felt as tiny as a star in the night. Galleried walls rose up on every side. A piano sat, mute, in the wings of the stage. Oil lanterns spilled pools of light and shadows that shimmered.

'The Company are waiting,' their companion began. 'Let me bring them to you now.'

After he was gone, Nell watched Sophia step lightly around the edge of the stage, as if to mark it with the points of her toes. As for Nell herself, she did not dare venture into the stage's empty heart – not until Sophia beckoned her onward. It was safer, somehow, to remain in the shadows. That was where a rag-girl belonged.

'I want you to listen carefully, Nell, and hold on to all that I say. Close your eyes, little one. Picture it if you can.'

Nell did as she was told. Somehow, she could still feel the vastness of the auditorium in whose centre she now blindly stood. The feeling of falling came over her, as if she was falling into the story – but here was Sophia, with her arms open wide, ready to catch her.

'The music strikes up. The curtains draw back. Imagine, Nell, a poor peasant girl – destined for a life in the vine-yards: a simple life, *the* simple life. The gamekeeper's lad is in love with her. She ought to marry him and be happy. But then –'

Sophia had fallen silent, so Nell said, 'Then what?'

'Then along comes another. He's worldly. He's wise. He's a peasant boy too – or says he is, because none really knows that he's a nobleman already betrothed to another. But men, Nell, men are either foolish or wicked – and there's nothing that makes a man more foolish or wicked than when he decides he's in *love.*'

Nell opened her eyes. In an instant, the spell Sophia was weaving was broken.

'What is it, Nell?'

She had thought, for a moment, that Sophia was spinning her own story again – but, of course, it was not so. She shook her head, inviting Sophia to go on.

'He woos our peasant girl. He courts and cajoles her. And bit by bit, though her mother pleads with her not to, though the gamekeeper's honest son would make her a better life, she falls for our nobleman too.

'Oh, but I have already told you: men, Nell, men reveal themselves once they have what they want – and when she discovers she's been deceived, that her lover isn't truly who he says he is, the grief of it destroys her. She dances, Nell. But it's wild dance. It's disordered dance. It's unstoppable dance. She dances until her heart gives in. Dances until she dies.'

'But Sophia, that's terrible –'

'Oh, but Nell, this is *ballet*, and she isn't finished yet. Close your eyes again. Picture it, now. Here come the Wills . . .'

'The Wills?'

'The spirits of maidens deceived and betrayed. The echoes of lovers who died with hearts broken. They've come to take our girl into their number. To make Giselle one of them. They'll scour the land, Nell, to exact their revenge. And any man who chances across them – well, he'll perish like poor Giselle perished, with his feet worn down to stumps, his mind cracked open by endless dance.'

Nell basked in silence, as the story tied its knots around her. 'But isn't it sad?' she finally asked.

'It's ballet,' Sophia replied, and in her tone was all the wonder of the occasion, all the promise of the future for which she'd been waiting. 'It's sad *and* beautiful, and that's precisely the point.'

At once, the sound of applause could be heard in the wings of the stage. Nell startled around, losing her purchase

377

on the boards – but Sophia held her fast as she rose to meet the newcomers.

A host of faces were gliding across the stage, the man who'd first greeted them leading the way. If he had meant to make an introduction, it quickly transpired that his services were not needed. A rake-thin gentleman, with hair as pale as his complexion, detached himself from the dancers and bowed to Sophia. 'They send us an angel,' he began, to laughter from the dancers behind. Whether it was nervous laughter, or hiding some secret aggrievement, Nell could not say. The faces she was staring into were of glacial and uniform beauty. She tried to bring them to mind, as they'd fanned out with such elegant precision across the boards where she was now standing – but seeing them up close was so different from how it had been from on high. She was not sure which was real and which was fantasy, up close or far away.

'So, then,' Sophia began, and Nell was quite sure she detected some frisson of nervousness in her for the very first time. The dancers gathered round; Sophia's arms made a cage around Nell; the Alhambra attendant seemed to be whispering prayers, as if to ward off some prophesied disaster. 'Giselle. The Wills. I have not seen your performance, though I *have* seen you, each and every one, when you danced in Paris last season. It is not right what has happened to you this journey . . . but since when did things ever go right on the stage? We have, all of us, been dancing to disaster.' Something had changed in her voice; at last, Nell detected the revival of ambition, triumph, hope. 'I should be honoured to do what I can, so that Giselle can dance tomorrow night. But time is against us. The hours are in short supply. We must, I believe, begin.'

Voices exploded, chattering in a language Nell did not understand; there was laughter and cheer – and, if there was some suspicion among the congregation of the Neva Ballet, it had evaporated by the time Sophia parted her arms, revealing Nell to the throng, and announced, 'My assistant, Miss Hart. You're to treat her as your own, until the music begins.'

Then the dancers were appraising her as well, venturing smiles, ostentatious bows, their gaze like the limelights that Nell had seen picking each of them out as they danced upon this very stage.

It was a feeling like drowning. Nell wasn't sure where to turn.

'But Sophia, what must I do?' she whispered

Sophia touched her cheek. 'Serve the Company,' she said. 'Serve – and *observe.*'

*

A coachman could not drive his horses by night, but it was nothing for a lone wayfarer to pick his way through the long winter dark – and for a wayfarer beset by bad dreams, it was easier still. Every time he lay down in some hollow, those dreams returned; every time, he clawed his way up, out of the Palace in his mind, to find the night cold and vast, and willing him onward. Sleep was no refuge – not for Minos, not tonight. So instead he opted for the impossible: to outrun nightmare, to leave memory in his wake. By dawn he was staggering past the coaching inn where

Murdstone had secreted him in a stable; by full light, following the low road under the downs. Midday was grey as the river as he watched the carriage carrying Murdstone rattling past, and lifted himself from the ditch where he'd been hiding to watch it fade into the north. The farm roads were safer, but no road was safe now – for, where Murdstone went, his story travelled. Two men dead and a Minotaur risen. No, Minos thought, he didn't need to sleep to find himself in a nightmare. Every piece of him had awoken now.

'I've come to stop this.'

The downs were busier by day. Other wayfarers ploughed the same roads; a farmhand drove pigs along the same tracks. The river Minos followed had swollen until it burst its banks, and consequently the trails on either side were heavy with water. Too often, he caught his reflection in the swirling silt. The blood in his hair came from no wound the footmen had inflicted; the new sharpness of his skull, like spurs of bone being born from the flesh. When he looked at himself too long, fresh memories stirred – *'He has horns, Ariadne. He's growing horns'* – but always that sword stayed in his side, and always the voice of that preening god.

He was bolder by night. Driven into the open – for the hedgebacks only tempted him to sleep – he shambled along the byways and bridle-paths, around the edgelands of hamlets and farms. Sometimes, the voices he was running from flurried up from the dreams he refused to sink into. From their depths came a mother sobbing, and a courtier's solid tones: *'Your heart may tell you he's your son, but tell me, my queen, what is the evidence of your own eyes?*' Or the muted whispers of guards just chanced upon a stable-hand covered in the gore of one of his geldings: '*Goats aren't enough any more. It will be the stable-boy next. Mark my words: something must be done about Pasiphae's bastard.*' Forty-eight hours' sleeplessness only made the veil that separated dreams from the waking world more porous – but to give in to sleep was to give in entirely.

So onward he went.

Left he turned; then right.

Forward he ploughed; then back.

It was strange how the whole of his History devolved down to the few inches in front of his face, the ability to put one foot in front of another. But it was by putting one foot in front of another that Minos chronicled another night in the long history of his life – until, when dawn finally descended, he could see the smog of industry blighting the horizon, the tell-tale serrations of a city coming into view. So unlike the cities he had known, he realized now. Carthage and Athens; Byzantium and Rome. London: the last great city in the world.

Distances were deceptive. The day was paling again by the time Minos reached the rookery of St Giles. He was grateful for the twilight, and for the rain laying siege to the city; both cloaked him as he picked his way to the narrow black door.

He hadn't expected Nell to answer, for the ballerina had surely not taken a lease on the entire building, but he had hoped somebody would bring her: disturb her from her dancing, announce his name and startle her out of this new dream she was living. The workman who answered was

381

disgruntled to be treated as 'that dancing tart's butler', but when Minos pushed his face forward and intoned the words, *'Bring – her – to – me'*, he vanished quickly enough. Now he stood alone, London beating at his back, the blood pounding through his veins. Of all the things he'd expected, it hadn't been that he would be nervous. And yet every piece of him was a-shiver – for wasn't there a chance she'd shrink from seeing him? His Nell of the river, who'd led him from dreams? He needed her to help him again, but he'd already absolved her of the duty. Seeing him would be like seeing Benjamin Murdstone: a hand beckoning to her future from her past.

'She doesn't love you, you know.' That voice did not come from the street. Nor was it speaking of Nell, though surely it was his need for her that had brought it to mind. He tried to shake it away, but the voice only persisted – and, when he closed his eyes, he could see the scene vividly as well: an atrium bordered by colonnades of white stone, and a little girl looking at him from a balcony above. *'How could she? You're the one that ruined her, so she can hardly even love* us, *and we're her real children. Her human children.'*

'Phaedra, you mustn't.'

Another voice, from somewhere beyond the first. He looks up and, in the corners of his vision, sees the curve of his horns; they are not mighty weapons, not yet fit to gore, but he feels a pride in them he does not fully understand. On the balcony above, another girl has appeared – some years older than the first, striking in her beauty, long and lithe as only the daughters of kings can be.

'Oh, why mustn't I? Look at him, Ari.' She leans over the

banister, to taunt him with words. '*You don't know what I'm saying, do you? You're just an animal, aren't you? That's all he'll ever be, Ariadne. No, don't! Don't tell me he's my brother. He's the thing that tore Mother apart. Ruined her in body and mind. Not even Apollo could bring Mother back to her senses now – and it's all* his *fault . . .*'

There was more to hear, but at that moment the workman reappeared, and Minos found himself wrenched back into the rookery of St Giles. 'There's neither one here – not your Nell and not your ballerina. You'll have to look elsewhere, and get off our step. They've taken some job. Barely been seen.'

'You must know where—'

But the door was already closing.

He could have reached out. Could have forced his way within. And perhaps he would have done just that, if only those voices weren't growing in fervour again, rising up from the miasma at the back of his mind.

If Nell wasn't here to help quell them, he would have to outrun them again.

And there were yet others who might know where she'd be.

The water was high on the beckoning river. Minos followed it into the east, certain that, by the time he arrived, the mudlarks would be scattered from their daily trawl. If Murdstone had returned to the city, perhaps he had returned to the mudlarks too – though, with dead men and failed enterprise behind him, Minos wondered if there were more pressing matters at hand for Benjamin Murdstone. He would have to keep his distance, then, have to pick his moment – but, when he arrived, he found their stretch of the river empty, save for the street dog picking its way through the rock pools. It was in the streets that he would find them, then. The one called Gander, or else Sally-Anne.

It was just Minos's luck then that, outside the haber-dashers at St George in the East, it was Noah's face that he found.

The boy had already emptied his bucket when the great shadow fell across him. Though he startled, he had no courage to run. 'Take it,' he said, rummaging in his pockets to unearth the pennies he'd earned. 'Have it all, I don't—'

'I don't need your money.'

Noah could not bear to look him in the eye. He cringed to the side, as if expecting some blow.

'Is she here?' Minos whispered.

'Who? What—'

'Is – she – here?'

The way he spoke the words, it was like tearing holes in the air. Noah had little breath to reply – for at last he had taken in Minos's visage, seen the crimson stains at his temples, the new haggardness of his build – but he found enough to say, 'Murdstone took her. There was a carriage, came to cart her away. We haven't seen her since. Haven't seen Murdstone either.'

A new sensation prickled in the nape of Minos's neck. He turned over his shoulder, to see two other mudlarks appear from the gloom.

'Are you lying to me?' he intoned.

Noah had found courage enough to take two faltering steps. 'I've no need.'

'I need to find her.'

'I've told you, we—'

384

'If you see her, tell her – tell her I'm going to ground. But I'll look for her at our old places.'

'I will,' stammered Noah.

Minos looked him up and down.

'If you're lying,' he whispered, 'I'll kill you.'

The words had come out before he knew what he was saying. Perhaps it was right that, of the two, Minos was the most shaken; Noah seemed to take it as self-evident that his life was in danger. Monsters killed; it was what they were bred for. He skittered backwards, saying, 'She's gone, gone from the river,' and took off up the street. If there was no real safety with the other mudlarks, at least three died harder than one.

But Minos did not move – because, suddenly, Minos wasn't in Ratcliffe at all.

The ballroom manifests around him: the vaulted ceiling and marble walls in the very heart of the fortress at Knossos. His sisters like dancing. They turn across the interlocking tiles of the dance floor, itself a creation of the grand artificer Daedalus, and he enjoys watching them as they swoop and glide. He might not understand their words, but dance is a language he can comprehend. Dance is the expression of emotion, pure and simple. It is more like crying or howling than it is like words. Yes, on the dance floor he can be like the rest.

He only wanted to join in.

To whirl and pivot like the others.

To let his yearning pour out in thrashing arms and kicking legs.

Now, Phaedra takes flight (just like Noah takes flight) and crashes into the arms of their waiting sisters. Callis is consoling her, 'He didn't mean to, Phaedra; he doesn't know his own strength', while Ariadne nurses the purple bruises blossoming on the side of her face.

'It's like he lost control,' says Ariadne. 'He doesn't know how big he is.'

'He shouldn't be dancing,' snaps Phaedra, 'he shouldn't be in the palace at all. Send him to the stables. Or – or build him his own palace! Send him there. He can dance there, can't he? And – and I'm going to tell Father!'

When he came to from his reverie, the three mudlarks were still staring. He wanted to go to them – just like, once upon a time, he had wanted to go to his sisters – but, just like in the once upon a time, he turned and he ran.

It was instinct that carried him. Left he turned; then right. Forward he ploughed; then back. Darkness had hardened on Ratcliffe, just as it had hardened across the rest of London. The lamplighters were out, to fight their useless war against the night, but the stretches between the gaslights were deep and vast, just like the Forever Dark in that Palace of old. And, just like the Forever Dark in that Palace of old, he found his way across them by scent, by touch, by the atlas scored into his mind.

Until he stood outside the familiar hoardings on the outlands of St Giles.

Beresford Kale had already snuffed out his lantern, ready to depart for the night, by the time Minos lumbered through. His porcine eyes opened in fury upon seeing the stranger's return. 'No,' Kale announced, defiant only because he hadn't the sense to remember the last time he challenged the beast. 'We've been here before, sir. Twice you've absented yourself from this site. Bullied me into rehiring you once, you might have done – but I won't be bullied twice. Remove yourself from this site, Minos. It's proscribed ground.'

The man wasn't worth confronting – too many voices buzzed already at the back of Minos's mind – so instead he stalked past, over the sandbags, and onto the scaling ladder that led down below. The last thing he heard was Kale's voice fading: 'You've no right, sir. There'll be no pay packet. This is trespass, and you shan't be forgiven. I'll bring men to rat you out –'

The darkness in the sewer embraced him. Yes, of course; there'd been a reason he was drawn to the comfort of tunnels, the dark crevices beneath the ground. Old men always harked back to their childhoods. Never mind his mother, his sisters, the fortress at Knossos. The Labyrinth was his crucible; the Labyrinth, the place he'd been born.

Left he turned; then right.

Forward he ploughed –

Something was different in the tunnels. The walls he hunkered under were shimmering and wet. By the time he'd lost himself in their turns, he fancied he could smell the river – and, of course, he could, because London's lost rivers were around him now, culverted and dammed and tamed by the city. But he hadn't tramped through roiling water the last time he was here. It trickled and flowed around him: all the snowmelt from above.

– then back.

If he couldn't have Nell, he could yet have a little peace. Just some sanctuary, until he knew what was next.

Somewhere to take stock. Somewhere to feel safe. Somewhere to . . .

No, not *sleep*. Sleep was where the memories awakened. Sleep was where torment arose.

But here came his third night wakeful – so, however much he struggled, sleep took him under, all the same.

22

The Wills

London, January 1862

The limelight followed her as she danced.

Nell sat in the shadows of the empty auditorium and watched. Some of these steps she recognized from Sophia's perambulations of the garret in St Giles, but in the Alhambra it seemed so different. How could it be that a single body filled up the entire stage? How could it be that, by something so simple as dance, a mortal woman could take flight? Of course, Nell told herself, it was all just a trick of the imagination. But what magic the imagination could wreak! Up there, Miss Chrétien wasn't really Miss Chrétien at all; she was ghostly Giselle, brought back from the dead, uncertain whether she should renounce or forgive her faithless lover.

A waif-like creature, the youngest of the Neva Ballet, was watching from the edge of the stage. She was the first at the theatre this morning, though every one of them had been here long past the midnight hour, outlining the dances to Sophia, reworking them in new combinations as one dancer assumed another's role, as the corps were stretched and redeployed. Throughout it all, there Nell had been, scampering between the store rooms on errands, on her hands and knees in the dust-filled catacombs beneath the stage, or angled and poised by Sophia as she sought to show some intricacy of dance to her corps de ballet. Now, fighting the weariness of last night's endeavour, she watched as Sophia invited the young Neva dancer onto the stage and ushered her into the light.

'She's good,' Sophia had told her, as they picked their way home through the sluicing rain of midnight. 'Untested, perhaps. One day, you'll discover how different it is to dance alone than to dance among the corps. Giselle is a coveted role. A part of her will be thrilling, but another part – the bigger, if I'm any judge of a dancer – will know she isn't ready. Not yet. But the Company needs her, so it's what she'll have to do.'

'You could step in, couldn't you, Sophia?'

'But it would be a betrayal of the Company, to import someone from beyond their own corps. No, I'll dance among the Wills when the moment comes – but Alyona will need to find her steel, if the Neva is to prosper.'

The chemical glow of the limelight made Alyona ghostly as she danced. Nell had seen nothing like it; it was like the moon being marshalled by man. When the rest of the Company arrived and fanned out around the auditorium, Nell felt certain they were watching the detail of her steps, seeking inspiration in the precision and mathematics, but Nell had given herself entirely to the fable. Weren't tears the most amazing things? They cascaded out of you when you were wretched, but sadness wasn't the real reason they came; tears were simply an excess of emotion, emotion being exiled from the body. Nell hadn't known, until this night, that something beautiful might make you weep.

She was weeping still when Sophia called her name from the edge of the stage. 'Fresh slippers, Miss Hart.' Nell hadn't seen through her tears, but Alyona had stepped out of her own. 'These ones are losing their shape.'

What a decadence it was to notice these things. On the river they would never understand.

By this second morning, Nell had a rudimentary knowledge of backstage at the Alhambra. The magnificence at the front of the theatre, where the patrons would be welcomed and fawned upon, gave way behind the stage to a higgledy-piggledy ruin of passageways, stairways and halls not unlike the teetering chaos at the Water's Edge – only, instead of sailors, traders and street-sellers, here there were corners for props, set dressings, and costumes. The flotsam of a thousand shows, Sophia had called it. 'All theatres feel like it. They carry the ghosts of the stories played out in all the seasons before.' So it seemed to Nell. The Alhambra had courted illusionists and jugglers, singers of the highest renown; acrobatic acts, Nell was told, who spun above the heads of spectators on nothing more than ropes and wires. But none of this compared, in Nell's imagination, to the knowledge that the gowns her mother stitched had once been worn on this very stage; that, perhaps, they were hanging in the wardrobes right now – echoes of the dances that used to be, the ghost of her mother still stitching every hem.

Nell slowed as she approached the costumes hall. The theatre's resident seamstress was no doubt within, tending to her gowns like a shepherd to his flock. Nell had longed to ask her if she remembered her mother, but more than once she had been met by some waspish comment as she picked her way through the racks, searching for some head-dress or trinket Sophia had described. Yet tonight, as she came to the door, she did not hear the tell-tale muttering of the seamstress at work. A regal lady, twice Sophia's age – and consequently ancient as the city to Nell – she rambled as she worked, constantly counting as her mother used to do, or else in spirited conversation with the garments she was tending. The memories it stirred might have been a comfort to Nell, if only the seamstress had exuded the same warmth as her mother. But there was a difference between working your magic in the back room of the hovel where you lived, and ruling over a fiefdom of silks and lace at the Alhambra Circus. In one, there was a place for a girl like Nell; in the other, only suspicion and discomfort. 'You're her lady-in-waiting, are you? Our Parisian princess?' Those, the seamstress's first words to Nell, the day she'd arrived at the theatre. She'd appraised her nails bitten down to the quick, and quickly held her at the door. 'No ragamuffin's going to get her grubby hands on these gowns. You tell me what you need and I'll fetch it.'

It didn't matter that Nell's hands were scrubbed raw. To some, you never really left the river.

That was why her heart skipped a beat when she realized the seamstress wasn't here.

Nell pushed open the door. No light illuminated the costumes hall, so instead she found her way by the oil lantern she had carried from the stage. By its orange glow, she passed between racks of hanging silks; she gazed at the stands where top hats and bowlers lined up; she startled at seeing the faceless white mannequin, draped in fox furs, who stood in the corner as if guardian to the room.

Shoes and slippers dangled in pairs from a forest of hooks. Nell knew she ought to have gone straight to them, but the rustle of silks was too tantalizing. She fancied, for a moment, that she might recognize her mother's stitching in the hems – and was on her hands and knees, running the fabric through her fingers, trying to feel for her mother's ghost, when the door opened up and the seamstress returned, wearing her displeasure with pride.

'Thieving fingers live on thieving hands,' she said, bustling close. 'On your feet now, Nell. Pockets emptied. Hands upturned.'

Nell scrambled up. 'Miss Chrétien sent me for slippers.'

There were none of these slippers more graceful than the ones her mother had stitched.

The seamstress glowered, 'You won't find slippers rifling through silks.'

'My hands are —'

The seamstress had snatched a pair of slippers from a hook. Now she thrust them at Nell. 'Magpies, that's what your sort are. Can't see a pretty thing without having a touch of it.' The seamstress might as well have had a broom; by bustling skirts, she swept Nell towards the doorway. 'If I'm not here, girl, you wait. Your pretty lady might have made a pet of you – but I'm not as easily deceived. You can't put a diamond collar on vermin and call it a lapdog. A thing is what it is. A man struts out on stage a dame, but the moment he steps off it, he's a man again. A guttersnipe is what a guttersnipe is.'

Here was that excess of emotion again. Nell tried to swallow it as she scurried back to the stage. Mr Murdstone would have had an argument with the seamstress. He'd have told her that knights could rise from the river. But, then, he'd found himself back there, hadn't he? At the end of his life, walking with the same tides he'd once escaped. And perhaps that was the fate of all those who tried to change their lives: just like the tide, life kept ebbing and flowing.

No matter; there was majesty enough in the theatre today. By the time the morning was old, musicians had started arriving, to fill the cavernous expanse with the sound of piano, of mournful violin, wistful flutes and horns. By the middle of the afternoon, ushers and ticket-collectors flocked through the Circus; pages, shoe-shiners, the entirety of the Alhambra's army, preparing the way for the battle of the night. To Nell, it seemed as if she was in the hold of some great ocean-going vessel, where furnaces were stoked and a hundred hands worked to the same great purpose. Sweepers were out in the stalls; incense was being burned in the boxes; the private secretary of some minister arrived, to make special arrangements for his master's appearance.

'It's all for nothing, though, Nell, if it isn't for the dance.'

Some time before twilight, the dancers of the Neva Ballet gathered in the backstage hall. Nell watched as feet were bound in ribbons, the better to hold back their spreading blisters and cracks. She flitted between them as they stretched, walked through the fug of smoke in which they reclined, observed each going through the private rituals that prepared them for the show. Somehow, the Alhambra Circus itself, with all its manifold passages and store rooms, its landslides and dead-ends, seemed to have come alive. She could feel the theatre's own anticipation. Even in the back rooms, the boards trembled under her feet.

'Come, Nell.'

It was Sophia's voice, calling her from the door of the backstage hall. Nell hurried to her now.

'Miss Chrétien?'

'Come with me. Quickly, girl.'

Sophia marched, with Nell in tow, through the tangle of passageways, until at last they emerged into the auditorium. 'It will fill with patrons soon, Nell. It will heave.' Nell scurried after; she remembered it well, the press of bodies in this room, the feeling of so many eyes all drinking in the same ghostly vision. 'But before they come, I want you to know how it feels.'

The moment Nell reached the centre of the stage, trailing from Sophia's hand, the music struck up. Her eyes darted around, seeking out the piano player hidden in the depression in front of the stage. It was only one man, but he was conjuring starlight. 'Come, Nell, nobody's watching.'

She'd danced on this stage before; danced, once upon a time, with Sophia herself, while her mother looked on. But this time, when Sophia led her around the stage, lifting her to sail, to turn and bow in perfect imitation of the ethereal host who would very soon hunt wicked men across these boards, it felt real.

Perhaps it lasted mere moments, but in Nell's heart it felt like for ever.

When the dance came to its close, and Sophia's hand slipped from her own, an instinct told her to look for her mother in the stalls. *They said you were a natural. My dancing girl.* But of course she was not there: Sophia was the one to gaze at her tonight, as the music faded and the limelight died.

'They'll open the doors soon,' said Sophia, 'and the stalls will fill up. Waves of noise will crash over this place – but, the moment our Giselle takes her first steps onto stage: silence,' she pronounced, with the power of a magic spell. 'What do you think, Nell? It takes much work. There will be days, countless days, when the punishment is enough to make you want to turn tail and flee from the stage for ever. Is it what you want?'

Nell said nothing, only lifted her eyes.

'I believe they like me,' Sophia whispered. 'Perhaps . . . St Petersburg,' she dreamed. 'I never got to dance at the Hermitage Theatre. The Kamenny, out there on Carousel Square. The Imperial Ballet has opened the Mariinsky, a theatre for the world. Yes, St Petersburg. It sounds like the future, doesn't it, Nell?' Sophia lay her spoiled hand in her lap. 'There might be no place for a butchered ballerina on their stage – but if I prove my value as instructor . . .'

'Will I always be vermin, Miss Chrétien?'

The words tumbled out of her. Nell hadn't meant to say them. Upon giving them voice, she felt suddenly foolish, and shrunk away from Sophia. But to shrink made her feel more foolish yet – so soon she was spilling everything the seamstress had said, the thoughts that had been needling her throughout the long day.

'I've known so many like her,' said Sophia at last. 'They look at us, when we're young, and tell us the world is as it is, as it's always been and ever will be – and that they themselves are but pieces of that. That nothing can be done, but to abide. But they're wrong. The seamstress sees a wonder in you, Nell, and it unnerves her – because her life story is spun, and yours has only just begun.'

'You mean to say – she wants what I have?'

'The old see possibilities in the young. They'd drink up our lives if they could, but they can't – so instead they learn bitterness, and envy, and sometimes hate.'

Nell dangled her legs from the edge of the stage, gazed up into the infinite surrounds.

'But do you think I'll ever be more than a mudlark? When people look at me, it's all they see.'

'You'll change, dear Nell. And therein lies the beauty. You weren't a mudlark, once. You were a dressmaker's girl. You'll be a hundred different things in the course of a life.'

Like the river had once been a stream; like the river would one day become the sea.

'But I want to be me.' It was the thought of being a dressmaker's girl that had done it. Life was dragging her inexorably away from her mother's bedside. Might there come a day when she had forgotten that bedside, or looked on it only as a dream? She thought, suddenly, of Minos and his ravaged mind: first one thing, then another, all of it fading behind him as time swept on.

'You'll always be you, dear Nell. It's just that . . .' Here Sophia paused; this particular thought seemed as elusive as the dance she'd be charting tonight. 'There's an old story. "The Ship of Theseus". Perhaps they don't tell you stories on the river?'

'I've heard the name,' whispered Nell. She had as well; she'd heard it on Christmas night, in the good doctor Bantam's voice. Theseus, the killer; Theseus, the hero who smote . . . What was it they called him? The Minotaur.

'When Theseus sailed his ship back to Athens, victorious from his adventure in Crete, his ship was kept in harbour, even unto his death, as a reminder of the great deeds he'd accomplished. But a ship does not last for ever. As the years passed, the timbers turned to rot. One after another, they had to be replaced – until, many years later, not a piece of the old boat remained.' A door opened, somewhere between the stalls. The ushers were getting ready. The noise from beyond had grown in fervour as they danced: patrons, milling in the hall, taking drinks together, readying themselves to be spellbound within. 'And yet – it's still the same ship, is it not? We all change, Nell. But we're still us.'

More doors were opening. The auditorium, which until now had been a cavern of darkness, was scythed with lights as ushers drew back curtains, revealing the portals through which the night's patrons would arrive.

'But *you* fell back to the streets, Sophia. Mr Murdstone might have been a sir, but then it came to doss-houses and gambling dens, the river all over again.' It was what Sophia had said about the claws of the past, trying to drag a soul backwards. 'The mudlarks used to say we belong to the river. We'd live by its gifts and, by the river, we'd die.'

Sophia gripped her more tightly. 'And is that what you think, Nell?'

She never had done, but being here, seeing the splendour all around her, only cultivated the doubt.

'Lean into the dance, Nell,' Sophia said, drawing her close. 'I might have fallen from on high, dear girl, but one thing's for certain: missing finger or not, I wouldn't trade having flown.'

A wave of noise hit them. Patrons jostling at every door.

Sophia lifted herself artfully upwards, urging Nell to do the same. 'It's beginning, dear girl. Fly, now. Tell the

Company the moment draws near. And Nell?' Nell had already started scuttling offstage; now she looked back. 'I shall need your help in the wings, so prepare yourself too. Our future may depend on how bewitched this audience is, how spectacular this night.'

*

He'd known men murdered before, but never had to take meetings with their master.

The carriage was already waiting on the street of Chinese lanterns, the body being made up so that it seemed he had died without pain. Murdstone was no skilled undertaker – certainly not skilled enough to make the dead seem peaceful in their repose – but the apothecary Lynn had had more cause than most to practise this trade. The Highway was not short of men who met unfortunate ends. Now, Murdstone sat in the apothecary's back room, imbibing some brew Lynn had provided and hoping it steadied his hand. It was the travelling, he'd been telling himself – but, of course, it wasn't the journey into London that was diminishing him; it was the journey through life.

He'd known no other place to come, not unless it was Bantam's surgery – and there would be no welcome there, not any longer. The Water's Edge would not do, the Lowood coach house was lost to him – and he was in desperate need of somewhere to *think* before he faced his defeat in Farringdon Within. So the street of Chinese lanterns it was. Lynn had rubbed his body with oils. Shovelled sailors and derelicts back to the Highway, so that there was a cot for Murdstone to sleep in. Powdered bone and burned moss to make what remedies he could. 'Bantam's finished with me now, but I've still got you, Lynn. Just to grease the wheels of this old body. Just to keep it in life until . . .' He could not finish that dream; it was almost beyond him now. Briggs's death he could have coped with: an unmarked grave in the manor grounds would for ever hide his shame. But the devastation of Elkington's man could not be over-come. 'This man, Lynn. You have seen nothing of his like. He's lived for centuries. Empires have risen and fallen. Stars have flourished and faded away. And yet he goes on . . .'

'It would be a curse to live for ever, sir.'

'Well, I don't need for ever.' Murdstone looked up, through the opiate smoke. 'Just give me a little longer, Lynn. Bantam's quackery be damned!'

'History is littered with men who tried to defy death,' said Lynn. Having helped Murdstone perform his ablutions, he had returned to the matter at hand, hovering over the footman's body and rearranging every stray hair. 'There was an emperor, Shi Huang, who dreamed the same dream. He commanded armies to scour the Earth for the herbs which would give him eternity. The fable said they grew only at the heights of the world, tended by spirits and gods.' Lynn paused. 'But Shi Huang's army never found the elixir they were sent hunting for, and Shi Huang wasted his life in waiting. By the time his armies returned to report their defeat, he was waiting in his tomb.'

'I'm already nearing my tomb,' Murdstone snapped. He had joined Lynn at the dead man's side, and thought: how easily it might have been me. 'I told Elkington he could throw me into the river, were I to fail. But I haven't failed yet.'

Those last words, so filled with forlorn hope. He began brushing down his fustians, ready to prostrate himself in front of Elkington one last time.

'There's always a chance, Mr Murdstone. Listen to the lessons of your own life: there must be something left for you to trade.'

But no, thought Murdstone, as the carriage carried him into the west, the cadaver at his side. For the first time in his life, the simple rules of commerce would not be enough. The trades had come to their end. No glorious gambit awaited him in Farringdon Within – only a plea, a petition, a prayer.

Elkington had received the instruction at dawn, and consequently he was already in his study when Murdstone arrived. The footman had had no wife – there were always small mercies, for Fate was a sentimental fellow – but his sister was waiting in the parlour to receive her brother's body. It had been deemed improper for Murdstone to be present when she looked upon him, but he was not spared the full expression of her grief. The howling echoed through the townhouse walls, filling up the drawing room where Murdstone waited for Elkington to begin.

'History repeats itself. Isn't this what the scholars tell us?' Elkington's weariness was the kind ordinarily worn by much older men. He shuffled behind his desk, playing with a letter opener styled like some medieval dagger. Theatre of the most obvious kind, thought Murdstone – but perhaps now was not the moment to scorn it. 'I remember the last time bad news crossed our path. Your solution was the same back then. I'd forfeited two clippers in that first trade we made – but you, sir, persuaded me to risk four more. Two to fulfil the contracts lost, and two to reap the profits that should have been ours. The risk, you told me, was calculated. I didn't know, back then, that it was calculated only in the way a drunkard calculates his losses and gains at the roulette wheel. That you were just rolling the dice. We thought there was wonder in you. Only a man blessed by good fortune could live the life you'd lived. None of us realized, until it was too late, that you were just another mountebank. That your only real talent was for taking a swindle made for the streets and replaying it in Society. That you hadn't really *changed*.' The dagger flew from Elkington's hand, to bite into the surface of his desk and stand there proudly. 'And now you want to play the same trick. One man dead, and you ask me for others.'

'It's different this time. We are not gambling with the seas.'

'No,' Elkington scoffed, 'we're gambling with legend.'

'If you'd only seen what I saw. Ask your footmen, those who survive. They know him for what he is, just the same as I do. Fate has been unkind, sir – but to let him go now would be to sacrifice all.'

Elkington shook his head. 'A man can cut his losses.'

And Murdstone seethed, 'Then a loss is all you will ever have!' He would have let the silence linger, were it not for the wailing still coming through the walls. A thing like that could sway a man's heart, so Murdstone barrelled on, 'It hasn't been in vain. It *hasn't*. If the cost has been great, it pales in comparison to the rewards we'll reap. I know what he is, now. I know it's no fraud. He knows it too. That's more valuable than I'd wagered. Were you to see it, sir, you would not doubt. The man is changed, even from the monstrosity we found on the river. With every ill act, the Minotaur manifests in him. He attacked my ward off the Highway in Ratcliffe, and the beast came out. These murders – yes, sir, *murders*, for that is what they are! – will work their magics on him too. You'll have to convince no man that he's real. Together, we'll build him his Labyrinth. See the old world reborn. And men will come, from far and wide, to play Theseus. I'll coax it out further, if I must – coax him, until the horns stand proud upon his head, and all faculty for language is gone. But I can't do it alone. I need capital. I need *you*.'

'The old lines, Murdstone. The old lines!'

'I'm not talking about teas and sugars, sir! I'm not talking about opium from the East. What worms we were, to dream of empires built out of cargoes and clippers! There's no wonder on Earth could compare with what we have here. I've seen it, with my own eyes. I'll show it to you. Sir, I'll show it.'

Elkington paused. That hesitation, it was all Murdstone needed. It was like a buoy. A rope cast out to an overboard man. He clung onto it.

'You're not in possession of the beast,' Elkington said. 'The Minotaur fled.'

'Yes, but I've *learned*, sir. Learned that he's frightened. That he's always been petrified of what he is. He simply hasn't known it – until we showed him the way.'

'What use is fear, Benjamin, when it leads him to this?' Elkington swirled a condescending finger in the air, to indicate the weeping in the walls.

'The Labyrinth couldn't keep him. Neither could words. But *fear* might.'

Murdstone could not be certain, but he thought he detected some flicker of intrigue in Elkington's eyes. The man was a fool: he still hadn't learned his lesson. Temptation undermines the best of us, but the worst of us welcome it in.

'Fear turns the greatest men to killers,' said Elkington. 'There's enough poor souls come back from India to prove that. Imagine what it does to a man already hiding a beast inside him. Once a monster . . .'

Murdstone took a breath. 'What if I could control his fear?'

He'd thought he had no gambit, but here it was, unfolding in front of him.

'And how would one go about that?'

'Listen to me closely now —'

'You mean to frighten him into your service? This man who's lived millennia? You, Benjamin Murdstone, mean to terrify the Minotaur?'

'No,' declared Murdstone, railing against the impertinence. 'I mean to save him from it.'

Elkington glared.

'There's a girl. One of my mudlarks. She's the one who drew him from the river. She spoke to him in dreams. I've seen her calm him. She saved me, down on the riverside, the first time I tried to own him. I'm certain she saved Noah's life, off the wharf-sides on Christmas night. I don't know what connection they share, but I know it's real. So I'll turn her into my weapon. She'll be the one to soothe the Minotaur in him, so that the Man can hear reason.'

'You'll have to find him first, of course.'

'That's why I need men.'

Elkington was frozen. 'How can I send them after him, when he already flayed one life?'

At last, a question for which Murdstone had no answer. 'It's the only way.'

Elkington's attention was momentarily diverted by footsteps at the drawing room door; they tolled louder, then faded again, as some figure moved past. Perhaps it was the thought of his wife's approach that prompted him to say, 'The New Year is already growing old. Our terms were Christmas night. How much longer must you be indulged before I—'

'A merchant ship has to move with the winds. This is no different. And I'm close.'

'You leave bodies in your wake!'

'These are *footnotes* to the story we'll tell!'

Silence resumed. Even the muffled weeping had come to a stop now.

'You have twenty-four hours, Benjamin, and whatever men will freely comply. I have no will to force them, but perhaps vengeance for their friend might be compulsion enough.'

'Twenty-four hours may not be enough. I need to find him first.'

'And yet twenty-four hours is the limit of my indulgence. Do you understand me this time? You think me weak-willed, but I am not. You think me easily swayed, and yet here I stand – on ground that does not shift like your tides. I know you, Benjamin Murdstone. This Minotaur has not changed since the days of its youth, and neither have you. You're a swindler. You're a cheat. You were born a scapegrace, and a scapegrace you remained – whether you're out mudlarking or dining with ministers.' Elkington plucked the dagger back from the table, while Murdstone tried hard not to betray his contempt. 'The clock says 9 p.m. Mark it, Mr Murdstone. I'll send men to do your bidding – but, if you have not delivered on your debts by this hour tomorrow, their instruction to support you will automatically revert to our original terms. To whit, Mr Murdstone: they will toss you in the river.'

Murdstone gave a single, curt nod. Twenty-four hours was more than he had hoped for upon entering this building. At least, now, he could see the shape of this endeavour.

He had reached the door, his mind spinning with all he would have to do, when Elkington added, 'Of course, my wife insists on summoning the Metropolitan Police. I mayn't be able to stop her. She fancies the thief-takers are already alert to what happened at Amberstone House. It might be that they're hunting your Minotaur as well.'

Murdstone had to compose himself before he replied. He had already learned that the woman would not be dictated to; it was she who dictated.

'That might be to our advantage still, sir. A legend must be spread.' Yes, he thought, and was pleased to find he could see the commerce on the other side of this once more. A man's life was spent, but that only propagated the legend. Let every thief-taker in London take to the streets in search of him. Let rumour spread like cholera through Soho. All it did was prepare the stage.

A thought occurred to him. 'You should announce a bounty. A price on the Minotaur's head. Not before I know where he is, of course. It must not be some other Theseus

who finds him. It can only be me. But a bounty for a creature like this? Sir, we'll have London eating from our palm.'

Outside, rain moved in a roiling curtain across the city,
the road itself a river as Murdstone set out. The carriage
which had brought him had long since departed, ferrying
the cadaver onward to its final rest, and Murdstone had to
wait some time before a passing hackney deigned to pick
him up. He climbed aboard, counting down the seconds.
Twenty-four hours. That it had come to this: one last game
of pitch-and-toss.

'Mr Murdstone, isn't it?' the coachman asked.

The man lifted his lantern to better illuminate Murdstone's
own face.

'It is at that!' he crowed, in wonder. 'I never forget a
face, and certainly not one as particular as this. Sir Benjamin
Murdstone, by God. You won't remember, sir, but you hired
me as your driver, once upon a time. And here I am, your
driver again. By God, the nights I waited for you – nights
such as this, if I've any memory. Sitting out on Hanover
Square, or down on the Horse Guards Parade. Outside
Almack's, or the Reform back when it was new. Underneath
Westminster itself, when there was some pageant or another.
I was sad to be let go, sir. Put a roof over my son and his
daughters, on the back of what I done for you. My sister
couldn't stand the smog no more – doctor said she needed
sea air. I helped her with that too.' He shrugged. 'But if
you didn't need a driver, you didn't need a driver. We all
rise and fall in life. That's what I've learned.' As the man
had been rambling on, Murdstone cringed from the light.
'So where's it to be tonight? Boodles, is it? Berkeley Square?'

Murdstone settled in the carriage, finding shelter under

its awning. This time, when the coachman lifted the lantern to his face, it revealed him not as the gregarious benefactor of Hanover Square, but as Murdstone of the river: broken, drawn, clinging onto life by power of will and ambition alone.

'Seven Dials,' he muttered, 'and make it quick.'

The hours of his life were like sand through his fingers, and Murdstone had a girl he needed to find.

23

Theseus the Destroyer

London, January 1862

The rain that coursed across Benjamin Murdstone had already turned the streets of London to an atlas of shimmering arteries – as if the tide, for this night alone, had reached out to cover the city. Yet the roads over which Murdstone's carriage took him could no longer hold the rainwater that pooled upon them. The gutters were subsumed, the ditches turned to quagmires; and London itself would have drowned, were it not for the old cities upon which it was built, the Londons that belonged to legionnaires, plagues and mad kings, opening their jaws to draw the water down.

Follow that water now . . .

Down through cobbles and stone, down through plague pits and the ruins of great fires, down into that world of lost London rivers, culverts and dams, where Minos awaits.

The brickwork around him was weeping, the tamed rivers Tyburn and Fleet frothing behind their walls – as if remembering the wild, free rivers they used to be.

Nor were they the only ones remembering.

The limelight flared. The tumult of voices in the auditorium died. In the wings, Nell waited, braced beneath Sophia's

409

arm, as the first sounds drifted up from the orchestra: playful flutes, heralding the delicate piano to come. Around her, the dancers of the Neva Ballet formed up: like soldiers, awaiting battle; like mudlarks, gathered at the storehouses to display their finds. It was their silence that astounded Nell. The rise and fall of backstage conversation was gone; so, too, the shadowed looks of uncertainty that had flitted across the halls. 'Now we come to it,' Sophia whispered into her ear. Then, as if summoned by a single note, two of the dancers broke free from the ranks and sallied onto stage.

The limelight found them.

A flood of other lights illuminated the wider stage, to reveal a woodland approaching autumn: the faces of simple houses sitting neatly among sketches of trees. Between them, the dancing began.

'Albrecht,' Sophia whispered, 'our ignoble duke. But he hasn't done wrong yet. He hasn't entrapped Giselle.' Sophia was still, and it seemed to Nell that she was already captivated by the story being woven out on stage. 'Oh, but he will.'

The music reached a new peak, punctuated by the sounds of horns. Hidden from view, Sophia and Nell remained resolute as the corps parted around them, then fanned out into the same woodland scene. The harvest was beginning. The vineyards being reaped. Last of all to sally out was Alyona. Nell could see the fearfulness written on her as she hovered by their side – but she would not accept Sophia's consoling hand, for now she would have to dance alone.

Off she went: Giselle, towards her fate.

And it was as Nell watched her spinning through the corps de ballet, taking her part in the imagined harvest while Albrecht and his squire looked on, that the music really reached her. Until now, it had existed out there, cascading over the stage; now, it seemed to rush through Nell herself. The stage trembled beneath the dancers' feet, the rhythm they marked out echoing the music as it rose and fell.

'Can you imagine, Nell? To be out there, among them?'

The music was drawing her on. She could feel it tugging at her, with all the force of the river. Perhaps that was why Sophia's arms stayed folded around her, to keep Nell from drifting onto stage.

Out there, Albrecht met Giselle. He took her hand.

Nell felt a burst of untold emotion. Was it the lies Albrecht was telling? Was it the yearning Giselle felt, just to be loved? Was it music? Was it dance?

Or was it simply the fact that on Christmas night she'd wished goodbye to the one true friend in her life, and returned to the river alone – and now she was standing here, where dreams were being born.

Giselle fell into the dance.

So, in her heart, did Nell.

Beneath the streets of a rain-drenched city . . .

In the heart of a London sewer . . .

Behind the eyes of a sleeping giant . . .

Memories flicker.

There is a certain chamber, in a certain wing, in a certain corner of the fortress of Knossos, where he knows he is not supposed to go. His step-father has forbidden it and his

411

step-father's rule is law. And yet, at a certain hour of a certain day, when a certain guard known to favour pity over disgust is stationed by the door, he might shamble past without being harassed. On days like these, if he dares, he can push through his mother's door. Perhaps she is in her bedchamber. Perhaps her parlour. There is a place where she can take the sun, and yet still be hemmed in by walls. He will know lots of walls like this soon – though, naive as he is, he does not yet know it. But his mother is so rarely seen in the fortress at large and this is the only place he might go to her without being accosted and taken away. They say his mother is mad now. That in conceiving him she was driven to some fit of insanity that reached its terrible climax only when he was birthed, his budding horns ravaging a body once blessed by the gods. Seclusion, the healers say, is the only path back from madness. Seclusion from all but those closest to her. And yet, of all those who dwell in the fortress of Knossos, it is her lastborn she is forbidden to see. He who was, until months ago, cradled inside her may now go nowhere near.

They say he is growing much more swiftly than he ought; that, when Ariadne and Callis were his age, they were still babes in arms. By the next half-moon he will be big as Phaedra.

Through the doors he comes.

Onward he goes.

Left he turns; then right.

And there is his mother, turning to greet him.

Her eyes light up.

'Hello, my sweet.'

He will not stay here long. They will come for him soon. But perhaps he will have time to rest his head upon her lap, to feel her hands running through the fur that cloaks his body, to hear her call him her son.

If this is madness, then he has never understood the word. This? This looks like love.

'They're not here,' the workman at the doorstep bawled. There was gin on this man's breath; gin and bitterness, the heady scent of Seven Dials. 'That dancing tart's got too many visitors, if you ask me. Treats us like her house staff, opening the door at all hours. But she isn't here – her and that whelp of hers, they're gone.'

Murdstone stood in the doorway, the carriage at his shoulder his only protection from the driving rain. 'Gone?' he asked. 'Where, sir?'

'I'm not the slattern's keeper. Instructing her whelp in her business, I shouldn't wonder. But there's harlots aplenty on these streets, you old rogue. You'll find what you're after, soon as you get off my step.'

The man moved to close the door in Murdstone's face, but he had thought too little of the septuagenarian who stood there. Out came the driftwood cane, to keep the door from closing. Murdstone levered it back open, hoisting himself onto the step. His body was brittle tonight, but his desperation thrived. 'I must find her. Her quarters, show them to me. There may be some trace of where she's gone.'

'Out, damn you!'

The man lunged forward, to wrestle with Murdstone's cane. It was the gin that propelled him, and the gin that made him tumble too. He was still finding his feet when a voice behind him said, 'Here, what's this?', and a woman – with more brawn about her than Murdstone and his attacker combined – loomed in some inner door. 'He's after the harlot,' said the workman, 'like that brute of before. Fists at this door, every hour, seeking her out.'

Murdstone had been preparing to pick his way past, to take to the stairs and hammer on each door, but the word 'brute' waylaid him. 'There was another here?' he whispered. 'A giant of a man? He would have looked—' He stopped – for how *would* he have looked? With two dead men on his conscience, that conscience which worked such wonders on his body? 'He would have cloaked himself, but there'd be no mistaking him. A head taller than you, sir, and built like an ox.'

The workman had righted himself at last. 'Aye, sir, and I sent him packing – with the same flea in his ear I'm giving you.'

'Where?'

The man stared.

'Where did you send him?'

The workman snorted. 'Strange, but he gave me the same black-eyed look you're giving me now. Brothers, are you? Twins, 'cept it's only him who got to suck at Mother's teat? I told him the same, sir: I neither know nor care where—'

'She's at the Alhambra Circus,' came the voice of the woman in the hall.

Murdstone's gaze left the dullard posturing in front of him and picked out the silhouetted woman. By God, but he could smell her from here. That was how the shape of her was defined: in shadows and stench.

'The . . . Alhambra?' he mouthed.

'I heard them talking, her and that girl she's been keeping. Both of them dancing girls, and not the sort who keep tables at the Courage. Don't listen to him. Harlot she might be, but not under this roof. She's taken work. She's there right now.'

Murdstone pitched forward, one step deeper into the blight. 'And the girl?'

'On her mistress's heels, master. Pretty little thing, once she got scrubbed up. And good luck to 'em, I say. There's some here,' and she looked at the workman, 'who'd drag the rest down, to rot together. But there's others who'll cheer a fugitive on. Let 'em run, that's what I say. Let them fly.'

Now it was Murdstone who flew. A few short minutes later, he was disembarking the carriage in the heart of Leicester Square, stepping out again into lacerating rain. Through that veil, the Alhambra Circus seemed a flickering mirage. So, he thought, gazing up at its turrets and dome: this was the place. The trade had been even more favourable than Minos could have imagined. If only he'd kept to his side of the bargain, Nell's future could have been here.

Beyond the colonnade, doors stood open, spilling incandescent light. Would they, perhaps, believe him a gentleman if he sauntered directly through? Lynn had bathed him, laundered his fustians, soothed every wound. Or would they think him a vagrant, chancing his arm?

There was but one way to find out, so Murdstone bowed beneath the umbrella he took from the carriage and made the approach.

The stage was Alyona's alone. In the wings, Nell watched as the single pool of limelight tracked her across the boards.

The harvests were over. The festivities done. The great

hunt had come to its rousing conclusion – and, somewhere in that chaos of movement and song, poor Giselle had learned the truth: Albrecht was nought but a man, and like a man he had lied. Now, on her own she danced – and out of her poured the frenzy of longing, grief and regret that would mark her last moments on Earth.

Until this moment, all Nell had known of dance was joy; only now did she see how it could conjure devastation as well.

The whole of the Alhambra was holding its breath. All that Nell could hear was the music as it climbed in fury, growing faster and faster, filling the auditorium with the torment in Giselle's heart.

Giselle danced.

She turned.

She bowed.

She jumped.

And then, just as the music reached its peak, she died.

The music died with her. There lay Giselle, perishing in the light. Then it was the light's turn to die as well. Blackness consumed the auditorium – and, a single breath later, waves of applause broke over the darkness. Voices were raised in celebration, feet stamping so that, to Nell, it felt as if the world was a-quiver.

In the darkness, Alyona slipped into the wings. Her eyes met Sophia's, and then each fell into the other's arms. 'You did well, my girl,' Sophia said. 'Giselle has never died finer.'

Out in the auditorium, the audience were shifting. A horde moved through the stalls, bound for the foyer and bars.

'My feet, Miss Chrétien,' Alyona ventured. In the gaslights

backstage, she bowed to remove her slippers, then peeled back ribbons sopping with blood to reveal feet pulverized by the dance.

'You are truly Giselle,' Sophia smiled, 'but you haven't danced your way into death yet. Your ghost will need to dance again.'

Alyona nodded.

'Time to serve the Company, Nell,' Sophia proclaimed. 'Ribbons, and fresh slippers – and quickly, now. They'll be coming back to their seats ere long.'

Nell was filled with purpose as she scurried through the reeling dancers, out from the hubbub backstage and into the warren of passages beyond. The trepidation she felt at confronting the seamstress again was as nothing compared to the elation on which she sailed. Serve the Company, Sophia had said. Well, this was how.

The door to the costume store was ajar, and there was the seamstress, tending to her flock. This time, though there was still disparagement in the look she gave Nell, she did not resist the girl venturing within. 'You'd better hand the soiled slippers here, girl. Most can be saved, with a bit of love.'

This time, Nell had no notion to dally. She hurried for the forest of hooks where slippers hung in pairs, tethered by ribbons. The soiled ones matched exactly a pair hanging from the uppermost hook. She took them down, filling one with fresh silks to bind Alyona's foot. Then, as she was scurrying back through the door, the seamstress called out, 'That's it, girl. At least you know your place, now. A pauper can make a good handmaiden, once the workhouse's been beaten out of her. Off you hop, off to your mistress.'

Nell hovered in the doorway, stole a look over her shoulder.

Perhaps the seamstress was goading her, or perhaps it was like Sophia had said: only her own bitternesses leaking out. Either way, Nell knew what she would do whenever this same fear was stoked inside her, whenever the past clawed out to drag her down. 'No,' she whispered – and, ignoring the seamstress's bewildered look, cantered on. There was a show to resume. The Wills and their merciless queen Myrtha were rising up to Giselle's defence. And every man who'd betrayed them would soon endure the devastation of dance.

Good fortune, at last. It had been in scant supply since the river. By the time Murdstone reached the Alhambra doors, patrons had started flocking out of the auditorium, filling up its grand receiving hall with folly and cheer. It was easier to slip among them than it might have been through an empty hall; easier to ape them as he avoided the eyes of passing drinks-men and guards. This place was not so grand, not really – not nearly as opulent as the Moorish palace after which it was named. His eyes took in the vaulted ceilings, the cherubim carved into pillars, the ostentatious sweep of the stairs leading above, and the Murdstone-that-was knew it for the lowly playhouse it really was. Hardly a place for the Shining Light of the Paris Opera Ballet. Hardly a place for ministers and kings. He'd dined in finer townhouses, and he opened himself up to the memories of those times now. Sometimes, you could imagine yourself into being. However dishevelled he appeared, they would think him a gentleman as he blazed a path among them. He would direct it to be so.

The tide moved against him as he picked a path to the auditorium. That seemed apposite, somehow, for the tide had been against him too long. No matter: the tides changed, just like men. He reached the stalls to find them half denuded, what patrons remained engaged in lively discourse on the plight of poor Giselle. Giselle: yes, Murdstone remembered this one; the ghosts who were the scourge of men. He had learned to admire the fine things, once. So would he again.

Murdstone reached the stage's edge, where musicians still milled in their pit, and marvelled at the wooden houses, the paper trees, the fraudulent vines that hung from the boughs. All fantasy, of course. But what value was there in fantasy when he was about to release myth back to the world?

He scoured the edges of the scene, the shadows that crowded every corner. The girl would be on the other side of all this, no doubt scurrying after the ballerina through some back hall, but he would not pick his way across, not and risk the ire of an attendant. Instead, he sought out a back door – and found one, at last, nestled at the edge of the stalls.

The handle hung free; he twisted it and limped into the gaslit darkness beyond.

The scents here were so different: grease and perfumes, as sickly sweet as the jars in Lynn's apothecary. The noises were different too. Some chatter reached him along the hall; a little further on, he was certain he could hear the ballerina herself. Other voices spoke a tongue he did not understand: some faraway language, some dancers' cant. If Nell was with them, he would have to confront them all – but, though

419

he followed the sound of their voices, he did not hear her among the throng. That gave him some conviction: Nell was a girl who had found her tongue and been too ready to use it, in the weeks that had passed. Perhaps she was not with them, then. Perhaps separated from the pack.

Left he turned; then right.

Forward he ploughed; then back.

A bell was ringing, somewhere in these halls. Murdstone froze. That had to signify something. The performance was about to resume – yes, he remembered as much from his own time indulging in places like this. Footsteps were tumbling past, some distance ahead. They echoed and echoed again, so that he could not say whether they were coming or going, hunting him or taking flight. But there were shadows aplenty in the Alhambra Circus; he pitched into them until the moment passed.

He had limped a little further when he felt the breath of winter against him; there was a back door here, being opened to the rain coursing down over Charing Cross. He turned against it, for Nell was surely in some deeper cranny, not going back to the night.

That was when he heard her.

'No,' she said.

No, thought Murdstone. *No*, he grinned. Yes, that had become her word, hadn't it? Like an incantation of old, something she used to ward off evil. Well, it wouldn't work tonight. A contract had been broken. The scales had to be balanced; a debt repaid.

He turned the corner, and there she was – scurrying along with a pair of satin slippers clutched in her hands.

'Hello, Nell.'

Nell clattered to a stop, mere yards from where Murdstone stood. There was no picking past him, not here in this narrow network of halls. She staggered back. The shock of seeing him must have robbed her of every word, because all was still, all was silent. The ringing of the bell stopped abruptly. Five minutes, thought Murdstone. Five minutes until the performance resumed. They'd want her before then – but that tradesman's door he'd sensed, it had to be near.

'Don't look so startled, my dear. I've come to fetch you.'

Murdstone did not dive for her, not at first, for the man had spent all his energy sneaking through these crooked halls. It was his eyes, not his hands, that trapped her.

'Fetch me?' she floundered. 'Mr Murdstone, Sophia's waiting.'

'Well, dear, she'll wait a little longer. It's me you're coming with now.'

That was when he lunged.

Nell tumbled backwards, sliding out of his grasp. Two yards away, she crashed into the wall, if only to save herself from falling. '*No*,' she said. That little word again – but what did words matter?

'Let's not argue, Nell. You've an oath you must keep. What was it you promised your mother? To stay out of trouble, to do as Mr Murdstone says. Well, here I am – and I'm telling you to come. You've been living under some misapprehension, Nell. You're not here out of talent or charity. You're here because of a trade. Yes, that's right – your friend, the savage. The cut-throat. The Minotaur.' He let the word hang in the air. 'Don't look so surprised, Nell. He cares for you deeply. Lord knows what you did to inculcate such loyalty in a creature like him. But he came to me on Christmas night: his life offered, in exchange for your freedom.'

He could pinpoint the moment Nell's disbelief vanished. That was when he closed the gap between them, clawing out for her collar.

'He broke our contract, Nell.'

Nell stuttered, 'W-what?'

'Yes, that's right. Betrayed every promise he made on your account. So you're to come to me now. The agreement is void. The contract forfeit.'

'*No*,' she said.

Murdstone lifted his driftwood cane. 'Don't test me, Nell. There isn't time for—'

'*No!*' she repeated, and cast the slippers into his face as if something so paltry might beat him back.

Murdstone pitched forward. 'I've been good to you, Nell. If I've seemed hard and cruel, why, that's only been for the good of you. For the good of all my mudlarks. The river is hard. London is hard. What goodness comes from lying?' With each phrase, a faltering footstep. 'So I'll stop lying to you now. Here it is: the unblemished truth. He's in trouble, Nell. Your gentle, caring Minos killed two men. That's two families grieving on his account. Two families wanting justice. There's thief-takers across this city hunting for him now.'

Nell spat, 'You're lying!'

But Murdstone shook his head. 'There's but one hope for him now.'

Was doubt the most powerful force in a human life? Nell felt it swelling inside her; swelling like a river in torrent, ready to burst its banks.

'He needs you, Nell.'

The bell had started ringing again.

'That's the performance to start. Mr Murdstone, I'm to bring them those slippers.'

At last, Murdstone saw how it had to be. He folded his hands, feigned understanding. 'But then you'll come with me, Nell?'

She was cautious as she inched forward, more cautious still as she retrieved the slippers from where they'd fallen. Poor, trusting Nell, thought Murdstone. She thought she'd tricked him into some pact of her own, and of course she meant to betray it. She thought she would reach the dancers, tell them he had come, and the dancers would fold around her – and then there would be ushers and guards, desperate to drive Murdstone out.

That was why, the moment she got close, he drove the driftwood cane into the small of her back, to pummel the breath out of her, to force her to the floor. It was easier, down there, to wrap one arm around her breast while the other clamped shut her jaw. Easier to whisper into her ear that he would break her neck – because, even dead, she would serve his purpose. A lure, he told her. Bait for a trap.

'To bring your monster into the open, one last time. To make him come to heel.' He lifted her up, braced so hard that her pain and his became one, two knotted bodies lurching down the hallway together. 'Now,' he breathed, 'the door, Nell. Which way to the tradesman's door?'

It isn't the first time they've torn him from her. He doesn't remember the horror of the birthing chamber, the revulsion of the midwives – but he's heard tell of it because, even though he can only make mangled speech, a bovine lowing, somehow he can sense the meaning of their words. 'She tried to feed him milk, but all he wants is blood.' So they tore him away from her then – and they've been tearing him away from her ever since.

Every time he gets near: 'My queen, step back now.'

They drive at him with labrys and sabre.

Every time she tells them, 'This is my child!'

They dare to wrestle him by the horns.

'He gored the king's stallion last night. There's no telling what he'll do.'

'They feed him on gristle and bone, but his hunger is too much.'

So it is said, all over Knossos: something must be done about Pasiphae's bastard.

'My queen, you are mistaken. This isn't your son. This is an aberration. The gods have turned you into a folly, and all to punish the hubris of the king.' A pause, while her hand-maiden (a bed-mate, she is sure, of her husband's) tries to make her see. 'It's not your fault, my lady. You mustn't punish yourself so. It is Poseidon. It is Aphrodite. It is . . . madness.'

But if we define madness as a devotion which no other understands, aren't all who love mad?

He had to wrestle her back to the square, and all the while Nell thrashing in his arms. By the time he cast her into the waiting carriage, his own body was broken. One last effort, he told himself; one last mountain to climb. He saw the aghast look on the coachman's face but commanded his silence with a single bark. 'My bastard daughter,' he lied, 'but I'll kick some sense into her yet.' The coachman knew, of course, that it was a lie – for wasn't it said that Benjamin Murdstone had sired no sons or daughters at all, and this despite the breadth of his romantic associations? – but it made sense to feign agreement. He muttered some sympathetic remark, then returned to his task and drove the horses out towards the river.

Nell saw it rushing past. A part of her thought: I could throw myself out, take my chances with the night. But another said: there must be some truth in it; what else, if not truth, had brought Mr Murdstone to the Alhambra tonight? But the moment he saw her hand dart for the carriage door, Murdstone lifted his cane, beat her back to the floor. 'Leap if you can, Nell. Let the road break you. There's plenty of guttersnipes been crushed under a cartwheel in this city. It serves me just as well.'

'But who died?' she said, nursing her split lip, her swelling eye. 'How? Why?'

If Murdstone had answers, he was steadfast in keeping them hidden. 'He'll come when you call him.'

'Mr Murdstone, where is he?'

Murdstone gave no answer. Instead, he extended the tip of his cane again and, pressing it to Nell's chin, lifted her gaze to meet his. 'He'll come when you call, girl. But a warning word: you won't find him the same as he was, washed up on the tide. Whatever you think of your friend, change comes to us all.'

'Here,' said Sophia, 'these will fit.'

The music had already begun. There crouched Alyona, draped on her compatriot's shoulder while one of the lowlier dancers redressed her feet. In Nell's absence, Sophia had taken the slippers from her own feet, and now she handed them over; there was yet time for her to dart to the costume store and back before the Wills made their fateful appearance on stage. 'Alyona, it's time.'

The audience had settled again. The piano was joining mournful violins. The dancers of the Neva Ballet were steeled for the wild second act, for Giselle to be coaxed up from the unhallowed ground.

'Thank you, Miss Chrétien.'

But Sophia couldn't stay to see Alyona return to the grave, nor watch, through shimmering eyes, as the local gamekeeper's lad, Hilarion, wept over the burial mound. Instead, she sailed into the back halls, turning left, turning right, until she came to the costume store. 'Nell?' she asked of the seamstress inside. 'Was she here? What happened?'

The seamstress gave a likely look, as if this was something she'd expected all along. 'You can't trust a rag-girl, madam. She was here, right enough. Walked out of here with a pair of my satin slippers. But I daresay something else caught her eye on the way. Something shiny she had to lay those fingers on. Once a rag-girl, always a—'

Sophia marched into the store, robbed a pair of slippers from the hook, and sallied back through the Alhambra. No Nell in the shadows; no Nell nursing some discomfort in the dressing salons. No Nell here, no Nell there – but, back at the stage, the audience were waiting, and a host of ghostly dancers required their queen.

Sophia stepped among them. 'Are my Wills prepared?'

They crowded her side: nine dancers bedecked in white; nine spectres, ready to set sail.

The pianist hit some discordant chord. The beauty in

the music evaporated, for but a few fleeting moments. That was the summons; that was the moment when the realms of the living and dead met, and the Wills tore the caul separating one world from the next.

'Then come,' said Sophia.

How long had it been since she danced upon this stage? How long since any stage at all? Sophia flew out, the ghosts trailing after her, and felt the glare of a thousand eyes. There was fear in her, but that was only as it should be. The fear was what gave her focus.

She had quite forgotten what her body could do. She felt light, free, filled with the infinite possibilities of dance, as she reached the heart of the stage, and the mound where Giselle's body lay. The corps she'd sailed out with fanned around her, swirling towards those who cascaded from the shadows on the stage's opposite side. Now they would dance the incantation; here, in this ethereal light, they would summon the spirit that was once Giselle.

Sophia began.

Nell vanished from her thoughts, for but a moment. The girl had got nervous; the girl had grown scared. The doubt that had been eating away at her had overcome her, at last. Like so many others, she had been confronted with the realization of a dream – and, rather than rush into its embrace, she had cowered. Well, there was no shame in that. Fear gets the best of us all. Sophia would find her, once her work here was done, and lead her back to the life she deserved. It was the duty of all who had escaped penury to reach back into the mire and drag up their sisters and brothers. One day, it would be Nell upon this stage.

For now, though, all Sophia could do was dance.

So she danced with the Wills, as they brought Giselle back from the grave. She danced with the Wills, as they inducted Giselle and set about hunting their false-hearted lovers. She danced, as sweet Hilarion was driven to death; she danced, as they swarmed deceitful Albrecht.

And it was as the Wills swarmed Albrecht, compelling him to dance until his body was but a broken marionette, that Sophia turned to the thousand staring eyes of the Alhambra – and among them picked out one pair in particular.

Eyes, watching her from the gallery above.

Face banked in shadow, but recognizable all the same.

The same spark of recognition in his eyes as had flared in her own.

The Wills danced on, driving Albrecht towards his death – but it was their queen whose heart had stopped.

It was Sophia who breathed in the horror of that forest at night.

Soon it was Ratcliffe rushing past the windows; soon, flashes of the river under its ceaseless curtain of rain. Scarcely an hour had passed before Nell was being disgorged from the carriage, Murdstone's boot in her backside as she was driven into the familiar lodging house surrounds.

They must have sensed her coming in the attic of the Water's Edge – for, when Murdstone forced her up the ladder, the mudlarks were already awake. Sally-Anne wanted to rush to her – Nell could see the emotion colouring her face – but then Murdstone appeared and not a soul dared move.

Twelve ragged faces looked upon her. Twelve searching

sets of eyes. To travel from the cusp of a dream to the cusp of a nightmare had taken less than an evening's length.

'Put her at the window,' Murdstone barked. At first, the mudlarks were unmoved – but what Nell thought was protest was merely confusion. 'To the window, Nell!' he thundered – and out came Noah's groping hands to goad Nell back towards the bed where so many nights of her life had been spent in dreaming and dread.

'Empty your pockets,' Murdstone bawled as he paused to catch breath.

Days and nights spent away from the river were uncommon in Murdstone's life, and the suspicion that he was being cheated only grew with each hour away. He composed himself as pennies and farthings filled his fist. The truth was none of this mattered – before he saw another night fall, he was either risen or defeated – but something in the ritual soothed him.

When the mudlarks were done, and Murdstone's heart beating less wild, he fixed his gaze on Nell. 'She's to stay where she is through the night. In the window like that, where she can be seen. There's not one of you to sleep. You'll all stand guard. Prop her there, if she tumbles.'

In the window, Nell trembled. 'He's using me as bait,' she cried out. 'To trap Minos.'

Murdstone sighed. She had always been clever. Always had an imagination. He'd liked her for that, once upon a time. And at least she saw, now, how it had to be; no doubt that would help. He'd decided it as the carriage took him into St Giles, Elkington's edict still ringing in his ears. Minos hadn't simply fled Amberstone House; he wasn't simply running away. He was running *to*, and the only destination he had was Nella Hart.

'Aye,' said Murdstone. He limped an arc around the room, to take in all of the mudlarks at once. 'The beast is coming back to Ratcliffe. He'll come for Nell. And when he does, you'll need to be ready. I don't care how big you are. How small. I'll take you all with me when I leave the river – but you must do this for me tonight.'

There was silence in the attic. In the corner of her eye, Nell saw Packrat Jack and Potato Rot hanging their heads, as if desperate not to be seen. Then, into the silence, Noah said, 'Sir, we've already seen him.'

Nell's hands turned to fists. There was such tightness in her that she felt as if she was still held in somebody's grasp: Murdstone's clawing hands, Sophia's protective embrace, Minos taking her in hold.

Murdstone said, 'Minos was here?'

'He came to the river,' Noah stammered. 'It's like you said: he came looking for Nell.'

'And?'

'And he said he'd kill me.'

'*Liar!*' Nell could keep silent no longer. Her fists opened to raking claws.

'He isn't lying, sweetpea,' came Sally-Anne's tender voice. 'We heard him.'

'I told him we hadn't seen Nell, that she was gone from the river. You're right about him, Mr Murdstone. I don't know what he is, but he isn't a man. He's worse, worse than before. It's in his eyes. And he said – he said to tell her,' and here Noah turned to Nell, 'he'd look for you in your old places – but that he was . . . going to ground.'

Nell's imagination was in cascade. *Their* places. The seaward cave. The churchyard at St George in the East. Was it possible he'd been so foolish?

But it was Mr Murdstone's eyes that were alight. 'Gone to ground?' he whispered.

Yes, he saw it now – and, of course, he ought to have seen it before. As frightened children take flight for their mother's bosoms, so too do frightened men find comfort in their familiar haunts. Places they know by instinct; places, lodged in memory, where they feel safe.

There was no Labyrinth at Knossos any longer, but there was a labyrinth right here in London. Minos had been carving it with his own hands.

'Gather yourselves,' Murdstone announced, 'and Nell – to my side. It ends this night. And, tomorrow, we wake up changed.'

He's been hungry before, but it isn't until he's been shown to his Palace that the hunger speaks to him. Lonesome people (if he is 'people' at all) need company, and deprived of it they spirit it up. So it is that the hunger starts goading him. The yearning grows incandescent. He chases after every flicker of life in the Palace and, when he finds it, sets about it with teeth and horns. The boars they force down the Long Stair: part of him would pet them, but the greater part needs to tear them limb from limb. The billy goats, the braying ass – soon, he knows how to fill the yearning inside him. Later, he will be told that crying is how an excess of emotion releases itself from the body. Well, so is rage. The wild, uncontrollable feelings that pulse through him are exorcized only in blood and gore.

He learns to like the silence that violence can bring.

But then come the Athenians.

Seven men and seven women, forced down the Long Stair from the fortress above. He knows, straight away, that something is different. The scents, the sounds, the feeling in the air – all of it drives him towards them. And the yearning is different this time, too. There's hunger here, plain and simple, and that same chaos of feeling that ends with him slathered in viscera, lying sated on a carpet of bone – but there's a new need as well. Is it a need for explanation? A need to be known?

A need to touch and feel?

Perhaps it is all of these things, but he will never find out, for they scatter and scream at his approach. After them he goes, bellowing and lowing. All he wants is to hold them, but instead he feasts upon them all.

It is easier the next time.

It would be easier still the time after that, if only it wasn't for the hero.

The godly son sent to save them all.

Now he feels the piercing touch of Theseus's blade. A blade like this, the gift of a father, is already suffused in legend; that legend grows further still as it cleaves flesh from bone, as it carves patterns into the thick hide of his heart. Pain as bright as the birth of stars fills him up. This too spills out of him in rage. It is the fury that makes him dance. The blade that makes him buck and cavort. Stronger and stronger the anger grows, stronger and stronger the pain – until he isn't really here in the heart of his Palace at all; until he exists only as the purity of agony, the ecstasy of rage.

Then: blackness.

When he awakes, he is alone in the Palace, though the stink of their fear remains. His body is riddled with such scars that the god has surely left him for dead. And perhaps he really did die, only to be reborn, for the feeling in his heart is not one he has encountered before. There is some new contentment, some new awareness in him. And, as for the hunger, if it is here at all, it is dampened, more distant than since he was a calf, trotting after his mother in the fortress above.

And he gets to thinking, then, that something has changed. He picks himself up, to make a study of the brutalities wreaked upon his body: livid red welts, pulsing with heat; notches carved and fingers severed. But no, it is not the changes in his body that he feels most of all. This change is somewhere deeper, in his heart or mind. It is as if the yearning is spent, leaving only its traces behind. Like a human being who has cried too many tears and now lies parched upon their parlour floor. The god opened him up and out rushed the rage.

For the first time he thinks: what is my name?

Why am I here?

What am I for?

And it is as he trembles with these questions, making words in his mind where once was just feeling, that he looks down and sees it:

A length of string.

This Theseus, this destroyer, has left it behind.

By instinct he follows it. His body has been ruined, his veins bled dry, so he is weak as he staggers along the route it describes. This must be the path the destroyer took as he picked his way through the Palace. It goes in spirals, over the abysses and up the crumbled stairs, until it leads him into parts of his Palace even he does not know. Until he stands at the bottom of the Long Stair itself – and sees, up above, a tiny sliver of light.

He is trepidatious (when has he ever been trepidatious before?) as he climbs the Long Stair. He is more fearful (when has he ever been fearful?) as he reaches the light. It is here that the string reaches its end, knotted to the handle of a door that, in the Athenians' haste to get away, has not been closed.

Some piece of him believes he really is dead as he snouts his way through the fortress halls – for he sees no other soul, and this must mean he has woken as a shade, existing only in an ethereal Knossos. But he picks his way through the empty halls, letting his instincts lead him.

And his instincts lead him to a certain chamber in a certain wing, in a certain forbidden corner of the fortress.

There is no guard at the door. Not tonight. Perhaps there has been no need to guard here since they interred him in his Palace. So he shoulders into the chamber, still trailing blood.

And comes face to face with his mother.

How long has it been since he saw her? Time is without meaning in the Palace, but the years of his life have flown by. So too have hers. She looks different now. More empty, more withdrawn, pallid and grey. She, he thinks, is the real shade.

But her eyes light up when she sees him. There is terror here – for he has grown so large since they took him away – but there is wonder too. Love and fear, he will one day discover, so often go hand in hand.

'They said you were dead,' she gasps.

He opens his jaws to reply – because, for the first time in his life, his mind is formulating real words. But, of course, he cannot speak. He just lows sadly.

And there, in the pit of his stomach, the yearning reignites.
There and then he decides he will not let it overcome him.
He tries to swallow it down.

'Oh, my boy. The Athenians played a trick. They sent a
prince to kill you. My daughter helped him. Your sister helped
him.' His mother is breathless. She wants to cross the room to
be near him, but some invisible hand holds her back. 'Ariadne's
gone with the prince. They stole away at first light. The king
is beyond fury. He gathered the guard. He's manning the fleet
to reclaim her. And—' She lifts her hand to her mouth, to stifle
the sobbing. 'My son, what have they done to you? What have
they . . .' A sound startles her, but it brings her to some reve-
lation as well. 'Listen to me now. Hear me as your mother. I
never wanted this for you. The things they say about you —
well, I never believed them. If you have a monster in you, you
have me as well. You're of my flesh. You're your mother's son.'
She had started crying. He did not yet understand the meaning
of tears. 'So you must run. Don't look back. Don't think twice.
Run and keep running, until you've left this place, this
Labyrinth, far behind. You're more than they say. More than
they think. You're mine and I love you.'*

Beneath the streets of a rain-drenched city . . .

In the heart of a London sewer . . .

Minos awoke.

The cavity in which he stirred seemed smaller somehow.
Its brickwork, laid by his own two hands, glistened in what
lamplight remained.

He picked himself up. His body was telling him to run —
but surely that was just the dream, breaking forth into the
waking world.

You must run. Leave me here and run, my child.

435

Those words weren't for him, were they? That was what Nell's mother had said as she lay dying. His mind was spinning some fantasy, weaving together the threads of his life – stitching him to Nell, in the only way it knew how.

Nell.

He lumbered through the tunnel, back the way he had come.

Nell –

She was the one who could stop this. Take his hand and lead him from madness.

'Nell!'

Too late, he realized he had called her name out loud. His fever was raging. He was not, he thought, in his own body. This pressure inside him – in the dream world, he would have called it *yearning. Hunger.*

He hadn't meant to kill those men.

It was the Minotaur who had done it, not him.

But weren't they one and the same?

Something was changing in the edges of his vision. As the tunnel dissolved, he realized that the pressure was not only building inside his breast. It seemed to be here in the world around him, throbbing in the sewer walls.

But then those walls were gone – and, in their place, the black stone chasms of his Palace fizzled into view. He looked left; he looked right. He looked forward; he looked back. All he could see were his border fires and the depths of the Forever Dark. So onward he plunged, into the Labyrinth of his mind.

The rain sliced into Nell as she found herself kicked from the carriage, a tumult of other mudlarks at her hind. What hour it was, she did not know. The sky was a seething mass of grey, the sodden earth turned to swampland across the tracks of St Giles.

Murdstone was barking at her, his body rippling behind the curtain of rain. She barely heard his words, but knew what he was saying well enough. She turned to the hoardings. She supposed she was not very far from the Alhambra Circus – where, right now, the Neva Ballet would be taking their bows, where Sophia would be seeking her out backstage – but it would not do to brood on that, not now that Murdstone was propelling her towards the gap in the hoardings, and all the mudlarks watching as she went.

'I won't do it,' she cried out. 'Mr Murdstone, I won't!'

'You will, Nella. You'll bring him to me.'

Inside the yard, figures milled. The light of an oil lantern spilled from a lean-to pressed up against the hoardings, and yet more rose up from an open chasm in the ground. Mounds of scaffold and brick were crowned in canvases, scaling ladders propped against the walls. Sandbags, darkened by the rainfall, bordered a great pool where the falling rain thrashed.

And a half-dozen faces looked up from beneath their raincoats and wax caps to confront the intruders.

'What is the meaning of this?'

Nell watched as one of the men detached himself from the others and tramped across the yard, the glare of the lantern light obscuring his piggy little face. The man was no bigger than Murdstone, but a generation younger. He puffed himself up with authority as he approached – but, unlike Murdstone, he achieved no imperiousness as he walked. His voice broke as he said, 'You, sir? You again?'

'Out of my way, Kale,' Murdstone proclaimed, and hustled him backwards with his driftwood cane.

With one hand wrapped around Nell's neck, Murdstone staggered towards the sandbags that ringed the chasm. Too late, he realized that the men here were not Kale's workers, but officers of the law. A likely lot of Theseuses, they looked. He rounded on Kale and said, 'He's down there, then? The brute came back?'

'Scant hours ago. Vanished a second time, then just turned up and rampaged through. But this time we can't abide it. This time he's gone too far. I told him there'd be no pay. That I'd call for the peelers if he crossed that line. But the man never listened. He was lost in his own head. Waltzing in here, making his threats. A man like that, it's monstrosity. You don't know him like I do.'

Nell said, 'I'm the only one who does.'

Nell wriggled forward, freeing herself from Murdstone's grasp, and peered over the edge of the sandbags.

The Underworld, Minos had called it. The city beneath the city. The veins along which London's blood would flow. It was like gouging a knot out of your flesh and looking into the world within. Other men shifted down there; she could hear the echo of footsteps, a man's reverberating cry. She wondered how deep the tunnels stretched. Murdstone had said that the sewers would be the end of the mudlarks; that, one day, they'd wall the Thames and all of London would be tamed. If that was so, it meant these tunnels stretched north and south, east and west, that he might be hiding in any corner of a London much older than this. It would be easy to lose yourself down there. To turn left, then right; to plough forward, then back; to look up and realize you had strayed too far, that you had no way of knowing your way back to the surface. Not unless . . .

One of the peelers had grabbed her by the shoulder. It was always a man's hands wrestling with her, casting her down into the dirt. Only Minos had ever been different; only Minos had ever danced. And now they said he had killed two men.

'Back from there, brat.'

Sally-Anne rushed to pick her up. 'Sweetpea, give me your hand.' But, before Nell was on her feet, Murdstone reclaimed her. This close, the lines of his face seemed deeper than ever. It was Murdstone's features that were ridged, tonight; Murdstone's head that was sprouting horns. 'Nell, we must find him first. These men don't yet know what he is, but it's only a matter of time.'

Outside the hoardings, another carriage had appeared. Out of it poured other men: not peelers, these, nor thief-takers come to hunt a killer; Elkington's men, answering their summons at last. Murdstone had left a message at the gate as they coursed out of Ratcliffe, diverting through Farringdon Within. Only five had answered the calling, but five armed men was better than none. Murdstone saw these had come with old pepper-box pistols tucked into their waists.

'Do you know where he is?' Murdstone demanded of Kale.

'We haven't ventured far. The rains are too much. The clay can't take no more. It's standing water down there. But Minos knows that – these tunnels aren't finished, the rivers too full. He must have gone deep. He must know we'd come to unearth him.'

Murdstone crouched, face contorted towards Nell. 'You'll bring him to me now.'

'I won't!' she snapped, and fought to get free.

'You will, if you know what's good for you . . .'

Murdstone brought his hand back, as if to strike her for her insolence. Yes, he thought, if the beast heard her crying, then he would surely come. But he needed her closer; the beast needed to *know*. He lost himself in thought, then hissed, 'He's of no worth to me hanging from a rope. If you won't believe in the goodness of an old man's heart, then believe I would never sabotage the greatest trade of my life. I'll lift you from the river, Nell.' He braced her shoulder. 'I'll lift all of you.' Then he put his blistered lips to her ear and whispered, 'Except Noah, if that's what you ask. I'll leave him to rot. Just say the word.' He drew back, looked her in the eye. 'Whatever you want, if you'll do this for me.'

At once, the echo of some agonized cry erupted from the chasm. Up and ever upwards it billowed – until it seemed to Nell that the earth itself was screaming.

In the yard, the mudlarks froze. The peelers, Elkington's men, Beresford Kale. The cry went on and on – until abruptly it stopped, and all that was left was the percussion of the rain.

'I won't go down there,' said one of the peelers as he tumbled away from the opening. 'The man's lost his mind. I've a wife waiting at home.'

They were scrambling backwards when Murdstone said, 'I heard it, Nell. Did you?'

Against her will, she nodded.

'Then take the lantern, girl.' He had lifted one from the

sodden earth, where Kale had dropped it. 'He'll come to you. He needs you now.'

'And then you'll take him.'

Murdstone counted his army. Too few, of course, to imprison the brute – but there was another way. Fill the beast with shot, carve him with blades; weaken him, as he'd been on the river, and imprison him while he slept. If one or two lost their lives on the way, bringing yet more of the Minotaur back to the man, well, that might serve his purpose too. Ropes hadn't held him. Iron bars might. And Nell, held hostage, to compel him. Yes, there was a chance here. An ivory sundial in the dirt.

'Yes, Nell,' said Murdstone. 'Then he'll live up to his promise. Then the beast is mine.'

Murdstone's throttling hands compelled her back to the precipice. There she dangled, staring into the swirling darkness. The glowing orbs of the few peelers who had already ventured below were all but gone now. Only a faint luminescence remained.

He truly did need her, she thought. Because, somewhere beneath her, he was reeling from tunnel to tunnel, hunted and harried, his dreams of the seaward cave brought vividly to life.

And just like in those old dreams, he was chasing a phantom, begging for a little hand in his own, for a whispered voice to guide him.

Just like in those old dreams, Minos was calling her name.

24

The Key to the Labyrinth

London, January 1862

There was nothing but the Forever Dark in the Palace. No
fires to guide him any more – though there was water
enough, rising around his horned toes, coating the stone
passages through which he fled. There had been a time
when instinct was enough to guide him through the darkness, but not any longer. He kept roaring out, to hear the
echo of his cries resounding along the forked passageways
and ravines. He kept drawing in great breaths, as if to scent
the Athenians (but *was* it Athenians?) who were coming
down the Long Stair. But none of it was enough. He was
blind. He was deaf. He was falling, falling, falling.

Falling into dreams older than time.

Falling into history and myth . . .

'On with you, now. On with you, I said!'

There was no resisting the tide that swept Nell into the
darkness: Murdstone's hand around her throat, Elkington's
men flanking her as they entered the abyss. Gander and
Noah were somewhere in this melee, Potato Rot and Packrat
Jack lagging behind with the foreman named Kale. What
peelers had joined the party seemed not to care about the

442

way Murdstone forced her along the first tunnel. Not one
of them paid it any mind when the driftwood cane sent her
sprawling, and Murdstone hoisted her up from the effluent
now marking tributaries across the sewer floor. 'Call out
for him, girl,' Murdstone kept barking. 'Call his name. By
God, he calls yours.'

'I won't,' Nell spat. She'd seen the shot being fed into
the pistols. She'd seen the clubs and blades. 'I won't,' she
cried again.

'Then I'll make you,' Murdstone seethed, and took her
by the neck again. 'Which way from here?' he barked back,
and soon Beresford Kale was picking his way through the
footmen to reach the head of the column.

'South is towards the river. It's to follow the watercourse
from Charing Cross, all the way to the estuary. There are
other teams working to join us, but the tunnels don't meet,
not yet. That's where Minos was working. And, by God,
come and see.'

Nell had to strangle her voice three times as Murdstone
wrenched her on. Some piece of her wanted to scream for
him to run, but in the end a deeper fear won out: if she
screamed, Minos would surely come, and she did not mean
to be the bait in this trap. That was why she bit her lip
until it bled. That was how, staggering in front of Murdstone
with Kale's wavering lantern making a kaleidoscope of
shadows up ahead, she followed the forking passageways
into the city beneath. The further they delved, the deeper
the water that rose at her feet; she could sense some camber
in the tunnel, though her eyes could hardly perceive it. It
was the trickle of water that told her they were venturing
lower. The strange pressure in her ears. By the time she

bowed beneath an archway of brick – where the keystones shimmered, as if with dew – the pressure had reached a new intensity. Some spell of deafness had come upon her; if Minos was calling for her now, it was muffled by the gasp of her own breath, the roiling in her ears.

The cane in her back told her that Murdstone had been shouting. She looked up, through wildly dancing orbs of light. 'Call for him, damn you!' Now that she saw his lips, it was clear what he was saying. When Nell shook her head again, the cane whirled out to wrongfoot her. The only reason she didn't crash to the floor was that Murdstone himself was ready to catch her. Trip her with one hand, while protecting her with the other – yes, that was Benjamin Murdstone. She tried to break free, but he was holding her fast. Then, when the exertion was too much for him, he flung her bodily at one of Elkington's men, who snatched her up.

'Don't let the bastard go.'

Something had righted itself in Nell's hearing; these were the first words she heard. Very quickly, they were followed by a clamour of other voices as Kale beckoned the rest to flock through.

Under the archway, the footman barrelled Nell.

So, then, this was the place where Minos once laboured; the place, Nell remembered, where he had spent so many of his nights after washing up on the river. He'd described it only fleetingly, just his hole in the ground, and she felt ashamed, now, that she hadn't been able to picture it. He always conjured up such flights of fancy for her. He'd taken her to the courts of Rome, to the frozen north, to lands beyond the sea – but of this hole in the ground she knew nothing.

She tried to resist as she was cast into the oubliette, a cavernous bulb at the end of the sewer where barrows sat slumped and dust from the excavations had turned to sludge at her feet. The officers of the law had arrived first, and now they lifted their lanterns to reveal the walls. Murdstone was already voicing his wonder, but Nell had to crane her neck to see. Then the wonder reached her too. Across every wall, engraved upon every brick, ran the same interlocking lines that somebody had inked upon Minos's back: his Labyrinth, repeated over and over again, carved by chisel or flint and trembling hand.

'It's been living inside him,' Murdstone snapped. 'Don't you see it, Nell?'

The footman was still holding her fast. Nell wrestled against his hold, but it was no use. When she fought too much, he only struck her across the face.

'Leave her alone!'

Gander's voice, somewhere in the tunnel, was drowned out by the footman, who wrestled Nell so close to the wall that she could trace one of the labyrinths with her finger. The brick was jagged where the paths had been scored. Her finger caught a serrated edge, beading blood which ran with the dew in one of the grooves. She followed its path until it reached the heart of the spiral.

It was what he had been doing all his life, she thought. Trying to escape from this Labyrinth, trying to put its twists and turns, switchbacks and dead-ends behind him. Then along came Mr Murdstone, to take him by the hand and lead him back into its heart. 'You did this to him,' she started to say – but the footman shook her so hard that the words died on her tongue.

'Where did he go from here?' Murdstone demanded.

A constellation of lamplights filled the oubliette. 'He might be anywhere,' said Beresford Kale. 'One wonders if he himself knows where he is.'

'One wonders,' Murdstone replied, 'if he even knows what century he's in.' He took the tip of his cane and drove it beneath Nell's chin, forcing her to see. 'Call his name, girl.'

'I won't,' she stammered.

'Do it this moment, or you're damned.'

'*No*,' she said.

Murdstone swung his cane around, as if to clear the centre of the oubliette. 'I told you before, Nella Hart, that you served me just as well dead or alive. But I'm a fair man. Haven't I always been fair to you? Well? *Well?*' His eyes danced around, to take in the other mudlarks crowding the archway that led back the way they had come. Only half had ventured below, but none would look him in the eye. 'I'm offering you your life. Call his name, Nell.'

She had started shaking. Scant hours ago, in the wings of the Alhambra, she'd watched Giselle dance – but you always woke from a dream. It never lasted long. 'If you find him, you'll kill him.'

Murdstone shook his head. 'But Nell, what use is he dead?' He paused. 'The river couldn't kill him. What chance a man? No, call his name for me, my dear. Call his name and let's end this.'

'Then he'll – *he'll* kill *you*.'

There: she had summoned the fear, spoken its true name. Minotaur or man, she'd seen the fury inside Minos, and Murdstone said that two were already perished on his account. Summon him here, thought Nell, and he'd do the same. Right here in the Labyrinth, as in days of old. '*No,*' she said, and then started babbling the word, over and over again, until its magic was spun, until she could speak it no longer.

Murdstone heaved a sigh. To his credit, thought Nell, the thought of what came next did seem to pain him. It didn't stay his hand, but his eyes were filled with regret as he brought back the driftwood cane for its final, righteous purpose.

There is good and bad in every man.

In the world above, Sally-Anne cowered in the lean-to, three of the smaller mudlarks sheltering behind her. The rain came in waves, then beat a retreat, churning up the open earth in the yard. Sometimes, the cries from below erupted out of the chasm where the few remaining workmen and officers gathered – but the voices seemed to be fading now. Perhaps that meant all was safe, or perhaps it meant they had drifted too far into the underworld below. She was trying to calm the others, telling them that they'd be back in their beds before the night was through, when a singular scream – more vivid, more visceral than all the rest – echoed up from beneath, shaking the scaling ladders and sandbags.

'Is it him?' asked one of the peelers. 'The beast?'

The workmen had not got used to calling him 'beast' yet, so it was Sally-Anne who stepped out of the lean-to and said, 'That wasn't him. That was—' *Nell*, she didn't say, for now another bass rumble came from below. It did not sound like Minos calling Nell's name; indeed, it hardly sounded human at all. Not the cry of beast or man – more like a rupturing of the earth, the shattering of brickwork and stone, the release of some wild, pent-up pressure.

Sally-Anne was not the only one who had heard it. Such consternation crossed the faces of the men crowding the sandbags that Sally-Anne rushed to their side and forced her way between them – but all she could see was blackness below.

The first said, 'It might just be the rain. There's been so much.'

'Aye,' said the second, 'and snowmelt, swelling the rivers since thaw.'

'The river?' breathed Sally-Anne.

Everything came back to the river, she thought; the river, the world. But what had that to do with the earth underneath her, the tunnels in the old city, the Grand Endeavour?

'Not the Thames, you fool,' the elder workman cried. He brandished a lantern over the sandbags, trying to make some sense of what was happening below. 'London's a city of islands – or was, in the elder times. There's the Fleet down there. The Tyburn. The Effra and Black Ditch. All the old conduits and washes. Half of them buried by the time you were born, I should think – and the rest being buried now, and us doing the burying. Don't you see?' He cringed upwards, eyes narrowing against the rain, as if to judge the time by storm-laden skies. 'It's high tide, and all the buried rivers too full. The bulwarks aren't finished. The culverts too weak. I told Kale this could happen. Didn't I tell him?' His fellow nodded gravely. 'It isn't just the Thames that can burst its banks, girl. Put walls around a river and it's still a river. You might tell yourself it's tamed, but a river *remembers*. Hold a force like that back and it's bound to explode. It can only hold itself in so long. Listen to it, girl! It's happening right now.'

Minos heard her scream. He'd heard terror like this too many times in his long, storied life. Pain, and the fear of pain to come; that bass note was the desperation of someone who tells themselves they will not beg for mercy, but whose body betrays them when the agony begins.

He'd felt that fear. He'd fed off it so many times.

Why, then, did this feel different?

The pounding he could hear was the thunder of his own heart, but now another sound rampaged through the tunnels. It was like a distant wind stirring. Like a stampede of trotters, as some sounder of boars was driven down the Long Stair. He could not orient himself. He was lost, and that could only mean that he'd strayed too far, beyond those parts of the Palace he had always known: the heart of the Labyrinth, where the altar was cracked in two; his sanctum, with its carpet of bones. The border fires had all perished, but he had never been afraid of the darkness before. Indeed, he realized now, he had never really been afraid. And yet now it filled up his body, buzzing like carrion flies. Where was the hunger? Where was the *yearning*? It was all gone, and in its place only fear.

Then: that scream on the stirring wind. Not the scream of some sorry Athenian, muscle ripping from bone between his own jaws. The scream of a child: Nell, here in the dark. And he knew, in that moment, that this was not the Palace of his memory, that he was not lost in a dream. This was real, and he could scent her; she was close and getting closer.

Lights crossed the maw of the tunnel, somewhere ahead. A constellation of stars, sailing past with panicked footfall and voices in full cry. He scented other men too. Among them, one scent in particular clawed out. *Murdstone.* Yes, that was the man who had goaded him towards murder. The man who buried a knife in his side with one hand, then revealed a salve in the other.

Here was the hunger.

Here was the yearning.

He was about to take off after them, but at that moment the second sound crashed over him. He'd known sounds like this as well. Sometimes, the earth put up its own protest at the evils being wreaked upon it. Stairs crumbled in his Palace. Ravines opened beneath the knot of passageways Daedalus had connived.

Rivers burst their banks.

Now it wasn't just Nell that he scented. Now it was the Tyburn. Now it was the Fleet. The imprisoned rivers of London were rising up. You couldn't build a labyrinth for a river, any more than you could a Minotaur or man.

He started to run.

Lanterns lit the darkness.

'Not that way,' came the voice of Beresford Kale. Though Nell, hanging bloodied and limp in one of the footmen's arms, could see so little, somehow she sensed they had reached some strange imitation of Seven Dials above, where tunnels plunged in manifold different directions. The orb of Kale's lantern light inspected each in turn. 'There's standing water in the south. The Thames has been too heavy since the snow. And—'

'Mr Kale, this water is running.'

Nell peered around. One of her eyes was swollen shut, but the other saw well enough. The eldest of Kale's workmen was bowed at the interlocking brickwork of the sewer floor, his fingers trailing in the effluent. After some time, he drew his fingers to his nostrils and snorted in the scent. 'River water. It's ripe.'

'The earth's holding too much,' Kale ventured to explain. 'He won't be further south than here. We should take—' His lantern had been scouring the tunnel openings, divining the possibilities of each, but here he stopped. One of the buttresses still in place at the archway was cracked, the timber bowed where it had met some unstoppable force. Kale ventured near, running a finger along the splintered wood. 'This one,' he ventured.

Murdstone gestured to the footman. 'Down with her now,' he demanded, and Nell felt herself cast onto the floor.

The shock of it was nothing compared to the blows she had already endured. She did not have breath to cry out, and picked herself up only when Murdstone's hand was back at her neck. 'You'll lead, Nell.'

'No, Mr Murdstone. Mr Murdstone, please . . .'

'Yes, that's it, girl. Keep up the begging. Louder, now. Louder, until he hears.'

Nell sought out Gander in the crowd, but the tunnel was crowded, the light too inconstant. Before she had found a single consoling face, Murdstone was kicking her on. Each blow to her back brought some fresh bleating; each step, the driftwood cane clattering at the place where her feet had just been. The only way to keep from crying out was to scramble forward. One step out of reach meant one more step in silence.

The darkness dragged her on.

'Mr Murdstone!' Kale's voice, in the darkness somewhere behind. Nell looked back, to discover a border of blackness between her and the footmen. Murdstone was ringed in the lantern light. He barked for Kale to be silent, but Kale went on, 'We have to go back. Mr Murdstone, look.'

Nell looked down. She was aware of the water playing against her feet, but now she saw other shadows flitting in the edges of her vision. The dark chitter of rats, feet scrambling over the brickwork, reached her ears. She'd been breathing too heavily to notice until now, but the rats were too many. They were coursing past, taking to the walls, daring to weave through the forest of legs behind Nell. Through the light, into the blackness beyond.

'They're frightened,' said Kale.

'Of course they're frightened,' Murdstone returned, turning back to face the throng. 'They can sense him too.'

'You have the wrong of it, sir. A rat's no more afraid of a sewer-man than he is a gull on the river. They live here among us. They've skittered around Minos's feet since summer. It's not him they're frightened of.'

The voices behind her faded to silence as Nell peered into the darkness ahead. And the thought struck her, then, that this was her moment; this, her chance to take flight. Half-blind already – what difference would it make if she abandoned the lanterns, if she gave herself to the inky black? All it would take was a sightless scurrying forward. Lose herself in these tunnels, and they couldn't use her as their bait. Throw herself into the void, and what had they to lure Minos on?

Her body burned with the aftershocks of Murdstone's blows, but perhaps that didn't matter. She realized, as she took the first step, that she'd already made the decision. The feeling was not so different from that first night at the Water's Edge, having left him at the mercy of dreams in the seaward cave. It was in loneliness that you lost yourself; in togetherness you were found. When you were somebody's token, you did not give up on them so easily.

The voices faded behind her. 'You learn to trust the instincts of rats,' Kale was saying. 'Mr Murdstone, the water – look at it, what current there is. It's coursing this way. We need to turn back.'

The lights of their lanterns faded too. Even as she reached the next joining of tunnels, not one of them noticed she had gone. The paltry glow that reached her was almost gone now. Two roads diverged in front of her. She took the first step.

'Oh, but they haven't seen him like this,' Murdstone whispered, somewhere behind. 'Trust to your rats, Kale. Take us to whatever they're fleeing. We'll find our quarry there –' Murdstone turned back to the tunnel, only to find blackness where Nell had once stood. Then, suddenly, he was screaming her name. 'Stay there, Nell! Stay where you are! After her, you fools – she's the only reason you won't be killed down here!'

The darkness embraced Nell, but running through it was more difficult than she'd thought. It wasn't just the water, now rising above her feet, that slowed her; the blackness, too, seemed to have some impenetrable quality: thick and viscous, dragging her back the way she had come. She had stumbled twice already when she heard the pounding steps behind her; was picking herself up from the roiling water when the lantern light reclaimed her again. Then somebody's hands were all over her, dragging her back to her feet. Fingers closed over her mouth as she was turned to the light.

It was one of the footmen who strangled her, but Murdstone was here soon enough. Funny, but Kale and the workmen hadn't followed. She searched for the mudlarks too, but all she could see was Murdstone's face.

'I'm going to tell him to let go of you now, Nell, but you won't scream until I tell you. Do you understand?'

She only glared.

'Nell?'

The breath was fading from her. She nodded, fiercely, and gasped for air when the footman let her go.

'How long must we play this game?' Murdstone rasped. 'Call him, and let's be done with it.'

There was no silence in the sewer any longer, for the sound of surging water filled the air. Nell felt it pulling at her. Yet more rats darted in its channels. She wanted to say: I won't, Mr Murdstone. She needed to say: you'll have to kill me first. And perhaps she would have done just that, if only something hadn't drawn her back, in that moment, to those dreams Minos had had, back in the seaward cave. Dreams of tunnels just like this; dreams of being lost, afraid, hunted, alone. Dreams which, she realized now, were simply memories rewritten, the stories of his damaged mind – and, right now, the stories of hers.

'Well, Nell, what's it to be?'

'Don't breathe a word, little one,' came a voice from somewhere in the dark. 'I've come to end this.'

It was Gander who heard the scream. Kale's workmen were picking their way back up the tunnel, following the rats as they fled, but the mudlarks remained beneath the brick archway, holding onto each other in the single pool of lamplight that remained. 'We should go too,' Noah had said, 'we don't know the way back, not without Kale.' That seemed to be the opinion of the peelers who'd ventured beneath as well. 'Let the floodwaters flush him out. We've no duty here.' But all of them were silenced by the scream.

'That wasn't Nell,' said Gander.

No, because grown men screamed too. Here came one of them, caterwauling back up the tunnel, bursting out of the blackness into the glow of their own lamp.

He did not get a chance to breathe a word, because in the same moment he arrived came the eruption of shots being fired. Short, violent slashes in the black of the tunnel, each one distinguished by a flash of orange fire.

'Boys,' the footman said – and Gander saw, now, that one side of his face was dripping in crimson, 'you've got to run. It's him. It's him – and everything Murdstone said is true. Boys, he has horns.'

Murdstone's forearm tightened around Nell's neck. Thank the Lord – whose existence Murdstone had always denied – for the life he'd been given; it had bred into him the instincts of malice and self-preservation that those born to better lives too often lacked. In the same second the beast made his voice heard, Murdstone had snatched for her. Now he wrestled her backwards as Minos stepped into view.

The footmen had dropped their lanterns in their haste to draw the revolvers from their waists. All but one extinguished in the water at their feet. The one that remained lit Minos from below as he emerged from some ulterior tunnel. Hunched in the sewer's surrounds, it seemed to Murdstone that he had grown in size since the tragedy at Amberstone House. His body rippled with violence. His great hands, curled into fists, bore yellowed claws where the fingers once tapered to nails. Yet it was only when the footmen started firing that his true visage was revealed. In the flash of each muzzle, Minos's face was lit up. His eyes, brimming with purpose; his jaw, always protuberant, bearing its tombstone teeth; his temples, matted already with blood and sporting heavy, spiral horns.

The shots met his breast. Blossoms of blood coloured the footmen closest to him – one took flight, losing his revolver to the water – but Minos did not topple. His body was a fortress. His hide like armour. He bowed forward. The smell of shit filled the air. Apt for the sewer, thought Murdstone, but of course it was his own drawers that were filling up. 'I've come to stop this,' the beast had said, but there was only one way it would stop. 'Take another step and I'll kill her,' Murdstone said. 'You know I will, sir. I've nothing left to barter with. Nothing left to lose. I'll be dead by fall of next night unless we reach some concord, so here we stand – you and I, for the last time. We can stop this together.'

'Put her down,' said Minos.

Nell sank her teeth into Murdstone's finger. She'd done that once before, but tonight he seemed impervious to its effects, bearing the agony of it just as Minos bore the shots. What words she tried to scream out were strangled. She could taste his blood. But there was Minos, and everything Murdstone had said on Christmas night was true: the spurs of bone that crowned his head were undeniable now, horns that had broken forth just as his history poured out of him. The Minotaur, escaping its Labyrinth for the second time.

The footmen were hurrying to reload their weapons. Only one had taken flight; that seemed, to Murdstone, a victory of sorts. He stepped backwards, the water playing against his shins. When had it risen that high?

'Look at you,' he said, and Nell detected the wonder that still hummed beneath the fear. 'You sorry soul, you didn't even know it. But here you are and—'

It was only Nell who realized Murdstone was stalling for time; Minos strode forward, as if to awake the fear he now knew he was capable of invoking. Nell felt that fear all around her. She felt it in her own heart. But then the air was alive with gunshot again, and the flashes of each barrel robbed her of sight. This time, she heard Minos lowing. Murdstone tightened his brittle hold on her. 'Aim for his head, you fools! The bastard survived the river, he can survive this. But put him down. Give him all you've got! Blades, now! Cudgels, you dogs! He won't fight back, not when I have the girl.'

It was only when the muzzle flash faded that Nell saw the melee. The second shots had opened Minos's breast more deeply than the first. The shirt she'd peeled back so carefully in the seaward cave was awash in viscous red. For the first time, she saw how his breast was furred, coarse and black and shimmering wet in the lantern light.

The footmen, seized by either bloodlust or bravado – or else undertaking, by instinct, to fight instead of flee – had thrown themselves at Minos. Their revolvers were gone; now, they took to him with daggers and clubs. One of them was gored already, nursing his ruined shoulder against the sewer wall. The others swarmed him, like street dogs to a stray ass.

Now they were on top of him.

Now, forcing him into the water.

He reared up for breath, only to be driven down again; he palmed one of the footmen away, only for another to throw his weight upon his arm, then brace it beneath the water. 'Hold him there!' Murdstone was saying, still oblivious to Nell's incisors making meat of his finger. 'Hold him until he's no breath left.'

At last, Nell's teeth found bone – and Murdstone, alive to the pain for the first time, pulled his hand away. 'Minos!' she sobbed, in time to see his horns rise from the water, his open jaws inhaling as much water as air.

'Look at him,' Murdstone whispered, 'he won't fight back.'

Sewer water fountained from Minos's jaws. In the lamplight, his eyes found Nell. She gazed into him, into whatever he was. 'Just do it,' she cried out, 'just fight!'

But, 'No,' said Murdstone. 'He knows what happens if he does.'

'I don't care!' Nell cried. One of the footmen had found courage enough to wrestle with a horn now. His full weight on it was driving Minos back under the water. 'Stop it, Mr

458

Murdstone. Mr Murdstone, he can't breathe. I'll do anything. *We'll* do anything. Just−' Minos's head vanished. What fight was left in his legs seemed to die. His body bucked twice, but the ferocity was gone; the rage, bleeding out of him just as his life's blood pumped into the water. 'He can't breathe, Mr Murdstone. Let him up. Let him up. Let him−'

Packrat Jack and Potato Rot were already gone, tumbling over their own heels as they chased Kale's fading light. Gander knew he should follow, but every footstep was faltering. Then he heard the scream and stopped dead.

'Out of my way,' Noah cried out. 'I'll not stay here. I've fought the devil once already. I'll not do it again . . .'

He shouldered Gander aside, but before he could take flight, Gander snagged hold of his sleeve. 'That's Nell,' he said. 'Noah, that's Nell.'

'She's the one who brought it on us.' Noah tore his arm free. 'You're a fool, to die for her. You're a bloody fool.'

Gander watched him go, swallowed by the blackness further down the tunnel. Then he turned back to the desperation. At least there was light up there. Wan light, spilling around the next turn. And perhaps it was better that Noah wasn't with him. How many opportunities had he had to show his worth? How many chances to show he wasn't all rot? If there was good and bad in every soul, how often did the good win out? How often bravery over cowardice?

'Please,' Nell was begging, her little voice rising out of the tumult.

Gander plunged into the black. He hadn't realized, until he started fighting it, how urgent the current against his legs, nor how deep the waters had grown. Flailing through it was like picking his way through the shallows of the river – but at least this was the artistry of his life. He had to palm off the sewer walls as he reached the end of the tunnel, but he did not fall.

He turned the corner.

There stood Murdstone, directly in front of him, with Nell entombed in his arms. The tumult was beyond them. The footmen swarmed the beast. Gander could see so little, only arms wheeling out to drive back his attackers; limbs thrashing in the water, a head – the flash of horns, the gape of jaws – rising from the surface and gasping for breath.

Nell was bucking in Murdstone's arms.

But Gander knew what he must do.

There'd been fights aplenty on the river; you did not grow up on the streets of Ratcliffe without taking your beatings, nor learning how to dish one out. Yet every piece of him rebelled at the idea he might strike Murdstone. He supposed that was the teaching of Ratcliffe too – for dogs who bit the hand that fed them always starved in the end.

Something caught his eye: a flash of dull metal, turning in the water. He bowed to retrieve it. One of the footmen's pepper-box pistols, ice cold in his hand. He did not know how to use it, but that did not matter. Every blunt instrument was a weapon.

It did not pay to think. He raised it up and smashed it directly into Murdstone's skull.

Nell felt Murdstone's arms go slack. She plunged forward, found herself submerged in the current, then lifted herself, just in time to see Mr Murdstone crumbling against the wall – and Gander hanging above. Murdstone had let go of his driftwood cane with the blow. Nell felt it turn past her as the current took it in hold. Then off it went, eddying into the dark.

The old man was slumped, the water rising about his breast. Dazed, thought Nell, but not dead. He gave some guttural groan, but Nell paid it no mind, for now Gander was straining to lift her. 'We've got to go,' the elder mudlark was saying. 'Now, Nell, before it's too late.'

It was those words that told the footmen Murdstone was overpowered. One peered over his shoulder; then another, his entire being focused on bracing Minos's head below, dared to look. Perhaps it was that momentary change in the man's concentration that gave Minos his chance. Nell had thought his body was broken, but even men on the precipice of death find the strength to say goodbye. When his head broke through the surface, his roar filled the tunnel.

It had filled the tunnels beneath Knossos, once.

It had risen through the king's fortress.

Through the streets of the city beyond.

Across the oceans that divided one kingdom from the next.

A legend, being born.

The footmen tumbled back, felled not by his raking claws – for, yes, Nell saw that he bore claws now – but by his strangled roar. His body was still a ruin as he rose out of the water. One of his arms hung oddly from its socket, though the blooded muscles still throbbed. He staggered forward, swiping past the footmen – who either turned against the wall, unwilling to see their deaths, or fled into the deeper submerged darkness of the tunnel. Only one still clung to his weapon. The falchion blade trembled in his hand. Nell watched as he levelled it towards Minos, with the fading courage of the last Athenian left standing. If this is death, he seemed to be saying, then let me go to it fighting.

Noble thoughts, for such ignoble times – but it did not matter; you might hold the notion in your heart, but your body did not have to obey. There was no chance the footman could drive that blade into the beast that loomed above him; little chance of cutting cake, with tremors like these.

Only one step divided them now. Nell watched as Minos closed the gap, the water turning to waves beneath him. He bowed his head. His great horns glimmered. From the depths of him came sounds that spoke of agony and devastation, of hunger and rage. One moment a man, thought Nell (recalling, in that tortured moment, the words Sophia had spoken), but one moment something far beyond. She had to squint to make out the Minos she had nursed in the seaward cave. She had to squint still further before she could see the Minos she'd danced with, wreathed by the river's first snow.

He was but inches from the footman. At last, the man lost his grip on the falchion blade. Down it went, into waters ribboned with blood.

Down came Minos, to meet the man.

Nell had been crying out all along, but even she could barely hear it echo. Out poured everything Minos was.

And in the mind of a monster, memory stirred.

'If you have a monster in you,' she had said, 'you have me as well. You're of my flesh . . . So you must run. Run and keep running, until you've left this Labyrinth far behind.

You're more than they say. More than they think. You're mine and I love you.'

Words that had become like legend to him, ever since he saw his First Light. How many years had passed? What number of generations? Yet still he dreamed of them. Still, he made them his prayer. He'd learned to speak a little now – though there had been times he'd lost language along the way, then had to reclaim it again – but these were the words he said to himself at nightfall, whenever his faculties allowed. 'If you have a monster in you, you have me as well.'

One moment a monster.

One moment a . . .

In the sewer tunnel, Minos fell silent. The footman knew a moment of reprieve when he saw it; in the same second that silence fell, he fled into the same dank darkness that had swallowed up his brothers. Then there was only Minos in the tunnel. The fire in his heart slowly fading. The echo of his screams turning to ghosts.

He lurched towards Nell. Gander, who had been holding on to her, strained yet more fiercely to drag her away; when she resisted, so did he relent. 'I can't, Nell,' he stammered. 'Nell, I—'

Minos had seen Murdstone, still semi-conscious against the wall. Now he hovered above, considering him closely. Nell thought she saw the panic return to Minos's eyes, but perhaps that was only a reflection of Murdstone – for the closer Minos got, the more animate he seemed to become. Dying animals always seek shelter. Nell had seen it with rats. And, like a bludgeoned rat, Murdstone began dragging himself along the sewer wall, summoning some forgotten reserve of strength to lift himself to his feet.

'Sir,' begged Murdstone. 'Sir – sir—'

The base sound in the back of Minos's throat had returned. It rose to a pitch. Minos closed his fists.

'*No*,' he said, and left Murdstone to the blackness as he reeled to Nell's side.

Up close, she saw that the changes in him were many. It wasn't just the horns that had returned to his head; his cheek-bones were starker, the ridges in his brow pulled back in reflection of the eruptions above. His shoulders seemed vast; the hair of his breast had risen in coils to meet the ragged black beard which had always grown wild about his jaw.

Nell tried to tell herself not to be afraid, but now she shook like the footman with the falchion blade. By instinct, she reached backwards, as if to grapple Gander – but the mudlark was no longer there. The splash of his flailing legs was rapidly fading, somewhere behind.

The stench of Minos had always been of the stable-yard, the tannery, the butcher's block – but now it was riper than ever. She could see the cavities the shots had opened in his breast. This was a visage out of nightmare – yet then she saw his eyes.

'Minos,' she whispered.

'Yes, Nell,' he uttered in reply – and perhaps Nell was mistaken, but it seemed something had changed in his voice as well, as if the words no longer fitted his throat quite as neatly. 'It's still me. I'm still here. But listen to me, now. You can't stay.' He looked around; there were still sounds in the blackness, but he and Nell were alone. 'The bulwarks have broken. The Tyburn burst its banks. There isn't time, Nell. Run now—'

Perhaps there really was magic in the world, for as soon as Minos spoke the words, Nell could hear the rush of water, somewhere deeper in the maze. It was as if he had summoned it into being. A wave was tearing through the tunnel. She felt its herald in the waters now pooling at her waist.

'*Now, Nell*,' said Minos.

Minos was the first to know it was upon them. He opened his body, as if to fill the tunnel's expanse. The surge crashed against his back, but he did not stagger. Then it broke around him, deluging Nell. The last of the lanterns, which had been bobbing precarious by the sewer wall, was submerged. Darkness prevailed. Sightless, Nell started to scream.

'I've got you,' came his unearthly voice.

Then his arms were around her.

Then she was free of the water, being cradled against the warm stickiness of his breast as he started to run.

Sightless through the dark.

Sightless, through the Labyrinth, to the Long Stair that would lead him above.

Sally-Anne reached over the sandbags, grasped Gander by the hand and helped haul him above. 'Where is she?' she gasped. 'Where's Nell?' But Gander was only gabbling. He was gabbling, still, as they rushed past the panicking workmen to the lean-to where the other mudlarks cowered. 'And Mr Murdstone? The men who went with him? Where are they, Gander? Where's Nell?'

'I told you!' Noah raged, at last. '*He* came. *He* was there, waiting. Murdstone thought he was the one baiting a trap, but he wasn't.' His voice faded, rage giving way to fear's remains. 'He was the bait.'

The clamour of voices in the yard, Beresford Kale and his workmen dragging yet more sandbags to the chasm, died. Sally-Anne was still shaking Gander, trying to loosen the truth from his tongue, when she dared look up. The rain was heavy on the window glass, so instead she had to go to the door. There, through slanting grey, she watched as Kale rallied his men away from the crevasse. 'It's him!' Kale was crying – and what workmen hadn't already fled for the hoardings instead took up pickaxes, forks, lengths of scaffold from the slag heaps of the yard. The peelers had already gone, as peelers – the mudlarks had noticed – so often did, so at once Kale started remonstrating with the mudlarks to join them. 'You!' he barked, spying Noah through the glass. 'Come, come!'

Noah opened his mouth to protest, but no matter; it was already too late. The shape of horns had already appeared over the sandbags. The workmen, those whose nerve didn't immediately crumble, were already trying to drive him back below at the point of their picks.

It was Sally-Anne who understood.

She let Gander's hand slip from her own and staggered, gasping, into the pouring rain. 'Leave him! Leave him!' she bellowed. 'He has her. He has Nell.'

Minos appeared over the sandbags. Heads turned. Feet took flight. But there, cradled in his arms like a swaddled babe, was Nell. Ignorant of the scrabbling workmen, he carried her to the lean-to's scant shelter – and there, his body protecting her from the wind, he laid her down.

*

Nell looked up. Colour had returned to the world, though only the flickering oranges, shifting blacks and greys of London at night. Some of the mudlarks were fighting their way past, to chase the workmen out of the hoardings and into the streets of St Giles. Others vanished behind the slammed door of the lean-to. Only Sally-Anne and Gander remained, unmoving behind the curtain of rain – petrified, ossified by the sight of horns.

He'd set Nell down. Now he crouched in front of her. Perhaps it was only because of all the fear she had birthed in the blackness below, but Nell found she did not have room to be afraid now. She studied him through swollen eyes; she reached up to touch the spiral ridges of each horn; she cupped the jaw she'd been so scared of reaching into, all those months ago. 'I didn't believe it,' she stammered. 'When Mr Murdstone told me, I didn't believe –'

'Oh, but Nell,' he said, tenderly, 'neither did I. But then –'

How to explain it, in ways a child might understand? Of the old gods who had perished as men abandoned their shrines? Of an age when magic both enchanted and corrupted the lives of men? Of naiads and dryads, rebellious Titans, winged mares? Of the old enchantress, exiled to her island, and his mother's words, echoing through all time?

'Then I remembered. It was like being opened up. Like somebody found a key.'

He looked into her – and he realized, then, that he didn't need to tell her a thing. She felt it already.

Something drew his eye. Instincts had long ago taught him to expect huntsmen, but no workmen were coming for him with their pitchforks; what few remained, Kale among them, clung to the corners of the hoardings, as petrified as Sally-Anne. No, it was some other instinct that preyed on him. He looked below. 'Nell, sweetness. I've got to go.'

He would have bounded away, but Nell had taken his hand. 'You need the doctor. Bantam isn't far from here. He'll help you.'

Minos drew his hand from hers; there was no use in holding on. 'No,' he said sadly.

He was already at the sandbags when Nell realized where he was going. She tumbled after him, oblivious to Sally-Anne snatching her hand. 'Please,' she begged, 'don't go after him. He can't hurt me now. He won't. I'll go to Sophia. He won't come after. Won't hurt me again.'

Minos lifted himself over the sandbags. He was already sinking below when he looked back and said, 'I don't mean to hurt him, Nell.'

Then he was gone, returning to the darkness beneath.

The Labyrinth, welcoming its wayward son back home.

He'd hunted Athenians before. The guilt of those hunts coursed through him as he picked his way onward. Round one corner, then the next. Left, then right; forward, then back. Water half-filled the tunnels now. Where two sewers joined, it ran deeper still. But blindly he followed their scents. They had scattered into unknown darknesses, terror driving them to the sewer's dead-ends – but fear had a stench so much riper than the river through which he was wading. He fixed himself on it: fighting the current, fighting the tide, but no longer the hunger inside him, no longer the fire.

One of them was bleating, like a lost lamb. Minos came

upon him at some rubble-strewn landslide, where the water roiled through shattered brick. If the footman heard the thrashing in the water that told of Minos's approach, he did not understand it. Not until Minos touched him did he know he was not alone.

The scream did not echo, for the turning water drank it up. Then, as Minos wrapped his arms around him, holding him so fast he could not slip free, silence prevailed.

Minos felt the thunder of the man's heart. Somewhere between them, it joined with his own.

'Do you want to live?' he said.

And the man started weeping.

Then they went above.

It was the first footman's panicked scrabbling at the scaling ladder that alerted Beresford Kale to something emerging from below. No matter how much he cajoled them, the others would not sally towards the sandbags. At the first sign of movement, two more fled through the hoardings. Kale was still remonstrating about their dereliction of duty when the footman's hand reached the top of the scaling ladder, and he hauled himself out. There he lay in the mud, breast heaving, mouth gasping, body bucking like a child just born.

It was Sally-Anne who rushed to him. Nell watched from the lean-to, where she and Gander were smothered in old coats, trying to fight off the chill of the underworld below.

'He found me,' the footman was gasping. 'By God, I'm delivered. I'm delivered.'

Nor was he the last. Some time later, the footman with the gored shoulder sobbed for them from the bottom of the ladder; Kale and the mudlarks worked to heave him up.

Some time after that came the third, then the fourth. Each one fell into the yard's deepening mire and spun the same story. The devil came for us, they said. But the devil set us free.

'Then it's done,' Kale said, as one by one what mudlarks remained emerged from the lean-to. He looked up, at skies still impossible to see for the shifting clouds, and added, 'All that's left is the rain. The floods. The endeavour.'

Some of the workmen had found courage enough to help the men delivered from the earth. Sally-Anne was organizing Packrat Jack to hasten to High Holborn, and the address of the good doctor Bantam. A carriage would be summoned, one of the footmen declared, at Elkington's expense, 'for at least this night's brought one satisfaction: Murdstone, dead in the river, just as our instructions required.'

'But no,' said Nell. Until that moment she'd been framed in the door of the lean-to, teeth still chattering against the ice cold of below.

'No?' spat the gored footman.

'No,' she whispered, and picked her way – as a foal takes its first steps – to the sandbags and rising water underneath. 'He isn't gone yet. He's still looking. Don't you see? He'll bring Murdstone back too.' She looked around, at the bank of shadowed faces. 'It's the part of him that doesn't have horns.'

Not quite the townhouse on Hanover Square, then. Not quite the bedchamber garlanded in silks, with a boy to chew his grapes and a maid to mop his brow. The water had reached Benjamin Murdstone's breast, but there was a strange comfort to this; every extremity was numb now: beyond feeling, beyond pain. If it didn't provide the same consolation of a handmaid whispering into his ear the long litany of all he'd accomplished in his life, perhaps that was just. Perhaps that had been fantasy anyway. 'Never before has a foundling boy been knighted. Never before has a tosher built such an empire. Go to sleep now, sir. It's time for you to rest. Let the angels mop your brow. Let them sing sweet songs about Murdstone & Sons, and all the boys who came after you, to build empires of their own. Your name's a legend now.'

How foolish that seemed, down here in the forever dark. What hubris was it to think your name might go down in legend, when real legends walked the Earth? That some piece of you might go on for ever, when that beast had roamed for time untold?

The rising current lifted the water. He felt it roll above his shoulders, before it moved on.

Darkness had never felt like this before. He'd fled through the tunnels until he could flee no more, but the moment he ceased moving, the darkness seemed to grow thicker, deeper, more suffocating still. Perhaps, he thought, he was dead already. He was certainly in the Underworld. His mind spun back to all those myths he'd imbibed at Murdstone & Sons. Theseus had been trapped in the Underworld too, had he not? Yes, thought Murdstone, dragged there to fulfil some oath – and entombed in rock for his impudence, until Heracles came to release him. Theseus was a fool; the thought made Murdstone smile, delirious in the dark. All those they spoke of as heroes were but fools in the end.

'Do you want to live?' came a voice.

Murdstone thought he was dreaming, until the voice came again.

'It doesn't have to end like this.'

It was *him. His* voice, animal as it was, skimming across the surface of the waters that devoured him. He turned his head against it, but had no strength to flee. The waters had him entombed, just like the stones of Tartarus once enveloped Theseus.

'Do you hear me, sir?'

'I hear you,' Murdstone spat. His body was so cold it took all his effort just to speak. 'Come no closer, sir. I'll die in the water before I die at your hand.'

'I haven't come for that end.'

'Then why?' Murdstone snarled. 'You have the girl, don't you? You're not bound to me.'

'No,' breathed Minos.

The water rose again. Murdstone felt it at his lips. The panic that coursed through him told him there was yet life in his extremities. By God, the body wanted to live. He knew how death would feel now. Like hands pulling you under, while you tried to take flight.

'I would have treated you right,' Murdstone gasped. Though none could see it, he had turned his face up, to face the bricks above him. The water was driving him towards the tunnel roof. Soon, he would be gone. 'I'd have built you your Palace. Kept you in luxury, at its very heart. The world would have known you, sir. They'd have come from every corner of the Earth. Men need their magic. I would have – *we* would have – given it to them. And–' Here came the water again. He closed his lips against it, waited for the current to calm. 'I used to hunt in the sewers once. Oh, not the Grand Endeavour. Not sewers like these. Storm drains and ditches, what ginnels and coverts went before. Prince among toshers, that's how I fancied myself. You'd find bodies down there. Derelicts, or else men with knives in their hearts. I sold their belts. Took their boots. Everything the cut-throats left behind.' He snorted, but the water was so close he breathed it in, and soon his body was convulsing as it fought to find breath. 'So I'll die where I began. I've been fighting it all my life. Well, the fight's over now. I tried to prove otherwise, but we all sink back below.'

Something was moving against the current; Minos had started forward again, forcing his way closer.

'I don't believe that, Mr Murdstone.'

'Oh no?'

'*No,*' he breathed.

'Well, I saw you, sir. I saw you for what you are. The natural order reasserts itself, in the end. Why else do your horns return? Why else does it break free? It's like the river that drowns me. The fools thought they could tame it, but they were wrong. Everything bursts its banks. And there you stand. What new monstrosities are cloaked by the dark? How animal is your face, right now?' Murdstone gasped again; his body had started trembling, to keep away the cold. 'The veil that separates man from Minotaur is as thin as the veil that separates nobleman from scoundrel, killer from saint. It's just the ordinary truth of existence – and here we both stand, as test –' he gasped again – 'as testament to it.'

A hand closed over his arm. He had no strength to fight back. He bleated, miserably, as the second hand took him.

'I don't believe it, Murdstone. And I'll tell you why.'

*

The enchantress is his mother's sister, exiled by her father at the whim of some capricious god. It has taken him a generation to find this place, hunted and reviled as he is, and decades more to find a shipwright willing to ferry him to her island prison. Yet an enchantress like this lives longer than ordinary man, and when he finds her, she looks as young as Pasiphae did on the night he fled Knossos. He still remembers that night. He is not yet old enough that his first memories are buried beneath the landslides of time. And, since he has learned a little language, he can articulate the feeling of it too, the very last words his mother spoke for him.

He has been searching for someone who might help him ever since.

She is not expecting his appearance, this enchantress. 'Though, of course, I attended your birth,' she tells him, having first protected herself with spells. 'The world thinks you dead. Theseus proclaimed it, and it suits his legend for it to be so. And yet – here you are.' She pauses. 'You have learned to speak.'

And he says to her the words he will say to a thousand different souls across all the endless ages of man: 'I don't know who I am.'

Of all the things he expects, it is not for her to laugh. 'And do you think you are so very different from the rest of us in that?'

He glowers at her darkly, rising from the mound where he sits. In those times, he still sports his earliest horns. He is devastation's avatar. He is teeth and claws.

'You carry your mother's words with you, but you don't seem to hear them. So – sit. Listen to me. Or kill me, if it is

your pleasure. I have survived on this island too long. I do not know if I would not welcome death.'

But he sits, even so.

'You are not a beast,' she tells him. *'You are not a man. You are, child, lost. You escaped your Labyrinth, only to enter another – and every man, woman and child who exists upon this planet is wandering through it with you. Born to it, picking their way through its tricks and dead-ends – searching, cease-lessly searching, for the Long Stair, to rise into the knowledge of who they are.'* She pauses. *'Well, I can save you the journey. I can hand you your length of string. Would you like this?'*

'I would,' he lows.

'You are neither man nor beast. You are but a choice.'

'A choice?' He understands this word, but not her meaning.

'One moment a man, one moment a monster. This is just the ordinary truth of existence. And there you stand, on the line that divides one from the other, poised on the precipice – ready to choose.'

He had been borne from the water now. The beast's arms were his chariot, Murdstone cradled to his breast like a suckling babe. Along the tunnel they moved. The current crashed around him, submerging him one second, releasing him the next.

'A choice,' said Minos, scenting the air at each conjunction of tunnels. 'To be one or the other – and to be the one who decides.' *And through the ages,* she had told him, *you might waver from one to the other. Your monstrosity might manifest. But so too might your manhood. So too might decency win out over deceit. Until one day . . .* 'The monstrous gone for ever, and only the man.'

'A choice,' gasped Murdstone. 'Only a choice.'

'So I wandered. For centuries, I roamed. Sometimes, I let him fight. I let the Minotaur make war. But, when I could, I gave in to the peacefulness. I lost my horns. I lost my memories.' So too did the world. The old gods died. The magic withered away. Where once was enchantment and wonder, now there was politicking, mathematics, the discoveries of science. Where once Titans, now engineers. 'And soon, the only thing to tell me who I was, where I'd begun, were the scars the enchantress carved into my back. The Labyrinth she designed as a reminder.'

'To show you where you came from.'

'No,' said Minos, 'to show me where I *was*. Still in the Labyrinth. Still turning left, still turning right, still searching for the Long Stair. But now I know, for sure, how to escape it. How to make my choice. I'll shed my horns again. I'll change and keep changing, change until . . .'

Minos had fallen silent.

'What is it?' Murdstone bleated.

His body was suddenly rigid. 'You must hold on to me now.'

But there was no strength in his arms, so in the end it was Minos who closed himself around Murdstone. 'What is it?' Murdstone kept saying. 'Sir, speak to me. What is it? What is it?'

'It's the tide.'

In the blackness, the air disappeared.

The unstoppable tide.

The swell had been chasing them along the tunnel. Now, at last, it was upon them. Murdstone felt it close over his head. His body, which had suffered the same too many

476

times, must have been expecting it to pass – but this time, when the water came, the air did not follow. He opened his mouth to take breath, and in rushed the river.

The water pummelled and turned him around. He did not know, any longer, which way was up, or which way down.

But that didn't matter, because he was already falling.

Falling into dreams older than time.

Falling into history and myth . . .

Time; there was never enough time.

Nell stood at the sandbags, heedless of the voices urging her to step aside, and peered into the depths. 'He's down there,' she kept saying. 'He went for Mr Murdstone. He's bringing him back out.'

The footmen were already gone, the yard emptying by degrees. But Sally-Anne stood beside her, and Beresford Kale hovered near. Three of his workmen remained. Yet more sandbags had been dragged to the opening.

'I need a lantern,' said Nell, ripping her hand from Sally-Anne. 'I'm going after him. I need a—'

The hoardings trembled, and through the narrow gap between them, figures appeared. Kale turned to greet them, but Sally-Anne had already cried out. 'Doctor, quickly!'

Bantam looked as dishevelled as he did on any night he'd been unearthed from the Courage and Crown, but sobriety found him the moment he knelt at Nell's side. 'Who did this to you?' he stammered, as if he hadn't already been told. 'You must come with me now, girl. Let me clean this. I have salves.'

'No!' she thundered. 'No!', and 'No!' Each time he took

her hand, she skittered backwards like a cat being cornered. 'He's down there, Doctor. He needs our help. Well?' She turned to take in the ragged workmen. 'He brought those men out, didn't he? He brought *me*. But who's to bring him?'

Her voice cracked with sadness, for some part of her knew already what Kale was about to confirm. As she was pleading with the doctor, he had taken his lantern to the peak of the scaling ladder. Now, he beckoned her near.

The rest made way as she picked her way through. Then, up the sandbags she scaled. On the precipice, in the ring of lantern light, she looked down. She betrayed no emotion when Kale said, 'I'm sorry, girl, it's the river – you can't stop the river', only looked into the churning grey at the bottom of the shaft.

The tunnel was a deluge. The water still rising. The bottom rungs of the scaling ladder had vanished into its inky murk. One rung after another, the river approached.

Nell had not been there in the moment her mother died. Somehow, this second time seemed so much worse.

Before Bantam or Sally-Anne could reach her, Nell had vaulted from the sandbags, tumbled towards the gap in the hoardings. 'Sweetpea,' Sally-Anne cried after her. 'Sweetpea, let me take you home. We'll make it better. Make it right.'

Better, thought Nell. *Right. Home.* No, there was only one place she could go now.

It was the running that kept her from crying. Every time she had to stop for breath, she felt it fill her up: the tears like a tide inside her, rising up her gorge like the river through the sewer. By the time she reached Leicester Square – where the gaslights were half snuffed out, the Alhambra sitting silent as a monolith – the pain of keeping them in was too much. It had always been foolish to think she would find her here; the night had grown too old, the performance dead for hours: Giselle gone back to the grave, the Wills in retreat. But at least she knew her way from here. Now the tears cascaded out of her as she ran. They joined with the rain as she tumbled into Seven Dials. They choked her for breath as her little fists hammered at the door.

'I swear,' came a vengeful voice from beyond, 'the next man who comes to this door hunting for the harlot, I'll—'

The door opened up. There stood one of the tenants from below. He had his fists raised as if ready to deal some blow – but Nell's appearance must have taken him by surprise, and she ducked beneath his arm to scuttle above. Only his invective followed her up the stairs; the man himself was too broken, too bone-tired to pursue.

In a cavalcade of tears, she reached the door at the top of the stairs. She had not expected to find Sophia awake, but evidently it was so; candlelight still flickered through the keyhole, the sounds of some frenzy beyond. Her fingers seemed to resist taking hold of the handle, for fear had taken hold of her. Hours ago, she had abandoned them at the Alhambra – or so it must have seemed. What had Sophia thought, when Nell did not return to the wings? What was she thinking, even now?

At least that fear arrested the tears. She crouched and pressed her eye to the keyhole. There, in flickering candlelight, Sophia hurtled back and forth. One of her travelling trunks was splayed open, gowns being pressed inside. The candle guttered on the ledge.

Nell opened the door.

Sophia pirouetted, throwing herself forward as if to slam

the door in Nell's face. When she saw Nell, it was only her dancer's poise that allowed her to turn out of the attack. 'Nell?' She darted around to slam the door behind her instead. 'Nell, where have you—'

'I'm sorry,' Nell blurted out, 'Miss Chrétien, I'm sorry. It was Mr Murdstone. He came to the theatre, and – and—'

'Your face,' Sophia said, scarcely able to believe. 'Look at you, Nell.'

Nell trembled.

'I looked for you, after the dancing was done, but . . .' This time, it was Sophia who started trembling. 'He did this to you? Your Murdstone?'

So Nell told her it all: of the body on the tide, and the man who'd become her friend; of the trap Murdstone set for him, and the beast he unearthed; of the labyrinths, ancient and new, and the river that burst its banks. 'But I didn't mean to let you down. I didn't. And Sophia, I don't know what to do. I – I don't know who I am.'

Sophia had found rags to dry her. She peeled back Nell's sodden clothes, draped her in gowns and sat her before the hearth's faded embers. It was only then that Nell thought of the frenzy of the room, the travelling trunk with its innards spilling out, and said, 'Sophia, what happened?'

Some calmness had returned to Sophia since Nell tumbled into the room. Now she stood in the window glass, arms wrapped tightly around herself, and said, 'Mr Murdstone wasn't the only one at the Alhambra tonight. I saw him the moment I stepped onto the stage. All those thousands of eyes – and there were *his*, luminous in the dark. Brighter than all of the others, as if it was he alone I was meant to see.' She stopped. 'The letter I shredded, the letter you

480

burned in the fire – it was to tell me my husband was coming for me, that he sought some rapprochement. An entente, here in London. He would send his valet first, to establish an accord. And there he was, in the gallery, gazing upon me. It was all I could do to keep dancing. And afterwards, in the wings backstage . . .'

Sophia went to her travelling case, and took from it a small pouch of silk, fastened with silver thread. She brought it to Nell's side, allowed it to unfurl in the palm of her hand.

It took Nell too long to understand what the wrinkled piece of leather really was. She had seen the waxen flesh of the dead before, but never something like this; never a finger, sawn off at its stump, mummified and dressed in ribbon, a diamond ring still sparkling at its knuckle.

'He's coming?' Nell whispered.

'His valet would not leave without an assurance that I would undertake to meet with *him*, so I did the only thing I could think of. I reached an accord.' She folded the silk back around the finger and took it to the hearth. 'But it is not an accord I mean to keep.' Then she threw it into the coals. For a time, it simply sat there. Then flames took to the silk. Then the pouch disintegrated. Then, behind fire that danced more wildly than the Wills, the grisly appendage vanished. 'It will be several days before my husband makes his appearance. By then, I'll be gone. Giselle will have danced the final time, the Neva will set sail for home – and I mean to go with them.'

Nell only stared.

'St Petersburg. The frontier of dance. The Mariinsky opened but a few short seasons ago. The Hermitage Theatre.

481

The Kamenny, on Carousel Square. The Company speak of these places as home. Half a world away from where we now stand. Far enough, I hope, to be out of his reach.' She stopped. 'Nell, you must come.'

There was silence in the garret. Nell's eyes returned to the fire.

'I may not dance for the Neva, but I believe there's a future with them. As a tutor, perhaps. An instructress. And Nell, I shall be in sore need of an assistant.'

Her eyes might have been on the fire, but Nell's heart was still subsumed by the waters of the rampant river. She could feel Minos's arms around her. The thunder of his heart, emanating from his butchered breast. That vision of him, his head heavy with horns, as he returned to the underworld below.

He'd survived the river once. He'd washed up on the tide, and taken fresh breath. But she thought of him now, turning through the drowned tunnels of the Labyrinth, opening his great jaws so that the river coursed into his lungs.

Then she thought of tomorrow. The mudlarks, back on the river – for, even without Mr Murdstone to marshal them, where else might they go? Their nights in the Water's Edge, their days in the silt, the bread and the gravy and the days that followed days that followed yet more days to come.

She had always dreamed of her own treasure from the river: an ivory sundial to change her own life. How bitter-sweet was it to realize that she'd found it all those weeks ago, that it had come to her in the shape of a man who bore horns, the secret locked inside him, unknown even to himself. A treasure in the dirt, like the heart in the body of a monster, like the decency in man.

She took Sophia's hand. 'Yes,' she whispered.

And next night, when Nell stood in the wings and watched Sophia take flight, she understood there was as much magic in that word as there had ever been in 'no'.

25

Legend

Legends last forever, but stories – like the lives of mortal men – must come to an end.

But venture a few more pages with Nell now.

Her life may yet have one more twist to come . . .

Twilight over Deptford; strange swells in the river. The wherryman was guiding his boat back home when he saw the dark shape upon the water. Flotsam was as valuable to a wherryman as it was a mudlark, so he channelled the boat through the grey swell to reach its side. Yet, as soon as he got there, he knew it was no flotsam; a hand, strangled in seaweed, reached for his own – a hand that dwarfed him as it grappled for his forearm, his oar handle, the side of the boat; anything that might heave him aboard.

Such an enormous brute the wherryman had never seen. He near upended the boat in his attempts to get aboard. Only when he had finally crashed into the bow, and the wherryman triumphed in keeping his vessel afloat, was he able to study the poor wretch he'd helped out of the mire. If there were uglier men on the streets of London, he was yet to meet them. He sat hunched, with animal features and a misshapen head. A circus freak, a medical curiosity, a man to be kept in menageries or out of sight. But the wherryman was a good, Christian soul, and he had always believed in charity. This man might have had the look of some devil – and didn't the shape of his head somehow suggest the impression of horns? – but he would not decry him for that.

There was blood upon his breast. 'But you're living, sir, you're living,' said the wherryman. Some time later, in the waterside inn with the other wherry keepers, he bought him food and drink, told him there'd be a bed in the barn if he cared for it, that they could send a message to a loved one, if that was what he required.

'But who is he?' asked one of the other rivermen, for whom the appearance of the stranger was a welcome novelty at the end of a most pitiful day. 'What does he have to say?'

So they gathered around, marvelling at the appetite of the drowned man, and asked him that very question.

But when he looked up, his eyes – set altogether too far apart on his head – only looked black and forlorn. 'I don't know who I am,' he whispered.

'What's that, sir?'

The man shifted, as if the thought had tormented him. His black eyes darted. He started to shake. Yet, when he went to speak the words for a second time, something had changed in his demeanour. The panic was paling; the fervour, fading away. 'I don't know who –' And there he stopped. Later, the wherrymen would remark it was as if he had come to some striking realization, the way a man might enter a trance and emerge from it, having received some message from God. In that same second, he rose to his feet. Tables crashed into chairs as he lumbered through the inn, trailing the reek of the river – and something of the stable-yard – behind him. 'No,' he was saying, 'I know. I know.'

But what it was he remembered, the wherrymen would never discover.

*

Noah wasn't ordinarily the first to awake in the cramped, frigid attic above the Water's Edge. At seventeen years old, and half a lifetime since he slept in a bed made up by a mother's kindness, he had got used to the shifting of bodies around him, the sulphurous stenches that too often populated the night. But last night had been different. The landlady prowling below, the whispered discontent, the ripples of uncertainty dogging the dreams that filled the attic air – all of that had meant he hadn't slept at all.

That was why he was the first to the river that morning.

That was why it was Noah who found the body, washed up on the shore.

Just a lump of flesh, this one, bloated by the river. He turned it with his foot.

'Oh,' he said.

So the river really was a capricious old god after all.

Bantam was swirling the amber yellow of his own water in a small glass phial, seeking to divine the ravages this murderous year had done to his body, when the knock came at the door. The hour was not unholy, but no soul was expected – so that meant it had to be one of the derelicts, come to beg for some relief. Consequently, he did not mind tarrying on his way to answer. The knuckles had knocked three times by the time he turned the key and peered out into the sullen morning light.

There stood one of the motherless mudlarks, the turncoat boy who'd thought nothing of betraying both his fellows and his master.

'Which have you come for?' Bantam stammered. 'To tell me he lives, or that the moment has come?'

'Remember how he said you're sworn to him, Doctor? That you'd have to come?'

'Well, no more,' Bantam recalled. 'I told him I was unyoking myself back at—'

'Oh, we're all unyoked now, Doctor.' Noah paused. Bantam could see the merest flickers of disbelief, wonder – and, yes, horror, playing in the corners of his lips. 'I think you'd better come.'

By the time Bantam and Noah returned to the shores beneath Ratcliffe, the mudlarks had dragged him to the seaward cave – not because there was any hope of reviving this particular body, but because something in the symmetry of it seemed right. They'd coaxed no fire, except that which they needed to see by, mopped no brows, cleaned no wounds. And yet every one, save for Nell, gathered around, in complete disregard of the tide and all its treasures.

Bantam knelt at the body. Its every bone was broken. Days and nights in the river had bloated its flesh so that it seemed a crude mockery of a man. Yet there was no mistaking this amphibious look. Later, Bantam would feel foolish for it – but some old sympathy bloomed up inside him. Then it died away.

Perhaps some legends really did come to an end after all.

'What should we do, Doctor?' said the one called Sally-Anne.

Bantam said, 'There's a belt on him. There's boots. Reach your hands into his jaws, there – those teeth are false; there's a fish supper in those. Off with all of it, and down to the dolly shop.' Bantam breathed deeply. The air in the cavern was growing too close; he needed the ripe air of the river. He returned to the fissure, brimming with some emotion it would take him the rest of his life to decipher. Benjamin Murdstone – former rag-gatherer, former inmate, former gentleman, and former master of mudlarks from Woolwich to the Wapping dock – had accepted his summons to the Ever After.

He was still on the shale when he heard footsteps cantering after. Some strange chorus of horror and jubilation was erupting in the cave, but here came Sally-Anne, to see him off. 'Doctor,' she ventured, and he felt compelled to turn back, 'what happens to us now?'

Bantam cogitated on the question for too long. The river kept rolling, he thought. Time waited for neither Minotaur nor man. 'I daresay you keep hunting for your treasures in the mud.' But he had not taken three strides before another thought occurred.

Briggs's body lay buried for ever in the grounds of Amberstone House, but among the book-lined halls of his Oxford abode there were as many treasures as had ever lined the shelves at Murdstone & Sons: books collected across a lifetime, artefacts acquired by shadowy means; the archive that was Briggs's life's work, and its keeper never coming home. It would not, he thought, be very different from claiming what washed up on the river. There would be trades to be made, a profit to be reached – enough, no doubt, to drag the mudlarks from the mire behind him, just as Murdstone had done for him.

He looked back at Sally-Anne. No, they could not stay here for ever, not unless the Ratcliffe rot was to set in. How many would end up dead on the tide, just like their master?

'Wait for me at dawn on the seventh day.' That ought to be time enough, he thought, if the thaw went on. 'Keep the others safe until then. Make sure they don't throw you out of the Water's Edge. The nights are still too bitter.' There were a few coins in Bantam's pocket – not enough to sustain them, but it would help. He pressed them into Sally-Anne's palm. Then he looked over her shoulder, at the narrow fissure in the rocks. 'And throw him back to the river. Make him a problem for somebody else. That is, if the eels don't find him first.'

Then he walked away, feeling some fresh lightness – as if it was he, not Minos, who had shed heavy horns.

A cry went up. In the seaward cave, Noah had pulled out Murdstone's false teeth.

The river rolled on.

*

As soon as the carriage arrived, Nell scurried through the back halls of the Alhambra: past the store where the seamstress was arranging gowns soiled by the closing night's performance, past the hall where Murdstone had ensnared her, through the wings – where she caught a final glimpse of Giselle's restful grave – and into the dressing chambers.

489

Here, the travelling trunk was already packed. Two storemen had been employed to ferry it to the carriage, and Nell nodded to them now. Then, across the dressing chamber – where Alyona and the rest of the Neva Ballet were at once elated and exhausted by the end of their run – she caught Sophia's eye.

Until that moment, Sophia too had been wearing that look of wearied exultation – but, at the merest incline of Nell's head, a transformation came over her. She took each of the Neva into her arms, then followed Nell into the passageway without. Left they went, then right – but always onward, ever onward, until they reached the tradesman's doors. Outside sat the carriage that would take them so far away.

You did not always know when it was a last time in life, but that evening, as Nell watched the river coursing past, she knew in her bones that this was the final time she would see its bridges and bargemen, the sparkling lights on its wharfs. As the carriage jounced along the Highway, she became distinctly aware that never again would she see the storehouses or the seaward cave, the haberdashers at St George in the East. And yet – weren't they imprinted on her, just the same as the Labyrinth had been carved into Minos's back? Wasn't that what a person was made out of, flesh and bones and memories that ran deeper yet?

A fresh carriage was awaiting them in Ratcliffe, for Sophia had made such arrangements that they might never be followed. On disembarking the first, and gifting the coachman a diamond ring encrusted in ash, Nell helped to load the travelling trunk onto the second. From here, the long road led to Dover in the east; from there, to lands across the sea – and, from there, to further lands yet, by road and railway and steamer. Out there, they would join with the Neva Ballet, step with them into St Petersburg's grand theatres – and meet with the future, side by side.

But hold tight now.

It is about to begin . . .

Ratcliffe was still fading, London's great miasma beginning to pale, when the horses spooked. The carriage started; the coachman cried out. But his horses would not be driven – and, in their whinnying cries, Nell sensed something familiar, a quality of panic she had experienced only once before.

The carriage came to a stop, the coachman tumbling from his seat to rein his horses down. Out came a whip; Nell heard it crack three times, but the quiet it brought from the horses did not last long. They strained at their tethers. They rose to their hind legs.

'You, sir!' came the coachman's cry. 'Get out of the road!'

Nell clambered out of the carriage.

The road was dirt, banked in brambled hedgebacks, and cutting a trail directly into the light of a moon beached above the fields of the east. Silhouetted in that silvery light stood a man three times the height of Nell and burlier still. His shoulders were hunched, his head lolling forward with its strange, protuberant jaw. But no horns hung from this man's temples. No tail flicked behind. So it could not be the man that all Nell's senses told her it was. She had to be imagining it when the familiar voice said, 'Nell', and he started running towards her, bringing with him all the scent of the sewers and the stable-yard.

Minos swept her into his arms, balanced her on his

491

shoulder, danced ungainly with her in the rutted tracks while the coachman wrestled his horses under control.

'But I saw you,' she said, when Minos had set her down and was running his hands over every crease in her clothing, like a carpenter does his proudest work, checking for cracks, for splinters, for every little imperfection – and finding nothing. 'You went below. The water took you.'

'It did,' Minos whispered.

Slide inside his mind, one final time. Picture that swirling grey mire in which he was subsumed. See how he held onto Benjamin Murdstone, until he could hold no more. Watch how he cradled him as he died.

'But I came back,' Minos whispered. 'And I remembered.'

Nell was aware of another figure behind her. Sophia had emerged from the coach, and now she stood some yards away, daring to watch the spectacle unfold.

'It's Minos,' Nell told her, in fractured breaths. 'He's here.'

Sophia looked him up and down. Some little piece of this made sense now, for there had always been something fanciful in the story Nell had told – as if, perhaps, she had given herself too much to the fantasy of *Giselle* and wanted to spin some fable of her own. 'You told me he had horns,' she said, gently chiding.

Nell reached up, to run her hands through the crouching Minos's hair. Yes, she was certain: the calcified patches were there, more prominent than they'd once been, but the great spirals of bone she'd seen in the sewer were somehow in retreat. She allowed her hands to remain there, and looked into his eyes. 'I know,' he whispered. 'I know who I am.'

'But Minos, your—'

He didn't let her speak the word. Instead, he placed one

of his great, callused fingers on her lips and whispered her to silence. There would be time enough to tell her, if they would have him. Time enough to speak of his mother, of the enchantress, of the ordinary, unremarkable choices men and Minotaurs make every day of their lives. He looked up, beyond Nell, and said to Sophia, 'You've been good to her. There's too many haven't. You have my heart.'

Sophia moved forward, through scudding moonlight. 'Nell has told me something of your story – but I would hear it for myself. Children have a way of telling tales. They find magic in such ordinary things. They spin legends out of the everyday.'

Nell lifted herself. 'It's all true,' she declared, 'every last word.'

But Sophia will discover that for herself, soon enough. For Minos will stay with them as they voyage into the east and over the seas. It will be Minos whose hand Nell holds as she is first introduced to that faraway city of palaces and spires. There he'll be, loyal retainer, as she studies dance in the little townhouse they find off the Nevsky Prospekt. There he'll be, in the shadows of the Mariinsky, as she takes to the stage for the very first time. He'll be with her when she accompanies the Neva Ballet on their grand tours of Europe. He'll be with her as she grows from young mudlark to grown woman; as she takes her first faltering footsteps into the world of dance; as, at seventeen years old, she has her heart broken for the first (but not last) time.

He has existed for centuries untold, but never before has he lived. And perhaps it is this devotion to some other soul that makes his shoulders grow a little less hunched each season, the calcified patches beneath his hair fade into flesh, his tombstone teeth diminish, and his voice – once so full of whispers and cracks – become richer, more melodic, simpler to understand. On the day he arrives at the church house to see Nell married, he stands straighter than in thousands of years. On the day she introduces him to her firstborn child, and he cups the baby in hands that once tore sinew from bone, his eyes are no longer fathomless black, but feathered in a pale blue that will spread across the years to come: light chasing out the dark, for this is the new pattern of his life.

He is the one holding Nell's daughter as Nell takes her part in *The Sleeping Beauty*, in *Swan Lake*. He is the one who guards her from afar, as she grows up in this city where beauty and villainy go hand in hand. And when, many years later, one century turns into the next and Nell grows lined with age, he is the one to lead her on his arm around the city parks, or sit with her in the stalls of theatres as much younger dancers learn their trade, and remind her of how far she has come.

When her memory begins to fade, and past gets jumbled with present in her own fractured mind, he is the one who tells her the tale of the mudlark who rose from the river, and achieved everything her heart desired.

'It's just the Labyrinth,' he tells her, on the night that she dies. 'You get a little lost in life, sometimes, but you always find your way.'

He dances with her for the final time that night. If it is not as wild and exuberant as it once was, off the river in Ratcliffe, it is filled with a lifetime's love – and, when he sees himself in the mirror the next morning, his eyes are full and blue, his teeth so much paler than ever they were. Later, when he stands at the graveside and tells her that he will never forget, he teases two scuffed satin slippers between his fingers, and promises he will carry them until the end of his days.

Because he is certain, now, that one day – somehow – his own end will come. He has been feeling different, of late. Mortality creeps up on a soul. He remembers how Nell used to speak about dance as if she was taking flight. Well, that is how mortality feels too. It is not only the absence of horns that makes him feel lighter. He feels his history, coming to a close.

Grief is the echo love leaves in its wake. At first, he does not know what he will do without her – and, at his loneliest, he fears that, in the vacuum love leaves behind, the Minotaur will find some fresh foothold in his heart – but, of course, Nell has children, and they have children, and soon they will have children too, all of whom might need a guardian as their years roll on. And so he leaves St Petersburg behind, to follow where they go. He is with them in the war-torn fields of Europe when the nations of man seek to wipe each other out. He is with them as the violent century grows old, and mankind creates weapons more capricious and powerful than the worst of the old gods. He sits with Nell's grand-daughter in her old age and tells her the tales of her ancestry – 'Once there was an orphan girl who lived by the river . . .' – and, in years later still, he will spin the story for her daughter, and her son, who returns to London to live overlooking the same river where his ancestor once hunted for treasure in the mud.

But of course that city has changed – and, of course, so

has Minos himself. By the time a new century dawns, Ratcliffe is no more, the Alhambra Circus long since demolished, even the mightiest river tamed by man. No, the Thames will never again burst its banks. And nor will the beast whose kernel still resides inside him. Because, by now, mortality is but moments away. In a single act of kindness, ageing will begin. Perhaps Nell would recognize him now, but only by the feeling of holding him near; no other soul from those older times would see him for who he truly is. The jaw that once jutted forward like a beast's is now delicate, perhaps even handsome. The eyes of fathomless black that once sat too far apart are now the blue of a winter sky, brimming with hope and compassion. The body that rippled with muscle, the coarse fur that coated his flesh, the thick hide and even the Labyrinth tattoo – all of it is gone, and in its place stands a man of unremarkable appearance, content to drift through his days (turning left, turning right, forever moving forward) just the same as the shopkeep who sold you your water this morning, the office clerk whose eye you catch every time you take the train, the man who stops on the corner each evening to throw some pennies in a vagabond's hat.

He could be any one of them.

He could be sitting beside you, even now.

Acknowledgements

I couldn't be more grateful to my editor Gillian Green and agent Euan Thorneycroft for continuing to put faith in the the things I unearth from the back rooms of my mind. This novel wouldn't exist without the support of either one. Thank you, too, to Jessica Lee and all the folks at AM Heath & Co; to my old friends (and perfect sounding boards), James Clegg and Colin Chisholm, who never mind a longwinded bookish ramble; to Esther, who (though she doesn't remember it!) first prompted this book by requesting 'a ballerina book' when she was small; and of course to Rebecca Needes, Ellah Mwale and the wider team at Pan Macmillan who have worked so hard to bring *Once a Monster* to readers. I am in your debt.

My father, Geoffrey Dinsdale, read every story, published and unpublished, that I wrote since long before I first started submitting stories at eleven years old. Very sadly, he passed away before having a chance to read more than a draft of the first early section of *Once a Monster*. His encouragement, love and ceaseless interest in what I was up to (and not forgetting my mother, who would happily translate an eleven-year-old's scrawl to pristine English on the typewriter) was for many, many years the difference between keeping on writing and not. Whatever happened with a piece of writing, I always knew that it would never go unread – and I will miss that more than I can say. Thank you for everything, Dad.

Robert Dinsdale was born in North Yorkshire and currently lives in Leigh-on-Sea.

He is the author of five previous critically acclaimed novels including the bestselling *The Toymakers*, which was his first venture into magic.